Oedipus Tex

Oedipus Tex

Don Tomlinson

Copyright © 2000 by Don Tomlinson.

Library of Congress Number:		00-193157
ISBN #:	Hardcover	0-7388-5312-7
	Softcover	0-7388-5311-9

Text and cover photograph copyright 2000 Don Tomlinson. All rights reserved. No part of this book may be reproduced or transmitted in any form or by any means, electronic or mechanical, including photocopying, recording, or by any information and retrieval system, without permission in writing from the copyright owner.

This is a work of fiction. Names, characters, places, and incidents either are the product of the author's imagination or are used fictitiously, and any resemblance to any actual persons—living or dead—events, or locales is entirely coincidental.

This book was printed in the United States of America.
To order additional copies of this book, contact:
Xlibris Corporation
1-888-7-XLIBRIS
www.Xlibris.com
Orders@Xlibris.com

Contents

Chapter 1	9
Chapter 2	13
Chapter 3	20
Chapter 4	26
Chapter 5	42
Chapter 6	56
Chapter 7	63
Chapter 8	69
Chapter 9	78
Chapter 10	87
Chapter 11	92
Chapter 12	102
Chapter 13	106
Chapter 14	121
Chapter 15	138
Chapter 16	158
Chapter 17	173
Chapter 18	194
Chapter 19	209
Chapter 20	218
Chapter 21	240
Chapter 22	259
Chapter 23	264
Chapter 24	273
Chapter 25	292
Chapter 26	317
Chapter 27	325
Chapter 28	331

Chapter 29	339
Chapter 30	346
Early Epilogue	351
Later Epilogue	355

This work is lovingly dedicated to my father, Noel Purdy Tomlinson, 1904-1975, who had a lifelong love affair with language and creative expression and who should have been what I try to be—a writer, a photographer, a mass communicator, a singer, a songwriter, a musician, a professor. That he was prevented by circumstance from developing and professionally using his God-given talents in these areas was a tragedy of life. If there can be a measure of repair, it is that he passed these gifts to me, and I have not suffered the inability to use them, however modestly.

Chapter 1

August, 1994. Taz Sterling would not have called himself a "ladies' man," but his social life picked up rather dramatically at the beginning of his junior year in college at Texas Christian University in Fort Worth, Texas, when he became involved with Ginger Fontenot. Taz was completely mesmerized by this daughter of an oilfield-roughneck father and housewife mother from real-small-town Texas, a place called LeMieux in the extreme southeastern corner of the state, just across from Louisiana's Acadiana parishes. Many of the town's residents were of French extraction—"cajuns" or "coon-asses," as they were known—certainly to include the Fontenots.

But while Ginger may have been cajun by heritage, and while she may have had a died-in-the-wool coon-ass family, she had spent most of her young life seeking to "overcome" her heritage. Ginger had only the mildest cajun accent and had been able to repress all but a few coon-ass speech patterns and mannerisms. Curiously, Taz had thought more than once while visiting in the Fontenots' home, her parents didn't seem to notice how different from them Ginger was, or maybe they did notice, he thought, and just didn't want to acknowledge it, at least to anyone but themselves. Ginger didn't even look much like them. She was willowy at 5' 8," high-cheek-bone gorgeous with black hair and blue eyes, really smart, and for reasons that were entirely inexplicable to Taz, she wanted him.

He had known her passingly for the two years they had been in college together, but he had been as afraid to ask her out as his friends had been. Then, just as school was starting in their junior years in 1994 and out of the clear blue, Ginger asked a friend of hers to let Taz know that she wanted him to ask her out. Taz was dumbfounded but didn't waste any time in calling her. He was a nice-looking guy—brown hair, hazel eyes, boyish features. A decent high-school athlete, he was well proportioned at 6' 2." Even though his friends told him he was selling himself short, he didn't rate himself on a par with her. He just woke up everyday not believing his eyes.

Together, they learned about sex. It was like exploratory surgery, both in the role of surgeon and patient at the same time. Because Ginger was so gorgeous, Taz had assumed she knew all about sex, but he learned after their first sexual intimacy that she had even less experience than him. He had been afraid to get past the petting stage, but after they had been dating for several weeks, Ginger abruptly moved things along. They were laying on the couch at Taz's place after returning from the movies. Taz was on top of her, but they had their clothes on. They were making out hard, and Taz was massaging her breasts—awkwardly because Ginger had on a bra—when Ginger scooted out from under him a bit, took his hand out of her bra and placed it between her legs.

He felt as though he would explode at any moment, but he still wasn't certain Ginger wanted to make love. Finally, after what Taz later thought must have seemed an eternity to Ginger, he unsnapped her jeans and slid his hand into the warmth of her panties. It was a bit difficult to do, though, because Ginger poured herself into her jeans. Moments later, Ginger pulled his hand from the constraints of her jeans and panties, stood up, and with eyes dancing the dance of a thousand emotions, slid off her jeans. They made love on the couch. Reaching the top together took less than a minute.

"Oh God, Taz, go for it...go for it!" Ginger was exploding.

Taz was in a zone, probably unable to speak and definitely unable to stop. Afterward, Taz considered the idea that while his own sexual gratification had been awesome, he had enjoyed Ginger's pleasure almost as much as he had enjoyed his own.

Round Two—which followed almost immediately—was more like animals in heat than sensuality. Every nerve ending in both bodies was on alert. They found a rhythm, and they made the most of the moment. They were young and in great shape. The experience was exhausting, but more fun than either could imagine.

Ginger climaxed several times more and Taz once more before they stopped to rest, breathing hard. Ginger had not been a virgin before this last twenty minutes, but as they reveled in the afterglow of the moment, Ginger happily admitted a truth.

"I hadn't really enjoyed my few previous, ah, sexual encounters. But with you, God, it was way better than anything I ever imagined."

"Amazing," Taz said. "Just amazing. The sex was amazing, you are amazing, and I think it's more than a coincidence that I feel the same way. Sex with you is way better than ever before. No, not 'way better'—totally better, *fantastic.*"

They were giggling. Taz didn't say the words, but he was certain he was in love. He would do anything for her. And they were dripping with sweat. They had not been separated from one another during the entire event. When Taz became concerned that he might be heavy on top of her, he began to pull away. He was amazed to discover himself still semi-erect. Further evidence, he thought, of the true emotional connection.

As they began to separate, they realized almost simultaneously that the cloth couch might end up being the worse for the experience and themselves a bit embarrassed.

"Tell you what, babe. Put your arms around my neck and hold on tight."

She complied, and he entered her fully once more, lifting her long frame off the couch and delivering her to the waiting bathroom.

"Thanks," she said, just a bit shyly.

"Hey, think nothing of it, my dear. For your love, I would do anything."

Ginger was ecstatic.

Taz was somewhere beyond Mars.

They showered together and then decided they were tired and should retire to Taz's bedroom for the evening—so they unfolded the couch in his efficiency apartment. It was a long rest of the night. They were sore the next day. They were glad it was a Saturday.

Chapter 2

Ginger had the blackest hair and bluest eyes Taz had ever seen. And that classic high-cheek-boned face.... Her body was simply flawless. As they became completely sexually comfortable with one another, Taz sometimes begged Ginger to stand before him naked for a moment or two and twirl around so he could marvel at her flawlessness. She always objected—and always complied. Taz knew she liked it. He liked it, too. Ginger had it all—body, brains, beauty. It hadn't taken long for Taz to fall in love for sure.

Taz showered her with attention; she loved it. They made a handsome couple. Taz was "buffed" without looking buffed. His face was a paradox of slightly-chiseled features and the soft skin of a "baby face"—a trait common to both parents. It wasn't that Taz had any kind of swagger, but he was comfortable in his own skin, especially since Ginger.

Taz and Ginger were somewhat celebrated at TCU by the general student populace. Ginger—by male and female student alike because of her beauty, grace, and intelligence. A foreign languages major, she could speak most of the romance languages fluently, albeit the kind of fluency that to a native speaker would betray her prowess as academically derived.

Taz—by TCU's male student body because he was Ginger's boyfriend, a nice guy, and a popular political columnist for the student newspaper. TCU's female student body admired him for those reasons plus that he was a nice-*looking* guy.

Taz called himself a "radical moderate"—eschewing the left and the right for a serious middle-ground approach on most—though not all—issues. He understood the need for pushing the envelope from time to time, the civil rights movement and the women's movement being prime examples; in the main, though, he believed in compromise and in the idea that all good things come in moderation, as his mother had so frequently averred. He often wished his father felt the same way.

Their junior and senior years at TCU were like a whirlwind. In the end, though, the relationship hadn't lasted. Taz asked Ginger to marry him on the cool May night in 1996 they graduated from college. At the cul-de-sac end of a well-frequented lover's lane not far from the university, they were making love in the back seat of Taz's car because his parents and little sister were at his apartment and her parents were at her apartment.

They were great sex partners and enjoyed having sex in unusual places—in the photography darkroom at the student newspaper at TCU, driving down Interstate 35 in the middle of the night, on the floor of unoccupied rent houses they had gotten keys to from unsuspecting real estate agents. . . . It was always Ginger's idea, but Taz went along happily—even if he did get a bit paranoid at the riskier places instantly after the sexual high had subsided, usually suggesting that they leave quickly. Ginger usually wanted to stay awhile. Taz was adventurous until it was over, Ginger always thought. She was just adventurous.

They were giggling, always giggling—and with this night as no exception, they poked their heads above the back seat to see whether anyone else was around. They were alone. As always, the sex had been wonderful.

"Dang, it's crowded in here," Ginger said. "We haven't made love in the back seat of your car in a long time."

"Yes, well, I've been thinking about that. After we're married, we'll get to sleep together no matter where we are, right? But, you know, I bet—I hope—we'll always want to make love in strange places. I guess it's the risk of getting caught. Maybe we'll write a book someday titled 'Cool Places We Made Love.'"

Taz noticed Ginger's mood turn immediately somber. She began assembling her clothes.

"Was that a marriage proposal, Taz?"

"Ah, yes, I guess it was. Is something wrong? You don't look too pleased."

"It's not that I'm not pleased that you asked, Taz. It's just that I can't do it."

Taz was incredulous.

"My, God, why not? We've talked around it for two years now. Doing graduate school together—all that."

"Because I'm moving to New York in a few weeks to begin a modeling career—and I'm going alone."

In the space of a few seconds, all that had seemed so right to Taz for so long now lay in some form of ruin in the backseat of his car. His giggles had become bewilderment; Ginger, half dressed, began to cry softly. The windows were down. A mosquito buzzed. It was a hot Texas night—and getting hotter. Unconsciously, Taz raised his voice.

"No way! You can't do that, Ginger! You know I totally love you. And you've told me no fewer than a million times that you love me just as much. We're a team. We're meant to be together. What are you thinking?"

"Taz, I'm going—and I'm going alone."

Even though still crying softly, Ginger had repeated her intentions with a firmness that made Taz realize she was totally serious; it was a side of her he had not seen before—it was just a bit...dark, he thought.

Never one to scream and shout, Taz slowly put his free leg back in his jeans, pulled them up, zipped, and crawled over to the driver's seat. Ginger gathered herself, slid out the back door, opened the front passenger door and slid in.

Taz drove to her apartment in silence. Neither said a word as she exited the car. She closed the door as softly as she could. He knew she was leaving for LeMieux with her parents the next day. He sat—dazed—for a few minutes before leaving. There would be a front to put up at his apartment for awhile. His parents would be leaving within the hour for the trek back to Dallas. The Sterling mansion always beckoned.

Try as he did over the next several weeks, Taz could not dissuade her. On June 16th, 1996, Ginger flew to New York from DFW. She had sold her car and shipped her belongings. Taz was not at the airport to see her off. She had forbade it. Ginger had been signed by a modeling agency. Pretty As A Picture, it seems, had contacted her, having run across her in a Miss Texas pageant videotape, they told her. They couldn't guarantee her a lot of placements, but it was a great start, Ginger said.

Incredibly disappointed—wounded—Taz went off to law school at the University of Houston Law Center dragging a heavy velvet chain behind his every step. Ginger was to have gone to UH, too, to earn a master's degree in modern languages. Looking back on it now—from the vantage point of not having seen her for four years—he had finally concluded that all he'd really meant to her was "safe sex." It wasn't that she hadn't felt something for him, he had decided, but he had come to realize, from the perspectives of hindsight and a bit more maturity, that the level of emotional connection clearly had not been mutual.

While he hadn't been able to get Ginger completely out of his mind, he had reached a point where he was at least grateful to her for the sexual learning experience, for the many good times of all kinds they had shared, and for her having helped him develop a greater sense of self confidence, especially concerning relationships with women.

The sex was safe, he now was sure Ginger had thought, because they had pledged monogamy. He had been faithful to her, and while he couldn't *know* that Ginger had been faithful to him, he believed she had been. Sometimes he lamented not having *known* others himself during those once-in-a-lifetime last two years of college, but considering the fact that every friend he had would have killed for his relationship with Ginger, his sadness never lasted long.

The Fontenots—Boudreaux and Tailese—loved Taz, and he felt the same way about them, but none of that was surprising to Taz because, since high school, it had not been unusual at all for him to relate to his dates' parents as well or better than he related to his dates. Whether he always was or not, he usually had seemed the responsible type to parents. He always had enjoyed discussing things with parents on what probably seemed to them an adult level. More than once while in high school, he thought a mother's or father's encouragement of their daughter to continue to go out with him had caused the daughter *not* to want to go out with him again. He had understood what the parents meant, but he also wished they had left well enough alone because such comments had added to the "he's too nice" image he knew he had with too many girls. He knew he had the image, but he'd never understood it.

Taz's mother, Reauxanne, had thought Ginger was just about the best thing in the world; his father, Rance, hadn't said much—he never did concerning personal matters. Ginger had maintained an amicable relationship with them. Neither set of parents knew Taz and Ginger more or less had lived together for two years because Taz and Ginger decided early on to keep separate apartments; they had agreed—at least where their parents and other "adults" were concerned—that discretion concerning sex was appropriate. Each had a telephone extension at the other's apartment. Taz never answered Ginger's telephone at his apartment, and she never answered his telephone at her apartment. They rented the cheapest efficiency apartments they could find so they wouldn't have to have roommates. Their apartments were in different complexes a few blocks apart. Living in the same complex, they had decided, might cause their parents to become suspicious.

It had been four years, and the dawn of a new millennium, since Taz had seen Ginger Fontenot in the flesh, but he had seen her in some print advertisements. He imagined that she was traveling the world, becoming famous and rich. In fact, any time he passed "Another Hour with Fortune and Fame" as he was surfing Austin's digital cable system, he wondered wistfully how long it would be until he saw Ginger's story.

Every time he saw Ginger modeling clothes in those national advertising inserts in the *Austin Evening News*, he felt the pain of wishing for something he knew would never be, and he always felt a rush of other, conflicting, emotions, as well. He knew he'd never forget her, and he thought he always might drag a few velvet chains around with Ginger's name inscribed on every link. To some extent, though, he was disappointed in her because of what he had come to believe was deceitfulness on her part perhaps from the very beginning of their relationship.

At twenty six, for better or worse, most of his friends living in Austin were married, and some of their wives didn't seem to like it much when their husbands went somewhere alone with him, even to a Texas Drillers minor-league baseball game in nearby Round Rock. Taz had come to understand that they were afraid he, being single, would somehow corrupt their husbands. The irony, Taz knew, as his available circle of high school, college, and law-school buddies dwindled, was that any corrupting done would come a lot closer to being the other way around.

Taz simply was a one-woman guy. He wanted to be married, but he just hadn't met the right person. He hoped it wasn't Ginger's ghost that was causing it, but whenever he first would become intimate with someone new, he would be left with a feeling of emptiness that he wasn't sure was the result of a lack of real feelings, or the result of Ginger's legacy, or perhaps even something else altogether. In any event, none of his post-Ginger relationships had worked out. He remained hopeful.

Chapter 3

July, 2000. Taz loved his little sister. He truly believed she was special. Heather was only twelve, but Taz already had begun thinking about the slow and painful death to be experienced by the first boy who dared kiss her. When Taz first mentioned this idea to his good-looking little sister, she had wanted to tell him he was several boys too late in the "kissing" category but decided not to. Whatever love interests Heather had, though, she loved her camcorder a whole lot more. She took it with her everywhere, including to a restaurant in Dallas one day, a happenstance that would come to affect a lot of lives.

Because the Sterlings were wealthy, Heather had a much better camcorder than the average person might have. It produced excellent pictures even in low-light-level conditions, and it had two interchangeable on-board microphones, one of the omnidirectional type, which picked up sound from all around, and one of the unidirectional type, which picked up audio in a straight line but at greater distances.

On the sunny Monday morning of July 3rd, 2000, Heather had been conducting an "experiment" using the unidirectional microphone. After some measure of begging by Heather, her mother, Reauxanne, had taken her to the ten a.m. launching of some hot-air balloons at a regatta on Lake Lewisville, just outside Dallas. Heather wanted to see how far up in the air a hot-air balloon would have to go before she no longer would be able to pick up what its occupants were saying to each other. Her answer was that once a balloon got thirty-five feet or so up in the air, she would lose the audio. She made a mental note of the experiment. She also enjoyed videotaping the legion of colorful balloons that filled the skies.

After the launching was over, Heather and her mother drove to downtown Dallas where they were to have lunch with Rance Sterling, Reauxanne's husband and Heather's father. Heather loved the food at The Gatehouse, and she loved how fancy the restaurant was, but it was too cold in there, she thought, and the waiters always put the napkin in everybody's lap, which she didn't like. Amid all the fuss about the napkin being placed in her lap on this particular day, Heather bumped her camcorder, which she had carefully placed upright on the edge of the table.

Once the waiter had moved off, Reauxanne Sterling expressed her irritation with her daughter.

"Heather, *please* put your camera on the floor under the table."

Albeit politely, Heather refused.

"Ma-ahm," Heather said, drawing out the word, "if I do that somebody might step on it and break it, or trip over it and want to sue us—or both."

In mild exasperation and slight amusement, Reauxanne gave in.

"All right, Heather, but keep it on your part of the table. We can't ask the restaurant to seat us at a table for six at its busiest time of the day just so you'll have a place to put your camera. I don't know why you don't just leave it in the car. You'd think that tape contained something really important."

Rance Sterling didn't like the camera being on the table but said nothing to Heather about it. They'd had disagreements over her camera obsession before. Rance was an immensely private person, and he believed Heather invaded people's privacy merely by pointing her camera at them—whether she recorded their image or not.

Reauxanne's slight amusement had come from Heather's comment about lawsuits. Reauxanne wasn't sure Heather understood completely, but Heather mentioning that lawsuits could result from people getting injured was more than coincidental, Reauxanne surmised, given the fact that Heather's father was a second-generation named partner in one of Dallas' oldest and most prestigious law firms. Gentry & Sterling performed all types of big-law-firm work. Rance Sterling was the firm's managing partner. His personal specialty was trial law, principally insurance defense. He limited himself to trying just one or two cases per year.

Heather knew why she took her camera everywhere, but she wouldn't expect her parents to understand. What Heather knew was that photojournalists—whether would-be or professional—could not stand the thought of being too far removed from their cameras because one never knew when the next set of rogue cops would beat up the next hapless citizen without knowing they were being watched by the prying eye of a video camera. But what really kept Heather excited was the network TV shows that were based on airing "spot-news" video shot by amateurs. While Heather would never admit such a thing, her secret hope—and that of any photojournalist, she figured—was to be the sole photographic witness to an airliner exploding in mid-air and crashing to the ground. Not that she wished that anyone would die or be injured, but, when she could, she videotaped every airplane she saw passing overhead in the busy Texas Metroplex air corridor.

What neither Heather nor her parents realized in the restaurant—and as has happened at one time or another to virtually every camcorder operator—was that Heather had bumped the camera onto "one-touch record" as the waiter was placing the napkin in her lap. The camera, the very latest Super Hi 8 model, was carrying an on-board videotape that had thirty minutes of recording time. She had used almost the entirety of a brand-new tape on the hot-air balloons, leaving her to discover to her surprise late that afternoon that she must have left the camera on "record" after leaving Lake Lewisville because something had been recorded at the end of the tape.

When she looked at what she had not meant to record, to her real surprise there was Ginger Fontenot sitting at a restaurant table with some man. Heather realized she must have recorded their images accidentally as she and her parents were eating lunch at The Gatehouse earlier that day. Candid camera, and she hadn't even meant to do it, she thought.

She paused the tape to look at a still frame. The image was quite good under the circumstances; all those automatic features on the camera had kicked in. The snippet of sound she had just heard was of good quality, but she wondered what it was like the whole way through; besides, since she knew Ginger—and didn't really like her—she wanted to hear what Ginger and the man were talking about. Using the shuttle feature on her small editing console so she could see the image on the tape during the rewind, Heather ran the tape backward until Ginger and the man became hot-air balloons.

When she heard what they were saying to each other, she knew she would have to show the tape to Taz. The unidirectional microphone had worked perfectly. Heather didn't exactly know what it all meant, but it sounded to her like Ginger and the man she was having lunch with were trying to get some politician she had heard of in a whole lot of trouble using sex.

Ginger and the man were talking. From the look of the table, they had finished eating. Because the restaurant was dimly-lighted, the background was very much out of focus, but the foreground—Ginger and the man—was only very slightly out of focus.

Since the table where she and her parents had been sitting and the table where Ginger and the man were sitting were separated only by a row of mid-height floor plants, Heather was surprised she hadn't noticed Ginger seated so close by; after all, until four years ago, Taz had brought Ginger to the Sterling mansion many times. At first, she thought it was odd that her parents hadn't noticed Ginger at the restaurant, either, but then she thought that her mother might have seen Ginger but not wanted to speak. During Christmas break in his first year of law school, Taz had explained to a more than curious sister and mother that Ginger had refused his marriage proposal. Her father, Heather thought, might have seen Ginger but said nothing. Heather couldn't remember her father ever paying much attention to Ginger when she had been at their home with Taz.

Heather didn't know the man's name, but she thought she had seen him on TV, and she wasn't sure what he did, but she thought it had something to do with the government. Taz knew a lot of government people down at the state capital in Austin because of his job working for the state legislature. Heather was confident Taz would understand and explain to her what was on the tape. She started to show the tape to her mother but decided not to because she was afraid her mother would want to decide what was best to do with it, such as showing it to her father, which Heather just knew would cause it to have a close encounter of the quickest kind with the nearest videotape-machine erase heads. Everyone knew that Rance Sterling hated invasions of privacy *and* family controversy.

Chapter 4

Summer, 1987. Heather's conception had been a mistake, but there was no way she could have been more loved. The first act of love shown Heather was when Reauxanne Sterling decided not to have an abortion when she became pregnant at age forty. It had been a soul-wrenching experience for Reauxanne. She had spent decades as an advocate of legalized abortion, though not an activist; with a prominent Republican husband, that just wouldn't have worked and, besides, she wasn't much of an "activist" about anything, anyway. She thought she believed deeply in a woman's right to privacy in relation to her own body, but when she learned she was pregnant, the thought that she simply would have an abortion had lasted no more than a few minutes before she began to have a gnawing feeling that abortion might be right for other women but perhaps not for her. It was pro-*choice*, she kept saying to herself over and over.

Perhaps she had been affected, she realized, by those television commercials she had seen quite a bit in the mid-eighties about making room in life for another life. What she had liked about them was that they said what they said *quietly*, without preaching and without *a*-nnouncing "right" and *de*-nouncing "wrong." The commercials, she realized upon reflection, weren't really anti-abortion as much as they were pro-life. It was as though at least that group of pro-life supporters had given up trying to make abortion once more illegal, having instead decided to concentrate its efforts and its money on influencing individual pregnant women to make the pro-life choice. Funny, she thought, how she'd never looked at it that way before. She hadn't thought those commercials had changed her mind about anything, but perhaps they had.

At any rate, she simply hadn't been able to bring herself to have an abortion, and she had been glad beyond measure at her decision when Heather sprung from her womb seven months later in March, 1988, ready to take on the world.

While husband Rance had applauded her decision to have the child, he had not offered Reauxanne any counsel on the subject because she specifically had requested that he not offer her any. She knew what Rance's opinion of abortion was generally, but the subject had never come up as to what *they* would do—perhaps because, as Reauxanne had advanced in age, neither of them had thought the chance of her becoming pregnant was very high. While they still had a good sex life, they long since had given up on their once-strong desire to have a second child, so Rance had made no secret of his happiness when she told him she was going to have the baby. Partly as a result of this interesting "beginning," Heather had been spoiled beyond recognition in many ways. Spoiling children was easy for rich parents, but it was doubly easy when the child almost wasn't.

At age seven, Heather asked for a camcorder. As the years passed, Heather asked for the latest model every time a new one came out, and practically all her other childhood interests eventually gave way to video. She was into shooting, editing, special effects—everything. Her father worried that she would become involved in the motion picture industry, or, worse, in journalism. Her mother, who wasn't concerned about such things, was delighted that her daughter was showing such interest in fields of endeavor that mostly had been male-dominated to that time, with notable—but not nearly enough—exceptions.

The Sterling mansion was in Highland Park, old-money Dallas personified. It was truly a mansion. It had a full-time complement of four employees: cook, maid, personal assistant, and chauffeur. For special occasions, such as this evening, the staff might swell to six or seven. It was the early evening of Tuesday, July 4th, 2000, and a traditional family and friends gathering was in full swing. In attendance—in addition to the Sterling family—were an assortment of Gentry & Sterling associates, partners, clients, their significant others, and Texas Republican-party officials and operatives and their significant others. Rance Sterling was a major contributor to the party. At this moment, he was holding court by the pool, verbally assaulting the President of the United States. Everyone knew Rance intensely disliked Carl Billartern, and everyone knew why.

Heather had hold of Taz's arm.

"It's only three minutes," Heather whispered forcefully. "Please!"

"Oh, all right," Taz said, grinning and ruffling her blonde hair, although he truly did want to stay and listen to his father's evisceration of President Billartern. Not because he totally agreed with his father on the subject, but because his father was so articulately critical of Billartern. Taz and his father had little in common politically—a source of some controversy between them—but Taz knew there was value in knowing what his father thought. His father was putting down Billartern as well as talk-show host Linus Routt ever had—just in a classier and more eloquent way, Taz thought.

As Taz and Heather started toward the inside of the mansion, Taz's mind again turned to thoughts of how protective he was likely to become of Heather as she reached her teens. Heather was a blonde and Ginger's hair was midnight black, but they shared eerily blue eyes. Heather was a pleasure to gaze upon, but Taz sometimes wished her eyes weren't so reminiscent of Ginger's.

Heather's room looked more like master control at a small television station than it did a twelve-year-old girl's bedroom. Every time he went in it, he was struck by the idea that Heather's worth just in television production equipment probably exceeded his annual salary as a staff attorney with the state legislature. Taz enjoyed Heather's videos, but they were put together through the amateurish and youthful eyes of a child. As he sat down at the editing console, he figured—at three minutes—that the tape was a music video shot and edited to Heather's latest "favorite all-time song;" at least, at that short length, it wasn't her version of her latest favorite blockbuster film. Instead, what he saw and heard shocked him speechless, a condition he had not often known.

When he had witnessed all he could bear, he slapped the joystick on the tape machine, causing the tape to pause. He didn't say a word to Heather, who was looking at him with some bewilderment—and with a slight amount of fear mixed in. Dazed, Taz got up and walked around Heather's room for a minute or so. He didn't know whether to laugh or cry or throw up. He thought he must simultaneously have been feeling every negative emotion it was possible to feel.

There on the tape was Ginger Fontenot discussing with Jack Duvalier entering into a conspiracy with Duvalier to sabotage the upcoming general election campaign of Democrat Winford Thomas, the incumbent U.S.

Representative from the Thirty-first District of Texas who had just won re-nomination to the House *and* the Democratic nomination to the U.S. Senate. Ginger was considering conspiring with Duvalier to engage in the political blackmail of Thomas. . . . It was too unreal to comprehend. For God's sake, Taz thought, Duvalier was chief of staff in Thomas' Congressional office in Washington, D.C. And Ginger. . . . What he had heard before he paused the tape kept swirling in his head. He mentally played it back.

"Look, Ginger," Duvalier said, "this will make you, and it'll break him. Winford has had his eye on you ever since you won that beauty pageant at TCU a few years ago when he was one of the judges. Anytime we'd get anywhere near Fort Worth since then, he'd say, 'I wonder where that Ginger Fontenot is.'"

"Okay, Mr. Duvalier, so you've done your homework. The modeling competition in New York is a hundred times tougher than I expected it would be, and I owe a ton of money to everybody in New York. You must know that I've had virtually no modeling income this year and that I need this money so I can get paid up, have some breathing room, and reach my goals. I *am* going to make it as a model. But to seduce Winford Thomas and then let you videotape it so you can use it to get him out of politics is a bit more than I had in mind when I agreed to meet you here."

"Well, Ginger, I damn sure didn't fly you all the way down here to talk about *softball* politics. I'm offering you more money for a couple of days' work than you've earned altogether in four years in New York."

"Okay, okay," Ginger said quietly but heatedly, "I hear you. Tell me exactly what you expect of me. I really don't know if I can handle it or not."

With a finger moist from perspiration, Taz walked over and pressed "play" so he could hear the rest of the conversation. Heather's slight fear was turning to upset; she hadn't realized the tape would unnerve Taz so. Once more, Taz sat down at the console.

"It's real simple. You just come to Washington in a couple of weeks, and I'll arrange for you to run into the Congressman at a party at the Ivory Coast Embassy on July 20th. He goes to a lot of embassy parties—flowing booze, you know, and an excuse not to go home to his wife. He'll remember you instantly, and when he does you tell him that you've thought of him often ever since that pageant so long ago. When he asks, tell him you live in Manhattan but that you've been in the district for several days on a modeling assignment.

"Tell him you stopped by the embassy party on your way out of town because you wanted to find out what you could about Ivory Coast since you might be going there on a modeling assignment fairly soon. Be real friendly, but after a few minutes tell him you have to leave for New York. When he asks for it, and I'm banking that he will, give him your phone number. The rest ought to come pretty naturally if what I've heard about you and your college boyfriend is true."

"What the hell do you know about my college boyfriend?" Ginger shot back quietly but through clenched teeth. "I think I've heard enough. Excuse me, Mr. Duvalier."

As she began rising to leave, Duvalier rose from his chair just enough to grab her arm.

"Ginger, wait, please. Sit down. I'm sorry. I didn't mean to upset you, believe me. It's just that, well, when you're in politics at my level, you learn to play hardball. I'm sorry. I didn't mean to offend you, and I don't know anything about your college boyfriend—just what I was told."

"Just what were you told, Mr. Duvalier?"

"I really wish you'd call me Jack, Ginger. . . . All I was told was that you dated a guy for a couple of years that not many of your friends believed you were serious about. That you sort of used him for sex. Hey, we all use people from time to time. I don't even know who the guy was."

"Jesus, that's. . . . Let's get something straight here, Jack. My previous relationships are none of your business, and whether or not I go along with your little scheme doesn't have anything to do with anything I ever did or didn't do before. I've certainly never sunk to the depths you seem to occupy."

"Okay, I deserved that, I suppose, but let's not get off the track. Just tell me, do you want a hundred-thousand dollars or not? Because if you don't, I don't imagine I'll have a very hard time finding someone who does. I offered this deal to you first because I don't think the Congressman will be able to stay out of your pants if you give him an obvious chance to get in them. I don't have a lot of time to waste here, Ginger. What'll it be? More years of frustration while your modeling body goes downhill, or the best chance you'll ever have to make the dream come true you've probably been dreaming since you were a little kid?"

"I need some time."

"How much?"

"I'm going down to LeMieux for the rest of the week since I was able to come to Texas on your nickel. I'll let you know Sunday, the 9th."

"Well, you know where to reach me."

"You'll hear from me this coming Sunday."

Taz watched as the videotape revealed Duvalier pitching what probably was a hundred-dollar bill on the table, getting up and walking out of the camera's frame. Ginger sipped from a wine glass for a respectable fifteen seconds or so and then she, too, was gone from the camera's frame. Just after Ginger left, the tape ran out and stopped recording. Both of them were utterly unaware that their conversation had been recorded inadvertently by the candid camera of a twelve-year-old whose brother was the "college boyfriend." The framing was off a bit but definitely captured the moment.

Taz reached—this time slowly—for the joy stick to pause the tape, which was rewinding automatically, absolutely stunned by what he had seen and heard. His chest was constricting; he knew he wasn't, but it sure felt like he was having a heart attack. Ginger, he thought, my God, my God. . . .

Heather sat on her bed, not knowing what to do. Finally, after ten seconds that seemed like forever, Heather got up and walked over to Taz.

"Are you mad at me, Taz? Did I do something wrong?"

Heather had that flushed feeling in the pit of her stomach she always got when she wasn't sure whether she had screwed up, or, if she had, whether she would get caught.

Taz, still stunned, hadn't heard what Heather said to him, but her words awakened him from near shock.

"What did you say, Heather?" Taz asked her weakly, looking up at her mildly contorted face.

Heather repeated her questions.

"No, sweetie, I'm not mad at you, and you haven't done anything wrong." Taz rose from his chair but felt extremely lightheaded and sat back down.

"Where the hell did you get that tape, Heather?"

Heather explained as Taz stared at the floor, running his fingers through his hair. He simply could not believe what Heather was telling him. Of course he *believed* her, but it was all just so incredible. When Heather finished her explanation, Taz rose and paced the room to clear his head.

"Look, sweetie, I've got to have this tape. I've got to take it with me tonight. I don't know what I'm going to do with it, but I just can't leave it laying around. Do you understand what you heard? You do remember Ginger?"

"I'm not sure I completely understand what they were talking about. It just sounded to me like Ginger was going to have sex with that man they were talking about to try to get him in trouble. And how could I not remember Ginger? That's mostly why I wanted to show you the tape. You never knew it, but I never liked the way she just treated me like I was a kid who should just go away and leave you alone all those times you brought her over here swimming and stuff. You're my brother, Taz, and I know how hurt you were when she went off to New York without you, so I never said anything to you about her. If I ever liked her, I stopped liking her when she left."

Good Lord, Taz thought, he hadn't known that Ginger had treated Heather that way. And, damn, could Heather be this knowledgeable about sex? Well, he thought, why not? After all, she did have the new "R"-rated music-video cable channel right here in her bedroom. She had fibbed a bit to their parents about the nature of the channel, Taz knew. The channel was viewable only in Heather's bedroom because Heather had blocked it out on all the other TV sets in the mansion. Rance Sterling would never see her room, Taz knew, much less her cable premium services, the bill for which was paid by some secretary at Gentry & Sterling who could not care less who watched what.

But could Heather really understand what "having sex" meant well enough to use it correctly in this conversation? It made him shudder to think of little Heather as this grown up at age twelve.

"Sweetie, I'll explain all this to you some time but not right now. I need time to think. The man on the tape's name is Jack Duvalier. He works for a Congressman who's running for re-election and for election to the United States Senate. It's a nasty business, sweetie. Real nasty. And this is an example of just how nasty it can get, up close and personal. Who else have you shown this tape to? Who else knows about it?"

"No one. I waited to show it to you first because I knew you'd know what to do with it."

"I wish I did, sweetie. I wish I did. I just can't believe Ginger would even consider doing something like this. She must want to be successful a lot worse than I ever imagined. And Jack Duvalier—and Winford Thomas, for that matter—what scumbags."

Taz got up and embraced Heather, holding her head to his chest. He didn't know whether he was trying to comfort her in her angst or whether it was him who needed the comforting—or both. In any event, he thought to himself that the side of Ginger he had just seen made her using him for safe sex while in college look like child's play, but he had taken note of what he could construe to have been a defense of him when Duvalier mentioned Ginger's boyfriend from college. Taz was amazed that Duvalier knew anything about Ginger's college days. But, more importantly, why did Jack Duvalier want to sink the political career of his own boss? Weird, just weird, Taz thought.

As reality began to seep back into Taz's consciousness, he realized that questions concerning who had passed along to Duvalier an analysis of Ginger's college relationship with him was idle thought compared to the thinking he needed to do about the tape. Heather, calmer now, still needed an explanation, but Taz didn't have one yet. Taz held her by the shoulders and looked straight into her eyes.

"Listen, Heather, everything's okay; everything's going to be just fine. I just have to figure out what to do. You'll trust me with the tape, won't you?"

"Sure I'll trust you with the tape. Do whatever you want to with it."

"At least for now, I don't want anybody to know you taped all this, especially mom and dad. That's part of the problem. The other part of the problem is that I more or less work for the same political party that Winford Thomas belongs to. Right now, I just don't know what to do."

Taz moved back to the editing console, sat down, then swiveled the chair around and faced Heather, who had sat down on the edge of her bed. Taz placed his elbows on his knees and put his hands together.

"Sweetie, I need to explain something to you that I hope you can understand. It has to do with dad and politics and his career. And another part of it has to do with me. It's gonna take a few minutes, okay?"

"Okay, Taz, I'm listening. I'll try to understand, but I guess you know I don't understand dad very much."

"Yes, well. . . . Heather, you, of course, you know that dad is a lawyer—and me, too, for that matter. So this tape is a problem for me and dad as lawyers—although for different reasons—and it's a problem for me because of who I work for, not to mention that I still feel something for Ginger, as strange as that may seem to you—and maybe even to me.

"About the lawyer part. Some lawyers practice law all their lives, and some lawyers practice law for some years and then eventually become judges. Judges are the ones who referee what the lawyers do in the courtroom and who decide what the law is after listening to the lawyers argue about it. Things like that. In lawsuits, somebody wins and somebody loses, and it's the judges who eventually must decide who the winner is and who the loser is. And sometimes they have to decide who goes to prison and who doesn't. Do you understand all this?"

"Yeah, I guess so. You tried to explain it to me before when I asked you why you were going to law school."

"Okay, good. Now I need to tell you a story about dad that you may not have understood before. I'm sure no one tried to explain it to you at the time since you were just four years old, but now, since you're twelve, you'll probably understand it. What I'm going to tell you about is the time when dad almost became a federal judge. Do you know what I'm talking about?"

"No, not really."

"Okay. Well, I need to try to explain it to you now so you'll understand why dad must never know that you are the source of this tape. In 1992, Bob Granger was the President of the United States and George Parsons was a United States Senator from Texas. Granger is a Republican, and Parsons is a

Republican, and dad is a Republican. Basically, there are Republicans and Democrats, and they don't like each other very much. The reason they don't is because they both think they know how to run the country better than the other.

"Congress has some Republicans and some Democrats, but the president of the whole country is one or the other. Sometimes we elect a Republican as president and sometimes we elect a Democrat. And see, it's the president who gets to decide who the new federal judges are going to be. Obviously, the president would want to appoint people to be federal judges who belong to the same political party that he does. Dad wants to be a federal judge, but since he's a Republican, there would have to be a Republican president in office for that to happen. Make sense so far?"

"Yes, I understand."

"Okay. Now, in 1992, President Granger asked Senator Parsons to recommend to him a lawyer from Texas who would make a good federal judge. They needed a new one because somebody who had been a federal judge for a long time had retired. So, Senator Parsons told President Granger that he thought dad would make a real good one. A month or so later, the President called dad and asked him if he wanted to become what's called a federal district judge, right here in Dallas. Dad told him he very much would like to become a federal judge, and so the president then nominated him to be one.

"Anybody that the president nominates to be a federal judge has to be approved by a part of the Congress called the Senate. The Senate is broken up into committees which do particular things. There's a committee called the Judiciary Committee. One of the things it does is help decide whether people who have been nominated to be a federal judge by the president should be allowed to be one. Normally, dad wouldn't have any trouble being approved by that group, but here's what happened. Since the president was up for re-election in 1992, the Democrats on the Senate Judiciary Committee, who were in control of what went on, decided not to even discuss whether to let dad be a federal judge until they found out whether President Granger was going to win re-election.

"They were asked to decide about dad in June of 1992, but they waited until November without doing anything so they could see how the election would come out. What happened in November was that President Granger lost the election. He lost it to Carl Billartern, who is a Democrat. So, because a Democrat would become president in January of 1993, the Democrats on the Senate Judiciary Committee, who were in the majority, just refused to consider whether dad should become a federal judge. That way, once Carl Billartern became president, he could withdraw dad's nomination to be a federal judge and appoint someone who was a Democrat instead of a Republican. Does any of that make sense?"

"Yes, nobody ever explained it to me that way before. It sounds to me like the Democrats weren't playing fair with the Republicans."

"Well, I'd have to agree with you, but there's one more thing you need to understand. If the situation had been reversed, the Republicans would have done to the Democrats what the Democrats did to the Republicans. Both parties act that way all the time. It's happening this year in reverse. President Billartern is a Democrat, but the majority of the Senate Judiciary Committee now is Republican, so President Billartern's judicial nominees are now being held up waiting to see whether Gregg Andrews or Bob H. Granger, Jr., wins the presidential election in November of this year. I don't know who started it, but now I think they all view it as turnabout being fair play."

"They do? I'm not sure I want to be an adult."

Taz laughed. It was the first bit of levity he had experienced since Heather had shown him the tape. It was welcome. Heather was so smart, Taz thought. Not only had she understood what he had told her, she had recognized the basic lack of integrity involved.

"Let me finish explaining. What happened to dad didn't just happen to him. There were about a hundred people that President Granger had nominated to be federal judges from all over the country who didn't get to be one because the Democrats treated them the same way they treated dad. Lots of those people, including dad, still would like to be federal judges. As I said, there's a presidential election this year. If Granger gets elected, it's a pretty sure bet that he would appoint dad to be a federal judge—maybe even a real high-up federal judge.

"The reason it's real important that dad never be associated with the tape you shot in the restaurant is because if he got involved in a controversy like this situation could become, Granger might not want to make him a federal judge. It's more complicated than this, but let me explain it this way. Federal judges are supposed to be real classy people—just the kind of person our dad has always been. They aren't supposed to have been involved in situations like this that have to do with sex and the private lives of politicians, especially the political enemies of dad's political friends.

"The point to all this, Heather, is that dad would want to kill you and me both if we did something that kept him from being appointed to a federal judgeship. That's why it's so important that no one ever know you shot this tape. Understand?"

"Yes, I do."

Taz rewound the tape to the beginning of the restaurant footage and popped it out of the machine. He put it in a tape box and told Heather he was going down to his car to put the tape in his trunk.

"I'm going to have to ask you not to tell a soul, not a living soul, about this tape while I try to figure all this out, okay?"

"Okay. I'll do anything you want me to."

"Thanks, sweetie. Let's head on back downstairs."

As they made their way out of Heather's room, Taz knew he couldn't answer all the questions by himself. As he walked to his car, he began making a mental list of the obvious questions, wondering how many not so obvious ones would reveal themselves to him after he'd had time to think through the first set. Included on the list of obvious questions was: Should he ever tell anybody about the tape? If so, should he ever reveal how it had come to exist? Should his parents, his father particularly, have any say in the matter? Who owned the tape, Heather or her parents? Did he owe Ginger any consideration? What were his responsibilities to the Democrat party? Given all his possible conflicts of interest, should he turn all these problems over to someone else, if that was even possible? Should he advise Heather to erase the tape? He was an officer of the court, as all lawyers were. Had any criminal acts been committed? By Duvalier? By Ginger? Good Lord, Taz thought, and those were only the questions he had asked himself stream of consciousness. How many would there be when he'd really had time to think?

When Taz and Heather rejoined the group by the pool, Rance Sterling was still pontificating about presidential politics. He was on a roll. President Billartern hadn't stood a chance against Rance Sterling speaking in his own backyard to an audience of his choosing. Rance viewed himself as occupying the moral high ground and Carl Billartern as occupying the depths of moral depravity. On the subject of public policy, Rance regarded himself as wise and President Billartern as vacuous. Even though he was ideologically poles apart from President Billartern's wife, First Lady Renee Holcomb Billartern, Rance appreciated that, in contrast to her husband, she was truly interested in governance issues and not simply in the opportunities high elective office provides for the overdevelopment of id.

Reauxanne Sterling was in the kitchen with the cooks and servants putting the finishing touches on dinner. Heather sat on the edge of the pool dangling her tanned legs in the water. Taz hoped the water wasn't as hot as the water he thought might be about to engulf him. He couldn't remember his dad having gone on and on so, but, then, he also couldn't remember the last time he'd had such an attentive audience. Practically everyone there was beholden to him somehow—mostly concerning money and careers.

Neither Taz nor Heather said much during dinner. That wasn't unusual for Heather, who usually felt like a fifth wheel at such events because the nearest person to her age was more than twice as old as her. Taz had plenty in common with everyone, except political convictions, but he was preoccupied by one of the most perplexing problems sweet little Heather possibly could have dropped in his lap. He just couldn't stop thinking about Ginger—and the tape.

Chapter 5

Wednesday, July 5th, 2000. Taz had taken a day of vacation time. He had planned to spend the day with his family in Dallas, but begged off on that promise to his parents late the night before, saying there were some things in Austin he really needed to do. Everyone understood. Rance Sterling was proud of Taz, though he would never let on.

Taz had been given his first name by his father and his middle name, William, by his mother. Rance Sterling had been quite the football fan throughout his life and had admired a pass-catching end at Rice University around 1960 named Taz Karan. Rance, himself the bearer of an unusual name, had been intrigued with the name "Taz" and had decided that "Taz" would be the perfect name for his first boy-child. Besides, it fit the formula he and Reauxanne had come up with—the name had to be unusual, short, and incapable of abbreviation. "William" was for "Williams"—the maiden name of Anita Reauxanne Williams Sterling.

To arrive in LeMieux when he did, Taz had driven through the night. The Fontenots lived just inside the city limits of LeMieux. When Boudreaux and Tailese had bought the two-bedroom frame house decades earlier, it had come with enough land that the house sat in the middle of about two acres. As a result, they had no close neighbors. The Fontenots were quite friendly, but they also enjoyed the privacy that their partially-wooded land brought them. Taz had been there many times. It had been four years, but he still knew the way. He always would. During the long drive, he had done a lot of thinking.

He had considered visiting the Fontenots when Ginger was about to leave for New York, thinking perhaps they could help him talk her into staying, but he had thought better of the idea, believing it could ruin whatever relationship he and Ginger had left. Later, when he realized there was no relationship left, he started to call the Fontenots to see if he could stop by some time just to visit with them. He was quite fond of the Fontenots and looked upon them as friends, independent of any relationship he'd once had with their daughter. But he'd never made that call. He had told himself they could call him, too, although deep down he knew they wouldn't.

But here he was, at six-thirty a.m., pulling into the unpaved driveway of their home. He still didn't know exactly what he was going to say about why he was there, much less what he was going to say to Ginger about the tape, if anything. The more he thought about seeing Ginger again, the more he thought that perhaps the relationship could be rekindled.

God, did he still love her? he thought. His insides told him he did; at least, his emotions were sending him an extremely strong message of some kind. Perhaps he simply wanted to save Ginger from herself.

The strangeness of the feeling reminded him of the way the German Shepherd he had as a teenager had acted the only time he had taken her to be bred. When he had put the six-year-old Angel in the pen with the male Shepherd—a big, experienced stud dog—Angel had not known exactly what to do. She was scared, but seemingly not of Bo. It had looked to Taz more like she was scared of the situation; scared of the unknown. While Bo watched her with obvious interest, Angel had fretted, frowned, peed, pooped, and paced.

Taz could tell she was experiencing more different emotions and all at the same time than she ever before had experienced. So when, after a very few minutes, Angel sailed across the three-foot high chain-link fence around Bo's pen without touching anything but air, Taz knew the situation just wasn't right for her. Bo hadn't even approached her yet; he had just been watching her, with a look on his face that said "what the hell is *your* problem?" Taz believed he was feeling all the emotions now that Angel must have felt then: uncertainty, desire, fear of rejection, fear of the unknown, lack of self confidence, a hundred more.

Taz was glad to see the rental car sticker on the Ford Tempo in the driveway. Boudreaux's car, an extremely-well-cared-for 1958 Chevrolet Impala two-door coupe, was in the driveway, too. Taz was amazed that it still looked so nice. Boudreaux was very partial to the car, Taz remembered, always treating it gingerly and saying it was special to him. Tailese, who had learned to drive after Ginger went off to college, had a 1992 Ford Escort, but, as often as not, Boudreaux and Tailese could be seen driving the streets of LeMieux in the Chevy, which Boudreaux lovingly called "Lucky."

Taz remembered how proud the Fontenots had been when they had paid off the Escort loan and made the last house payment on the home mortgage they had taken out twenty-five years before. Both events, Taz remembered, had come within a few months of each other and just before he and Ginger graduated from college. With a bit of real-world experience under his belt and away from the comfort of his own childhood, Taz understood the significance of those events much better, especially as he sat in his $30,000 car with the $25,000 mortgage.

It had been light for awhile, and Taz knew the Fontenots either were up already or would be getting up any minute, so he just parked in the driveway behind "Lucky." He didn't want to barge in on them in their house robes, so he thought he would just wait until Boudreaux came out to leave for work to let his presence be known. The next thing he knew, someone was shaking him. Startled, he woke up to find Boudreaux laughing and calling out his name.

"Hey, Taz, it's good to see you, man. What the hay you doin' out here in the yard? When I look out the window and see a convertible car with somebody's head half hangin' out the window, I told mama Fontenot I thought whoever it was out there might be dead. Then I come out here and find out it's you. Man, I was happy on two accounts. Nobody's dead, and you come to see us."

Taz smiled groggily, straightened up, and shook hands with Boudreaux.

"It's good to see you, too, Boudreaux. I can't believe I fell asleep like that. My neck feels like it's been in a vice."

"Come on in the house, boy. Tailese is gonna be happy to see you, I mean. And Ginger gonna be real surprised, what chu tell me, mmmh! You pick a good ol' time to come because Ginger is here from New York visiting us ol' Fontenots. She's been tryin' to get us to come up there to see her, but much as I love my Ginger I tol' her it would take a big ol' gun to get me on one of them damn airplanes and an even bigger one if that plane I got on was headin' for New York, what chu mean! You is a sight for some kinda sore eyes. Mama Fontenot can get that ol' crick out from your neck. Get on in there and tell me what for. Breakfast will be comin' out soon. Mm mmmh!"

Even though his neck hurt like hell, Taz smiled. Boudreaux was infectious that way.

As Taz and Boudreaux headed for the house, Tailese Fontenot ran out the front door like the house was on fire. Before anyone could say anything, Tailese grabbed Taz and hugged him real tight. The muscle pain in his neck at least doubled in intensity, but there was no way he'd let on. He thought the Fontenots would welcome him, but he had no idea they would be this happy to see him. It didn't take him long to understand why.

"Lord have mercy, Lord have mercy," Tailese virtually shouted. "Oh, Taz, I could jus' cry all over you, I'm so happy. Taz and Ginger here at the house, jus' like it used to be."

Given the amount of pain he was experiencing at the moment, all Taz could muster was a somewhat weak, "Hi, Mrs. Fontenot, it's good to see you."

She hadn't heard him, anyway. She just kept on hugging him and mumbling to herself. She wasn't on the verge of tears—she was crying.

"How long you been out there in the drive, boy?" Tailese asked.

Boudreaux did not wait for Taz to answer her.

"Watch out, mama, you gonna break his neck, huggin' him like that. The boy got a crick in his ol' neck from sleepin' out there in the car and hangin' his fool head out the window. I told him you'd get it outta there for him, but I think you gonna break it shore 'nuff before you get the chance to fix it, mm mmh!"

Tailese always had been "fussy," but she was being so fussy at the moment that she started rubbing Taz's neck and shoulders before the trio had even made it into the house. When Taz sat down at the kitchen table, and before he had the chance to say anything else, Tailese, as only she could, placed the previous four years into perspective.

"Boy, I got to finish makin' the breakfast right now, and then I fix your crick, so unless the crick is hurtin' you too bad to talk, tell me and papa Fontenot about yourself. I want to know everything since I saw you last, goodness gracious! Ginger's still asleep, you know. There's no kind of tellin' when she'll get up. I know you come to see her, boy, but us ol' Fontenots are real happy to see you, too, what chu mean, so tell us about yourself before she come in here and take you away from us like she did when she fool thing ran off to New York."

Taz, incredibly tired from having driven all night and feeling quite groggy from having slept only an hour or so, begged a short reprieve.

"I'd love to tell you everything you want to know, and I want to hear about you, too, but could I go to the bathroom first? I really need to throw a little cold water on my face."

"Sure, boy, go on," Boudreaux said. "We'll be right here when you get back. You know where everything is. Nothin' don't change much 'round here."

As Taz heaped cold water on his face, it occurred to him how selfish he'd been when Ginger left for New York. In his own heartbreak, he hadn't given nearly enough thought to the pain and anguish the Fontenots must have suffered then and been suffering ever since. Ginger was their baby. She had an older brother, Alphonse, twenty eight, but he'd gone to work as a roughneck in the oilfields as soon as he got out of high school. Following pretty much in Boudreaux's footsteps, Alphonse had gotten married to a local girl, Giselle Poirot, and fathered three quick kids. He lived only a few miles from his parents. He was a nice guy, but he wasn't Ginger.

Maybe the Fontenots hadn't realized as Ginger was growing up just how special she was. With her intelligence, personality, and looks, it hadn't been very likely that LeMieux and environs could hold her. On the other hand, maybe the Fontenots had realized that Ginger would move away, just not so far. Taz surmised now that they had hoped she would marry him and at least stay in or near Texas. They probably would have settled for the south. But New York. . . . And alone. . . . Selfishly, he now realized, he'd never before viewed the situation sufficiently from their perspective.

Taz's thoughts were interrupted by one of Boudreaux's laugh inducers.

"Taz, boy, I got some coffee in here so hot, what chu mean, it'll make you awake as if you was alligator bait down in the bayou."

Taz laughed out loud. He always had enjoyed the Fontenots' cajun ways and speech patterns, especially Boudreaux, who used to get Taz so tickled when they would go off fishing that all Taz ever seemed to do was laugh. They never caught very many fish. Taz figured the constant laughing kept the fish scared away. On this day, Boudreaux was in rare form. It flooded Taz with the fondest of memories.

As Taz walked back into the kitchen—passing Ginger asleep in the bedroom they had added to the house when Ginger came along—and sat down to share in the Fontenots' breakfast, he remembered another reason he liked visiting them—Mrs. Fontenot's cooking. Where else, he thought as he ate, could he get bacon and eggs with all that wonderful cajun seasoning. Fat and cholesterol hadn't seemed to bother the Fontenots; they'd been eating like this their entire lives and were as trim as could be. Maybe it was true that the only cure for eating like that, other than not eating like that, was exercise.

Boudreaux and Tailese Fontenot probably would not have called it exercise, though. To each other, they probably would've called it hard-ass work. Boudreaux, who was fifty, had been working in the oilfields his entire adult life. He had started out adulthood at about a hundred and forty-five pounds and 5'10," but the years seemed to have taken their toll on his posture. He now bent forward a little, as though perpetually gazing down a drilling pipe. His leathered skin and weathered face were telltale signs. A few times, Taz had seen him come home so tired he barely had the energy to get his filthy clothes off. It wasn't like that all the time, but often enough, Ginger had told Taz more than once, that she knew she never could work like that. Taz knew Ginger didn't want to work like Tailese always had, either.

Tailese, forty nine, slender and diminutive at 5'2," was a housewife. She had been that and "backyard" truck farmer since marrying Boudreaux as a late teenager. Sitting at the breakfast table, half listening to Tailese's stream of consciousness banter, Taz chewed on the idea that the term "housewife" was quite broad. His own mother had been a "housewife" all her adult life, too, but Reauxanne Sterling had performed little labor that she had not wished to perform. Only in recent years had the Fontenots been able to afford the dishwasher Taz had noticed in the kitchen and the clothes washer and clothes dryer he had seen on the newly-enclosed back porch as he made his way to the bathroom.

Tailese had tended the backyard vegetable garden seven or eight months out of the year, using what she could, canning as much as she could, and selling the considerable excess she produced to the farmer's market in nearby Demonbreun. Boudreaux made the deliveries to the market several times a week. During the winter months, Tailese took in ironing to make up for the lost cash from having no fresh vegetables to sell at the market. And all that was on top of cooking meals, cleaning house, and supervising children, including many not her own. Ginger had told Taz that her house growing up was the one all the kids came to to play.

There'd been a place like that in Taz's neighborhood, too, Taz remembered, but it surely hadn't been much of a burden for the "lady of the house" because she had ample servants there to watch after her children *and* the visiting Highland Park kids.

With Tailese's fine cajun breakfast and several cups of Boudreaux's coffee in his gut, Taz was very awake if not downright chipper.

About ten a.m., Taz and the Fontenots were sitting in the living room trading new times and old when Ginger woke up and strolled into the room to see who was doing all the talking. Boudreaux had taken a few days off on the occasion of Ginger's visit. When Ginger saw Taz, she rushed over and hugged him just as tight as Tailese had. Since Tailese had mostly ridded Taz of the crick in his neck, Taz enjoyed Ginger's hard embrace. He couldn't believe the reception, but he sure did like it. Ginger was just as stunning without make-up as with, in Taz's opinion.

"What are you doing here, Taz? I can't believe it."

Taz had known Ginger would ask a question like this, and he still hadn't decided what his best answer would be, so he just blurted out his most recent thought on the subject.

"Well, it was a spur of the moment thing, Ginger. I had been to New Orleans over the 4th visiting friends—who just had twins—and as I was heading home on I-10 a few hours ago, I just decided to stop off and see your parents. I had no idea you'd be here, but it sure is good to see you."

Taz didn't know whether Ginger actually believed that story. He knew her parents did; they would believe anything he told them. He knew he was just going to have to play the situation by ear. Ginger showed no signs of disbelief.

The Fontenots decided after lunch that they needed to go shopping since Boudreaux had the day off. They left about two p.m. and told Taz and Ginger that if they went anywhere to be back by supper time because Tailese was going to cook up Taz's favorite food, cajun-fried shrimp. "Lucky" purred as they drove away.

Taz knew they had left to allow him and Ginger time alone. He didn't know whether Ginger realized that or not; he figured she did, but neither mentioned it to the other. Taz suggested they go for a ride. Ginger agreed, and they put the top down on Taz's Chrysler LeBaron and drove around, finally stopping at a city park. They sat on a swing set and talked for a long while. Ginger told Taz that she had done well in New York, that the competition was tough but that she loved it and was determined to make it to the top.

Much of what Ginger told Taz didn't exactly square with what he knew from the tape, which was in the trunk of his car, but Taz nonetheless found himself enraptured by her, as always. He also felt another emotion. It was as though they had never made love. He wanted to make love to her more than he had ever wanted anything—at least that's what his loins and perhaps even his brain were telling him—but he was afraid. It was like all the self confidence he had learned, mostly from Ginger, about how to handle the subject of sex suddenly had escaped him.

Finally, summoning considerable courage, he got up from his swing, stepped in front of her, stopped her swing, held her head in his hands and kissed her. She melted. Clearly, she needed him, too, Taz thought, knowing that she wasn't as successful in New York as she had let on and that she had other troubles, as well. At that moment, though, he didn't want to think about the tape.

"Let's go somewhere," he said.

"I thought for a few minutes I was going to have to be the aggressor again—like our very first time."

"Ouch."

Giggling. Holding hands. Old times.

It wasn't far to Demonbreun. The Fontenots wouldn't know, and even if they did, Taz didn't think they would care. In fact, as he drove to the motel, Taz was thinking that the Fontenots probably were hoping at that very moment that what was happening was happening. Just before Taz entered Ginger—neither had needed or wanted much foreplay—Taz, in a moment of courage brought on by the sexual high and extreme self confidence he was experiencing, stopped just short and asked Ginger to marry him. Ginger didn't answer; she just grabbed his hips, pulled him inside her hard, and held him tight.

After the sex, which was long, multiple, hot, and wonderful, Taz couldn't believe what was happening to him. There was that feeling again. Not the deep feeling of love that he had expected, but that unfulfilled feeling. And it was strong. He thought he finally knew what it meant, at least with respect to his relationship with Ginger. It was a sign that what he had just done had been out of lust, not love—not a particularly mortal sin, but something of an immoral act nonetheless. He knew he was not in love with Ginger; that he may have been at one time, but no longer.

The feeling was much more than a simple lack of fulfillment. It was a whole range of emotions: guilt, remorse, a realization of Ginger's seeming lack of character—both in terms of her ability to make love to him, not mean it, and have a good time—and exemplified by what she might be about to do to Winford Thomas. At that moment, Taz knew beyond doubt that he loved Ginger no more, that all he would feel for her in the future was pity at worst, twisted emotions at best.

Having no idea what was going on in Taz's mind, Ginger thought she'd better answer the question she had refused to answer just before they made love. She spoke softly.

"Taz, I've just recently come upon an opportunity that's going to help me tremendously. You're special to me, but there's just no way anybody could get me tied down right now. Not when I'm this close."

Ginger loved making love to him, Taz then knew for sure, but otherwise there was nothing there. He just got in her way. Taz realized that he'd never really known much about her mind. While he had traversed every square inch of her anatomy many times, he was having to admit to himself that he hadn't delved nearly as deeply into her intellect or her heart, wherein resided her character—or lack thereof. Funny, he sure had thought he knew her, but as he laid there beside her in a Demonbreun, Texas, motel room, he decided that she was the classic chameleon, varying her stripe calculatedly to achieve some ultimate end that Taz didn't understand and wasn't even sure she understood. But he knew he was through with Ginger. He spoke politely.

"Hey, I understand. Just forget what I said to you a little while ago. It was just sex talking, anyway. And even if you'd let me move to New York to be with you, I couldn't leave here now anyhow because the legislature will be meeting for several months beginning in January, and I'm poised to play a significant role in shaping the major legislation that should come out of this session. I'm real proud of that. Anyway, perish the thought about you and me as 'together,' but I guess we still make great lovers. Maybe neither of us will ever marry and we can meet somewhere every six months or so for a wild weekend."

Ginger took the bait, believing Taz finally was on the same page as her concerning their sex life. They showered—him first then her—got dressed and went back to the Fontenots' home. All was cordial.

Tailese had made Taz his favorite meal. Taz tried his best to be cheerful and to seem like he was enjoying the food; in fact, he couldn't taste it. Ginger didn't seem to have the least problem with the facade. The Fontenots were deliriously happy and didn't seem to notice that Taz was a bit more subdued than he had been earlier in the day, or if they noticed, maybe they just thought he was tired, what with his trip to New Orleans and all.

After dinner, Taz bade Ginger and the Fontenots farewell, reminding them that it was a five-hour drive from LeMieux to Austin and that he had to be at work the next morning. Ginger said she had a flight out of Demonbreun a few days later. Taz thought that probably meant that Duvalier had paid for Ginger's LaGuardia-DFW round trip and that Ginger had paid for her own DFW-Demonbreun round trip. She probably had chosen American Airlines for the New York-Dallas trip so that it would be convenient to fly American Eagle on the Dallas-Demonbreun trip. In any event, Ginger could tell the Fontenots anything she wanted about air travel because they certainly wouldn't know the difference.

When Tailese expressed grave concern for Taz's safety and beseeched him to stay the night, Taz pulled a package of over-the-counter caffeine tablets from his pocket—there from the night before—and told her not to worry. Tailese responded that she sure did wish she could see him more. Boudreaux echoed the sentiment. As Taz was about to get in his car, he hugged everyone goodbye. As he began backing out of the dirt driveway, Taz shouted to the Fontenots that he'd see them soon, but he knew he was lying about that.

Boudreaux hollered to Taz as he was driving away.

"If you don't come back to see us, boy, we jus' might come to the big city to see you, mm mmmh!"

Taz waved. Tears came to his eyes as he turned the first corner. It would be a long drive. The Fontenots hadn't asked either of them anything about their getting together after so many years, but Taz knew in reason that Boudreaux and

Tailese Fontenot were very hopeful that their dreams for themselves and Ginger—and him—might, just might, be realized after all.

Chapter 6

Jack Duvalier was trying hard to leave nothing to chance. If he was going to set up his boss, he might as well go all the way. Duvalier thought Thomas probably had not had much of a relationship with his wife, Linda, in recent years because Thomas bitched about her all the time. He knew Thomas, for political reasons, had not cheated on his wife in many years, but he thought Thomas might be susceptible to a tryst with just the right person. After years of probably little or no sex with his wife, Duvalier thought, Thomas was bound to be getting anxious. Duvalier knew, though, that he'd have to be crafty about this because with Thomas' best chance ever to be elected to the Senate coming up, Thomas would be real conservative unless he just couldn't help himself. Of all the women he and Thomas had met over the past few years, Ginger Fontenot was the one Thomas still babbled about from time to time. Duvalier believed if he could get Thomas to screw up, it would be with Ginger.

Friday, July 7th, 2000.

"Hello."

"Jack?"

"Yes, who's this?"

"Ginger."

"Hey, I didn't think you were gonna call. Where are you?"

"I'm outside a convenience store in LeMieux. I called you with one of those phone cards so there'd be no record of the call."

"Good. Sounds like we've got a deal."

"We do. Call me in New York on Monday so we can work out the details."

"Will do, Ginger. Glad to have you on board. Goodbye."

"Goodbye, Jack."

Ginger wasn't so sure how happy she was to be "on board," but she was damned happy about the money—$50,000 up front and $50,000 "after." With the ability to pay off every single debt and have a considerable grub stake left, she believed she could do everything she wanted to do, including for the Fontenots.

The few days Taz had been back in Austin after his trip to LeMieux were torturous. In trying to decide what to do with Heather's tape, he had come to feel quite alone. He knew the decision was his, but, Lord, what a tough call, he thought. Somewhere in the randomness of his thoughts, Taz remembered a way he might seek help without—at least literally—speaking with another soul. He was recalling an applied ethics course from college.

The professor had stressed, Taz remembered, that in confronting an ethics problem, the best approach was to return to the basics. The first thing to remember about ethics, Taz remembered, was that the terms "morality" and "ethics" were not synonymous. Morality was personal; most often, a person's moral code was based on religious principles—a basic set of "do's" and "don't's" learned through religious training as a child—and/or parental training; even the influence of educators and peers.

Ethics was not implicated, he remembered, until two or more of a person's moral rules came into conflict with each other; the duty to tell the truth, for instance, in conflict with the duty to cause no harm to innocent third persons. Once a moral dilemma had been identified and articulated, the idea of ethics—which should be thought of as a process—could be used to divine which moral precept to uphold and which to reject in that situation. The moral dilemma was to be considered using a framework of analysis based on a predetermined set of principles.

Taz knew he would have to re-gather the framework of analysis he had constructed for himself when he took the ethics course in college—he had learned little about ethics in law school—so he dug out his ethics text and read a few chapters each night after coming home from work. He had kept the textbooks he thought might have some lasting value. He quickly remembered that there were two theories in particular that he liked more than the others; one was a three-pronged test and the other was an ethical decision-making device called the "veil of ignorance."

The first step in the three-pronged method of wrestling with a moral dilemma was to check gut instinct—in other words, without consultation with fancy philosophical theories. At the gut level, Taz thought, Duvalier's activities as a political blackmailer were too important to society to suppress, no matter how many innocent people got hurt—but he just didn't want to put his family in harm's way if he could prevent it. The next step was to determine whether there were any alternatives to having to deal with the moral dilemma—he could think of none.

The final step in this model was to discuss the situation—either in an imaginary or real sense—with "everyone" involved. Since Taz could not have such conversations in other than an imaginary way—except with Heather—he couldn't know exactly what the feelings of the other people would be. The idea was to try to imagine their feelings.

Before having these imaginary conversations, Taz decided to use the other ethical decision-making device he liked from his college course, the "veil of ignorance." The idea underlying the veil of ignorance was that the actor—Taz—would blind himself to his own position in the situation; that is, he would step behind a veil of ignorance and not know whether he was Taz or any other relevant party. In this way, the decision would be the most "objective" possible. Taz knew most people acted mostly out of self interest; that most of the time it was difficult not to, especially when the actor knew she could be hurt in some way should self interest not be acted upon.

In the imaginary conversations among the principals and the objective decision maker from behind the veil of ignorance, Taz wanted to destroy the tape to protect his family, Heather wanted the tape made public so she would know something she shot was on TV, Rance Sterling wanted the tape destroyed immediately based on privacy notions and personal political considerations, Winford Thomas wanted Duvalier's duplicity known but not at his expense, Jack Duvalier and Ginger Fontenot wanted the tape destroyed so they would not be exposed, and the Fontenots wanted the tape destroyed to protect Ginger, but the representative of the voting public Taz had discussed the situation with demanded to see the tape even under the circumstance of never being able to know where it came from.

With the imaginary conversations over, and having considered other ethical decision-making ideas such as doing the "greatest good for the greatest number," the decision on whether to make public the tape was made from behind the veil. The conclusion of the objective decision-maker, everything considered, was to *not* release the tape.

It was only an academic exercise, Taz knew, but nonetheless he was gratified that the objective decision-maker's decision comported with what he himself considered appropriate under the circumstances.

Saturday, July 10th, 2000. Taz called Heather to let her know his decision.

"Hey, sweetie, how've you been?"

"I'm fine, big brother. What've you been doing?"

"Well, I've been thinking a lot about your videotape, of course—and I've finally figured out what I think we should do."

"Okay, what? I hope I know what you've decided."

"Well, I think you do because if my decision was to somehow make public the tape, I would be calling to talk to you about it rather than just calling to tell you what I had decided."

"That sounds like you've decided that no one but me and you should ever see the tape."

"You've got it, sweetie."

"Good. I've been thinking about it, too, and, you know...like...I know dad loves me and everything, but I never talk to him very much or anything, and. . . ."

"You don't feel real close to him like you do me and mom."

"Yes, is that bad? Anyway, I wouldn't do anything to hurt him or anybody else in my family, so if letting anybody else see this tape might lead to a bad situation for anyone in my family, then I've decided we shouldn't let anyone see it. So I'm glad you feel the same way."

"Yeah, your thinking is the same as mine. There are lots of good reasons to let people know about what Jack Duvalier and Ginger are planning, but, bottom line, we have to protect our family."

Taz noted mentally that his conversation with Heather from behind the veil of ignorance had her wanting the tape to be released. Taz was extremely impressed with his little sister that she had made her decision on a basis other than pure self interest.

"So where is the tape now?" Heather asked.

"It's right here in my apartment. I think we should destroy it, but I don't want to do that without erasing it first. I don't have a Super Hi 8 machine, just a regular VHS VCR, so what I'll do is bring it to you here pretty soon so you can erase it on your machine and then we'll destroy the tape. I guess I could burn it or something, but that's messy and it stinks. It won't hurt anything to just leave it right here until I get to Dallas next. I know I'll be there on Labor Day and maybe even before then. Is that okay with you?"

"It's fine with me, big brother. I'm just glad I don't have to worry about it anymore. I'll see you in a few weeks. Are you bringing anyone with you?"

"Hell, sweetie, I haven't been thinking about women at all, if that's what you mean. Are you worried about me?"

"Well, I just don't know why every girl in Austin isn't after you."

Taz laughed a belly laugh.

"Heather, you are amazing. I need to get you down here to be my agent. Maybe you could rustle up some women for me."

"Yeah, right. Well, if you need any advice in the female department, just ask."

"Listen, I'd better not be able to get any serious female advice from you because you aren't old enough to give me any. Understand?"

"I hear you, but you never know. I run with a pretty fast crowd."

"Heather, if I didn't know you were kidding, I'd be up there tomorrow to wrap you in chains. But since I don't believe you, I'll see you soon, okay? Oh, Heather, by the way, I could of course anonymously tell Winford Thomas what Duvalier and Ginger are planning, but I've decided just to stay out of the whole thing."

"Okay, big brother. I love you. See you soon. Bye."

"Love you, too. Bye."

Chapter 7

Embassy parties were a part of Washington life. Foreign embassies were very much in the business of trying to curry favor with Congress and the executive-branch elite for a variety of reasons, not the least of which had to do with foreign aid of various sorts and other advantages such as favored-nation trade status. Embassy parties reminded many newcomers to Washington of "happy hour" at the back-home watering hole, with two major exceptions: the drinks weren't weak, and they weren't two for the price of one—they were free.

Embassy parties almost always began in late afternoon and ran into the early evening. Usually, there was little or no formal program; just alcohol, meal-level *hors d'oeuvres*, and talk. Many new members of Congress seemed to feel an obligation—or just sensed a political opportunity, perhaps—and therefore tried to make all or most of the major-country embassy parties, which was practically a full-time, late-afternoon job.

It had happened that some members who didn't drink much before moving to Washington developed drinking problems from consuming so much alcohol at embassy functions. For those who wished to appear to be drinking but who had no interest in alcohol—or an interest in avoiding it—there was an open secret: slide the bartender a $20 bill and then say, discreetly, "Coke and water." Then each time the drinker stepped up to the bar to order that most favorite of Washington, D.C., drinks—scotch and water—what the drinker would get was a tablespoon or so of Coca-Cola in a glass of ice water—mixed under the bar—and, by sight, a quite reasonable facsimile of the real thing.

Wednesday, July 19th, 2000. Jack Duvalier and Winford Thomas were attending an embassy party sponsored by the Ivory Coast ambassador. Duvalier had accompanied Thomas to the gathering to make sure Thomas actually went because Duvalier knew that Thomas considered Ivory Coast political "small potatoes" to an important Congressman like him. Duvalier had chosen an Ivory Coast embassy party for the rendezvous because that party would attract fewer lobbyists and other such types who would seize the opportunity to buttonhole Thomas, perhaps keeping him too occupied for Ginger to comfortably move in. This way, Duvalier believed, he was lessening the risk that Thomas would not get to interact sufficiently with Ginger.

It was not at all unusual for Congressional staff employees to attend embassy parties. Many "staffers," as they were called, especially the lower-paid ones, ate "dinner" several late afternoons a week at embassy parties—another oddity of life inside the beltway and partly the result of the outrageous cost of living there.

When Duvalier and Thomas arrived at the party, Ginger was there already. With her beauty and elegance as calling cards, simply walking into the embassy had not been a problem for her. Duvalier noticed Ginger immediately and moved away from Thomas, fishing in his pocket for a $20 bill to slip the bartender. Ginger saw them come in and wasted no time moving in on Thomas after his quick trip to the bar for a scotch and water.

"Excuse me, but aren't you Congressman Thomas of Texas?"

"Why, yes, I am, and I'm certain I should know you; I'm embarrassed. You do look awfully familiar—and awfully nice, I might add."

"Why, thank you, Congressman. We've met, but you wouldn't have any particular reason to remember me. It was years ago in Fort Worth. I was a contestant in the TCU. . . ."

"Stop. . . . You're Ginger Fontenot. Of course I remember you. How could I forget someone so gorgeous as you? I was quite sad that you didn't win the Miss Texas pageant. I didn't get the chance to see it that year, but I can't imagine anyone having been any more talented than you. You did a Russian gymnastics and modern-dance routine at the TCU pageant. I thought the combination of the two concepts was fascinating."

"Thank you, again, Congressman. . . ."

"Winford, please, please. . . ."

"Okay...Winford...for remembering me so well. I guess I'm grown up enough now to call my Congressman by his first name. I am from your district, you know. The great metropolis of LeMieux. Of course, pretty soon I guess it won't matter what town in Texas a person is from they'll still be your constituent, you about to become a Senator and all."

"Ginger, Ginger, you flatter me too much. I haven't been elected statewide just yet. It's so great to see you. Tell me about yourself. What in the world are you doing here?"

"Well, as with most things, there is a logical explanation. After I graduated from TCU several years ago, I moved to Manhattan to see if I could talk the fashion world into allowing me to have a modeling career. I've been fairly successful.

I've been in Washington for several days on assignment. The reason I'm at an Ivory Coast Embassy party is that I may be going there soon on assignment to do some swimwear shoots, and I thought I might meet some people here from Ivory Coast who could give me some insight into the country."

"Fantastic, Ginger, I'm so happy for you. I'd be happy to introduce you to the Ivory Coast ambassador, but first I want you all to myself for a little while."

Damn, Ginger thought, she hadn't anticipated—and she should have—that this fool would want to introduce her to somebody from Ivory Coast, especially the ambassador. Well, she'd just have to finesse her way through that conversation, she thought. She couldn't speak any African languages, but she was fluent in every romance language except French. Maybe the ambassador knew one of them, she thought, and they could spend their time conversing in a tongue native to neither of them. That might be enough of a distraction, she thought, to prevent the ambassador from asking her too many questions.

"You know, Ginger, I get to New York fairly often—fundraising trips for my Senate campaign, you know. I'd love to take you to dinner some time. I'll bet I could introduce you to some folks who could help you in your career. Not that you need any help, I'm sure, but it never hurts to know the right people."

"That would be great, Winford, but I'm not in the phone book—you know New York; it wrote the book on weirdos."

"I understand completely. Everybody living there ought to be scared. I don't know how you feel, but every time I'm there for very long, I get this overwhelming compulsion to just go out to LaGuardia and get on a plane, any plane, heading south. But, hey, listen, I've got a pen here. Why don't you just give me your number, and I'll put it in the private address book that I keep hidden away in my office credenza."

"Okay. It's 212.555.3858. If you'll give me a few days' warning, I'd love to have dinner with you some time. And if you misplace my home number, you can always leave a message for me at my modeling agency. Here's my card."

Thomas glanced at it. "Ginger Fontenot. Pretty As A Picture. 212.555.8725."

They talked another five minutes or so before Thomas spotted the Ivory Coast ambassador, who was all too happy to talk to the gorgeous constituent of a member of the House Foreign Affairs Committee who was running for the Senate. The ambassador was delighted to learn from Thomas that Ginger might be visiting Ivory Coast.

Thomas was glad he had spotted the ambassador. Thomas had been a Congressman for nearly twenty years, and, as far as he knew, he was above suspicion; he certainly wanted to keep it that way. He didn't even want Jack Duvalier to notice how long he had been talking with Ginger. After introducing Ginger to the ambassador, Thomas made an excuse to leave. On his way home, all he could think about was how long he should wait—what would the appropriate minimum interval be?—before he called Ginger to ask her to dinner.

Interestingly, Ginger thought, her conversation with Ambassador Anani Oulatè had been elucidating. He had made Ivory Coast seem a really fascinating place to visit. The conversation had lasted about ten minutes. Ginger thanked her ever-so-gracious host and made her exit. Their common non-native language was Portugese. The ambassador had been surprised that anyone fluent in several romance languages and with the last name of Fontenot did not speak French. He had invited Ginger to check whether he might be in his native country on a visit when she traveled there on her modeling assignment. She told him she'd certainly try to look him up were she ever in Ivory Coast.

During Ginger's conversations with Thomas and Ambassador Oulatè, Duvalier had been conversing with Michael Fletcher, a low-ranking member of the White House staff, but Duvalier had kept an eye on Ginger at the same time. Duvalier was interested in Michael, but he didn't desire to start a new relationship right then. Michael was interested in Duvalier, too, but Duvalier told him any significant friendship would have to wait. Michael didn't exactly understand the need to wait, but he was willing to play along awhile. Both had experienced painful break-ups in the recent past, and Michael thought Duvalier might still be carrying a bit of a torch.

Chapter 8

Sunday, July 23rd, 2000. After what he hoped was a respectable interval of several days, Thomas, alone in his Congressional office, called Ginger at her apartment. He simply could restrain himself no longer. They made a dinner date for Thursday, July 27th, at the Tavern On The Green restaurant in Central Park in Manhattan. Great restaurant, Ginger thought, but its popularity with tourists was a dead giveaway that Thomas didn't get to New York much.

Thomas practically was beside himself with anticipation. This he had fantasized about. This could be a rare prize. He could steal away from the district for a night in New York. The campaign would not suffer. Candidates weren't as important to campaigns on a daily basis as they once were, at least in big states like Texas. The races there were won and lost via fund raising and via political commercials on television. Besides, things wouldn't heat up for another month or so; it was still a long time until November. Given their relationship, his wife probably wouldn't even notice that he was gone.

The next day, Thomas told Duvalier he had to go to New York on Thursday for an overnight fund-raising trip. When

Duvalier asked him who he was to see, Thomas told him he was to meet with a confidential supporter who said he might donate a bundle to help him win the Senate race. Duvalier laughed to himself, knowing that Thomas was going to see Ginger. Ginger had called Duvalier at home—using a phone card—with news of the "date" just after she had spoken with Thomas on the telephone.

Duvalier was ready. His agreement with Ginger was that he would position a camera in the window of the hotel room directly across the street from her apartment building in midtown Manhattan. There would be no video of the lovemaking session itself, but it would be recorded on audiotape recorders positioned under the couch in the living room and under her bed. Thomas, after all, might be one of those "couch lover" kinds of guys. Lots of gays were, and Duvalier knew a whole lot more about that than he did heterosexual activity. That there was a hotel directly across the street from Ginger's apartment building was a lucky coincidence. Ginger was to make sure she spoke the Congressman's name several times during the lovemaking; "Winford," after all, wasn't "John" or "Joe" or "Sean."

On the appointed evening, Ginger took a cab to the restaurant. Thomas was waiting in the small gift shop just inside the restaurant's entrance. He was feigning reading a magazine and glancing furtively at the front door of the restaurant each time it opened. Ginger wondered if he had been there all afternoon. She was at her elegant best. Her dress—formal but not too—was a sheer pale blue with black accents that complemented her features immaculately. The outlines of her to-die-for figure were sufficiently evident to leave Thomas as weak as soft butter.

Thomas had reserved a table for them with a good view of Central Park. He was on his best behavior, Ginger thought. The dinner conversation had been halting, but it got better as the scotch and waters began to flow. During the after-dinner-drinks phase, Ginger seized the opportunity to cut to the chase. She knew how. Leaning over the table, Ginger gazed at Thomas as dreamily as she could conjure. She mostly whispered.

"I guess I've had just enough to drink to be bold, Winford. I've never made love to a Congressman, much less a soon-to-be Senator. I'm a big girl now, and I'd like to thank you for what you've done for me already and for what I'm sure you'll be able to do for me in the future."

She was squeezing his hand ever so lightly. Thomas was speechless—but not so speechless that he couldn't order their check. He spoke in such loud tones in requesting their nearby waiter to bring the check that the occupants of several adjacent tables momentarily looked his way.

God, Ginger thought, please don't let anything break the spell.

Her worry was for naught. The combination of Thomas' arrogance, the alcohol, and his melted-butter emotional state simply would not allow him to be suspicious of Ginger's "offer." Duvalier had told Ginger not to worry about Thomas being wary of sexual boldness; that people lied to politicians so often that when a person had been a politician for nearly an entire lifetime, as Thomas had, the truth wouldn't be recognized if heard. Politicians' colossal egos oftentimes made it easy for others to use them, Duvalier had told her, because politicians truly believed other people saw them as special since they saw themselves as special.

With the pretenses now aside, Ginger told Thomas that it would be better if they took separate cabs to her apartment—that she needed a few minutes there before he arrived. That statement served only to excite him more; a dozen new thoughts running through his already-racing mind. She gave him the address on a card. They left the restaurant together. Ginger took a cab. Thank God for liquid courage, she kept thinking on the way to her apartment.

Thomas waited a few long minutes before hailing a cab. He had struggled with himself not to jump in the first cab available. He kept recalling the Southern adage about "many a slip between the cup and the lip," and Winford Thomas wanted no slip-ups here. Ginger Fontenot would be his. Duvalier's operatives had been instructed to videotape Ginger and Thomas getting out of their cab and disappearing into Ginger's building. Then, without turning the recording device off, to swing the camera into position to see through Ginger's open bedroom window—on a hopefully pleasant New York summer evening. Ginger would lure Thomas into the light by the open window where she would embrace him and begin taking off his clothes. Ginger's deal with Duvalier was that, after a just-long-enough time at the window, she would allow her cover-up to fall off, then move away and release the mini-blinds. She would make sure her back was to the camera. That way, she would be exposing herself at a minimum and Thomas at a maximum.

When Ginger arrived by herself, Duvalier momentarily was afraid something had gone awry, but he clung quickly to the idea that Ginger probably told Thomas they should travel to her apartment in separate cabs. Duvalier told his camera operators to stay sharp. A few minutes later, Winford Thomas arrived. All was well.

Duvalier's main camera was outfitted with a zoom lens sufficient to capture a nice close-up of any activities in front of the window. Additionally, Duvalier had a second operative with a disguised miniature camera on his eyeglasses inside the lobby of the apartment building now waiting to ride the elevator with Thomas to Ginger's floor. He would get off there, too, and hopefully be able to videotape Thomas ringing Ginger's doorbell and perhaps glancing nervously about as the operative passed on by and turned the corner into another hallway. If all went well, Duvalier had told Ginger, the public never would see the tape, and Ginger's participation in the scheme would not come to light.

Ginger knew it was a high-stakes game. Duvalier had promised Ginger that the tape would not become public unless Thomas refused to get out of politics. Even then, she would not necessarily be identified. She wasn't sure she could trust Duvalier, but she really needed the money. That morning, a personal courier had arrived at Ginger Fontenot's door. She tipped him $50 for the package. Why not, she thought, $50,000 in cash demanded a good tip.

Duvalier's videographer, on alert after seeing Ginger arrive, had been videotaping every cab that pulled up to the apartment building. Once Thomas arrived and got inside the lobby of Ginger's apartment building, Duvalier's other operative had no problem videotaping Thomas with the miniature camera attached to the side of his eyeglasses, the signal from which was being transmitted live to a small recording device in the pocket of his suit jacket.

The operative followed Thomas onto the elevator. Thomas, who positioned himself in front of the floor-selection panel, asked the elevator's only other occupant for his floor number. Thomas already had punched Ginger's floor number—three. The other occupant, nodding in the direction of the illuminated third-floor button, said, "That's my floor, too."

When the elevator door opened on Ginger's floor, Duvalier's operative silently motioned for Thomas to exit the elevator first. Thomas exited and was followed down the hall at a respectable distance. When Thomas stopped at Ginger's door on the right side of the hallway, Duvalier's operative turned his head so as to record Thomas' actions. As hoped, the look on Thomas' face was something akin to the cat who ate the canary as he glanced about while waiting for Ginger to open the door. The operative was recording audio, too, and had picked up Thomas' few words on the elevator. He had hoped he would be able to record Ginger's voice when she opened the door to let Thomas in, but he was out of range by the time she opened the door.

It mattered not that he was out of range, though, because Thomas and Ginger had said nothing when Ginger opened the door and beckoned Thomas into her living room. Thomas said nothing because his heart was beating so fast he might not have been able to speak. Ginger said nothing because there was nothing to say.

Thomas took Ginger in his arms and kissed her passionately. He wouldn't have known whether she was responding. That Ginger had changed into Victoria's Secret was all Thomas needed to fly into sexual orbit. He was on automatic pilot. His wife walking through the door wouldn't have prevented him from attempting to finish what had been started.

After the kiss, Ginger took him by the hand and led him to her bedroom. In his emotional state, he would have followed her anywhere. Sensing this, Ginger walked directly to the window, which was near the bed, casually turned her back to it and embraced Thomas once more. After a short kiss, Ginger stepped back slightly and began removing his already-loosened necktie. Thomas pushed both her shoulder straps aside, causing her cover-up to fall to the floor. She worried that they hadn't been in front of the window long enough. She should have anticipated, she thought, that this pervert would jump the gun. She dropped to her knees. When Ginger knelt, Thomas noticed the uncovered window and stared straight through it into the darkness. He reached forward and released the mini-blinds just as Ginger's nimble fingers unzipped his pants. For the briefest of moments, he was reminded of a young girl named Sophie Minden—from so, so long ago.

If Duvalier's camera operator was any good at all, Ginger thought, he had everything on tape, and Duvalier surely had gotten what he wanted, even though the plan had not worked exactly to perfection. Ginger hoped Duvalier appreciated her improvisation.

He did.

Duvalier had slipped into New York just after Thomas and was secure in the hotel room across the street while Thomas and Ginger were still at the restaurant. Anticipation had mounted as first Ginger then Thomas arrived at her apartment building. Now, as he and the others in the room listened to the lovemaking live, they watched the video playback from the previous few minutes. All were ecstatic. The images of Winford Thomas slipping off Ginger's cover-up and then staring out the window with a look on his face that would define "lascivious" were perfect, just perfect, Duvalier exclaimed to his cohorts. Winford Thomas, Duvalier believed, was as good as gone from Texas elective office.

Duvalier knew Thomas would be leaving Ginger's apartment at some point the following morning because Ginger had told Duvalier she would tell Thomas she had an early assignment. Ginger also had told Duvalier that, for the sake of appearances, she would tell Thomas to stay in her apartment as long as he liked before leaving.

Ginger left her apartment a bit after seven a.m. It was Friday, July 28th. Thomas had awakened her once during the night to make love, and she had endured that. Thomas was ready to go again as they awakened that morning, but Ginger explained that, much as she would like to, she had to be on location and ready for a photo shoot by eight a.m.

Thomas lay in Ginger's bed for awhile, just relaxing. Somehow, just being there was a turn-on. He masturbated. He vocalized. He was screwing Ginger again and talking to her all the while. The audiotape recorders were still rolling. What an unexpected bonanza, Duvalier thought, as he and his friends roared with laughter as Thomas selfaggrandizingly vocalized while handling himself. This tape, Duvalier knew, would be the party favorite of a certain large subculture for many years to come.

Winford Thomas had had one helluva good time. Ginger was some lay. He just had to figure out how to keep the relationship going. He couldn't tell whether she meant for the liaison to be an ongoing one or whether he simply had been treated to a one-night stand. He didn't feel comfortable asking the question, either, mostly because he was fearful of the answer. After finally exiting her bed, he spent some time looking around Ginger's apartment. It was a bit Spartan, he thought, for someone doing as well modeling as Ginger was.

He took a shower, shaved, and put on the change of clothes he had brought in his otherwise nearly-empty briefcase. When he exited the front door of the apartment building, Duvalier's cameras were recording. Thomas had to wait several minutes before the doorman was able to hail a cab to take him to LaGuardia. The video images of Winford Thomas squinting in the bright sunlight while standing in front of the sign announcing the name of Ginger's apartment building—The Regency—were quite crisp.

Duvalier couldn't leave New York too quickly on the heels of Thomas for fear Thomas would see him at LaGuardia. Duvalier knew Thomas likely would be on the Seaboard Shuttle, but he didn't want to chance anything, so he waited awhile in his room at the Paul Senning Hotel before leaving.

About noon and shortly after Duvalier had boarded a flight back to the district, there was a knock on Ginger Fontenot's door. She tipped the courier $50. After opening the package to count the second $50,000 she had been paid in cash in two days, she remembered to check her apartment to see if Duvalier's people had removed their audio-recording equipment. It was gone. By noon the next day,

Ginger's front-door lock had been changed. This was a creepy business, she thought. It seemed prudent not to take any more chances than she had to. Her lease was up. She would be in her new digs in a few weeks.

Chapter 9

Saturday afternoon, July 29th, 2000. The meeting was taking place at a GAYPAC-owned cabin on a beautiful lake in Northern Virginia. Jack Duvalier, producer of this special project, was gloating. Harriet Salley was in stitches. Sandy Jamanski was coming unglued. Tony Jasmine was laughing really hard. In fact, the entire ten-member Board of Directors and the various invited members—everyone there—was excited. They had just finished watching the "Ginger" tape, as it had come to be known in telephone conversations.

At a Houston media conference the previous month, Congressman Winford Thomas had made the statement that he was a loyal and faithful husband, that he had a strong relationship with his wife, had never strayed in twenty-one years of marriage, and never would. Thomas didn't invite the media to follow him around, but he had made his points forcefully enough.

The news media had been hot and heavy on the "infidel-womanizer" theme again because of the continuously "outed" private life of President Billartern. The previous week, the president had been caught on audiotape telling a supporter and former employee that he had "a lot of catching up to do" once he left office in January, 2001. The president had added, "Hell, I might even get old Gloria to come see me," clearly referring to an earlier sexual outing. As a result, in this election year, many politicians were making statements like the one Winford Thomas made at the Houston media conference. Some were lying. Some were telling the truth. And some were partly telling the truth and partly lying. Thomas belonged to the latter category.

Duvalier had juxtaposed footage of Winford Thomas at the Houston media conference telling the world what a faithful husband he was—the director of the UTS Network archives was a GAYPAC member—against the footage of Thomas at Ginger's apartment, finishing it off with audio of the lovemaking session and the bonus masturbation session juxtaposed to relevant video from a porn film. Of course, in the event the project had to be released to the media, the porn video would not be included, but the GAYPAC folks thought it was fun to look at while listening to Thomas heaving on Ginger's bed.

This was to be the first major "outing" of a non-gay. As a term of art, "outing" had come to mean more to the activist gay community than simply revealing to the world that some prominent person was a closet homosexual. It also had come to mean the "doing in" of prominent gay haters and gay bashers, especially if they happened to be makers of public policy. Winford Thomas fit the bill perfectly except in one way. He was a Democrat, and Democrats weren't supposed to be gay bashers. They were supposed to be liberal, and being liberal meant being for gay rights and gay acceptance. Republicans, not Democrats, were supposed to be the "homophobes" who regarded gays as threats to the very fabric of society.

Trouble was, in real politics, it didn't always work that way. Winford Thomas was a Democrat, all right, but he was a southern Democrat. Ideologically, he probably didn't know what he was. Usually, he was for whatever seemed popular at the moment. Like President Billartern, he mainly responded to pressure. Whatever special interest group was applying the most pressure at the moment usually got its way—at least somewhat and at least for awhile.

On the "gay" issue, Thomas tried his best to have it both ways. When he was appearing before liberal Democrats outside Texas, he was all for gay rights. When he appeared before liberal constituencies in Texas, in cities like Dallas and Houston and Austin, he was quietly for gay rights. But when he was in his own Congressional district, when he appeared before the people who had elected him to Congress ten times, he was a quiet gay basher. Quiet, because he didn't want his duplicity known. The news media, probably out of simple ineptness, had never given him away.

What Thomas truly felt inside concerning gays was revulsion. He never failed to tell Duvalier how repulsive he thought "queers" were once he and Duvalier were safely away from any setting in which Thomas had just voiced his approval of homosexuality. Politicians, especially liberal politicians, almost always thought their staff members believed exactly as they did, having no minds of their own. In any case, it would have been difficult for Winford Thomas to have a staffer who thought exactly as he did because Thomas flip-flopped so often on so many issues.

Staffers in Thomas' offices, after having worked for him awhile, usually came to the conclusion that he had no—or few—truly held beliefs. Winford Thomas was for Winford Thomas' re-election, nothing more or less, they came to believe. Mostly, however, such staffers didn't quit when they made this "discovery" about Thomas because Congressional staff jobs generally were coveted and, besides, the egomania of members of Congress was closely rivaled by many of their staffers. There was rarified air all around.

The Gay Alliance Political Action Committee, or GAYPAC as it was known, had learned the lessons of negative political campaigning well. Its hierarchy had paid considerable attention to the ultra-right-wing PACs of the eighties and nineties that had targeted particular U.S. Senators and U.S. Representatives for defeat. Smartly, the right-wing PACs had concentrated their efforts on those few individuals they viewed as being particularly antithetical to their causes and that seemed the most vulnerable to defeat. They had been quite successful. GAYPAC had decided to become even more ruthless than the right-wing PACs. It had decided to stop at virtually nothing, including political blackmail.

GAYPAC may not have been quite as financially well heeled as some PACs, but GAYPAC wasn't poor, either. So many heterosexuals either didn't know it or didn't like to think about it, but—depending on which research was believed—gays made up from two to fifteen percent of the population and were involved in every facet of American life, including the American dream. Many were wealthy, especially those who were involved in the arts and various retail industries, and most of them were quite willing to support GAYPAC's efforts in ridding Congress of the Winford Thomases of the world.

In 2000, GAYPAC had targeted several Republican members of both houses of Congress that it planned to take on in the general election with extreme negative advertising. Additionally, its board of directors had approved one special project. Because Jack Duvalier, a respected member of the organization's inner circle, had such excellent inside information on the true feelings of Winford Thomas, because Winford Thomas had a reprehensible voting record on issues affecting the gay community, and because there was a distinct possibility that he could be elevated to the Senate in 2001, GAYPAC had decided to expend considerable funds orchestrating his removal from politics. But it would not be by negative advertising.

GAYPAC could handle Thomas being in the House where he was but one of four hundred thirty-five, but in the Senate, he would be one of one hundred. There were some very important gay-rights legislative initiatives coming up in 2001 and beyond, and GAYPAC couldn't stomach the idea of Winford Thomas voting against them as a U.S. Senator. The reason GAYPAC couldn't use conventional political warfare against Thomas in the Senate race was because Thomas was a Democrat, and to the extent the gay community had real friends in Congress, they almost always were Democrats. It would be far too unseemly for GAYPAC to be seen as supporting Republican George Parsons by campaigning against Democrat Winford Thomas. So this had to be done surreptitiously.

Senator Parsons was not homophobic, and he wasn't a gay basher. As a Texas Republican, he couldn't come out *for* gays, but he went out of his way not to bash them. In terms of his votes in the Senate, any time he politically could get away with voting with the gay community, he had done so. There was to be a very important anti-discrimination bill introduced in 2001, and GAYPAC wanted George Parsons in the Senate to vote for it. He had indicated privately to GAYPAC that while he could not openly support the bill, he would vote for it because he believed he could sell enough of his critics on the idea that discrimination in any form was intolerable. It was not an issue that anyone politically knowledgeable thought would cause his later defeat for any public office.

Winford Thomas probably was not subject to defeat in his home Congressional District. His district probably was the most strangely shaped of all the four-hundred thirty-five districts in the country. It ran from Rhinehart on the north to Demonbreun on the south. In order to accomplish that, it was no longer than a mile or two wide at some points. To say the district had been gerrymandered or designed for him would be the understatement of the decade in Texas politics. Winford Thomas knew exactly which kind of people supported him and which kind didn't, so when the Texas legislature had been faced with the task of reapportioning the Congressional districts after the 1990 census, Thomas had called in a horde of chits to get his new district carved in the exact shape he wanted—reflecting a sizeable majority of poor workin' folks, black and white, who were particularly susceptible to his populist message of fightin' the big Republican special interests and granting relief of every kind to the little man—"the backbone of this great nation," Thomas liked to call them to their faces.

He was opposed for election to the newly-formed district in 1992 by Terry Dunedin, a moderate Republican lawyer from Demonbreun who detested lying politicians and political and governmental extremes and excesses as solutions to anything. He spent the entire campaign telling the honest and simple truth as he saw it. He got eighteen percent of the vote in the general election and retired from politics. The exposure surely would bring the firm a few more clients, his law partners had told him after his rather ignominious defeat.

Thomas definitely would vote against the anti-discrimination bill were he in the Senate. He would vote against it in the House, too, were he a member of that body in 2001, but GAYPAC knew his negative vote would count for a lot less there.

GAYPAC had bypassed any involvement in the Winford Thomas House and Senate primaries. It knew Thomas would be easily nominated for re-election to the House, and it actually wanted him to win the Democratic nomination to the Senate. Thomas was backed by powerful oil interests in east Texas and elsewhere in Texas. He had not won the Senate nomination easily, but he had pulled it off. His principal opposition had been Lt. Governor Felicia Mayes and Land Commissioner Samuel Rodriguez. The "running for two offices at once" issue had not been much of a factor because while Thomas was the only Democratic Senate candidate who needed to invoke the law in 2000, *all* the major candidates in the Democratic Senatorial primary had used the law at one time or another in their political careers. Knowledgeable voters were mad as hell over what the law allowed, but there weren't very many of them.

Several special interest groups had promised to lobby the state legislature hard in 2001 for the repeal of the law, known as the "MTK" law. It had been enacted in 1960 by the Texas legislature at the behest of Democrat U.S. Senator Marlon Tynes Kirkland who desired that year to run for president or vice president of the United States and for re-election to the U.S. Senate from Texas at the same time. In fact, he was elected both Vice President of the United States and U.S. Senator from Texas in November, 1960. To assume the vice presidency, Kirkland resigned from the Senate, and a special election had to be called to fill the Senate vacancy. There were several dozen candidates. Good ol' Texas chaos. Ironically, a Republican won the special election, giving Texas its first Republican U.S. Senator since reconstruction.

GAYPAC wanted Thomas to be Parsons' opponent for the Senate. That way, if GAYPAC could do something to cause Thomas to lose the Senate race, Parsons would be in the Senate to vote for the anti-discrimination bill the following year. Marlene Davidson, Thomas' Republican opponent in the House race, likely would win that seat with Thomas not in the race and against whomever the Democrat party of Texas appointed to run in Thomas' place. By the dawn of the twenty-first century in east Texas, many persons who once considered themselves "yellow-dog" Democrats now were turning to the Republican party as the Democrat party seemed to them to be moving further and further to the left. To GAYPAC,

Marlene Davidson seemed a fairly moderate sort who might vote for GAYPAC's issues when she could, much as Parsons had.

The timing on all this had to be just right. The Democratic National Convention was set to begin Sunday, July 30th, in Boston. The "outting" of Thomas needed to take place after the convention so that if GAYPAC had to make the "Ginger" tape public, the convention itself and Gregg Andrews' nomination as president would not become secondary to and tarnished by the Winford Thomas situation.

GAYPAC would confront Thomas just after the convention. If he didn't resign within a week, GAYPAC would—anonymously—cause the release of the "Ginger" tape. GAYPAC also would show the tape to several top Democrats who themselves were gay and who knew of Thomas' true feelings regarding homosexuals and the gay community. In that way, pressure from within the party could be brought on Thomas to resign, and the Democrat party of Texas could be given fair warning that it would need to appoint replacements for Thomas in the two races.

With Thomas out of the Senate race, there always was the slight possibility that a real liberal, appointed by the party to run in Thomas' place, would defeat Parsons for the Senate. And there was virtually no chance that the "powers that be" in the Democrat party of Texas, more than a few of whom were gay, would appoint a homophobic conservative to replace Thomas in either race, though the House race wasn't the principal focus of the special operation. In the final analysis, GAYPAC believed, the possibility that GAYPAC would be shooting itself in the foot by causing the political demise of Winford Thomas was practically nil.

After Duvalier, Salley, Jamanski, and Jasmine calmed down from watching the "Ginger" tape, Duvalier told them how Thomas would be confronted with it. The "when" would be the afternoon of Sunday, August 6th, just as Thomas returned to Washington from the Boston convention. The "where" was that Duvalier would lure Thomas to a hotel suite in Washington rented for the purpose of confronting him and showing him the videotape. Duvalier would greet Thomas at the door, usher him in, introduce him to the others and tell him they had a videotape to show him. The ruse Duvalier would use to lure Thomas to the hotel suite would be that a particularly well-healed lobbyist for the timber industry, east Texas' largest employer, had asked for the meeting.

Chapter 10

Sunday, August 6th, 2000. When the knock came, Jack Duvalier looked through the peephole. Standing there waiting to be let in was one Winford Thomas—in his Congressional uniform of dark suit, white shirt, and necktie fad of the moment.

"Come in, Winford," Jack said, opening the door.

Thomas looked around, saw no one and gazed expectantly at Duvalier. Duvalier shut the door and looked Thomas in the eye.

"Winford, there's no lobbyist here. In fact, there's nobody here but us queers."

Thomas laughed heartily.

"Oh, bullshit, Jack. Where's Verne Atkins? I'm tired, and I want to go home. I've been gladhanding fat folks and kissing ugly babies all week."

Before Duvalier could respond, the others walked out of the bedroom. Thomas did not recognize any of them.

"What the hell's going on here, Jack? Was that 'queer' remark a joke of some kind?"

"It's no joke, Winford. Let me introduce my friends. Meet Harriet Salley, Sandy Jamanski, and Tony Jasmine. They're all friends of mine, Winford. They're all queers, just like me. . . ."

Thomas interrupted.

"Wait a minute, Jack. What the hell are you talking about 'queers?' You'd better tell me what's going on here, Jack. I'm in no mood for bullshit or games. I'm too damned tired for. . . ."

Duvalier interrupted. He spoke loudly.

"Winford, come over here on the couch and sit down and shut the fuck up. This is one time you're going to listen to somebody else. And before you turn around to leave, let me tell you that there's a videotape in that machine over there of you and Ginger Fontenot that you just might want to see before you rush out. Now sit down, shut up, and listen."

Thomas, agape, sat down on the couch—slowly—and by himself. Everyone else sat in chairs.

"First," Duvalier said, "you hereby have my resignation. I've wanted to leave your employ since shortly after going to work for you and learning of your gross homophobia. But as time went by, I decided you deserved a better fate. And this is it. But pardon me, I'm being rude. Let me tell you something of my friends. Harriet here is an independent book publisher in New York. Very influential. Quite wealthy. Lesbian."

Harriet nodded at Thomas. Thomas stared at them all in amazement, and he kept glancing at the tape machine. The room was well air conditioned, but Thomas had begun to sweat. His lips were tightening.

"Well," Duvalier continued, "they're all influential and wealthy and homosexual, so I won't repeat that part every time. Sandy lives in Miami. She's general counsel for a nationwide chain of clothing stores. And Tony lives in Little Rock. He's a philanthropist and patron of the arts. And they all have one other thing in common, Winford. They constitute the executive committee of the board of directors of GAYPAC. Ever heard of GAYPAC, Winford? Sure you have. It's the political action committee run by all those queers. Remember how many times you said that to me, Winford? Do you?

"Well, we, yes *we*, at GAYPAC have a little surprise for you today, Winford. We call it the 'Ginger' tape. We've been enjoying watching it a lot, but we think it's time you saw it, so Tony if you'll turn out the lights—and don't worry, Winford, none of the queers in here has any plans on grabbing your dick or anything—we'll watch us a little short movie."

Thomas was frozen. He could say nothing. He was moments away from throwing up unless he could somehow control the urge. Sweat dotted the perimeter of his lips. He stared at the monitor. He could not believe what he had just heard. If Duvalier had on the tape what he feared was on it, Thomas knew he would be watching his political career passing in front of his very eyes.

His worst fears were confirmed. There he was telling the world he was no infidel in one sequence and clearly slipping off Ginger Fontenot's cover-up with his face to the camera in the next sequence. He had been set up. He wanted to kill every God-damned queer in the room to start with and then rid the entire world of every other queer with his bare hands, one motherfucker at a time. He wanted to kill Ginger Fontenot, too. For her, he would reserve a special death.

After the showing—the GAYPAC people hadn't been able to keep from smiling during the porn-video part—Duvalier was the first to speak.

"Well, Winford what did you think of that? Nice little set up, huh?"

All but Thomas laughed. He was sitting on the couch, sweating profusely, nauseous, holding his face in his hands.

"What do you want?"

"Our terms, Winford, are quite simple. You are going to resign from the Senate and House races by this time next week. Given who you represent in the House, showing this tape there might make you a hero, get you more votes than you normally get, but that ain't gonna matter 'cause you ain't gonna be in the race. Statewide, you and me know damned well that you couldn't get fifty-thousand votes against George Parsons if this videotape ended up on TV. And if you don't resign, this tape—minus the porn part, of course—*will* get shown on TV. Texas TV. 'The Texas Truth.' Lots of times. You can count on that. You're politically dead, Winford. You died today. Right here. This moment. One more thing. Just in case you think you might be able to finesse this somehow, think again. Tonight, this tape is being played for a number of the higher-ups in the national Democrat party. In case you're interested, they're homosexuals. Yes, Winford, there are homosexuals in your own political party. And at damned high levels, too.

"We think you should resign from both races tomorrow, Winford, but we know you won't. You'll leave here in a few minutes and go on off somewhere and get by yourself so you can think. That's fine. Go right ahead. But it ain't gonna change a thing. You're gonna resign from politics by the end of next week, or you're gonna see this videotape playin' on every TV station in America. Go quietly, Winford. Be smart. Oh, yeah. We are gonna let you serve out your term in the House 'til the end of the year so you can have your retirement boost. But don't get smart. Even after you've resigned from politics—and that's forever, by the way—you still wouldn't want your wife and your children and your old papa down there in Rhinehart to see this tape, would you, Winford?

"And you have no chance of trying to expose GAYPAC without the 'Ginger' tape getting shown to everyone, including your family. You're not real smart, Winford, but you're smarter than that. So just go on off now, and spend your time wisely. Figure out what you're going to say when you hold that media conference in the next few days. One last thing, Winford. I've been a homosexual all my life. Yes, I was married once, but it was a facade. In the seven years I've worked for you, not one time did you consider that I might be gay. You just assumed that I was wedded to you and to my job. And all those times you told me how revulsing queers were to you, I wanted to die inside—just die. But revenge is sweet, and I'm having mine now. So get on out of here before I forget my manners and kick your ass."

The room fell silent. Slowly, Winford Thomas stood up. Slowly, he walked to the door, opened it and stepped into the hallway. Slowly, he closed the door and moved off down the hallway. His life kept passing in front of him as he walked. Why me, he just kept thinking, why, why me?

Chapter 11

Taz Sterling was a staff attorney with the research and drafting arm of the Texas legislature. He had taken the job the previous year after graduating from law school and passing the bar examination. Rance Sterling had wanted Taz to join Gentry & Sterling—even if they didn't see eye to eye politically—but Taz didn't think he could handle the culture of a mega-lawyer firm, even if his last name had been on the firm's front door for two generations. Once again, he knew, he had defied his old-line law-firm family's wishes in a significant way. The first time had been when, as a third-generation legacy, he hadn't pledged Delta Sigma Phi at TCU. Now, how would his father explain *this* at the country club, Reauxanne Sterling had disappointedly wanted to know when Taz took the government job in Austin.

Taz had been hired by Ed Land, chief of the Legislative Research and Drafting Service. Land served at the pleasure of the Speaker of the House and the President of the Senate—both Democrats; there hadn't been a Republican serve in either office since Reconstruction. Ed Land, too, was a

Democrat. When Taz flew from Houston over to Austin for his interview with Land in March, 1999, he had worried that Land might not hire him because of the big-time Republican politics of his father. He decided to mention it during the interview.

"Mr. Land, if you don't know that my father is Rance Sterling, I think you should."

"Why is that, Taz?"

"Because he's quite the Republican."

"Yes, well, Taz, I know who your father is. I wouldn't have survived in this job for twenty-three years had I not been any better at Texas politics than that. But let me explain something to you. I'm a *Texas* Democrat. You know, that's a bit different from being, say, a Massachusetts Democrat. Your father is probably way too conservative for me, but we probably agree on many issues. Besides, the job you are interviewing for truly has little to do with politics. You would be doing research and drafting bills as requested by members of the legislature. There's little room in the job for personal political views. In fact, that's one reason you made the list of finalists for the job."

"How's that, sir?"

"Well, from the research we've done on you, we've discovered that, in political terms, you think of yourself as a 'radical moderate.' Whether you're actually radical or not, we find it interesting that you view yourself as a moderate. Not only are there conservative Republicans in the legislature now, but there are Democrats who are conservative, Democrats who are liberal, and Democrats like me —Texas Democrats. You would be working with all these members, Taz, so the ability to draft bills from their particular point of view would be a great asset in the job. We have found that young lawyers who are too ideologically driven don't do well here."

"Wow, you certainly checked me out. I'm flattered. And I want you to know that I feel entirely capable of performing this job. I really hope I get it. I'm very interested in the governance of Texas, and I would be proud to be a part of helping the legislative branch function well."

"Fine, Taz, fine. We'll let you know our decision in a week or so. C'mon, let me show you around."

More than a year later and having been through a called special session of the legislature, Taz had grown confident and comfortable. He had learned an immense amount about the legislative process, about drafting legislation, about state government, and about politicians. His impression of politicians had not improved, and any latent desire to himself run for public office had evaporated. His view of Ed Land, however, was another story. Land's job was quite difficult, walking a political tightrope between those at whose pleasure he served and everyone else, Taz thought. Taz had great respect for him. He also was beginning to identify with the folks around there, like Ed Land, who called themselves *Texas Democrats*.

By any history, Shannon Gillette was not Taz Sterling's cup of tea, but Taz had been powerfully attracted to her from the moment they met. She certainly was good looking; no one would deny that. Her dirty blonde hair was natural, her blue eyes weren't, and she was very sexy. At about 5'5," he thought, she was slinky, looked just a bit kinky, and hopefully was. At twenty eight, he discovered later, she was two years older than him and that was somehow attractive to him, too.

Shannon Gillette was a television reporter, but not for some local station. Shannon was the principal correspondent on "The Texas Truth," a syndicated, twice weekly, half-hour prime-time show produced out of Austin that aired in every major Texas television market from Amarillo to the Rio Grande Valley and from Texarkana to El Paso. In Austin, Dallas, Houston, and San Antonio, it was a real ratings grabber because its principal fare was politics by way of investigative reporting. The show had been a force in Texas politics for a decade. Shannon was its latest star, having been there three years. "Triple T," as it was known, was owned by Diversicom Corporation and was worth millions. Diversicom owned similar programs produced in other states, but Triple T was its crown jewel. Diversicom's owners were corporate bean counters and investment bankers in Atlanta who could not have cared less about the program's content. To them, the program was nothing more than a national concept that they had applied in large local markets, like the Texas market, which was more like a region than a locale. The bottom line: Triple T made a lot of money.

Shannon was fearless. She took on anyone and everyone in the political and governmental establishment of Texas that she thought needed a comeuppance. She had revealed corruption from the highest levels of state government to the lowest levels of city hall—and all over the state. She had been sued for libel and privacy invasion more than once. Mostly, the cases against her and Triple T had been dismissed pre-trial for lack of proof of intentional tortious conduct, the legal standard in such cases. Of the few that had proceeded to trial, she had lost every one and with jury awards to her "victims" in the millions of dollars. If juries didn't hate her, then at least they hated her tactics. In each such instance, however, Triple T's media attorneys had appealed, and, each time, an appellate court had reversed the award and dismissed the case, finding no intentional tortious conduct. She seemed invincible. By the political establishment, she was feared, loathed, respected, and admired—all at once.

Shannon's network of informants was a mile wide and an inch deep. The unsolicited calls she and her producers got usually were from folks who described themselves as "little people" and "ordinary workin' folks" who just happened to know a little something about something corrupt. Usually, they were right; Shannon could get to the bottom of anything.

Triple T was not to be confused with "tabloid TV;" that, it was not. It could be described more aptly as "in your face" journalism; not some whitewashed or varnished form of the truth, but—"The *Texas* Truth." With "victimized" taxpayers, Shannon was as gentle as a lamb; with government and political types, they were lambs to the slaughter if she thought them corrupt and they allowed themselves to be interviewed by her.

As a staff attorney, Taz was not Ed Land's media assistant, but the Legislative Research and Drafting Service had no PR person, so whenever a reporter inquired about something, the media-relations function fell to Taz—as new kid on the block and because of his college newspaper column-writing experience.

On an otherwise routine August 9th, a Wednesday, Taz answered his line about ten a.m. to discover Shannon Gillette on the other end.

"Is this Taz Sterling?"

"Yes, it is."

"Hi, I'm Shannon Gillette with 'The Texas Truth.' I was told by the secretary there that if I wanted to set up an interview with Ed Land, I'd have to go through you."

"Well, that's because I'm sort of the default media-relations person around here. What can I do for you?"

That Shannon Gillette was on the telephone would make anyone nervous, Taz thought. That she wanted to interview his friend Ed was truly angst-inducing.

"Like I said, I want to interview Ed Land."

"Can you tell me what about?"

"No."

Taz laughed. He couldn't help it, even if his ineptness as a media-relations person would not serve Ed well.

"I guess that question deserved that answer. You can see that I'm no pro at this, but I will need to tell Ed something; after all, your reputation as an interviewer does precede you."

"Yes, well, that's certainly been said to me before. Look, what I need to interview him about is not controversial as to him. May I tell you something in confidence?"

"Sure."

"You understand confidence—confidentiality?"

"Ah, Ms. Gillette, whatever else I'm not, I am a lawyer, so don't worry about my ability to keep a confidence, okay?"

"Okay, just so long as we understand each other. I'm working on a story that's going to say that the generic drug law the legislature passed some years ago had an unintended consequence. It was meant to help senior citizens get a handle on the cost of prescription drugs by allowing pharmacists to substitute the inexpensive generic equivalent for the expensive name-brand drug. Doctors, you know, just know the brand name, so that's what they almost always write down on the prescription form."

"Ah, sounds good to me. What's the controversy."

"Well, seems as how the Medicare and Medicaid programs are getting ripped off by that law."

"How?"

"Try this on. The doctor gives the patient a prescription for a brand-name drug. The patient goes to the drugstore to get it filled. The pharmacist substitutes the less expensive generic equivalent and then bills Medicare or Medicaid for the brand name. The rip-off is that the pharmacist has dispensed a drug he bought on the cheap but tells the government he dispensed the expensive one, so the government pays him on that basis. If Medicare or Medicaid ever happens to investigate, the pharmacist simply shows them the prescription, which he has on file, where the doctor prescribed the brand name. The brand name goes on the pill bottle. The pills are consumed, leaving no evidence. It's a sweet scam. All I need Ed Land to say is something I'm sure you already know, which is that no matter how good legislative drafters are they can't anticipate the exact and total consequences of every statute they draft."

"Amen to that. Hey, that's a great story. When do you want to interview Ed?"

"Today."

"Okay, let me clear it with him for this afternoon. How about four p.m?"

"Cool. Call me soon. My number is 555.9735."

Ed Land's Shannon Gillette interview went smoothly. Few government officials interviewed by her could make such a claim. She had explained to Taz in their second telephone conversation that she wanted Ed Land in her piece making the "drafting is difficult" statement so that she could claim she wasn't being unreasonably critical of the legislature. Armed with this information and promise, Taz had been able to convince Ed to do the interview.

As the actual videotaping took place, Taz lurked in the shadows and watched. Always drawn to journalism somewhat, he was fascinated with the process. Shannon saw him watching. After the interview was over, she asked him if he would like to join her and the crew for a drink. Taz didn't know whether to be flattered, whether she was just offering a quid pro quo for his help, or whether she saw him as a possible source at the state capitol. At the moment, though, he really didn't care. She, he thought, was even better looking than on

TV. She was sexy as hell, and in the aftermath of his recent encounter with Ginger, he needed something new. Like the song says, he thought, if you can't be with the one you love, love the one you're with.

Sixth Street in downtown Austin, Texas, is famous—infamous, some would say. The bars might not be world class, but there is a world-class number of them. Every left-over hippie in Texas either works in one or is panhandling on the streets outside. Trying to make all the Sixth Street bars on a given outing is a guaranteed formula for achieving drunkenness.

Austin also bills itself as the "Live Music Capital of the World." A dubious claim, but it is true enough that Austin and Sixth Street offer lots of music and lots of different types of music. Everyone's favorite genre is represented somehow.

Within an hour of hitting Sixth Street with Shannon, Taz had noted two interesting developments: Shannon's crew had departed for planets unknown, and Taz and Shannon had discovered a shared taste in many forms of music. They decided to sample every genre Sixth Street was offering that night. Sampling the music also required sampling the alcohol. Drunk, they ended up at Taz's apartment, which was itself downtown.

They made love, but it was not a moment either of them would cherish—mostly because they mostly wouldn't remember it.

Thursday, August 10th, 2000. Six a.m. Taz's alarm went off. He hit the "snooze" button fast and clean. Shannon, startled by the unfamiliar clanging, opened her eyes just in time to see him in action. She decided that this probably was a morning ritual with him. A few minutes later when the alarm clanged again, four eyes came open to stay. Shannon, fighting grogginess but interested in where she had awakened, propped up her head with her elbow and hand and gazed at Taz. She was smiling. Taz was glad of that. Shannon spoke first.

"Oh, God, who are you?"

"Ah, my name is Taz Sterling. What's yours?"

"Shannon Gillette. Nice to meet you. Did we do what it appears we did?"

"Damn, you don't remember? I'm crushed! Gee, I can see you don't remember. Truth is, I don't remember much, either, but from our lack of clothes, I'd say we did or at least tried to. What do you think?"

"Well, I'd say if neither of us remembers, it doesn't count if we did...do...whatever."

Taz scooted closer, kissed her sprightly, and then backed off, leaving them face to face. He spoke.

"Hey, I had a great time last night. Let's go take a shower and see where this thing goes from here."

"Deal."

One hot shower and one hot love-making session later—diminished only by the hangover they were sharing—it was time for Taz to take Shannon to her car, parked somewhere near Sixth Street, and drive on to work. As Shannon was gathering her belongings—clothes and such strewn all over his apartment—her purse slipped from her hand and fell onto the coffee table, spilling much of its contents. With some irritation, she raked it all off the coffee table and into her purse.

Taz looked sharp in the olive-green suit he was wearing, she thought. She was sure she looked a mess—even having taken two showers that morning—because she had on yesterday's clothes and was wearing a hangover, as well. Her long, wet hair was in a ponytail. Oh, well, she thought, she'd be home soon, and besides, she felt no embarrassment. Taz was straight, yet strong and fun. She needed that. She liked him.

Chapter 12

Thursday morning, August 10th, 2000. Winford Thomas was in a cabin way back on his father's land in the piney woods of east Texas. Jack Duvalier, Thomas had concluded after several days of careful thought, had been right about some things and wrong about some others. Thomas knew his political career was over; Duvalier had been right about that. Thomas also knew that whatever decisions he made in the situation, his wife would divorce him. Even if he simply resigned, he never would convince her that he hadn't done something awful; he knew she was looking for a way out.

And he knew that divorce would be expensive. Real expensive—because the law in Texas was that courts had the authority, even the duty, to award property from a marital estate in grossly differing proportions based on the degree of fault in the circumstances. Depending on the judge, the various "faults" of his that she might prove could be the financial death knell for him.

He knew better than to be expecting any bail-out from his father. Except for some land and hidden cash that his father had been able to keep, Winfred Thomas no longer was a seriously wealthy man. In the late eighties, as he was preparing to retire, he was caught charging his customers grossly usurious interest rates, his whole scheme unraveled, and he was sued into oblivion by government consumer-protection officials and by individuals. Winford, with all his power, had not been able to help his father more than slightly.

Winford knew he was going to need a lot of money. In addition to the cost of divorce, he would need to work, and who would hire him? He had a law degree, but he never had practiced, and he would be too hot even to work as a lobbyist for a year or two.

The GAYPAC folks just thought he would be predictable, Winford thought. But he wouldn't. There just might be a financial way out for him in this whole thing. He would tell GAYPAC that he had no intention of resigning from a damn thing and that GAYPAC should release the tape. He knew he would be forced to resign after the tape became public, but at least then he would have a bunch of folks to sue. He was tired of his life and of all the political bullshit, anyway. He just couldn't trust anyone anymore. He was ready for a big change. Besides, lots of men he knew his age would give their eye teeth to have screwed Ginger Fontenot. Let the world know about it, he thought. Stuff like this hadn't hurt President Billartern any.

Winford Thomas might be in trouble, but he hadn't served in Congress for nearly twenty years not to have friends in various places. He believed they would help him so long as it wasn't public support. In that regard, he was persona non grata. *Very interesting*, he thought, when he learned that Diversicom Corporation was in the midst of the Kennecut negotiations. If Diversicom was a motivated seller, and he was betting it was, Diversicom might pay a pretty penny to get rid of a lawsuit filed by him. Duvalier had specifically mentioned

"The Texas Truth" in boasting where the tape would be broadcast.

The public, Winford was certain, thought he—like all members of Congress—was rich; in truth, he had been in Congress since just after law school, so he'd had no time to amass any wealth. True, he had raised millions in campaign contributions, but he'd spent that on television advertising getting re-elected. He had counted on inheriting half of his father's rich estate, but he could count on that no more. He wouldn't get rich off what he might win in a lawsuit, but it would be a start, and he had some money-making ideas.

Early Thursday afternoon, August 10th, 2000. Jack Duvalier was stunned when Winford Thomas told him to release the tape. Stunned.

Later Thursday afternoon, August 10th, 2000.

"Hello."

"Shannon Gillette?" a digitally-manipulated voice asked.

"Yes."

"Package for you in a locker at the bus station. The combination to the locker is on top of your left-front tire. It will open for you the best story you'll have this decade—maybe ever."

"What? Who?..."

"Goodbye."

Because Shannon knew that great stories happened just this way, she immediately walked outside to her car, glanced about, and felt the top of her left-front tire. She retrieved a slip of paper taped to the tire. On it was written the numbers "22-13-12" and "104." Without so much as another thought, she was on her way to the bus station. Locker 104 contained but a single entity—a Super Hi 8 videotape sealed in a small plastic bag. She stuffed it into her purse and headed home where she had a Super Hi 8 player. This videotape she would watch alone.

Once at her apartment, Shannon dumped out her purse to find the tape. To her mild surprise, two tapes fell onto her bed. Both were Super Hi 8. The first tape she picked up was not labeled. For a moment, she wondered what it was. She opened the plastic bag and removed the second tape. To it was affixed an adhesive label. The words "Winford Thomas" had been typed or computer-generated onto the label. Shannon walked over to the Super Hi 8 player carrying both tapes. The unlabeled tape went into the "recycle" drawer in her entertainment center. The labeled tape went into the player. "Winford Thomas," she said to herself. "This could be junk or it could be great." She sat down on her couch and pressed "play" on the remote control.

Chapter 13

Winford Thomas grew up in Rhinehart, population eighty thousand, one of the two largest cities in northeast Texas. During this time, his family had owned the largest chain of furniture stores in the whole of east Texas, selling expensive furniture, not-so-expensive furniture, and cheap furniture. Winford had an older sister, Jean, who grew up well and married well. Her husband of twenty-three years was president of the largest bank in Rhinehart.

That Winford, who was born in 1953, had had political ambitions since childhood was no surprise to anyone who knew his family. His father, Winfred Thomas, had wanted a political career, but wouldn't trust the business to anyone long enough to leave Rhinehart for any extended period. There was money to be made in the furniture business in east Texas, but only if the businessman understood the timber industry and financing. Winfred Thomas understood both.

He bought furniture frames from various small east-Texas companies. Since he was by far the biggest account each of them had, he dictated to them the price he paid for their frames. He kept them all at the point where they hated living with him but definitely couldn't live without him. They all had families to feed, so Winfred Thomas had dirt-cheap prices for furniture frames locked in. His suppliers contented themselves with the notion that at least they were working for themselves.

The same was true for the upholsterers except that they worked directly for Winfred Thomas. He paid slave wages, but the work was real steady, and The Thomas Furniture Company even had group health insurance and a retirement plan. The employees had to pay all of the health-plan premium, and the twenty-year-vest retirement plan was minuscule, but most folks thought a job at The Thomas Furniture Company was a career. After a few years of working there, no one wanted to lose out on the retirement money, even if the wages and retirement plan were nothing to shout about.

The patrons who bought the expensive furniture generally didn't need any financing. The middle-class folks who bought the not-so-expensive furniture usually needed some help, which Winfred Thomas was always ready to provide. The interest rate he charged them was usurious by about fifty percent, but no one seemed to mind because credit at The Thomas Furniture Company was plentiful. Winfred Thomas didn't get turned in by his competitors because they were doing it, too, just on a much smaller scale. It was the poor folks who bought the cheap furniture, though, who really took it on the chin.

First, they were charged premium prices for the furniture, then charged an outrageous interest rate—and then there was Winfred Thomas' favorite trick. Any time one of "those" customers would come fairly close to paying off his account, Winfred would send him a personal letter telling him what a wonderful customer he was and that because he was so wonderful, The Thomas Furniture Company was going to offer him a deal he couldn't refuse. Just come on down to the store, he told them in the letter, and pick out any single item in the store they might want. They could have it for *two-thirds* off the regular price and he would finance it for them to boot.

Almost no one could resist such a generous offer and most everyone viewed him as a good businessman with a kind-hearted soul. Little did they know, at least at the time, that when any new purchases were added to their existing account, everything they had ever bought there continued to serve as collateral securing the payment of the account since the account never had been paid in full. When a family that had been buying furniture there for years and years fell on hard times and defaulted on its payments, sometimes every single item ever purchased there was repossessed by the secured creditor holding the paper because it would take the used-market sale of all that furniture to satisfy the current indebtedness, what with the high interest rate and inflated original selling prices. The secured creditor was a company in Dallas.

When such a family would come to see Winfred Thomas to let him know what was happening to them, he would tell them he was sorry but that he'd been forced by the hard times he'd been having recently to sell some of his accounts to "that bunch of thievin' scumbags at that Dallas finance company" so he wouldn't have to lay off any of his employees. Many such families felt so much better after talking with Mr. Thomas that they bought furniture there again, on the credit, just as soon as they could or once they were discharged from bankruptcy. Not that it could be determined by ordinary means, but the Texas General Finance Corporation of Dallas was owned lock, stock, and barrel by Mr. Winfred Thomas of Rhinehart, community pillar.

By the time Winford was in high school, he knew for sure what he wanted to do and it wasn't stealing from poor folks in east Texas. Not that he minded that his daddy did it, he just didn't want to do it himself. Winford had a considerable ego. He came by it quite naturally. His daddy thought pretty highly of himself, his mother was president of the Junior League well beyond the age when a person wasn't supposed to be in the Junior League anymore, and his sister was at a snooty private school in Dallas learning exactly how to follow in her mother's footsteps.

Winford was smart. He made good grades, but they would've been a lot better had he applied himself to academics like he did to athletics and girls. He was a better-than-average athlete, but that was all. There would be no college athletic scholarship offers, not that he needed the money. He thought he might play on the golf team in college, just for fun, but he didn't want to play football. Football was rough, and Winford didn't want to get hurt. He had too many important things to accomplish in life to take any silly chances like that.

Winford Thomas was going to be the Congressman from east Texas, maybe even a U.S. Senator someday representing all of Texas. College for Winford Thomas would take place at the University of Southern California. His father had insisted that Winford go to one of the large state universities in Texas because friends made there could be politically helpful on a lifelong basis. And so it had been highly irritating to his father when Winford chose USC, but his father rationalized that a degree from a highly-rated academic school would have advantages, too. Winford figured he could handle the academics. He also believed he could handle the sun, the surf—and the women, who he figured might still be into the "free love" thing he had heard so much about in the late sixties.

During the summers between his freshman and sophomore and sophomore and junior years in college, Winford came home and worked in the family business. He didn't like the furniture business; it was way too confining. Halfway through that second summer, the summer of '73, Winford knew he was going to figure out a way not to spend the following summer in Rhinehart. He was hoping for a Congressional internship. After that he would be home-free because he would be graduating the next May and attending law school. Those summers would be occupied by law-firm clerkships.

There were plenty of girls for Winford to date in Rhinehart. Most of them thought he was arrogant and egotistical, but they went out with him anyway. He was nice looking. His coal-black hair and movie-star features were noticeable to anyone with eyes. He was too good a catch for the Rhinehart girls not to at least see if they could stand him. The one thing none of them would do with him anymore, though, was sleep with him. He was too irresponsible. He was having a difficult time overcoming the story that got around on him very early during the summer of '73 that he told a girl he was wearing a condom when he wasn't.

The story went that during the act, which was taking place in the back seat of his car, Winford and his partner became separated. They were near the height of pleasure and reached down almost simultaneously to re-secure the connection. She got there first and was mortified to discover that he had lied to her about wearing a condom. Given the moment, she let him re-enter and finish, but she spent the next few weeks being horrified that she might be pregnant. That just didn't happen to good Rhinehart girls, even with Winford Thomas. She had immediately told her best friend about the incident, swearing her to secrecy. The best friend told her best friend, swearing *her* to secrecy. Within a few days, every upstanding girl in Rhinehart knew Winford Thomas lied about wearing condoms.

As a result, Winford, who had a considerable sexual appetite and southern-California experience, found himself seeking satisfaction elsewhere. For most sexually-active twenty-year-olds, that would have meant spending more time alone with themselves. For Winford, though, elsewhere could have meant a whore house in Dallas or across the line in Bossier City, Louisiana, but he was too afraid he would catch a venereal disease to do that. He would find his sexual solace a little closer to home; not too close, though. A few miles out of town would do just fine.

Most of the girls who lived out in the country from Rhinehart didn't have much, so when they got the opportunity to go on a date with someone like Winford Thomas, most were all too happy to oblige. Not being as sophisticated as the "Rhinehart girls," they didn't place quite the same degree of emphasis on the use of a condom. Winford's favorite "country girl" was an absolute beauty named Sophie Minden, who lived near the Locust Grove community, south of Rhinehart.

She liked Winford, too. He had a new car, money to spend, he often took her dancing at one of those honky tonks out in the county, he was good looking, and he could make love for the longest time. She knew he'd never want to marry her or anything like that, but she was having fun. Life for her was too hard not to ever do what she wanted to, she rationalized.

Her mother, Nahlia Fern, was deceased. She had died at the birth of Sophie's little sister, Kathy. Sophie had two half-brothers a lot older than her that she didn't know very well because they lived a few counties over and didn't come around much at all. Their mother, Nelkie Sue, was dead, too. Folks around there said she drowned accidentally when she got bitten by a water moccasin and fell into a stock pond, but there were those who believed that Sophie's uncle, Mulie Minden, had pushed her into the snake-infested pond when she refused his sexual advances. Sophie was eighteen. She lived on the old home place with her daddy, Maurice Minden, and her little sister, Kathy, who was fifteen.

Maurice Minden had been a small-time rancher for most of his life, but he had lost almost his entire herd to disease a few years earlier and had been forced to take bankruptcy. Because of the homestead exemption in the Texas Constitution, he had been able to save the old home place and a few acres, but not nearly enough to continue ranching. He also had lost most of his furniture to the Texas General Finance Company in Dallas. Maurice wasn't at all dumb. For the loss of his furniture, he blamed Winfred Thomas. No Thomases were welcome on what little property he had left, that was for sure. Sophie didn't exactly understand why, but she knew her daddy hated the Thomases. That didn't stop her, however, from slipping off to meet Winford when he would call to say he wanted to see her.

Her daddy was getting old before his time, and he was getting bitter. The only work he could find was at one of the small sawmills that made furniture frames for Winfred Thomas. It wasn't much, but it was enough to keep his two girls and him fed and clothed. He was looking forward to the day when both his girls would go off from home so he could just sit on the front porch and get drunk when he wanted to, but he wanted Sophie to stay long enough for Kathy to get grown up. Sophie, who worked a part-time job in Rhinehart, was the woman of the house, doing most all the cooking and cleaning. Kathy helped out, but she was making straight "A's" at Rhinehart High School—her daddy had to pay extra for her to go there instead of to the county school that Sophie had gone to. Belatedly, Maurice Minden had come to place a high premium on a quality high-school education.

Winford liked to see Sophie about twice a week. Any more than that and he would be missed at some of the Rhinehart social functions. These were his future constituents, after all, and it was important that they perceive him to be treating them right. Nonetheless, Winford and Sophie enjoyed quite a few summer evenings naked in the back seat of Winford's car with the doors open in the quiet of a country pasture after dancin' and drinkin' the early hours away. Winford was no more careful with her sexually than he was with any other girl, but he was damned careful with her at the honky tonks. Every redneck boy from three counties wanted to date Sophie Minden. More than once, Winford and Sophie had to leave a honky tonk when the locals were just about to get drunk enough to take him on even if his daddy did own the biggest furniture-store chain in all of east Texas.

The cool breeze was always so nice on their naked bodies, and they could holler and scream all they wanted to when one did something the other one particularly liked. Winford wouldn't—couldn't—admit it, but he really liked Sophie. Sophie refused to let herself think about it. They were quite compatible, and Sophie really understood sex. According to the odometer in Winford's car, she could have his zipper down by the time they were no more than a tenth of a mile away from the last honky tonk and on their way to the pasture.

The only bad thing about the secluded pasture they usually went to was that it was always also occupied by cows—and fresh cow pies. The sex was so good, though, that after only a couple of minutes in the back seat, a cow could have been in there with them and they wouldn't have cared. They made love on the hood and in the trunk—with the lid open—and while Sophie was driving Winford's car through the open pasture. Dodging cow pies, they loved to run naked through the pasture on those evenings they got to the field before nightfall. It could've been a love story.

In late June, Sophie missed her period, but said nothing to Winford. She missed it again in July, but hoped it was just because of all the sexual activity, which she had heard could cause a girl to miss her period sometimes and still not be pregnant. In August, when she had missed it for the third month in a row, she told Winford about it one night after they had made love in an old tree house in a gigantic oak tree at the south end of their favorite pasture. As they were getting dressed for the drive back to where he would always let her out so she could walk the rest of the way home, Sophie told him she was pregnant.

"What?" Winford said. "You couldn't be."

"Why could I not be, Winford? We've been doin' this all summer, and you ain't used a rubber yet. You got me pregnant in June. I must be two months along by now."

"Jesus, Sophie, you just can't be. And if you are, there's no way it could be mine."

"What do you mean, Winford? You're the only person I've been with. Those other boys come around sometimes, but I want better. I know I could never have you for a husband, but I thought if I was around you, a little bit of what you are might rub off on me. I made up my mind a long time ago that I'm leavin' for somewheres just as soon as my little sister graduates from high school. That'll just be three more years. But now this. I don't know what to do."

"Are you sure you haven't been with anybody else this summer? Not even one time? Damn, Sophie, I can't have a kid with you. It'll screw up everything for me. Look, you'll just have to go to Dallas and get this fixed."

"Fixed?"

"Yeah, you know, have an abortion."

"Oh, Lord, Winford, I could never do that. I just couldn't. I don't want to be pregnant anymore than you want me to be, but I just couldn't do that."

"Sure you could, Sophie. I'll pay for it. It'll be real easy. You can ride the bus over there and stay in a nice hotel. I'll pay for everything."

"I don't think I'd better see you again after tonight, Winford. I've got to figure out what to tell my daddy about bein' pregnant. He's gonna have a fit. I won't tell him it was you, though. He'd want to kill you. He hates your daddy, you know. I may just tell him that I ain't gonna tell him who's baby this is. I guess I'll just keep it and raise it. I don't know how I'll support us, but I'll figure somethin' out. If daddy will let me stay on the place, I'll get a full-time job in Rhinehart and raise my child."

"Ah, okay, Sophie. Look, I tell you what. You think about what I said about goin' to Dallas on the bus and me payin' for it and all. If you don't do that pretty soon, the doctors and nurses that do this sort of thing won't do it. It is illegal, you know. They say the baby's too well developed after a certain time. Look, I'll stay in touch with you after I've gone back to California in a couple of weeks. We'll work this out, okay?"

It was dark on the road where Winford stopped to let Sophie out.

"Goodbye, Winford. Pray for me."

It was nearing spring break at Southern Cal. It was 1974. Winford's junior year had not been nearly as much fun as his first two years had been. There had been the fraternity parties after the football games and the panty raids at the sorority houses, but, somehow, Winford hadn't had as much fun as before. He knew why. Sophie had done exactly what she said she might. She had told her father that she was pregnant but that she was going to keep to herself who the father was because the father had no interest in marrying her. She had assured her father that she had been with only one boy.

Maurice Minden was becoming more bitter all the time. He had been harboring resentment against his brother, Mulie, for decades concerning his first wife. He had tried hard not to believe that Mulie had tried to rape her and then caused her death when she tried to fight him off, as some people believed. But with this background, Maurice got real suspicious when Sophie wouldn't tell him who the father of her child was. Maurice had promised Sophie faithfully that he wouldn't go shoot the father or anything; he just felt like he had the right to know.

Sophie told her father that she understood his feelings but that it would be best for all concerned if no one ever knew who the father of the child was. Sophie didn't know to tell her father that her Uncle Mulie wasn't the father because Sophie had no idea her father suspected him. Besides, there was no way Sophie would have allowed her Uncle Mulie near her.

By early March, it was clear that the baby could come at any time. Sophie had found a midwife who would deliver the baby for her at her father's home. Winford knew the baby was due. He was seriously hoping that Sophie would not have a change of heart and tell the world who the father of the child was. Winford had had months to think the situation through and had decided there was no way he ever could acknowledge being the father. There was simply too much at stake. He already had made preliminary inquiries into fabricating an alibi for all those nights with Sophie. It would be Winford Thomas and his elegant alibis against the word of a bunch of country yokels.

The baby came the night of a spring thunderstorm. It would be a loud beginning. Sophie would be having the baby by natural childbirth, not because she wanted to, but because she couldn't afford to do it any other way. She was in considerable pain. Kathy's excitement at Sophie's labor pains had turned to anguish as Sophie began to cry out. If the size of the pregnancy had anything to do with the size of the baby, the baby would be large. The midwife was trying hard to comfort Sophie, but it was going to be a bad night. The thunderstorm wasn't a soothing factor, either.

Sophie screamed. Sophie cried. Kathy cried. Kathy didn't know what else to do but squeeze Sophie's hand. The midwife, who had delivered hundreds of babies, was calm. Maurice was in the next room, ready to transport Sophie to the hospital if anything went wrong. Mulie had offered to come over to help if need be, but Maurice had told him to "just stay the hell away." Mulie didn't understand, but he'd never gotten along with his brother Maurice anyway, so he stayed home.

The baby came. It was a girl. A big girl, weighing in on the family scales at just under ten pounds. She was a full twenty-three inches long. The midwife was unfazed. Kathy was excited.

Sophie was glad it was over. After the midwife weighed and measured the baby and cleaned it up, she started to hand it to Sophie. Sophie looked away.

"Give it to Kathy, please."

Sophie was bleeding, and the midwife had been unable to stop it. She went to the living room to discuss the situation with Maurice.

"Mr. Minden, ten-pound babies ought to be born in a hospital. It split her up pretty good, and I can't stop the bleeding. You're gonna have to take her to the emergency room in Rhinehart to get her sewed up or she could bleed to death before the mornin.' The baby's fine. Kathy can stay here with it 'til you get back. The baby is very strong and healthy. It'll be mostly sleeping for quite awhile."

Maurice was suffering from seriously conflicting emotions. Here was his granddaughter crying in the next room. On the one hand, he badly wanted to see the child; on the other hand, though, he wanted the child to be gone when he returned from the emergency room with Sophie. He was a proud man, and this was a disgraceful situation. The child was a bastard. His daughter was no whore, but, at the least, she had been sleeping with somebody. At the worst, the child was Mulie's. It was easy to think the child was Mulie's because Sophie wouldn't tell him who the father was. Who else, Maurice thought, could it be that Sophie would be so determined for him not to find out?

He was getting old. He was tired. Why did this have to happen to him? All he'd tried to do in life was raise a family, work the cattle, get ahead, and be God-fearing. But this was just too much. At his age, he just couldn't take on the responsibility of rearing an infant, even if Sophie would be doing the lion's share of the raising. He had thought long and hard about all this.

When Sophie had been about six-months pregnant, just after the first of the year, he had told her that she was going to have to give the baby up for adoption, that he just couldn't let her stay there to raise the child. He just didn't have the money, and he just didn't have strong enough nerves to go through raising another child.

Sophie had responded that she would do all the raising, that he wouldn't have to do a thing. He lovingly placed his big hands on her shoulders and looked her straight in the eyes.

"Look, girl, you've made a mistake here. I'm real sorry about that, but I just can't let it control the rest of my life. Everybody will be better off if you just give it away. Otherwise, I guess you'll just have to go to one of those homes to live at or get on the welfare or somethin' 'cause I just can't handle it."

"Please, daddy, don't send me away," Sophie replied, bursting into tears. "I didn't mean to have this baby, but I'm going to. It's going to be my own flesh and blood. I can't just give it away."

"Sophie, life ain't always fair, girl. Sometimes it deals you a blow, and you just got to do the best you can. Right now, you're probably feelin' a lot like a lost ball in the high weeds—real alone, not knowin' what to do. My mama taught me somethin' once, girl, and it's stayed with me right 'til now. All anybody can ever do is get out a pencil and a piece of paper and write down the situation they're in. Then they can write down all the things they could do about it. After they've done that, all anybody can do is pick one of those things and then do it. And a smart person doesn't go back on his decision. You'll just keep yourself in a boil all the time if you do that.

"Now I've written all this down, and I've come to a conclusion for me. I just can't raise another child. I don't have that long left on this earth, and it don't seem fair to me, what with all the heartache I've suffered in my life, to have to spend my last days raisin' another child. I don't know what the circumstances were of your conceivin' this child because you won't tell me. But that don't matter. I just can't have another baby around here. So what you need to do is think about all the different things you might do if one of 'em ain't stayin' here."

Sophie was shattered. She knew she would need her daddy's permission to keep the baby at his house, but she had been scared to ask him about it, so the subject just hadn't come up. Now that it had, his thinking on the subject was like her worst nightmare. She couldn't have an abortion; she was way too far along. And even if she could, she didn't want one. Snuffing out a life once conceived just didn't seem right to her. There was no way she could raise the child on her own. All she had was a country high-school education and that hardly would get her a good enough job in Rhinehart to be able to afford room and board somewhere, much less be enough to support her and a baby.

She just couldn't see going to some "home" in Dallas where a bunch of people would be askin' her questions and talkin' to her about religion and morality and all that. And for sure she couldn't get on the welfare. Only blacks and the poorest whites did that. She didn't have to write anything down. The options were indelibly clear right there in her mind. There was but one thing she could do. She would have to give the baby away. But how? To whom? She didn't want just anybody raising her child. She would have to find the right parents before the baby was born. That's what she'd do. She told her daddy she wanted to think about what he'd said. She told him she was going to lie down. She went to the room she shared with Kathy. She cried all night. Kathy didn't sleep a wink.

Chapter 14

Spring, 1974. Frank Dailey was an oilfield roughneck. East Texas was oil country. When oil was discovered there in the thirties, the area boomed. Booms were good and bad. They brought money—usually to a depressed region. In the thirties, it would be fair to have thought of east Texas as depressed. Times never had been very good there, and the Great Depression had made things even worse. Ironically, only the most fortunate in the area even knew there had been an economic depression.

The good part to the boom was that jobs, decent paying jobs, were much more plentiful. The bad part was that the work was hard, there rarely was a day off to be had, and the oil companies mostly treated human beings like a lesser form of life. Another bad part was the riffraff which had migrated to east Texas in search of work. Prior to their coming, at least east Texas had been God-fearing and family oriented. There always had been a downside, but east Texas in no way had been prepared for the nature of the in-migration that had taken place.

The good part was that land that had once been valuable only as dirt farms suddenly was valuable for the black gold hidden in its depths. The bad part was that not everyone's land had oil under it, so only some of the people with land got rich; others were no better off than before except that they could get a job working for the Minrite Oil Company. The worst part was that oil didn't respect property lines and the oil companies didn't, either. There was absolutely no telling how many dirt-poor landowners had been defrauded out of how many millions of dollars over the years through such oil-company techniques as "slant drilling."

Frank Dailey was born in Edge County, about twenty miles from Rhinehart, in 1952. He was 22. His mama's and daddy's families were from Indiana. Like so many others, his parents followed the oil trail from the midwest to east Texas when the big fields were brought in there in the thirties. Frank was a roughneck. And he was rough. And he was gentle. He was one of those guys who could be so sweet one minute and a tyrant the next. But he was ruggedly good-looking and a hard worker when he worked, and Rena Kirkpatrick, nineteen, had fallen for him hook, line, and sinker because she really wanted to be married. They had gone to the county high school together her freshman year and his senior year. They had dated some then, but it wasn't until she had been out of high school a year or so that they fell in love.

Rena was working as a waitress at a diner in Barksboro, and Frank was roughnecking in the oilfields. As the oilfields around Edge County had become more and more developed, work was becoming more and more scarce. Frank and Rena decided to get married and move to somewhere near Demonbreun, in extreme southeast Texas, where the oilfield jobs paid better and were more plentiful because there also were refineries in the area. There was just one problem. Neither one of them had a pot to pee in or a window to throw it out of, but they wanted to get out of Edge County real bad.

Frank had a mean streak a mile long, and he was long on larcenous thoughts, too. One night after about a six pack, he told Rena about an idea he'd had.

"You know, Rena, when I was workin' down near Demonbreun a few months ago, I was workin' one day with one of those cajuns, a real sure 'nuff coon-ass. A real talkative kind of a guy. He got to tellin' me his troubles. Seems as how his wife got all screwed up havin' their first kid and can't have no more. Now she's wantin' another one real bad, and they can't have no more."

"So?"

"So, didn't you tell me about a girl you know down south of Rhinehart a little bit who's pregnant and doesn't know what she's gonna do with the kid when she has it."

"Yeah, I met her when I was down at the county health department in Rhinehart gettin' a penicillin shot that time you give me the clap. I sure as hell didn't want to go to the clinic here in Barksboro. Everybody woulda known you give me somethin.'"

"Well?"

"Well what?"

"Well, dumb butt, how does business work? You have somebody who wants something. You find out where you can get one of 'em cheap. One that's just like they want. And then you sell it to 'em for a big profit. Got it?"

"You don't mean that you want to sell that guy a baby?"

"That's exactly what I mean."

"You're crazy."

"What's crazy about it? I mean, look, the girl wants shed of the baby. The guy down there near Demonbreun wants a baby. We need the money to move down there and get goin.' You got any better ideas on how to get some real good money pretty quick? Maybe you'd rather keep on livin' at your mama's house and just seein' me every now and then."

"Wouldn't it be illegal?"

"I 'magine so, but who cares? Who'll ever know? Tell the girl that I can't have kids and that we want a baby. She's our kind of folks, ain't she? Don't you think she'd let us have it to raise?"

"She might."

"Then when we sell it, we won't tell that coon-ass where it come from. He wants one for his wife so bad, I don't think he'll ask no questions. Let's do it."

"Okay, but I sure hope we don't get caught, Frankie. What if we ever want to come back here?"

"I don't know about you, but I ain't never comin' back here once I leave. There ain't nothin' here I want. How 'bout you?"

"Yeah, I guess you're right. Besides, that girl told me she was leavin' for somewhere big just as soon as the baby was born and she found a home for it."

"Well, see, that's great. Nothin' to worry about."

"Hello, this is Boudreaux Fontenot. Tell me what for."

"Is this Boudreaux Fontenot?"

"Yeah, man. Who is this?"

"Boudreaux, this is Frank Dailey. Me and you worked together a while back on a drillin' rig down there near you. I'm from up around Rhinehart. You remember me?"

"Yeah, I remember you. What chu callin' ol' Boudreaux about, mmmh?"

"Well, remember how you was tellin' me about your wife not bein' able to have any more children an' all?"

"Yeah."

"Well, I know where there's a baby you might could get."

"What kind of...? What chu mean?"

"Well, it ain't born yet, but it's gonna be real soon. I know the girl. She's a real nice, good-lookin' girl that got herself in trouble, you know, and she just ain't in no position to keep it once she has it. It ain't no half-breed or nothin' like that. Are you interested?"

"What if I am? How would I go 'bout gettin' it?"

"I'm gonna be down there workin' next week. Could we meet somewhere to talk about it?"

"Sure. You know where the truck stop is on Highway 62 near where we was workin?'"

"Yeah."

"I'll meet chu there 'bout five a.m. nex' Monday. That okay wit' chu?"

"Yeah. I'll see you there."

Tailese asked Boudreaux who that was on the telephone, but he fibbed to her, saying it was one of his co-workers calling to complain about their boss. Boudreaux wanted this baby real bad. Tailese had been quite depressed over not being able to bear Boudreaux any more children. No cajun family around those parts had just one child. Everybody had at least two. Boudreaux felt like Tailese would feel complete if they had one more child. He decided to do everything he could to get that baby for Tailese.

"Boudreaux, over here, man."

"Hello. What chu say your name was again?"

Boudreaux slid into the seat on the other side of the booth.

"Frank Dailey."

"Yeah, that right, Frank Dailey. Tell me more 'bout this child, Frank Dailey."

"What all do you want to know?"

"I want to know everything you can tell me."

"Well, I can't tell you a lot. Its mother is a white girl from out in the country up near me. She's about nineteen or twenty. The daddy is somebody from around there. He's a white boy about the same age. There ain't nothin' wrong with either one of 'em," Frank said, lying through his teeth. He had no idea who the father was and had never seen the mother. Rena had said the mother looked okay to her. Real pretty and all, Rena had said.

"Coffee, please ma'am. Real hot," Boudreaux said to the waitress. "How do I get this baby, Frank Dailey?"

"Well, I can get it just after it's born. You can have it right then."

"But what 'bout all the legal stuff. Don't this have to go through the courts and all?"

"The courts? Are you crazy, man? This ain't gonna be no legal deal. She's just gonna have the kid, give it to me, and I'm gonna bring it to you. That's it."

"No, that ain't it, Frank Dailey. I wasn't born yesterday, and I didn't ride in on no turnip truck, either. What's in this for you?"

"Well, that's what we need to talk about, Boudreaux."

"You talk. I listen."

"Okay. Well, you want a baby, and I know where one is, and I can get it for you. Ain't that worth somethin' to you?"

"How much you got in mind? Lord knows I ain't no rich man. But you know that."

"Well, I was thinkin' in terms of five thousand."

"Thank you ma'am. That looks good and hot," Boudreaux said as the waitress walked away.

"Are you crazy, man? I can't pay you no five-thousand dollars. Ol' Boudreaux don't have that kind of money. There ain't no place I could get it, either, even if I would do anything I know how to comfort my Tailese's misery 'bout her can't have no more kids, mm mmmmh!"

"What's your car worth, Boudreaux?"

"My car? Man, I got to be able to get back and forth to work. What chu mean?"

"Well, is it paid for?"

"You talkin' 'bout that '57 Chevy what chu see in the parkin' lot out there?"

"Yeah."

"Yeah, it's paid for. It's my pride and joy, mmmmh! And it's in perfect condition, other than it's a little dirty. I could probably get five thousand for it, too, but if I was to sell it and give you the money, what would I do for a car?"

"Okay, here's the deal. You sell the car, give me three thousand and use the other two thousand to buy yourself another car. Tell your wife that the engine was going bad and that you got rid of it just in time."

"So now this baby is only gonna cost me three-thousand dollars?"

"Naw, it's still gonna cost you five thousand 'cause that's the amount I've gotta have. And besides that, this is a damn good deal. Where the hell else you gonna find a baby like this?"

"Nowhere that I know of, man, but where the hell you think I gonna get the other two thousand?"

"I don't know, Boudreaux, but I'm sure you'll think of something. Is this a deal?"

"How 'bout if I give you the three thousand and then pay you as we go on the other two thousand?"

"If that's the only way this will work, then I guess that's what we'll have to do. Is that a deal?"

"Deal."

"One more thing, Boudreaux. I'm never tellin' a soul I did this, and I ain't tellin' you nothin' else about this baby. And you ain't tellin' anybody anything, either, including your wife. Right?"

"Yeah, but what I gonna tell Tailese 'bout where I get this baby? What I gonna do, jus' walk in the house with it and ask her to look what I found on the front porch? My wife did not come in on the pumpkin truck, either."

"Just tell her some real poor people had the baby and knew you wanted one and asked you to take it if you would promise not to tell anyone where it came from. If you give her the choice of havin' it and not knowin' anything about it or not havin' it, what do you think she'll do?"

"I think all this is scary as hell, but I want my Tailese to be happy. I fix it up with her. You jus' bring the child."

"Listen, Boudreaux, when the baby comes, I'll call you that night and tell you to meet me with the money. I'll give the baby to you then. If you don't want it when you see it, I won't make you take it, okay?"

"If the baby look healthy and is a white baby, I take it."

"Get the money, Boudreaux. This baby will be comin' out pretty soon, and the longer between when you sell your car and when the baby comes, the less suspicious your wife will be."

"I'll sell the car this weekend in Demonbreun."

"Good. I'll call you when the time is right. See you, Boudreaux."

"I'll see you, Frank Dailey."

"Daddy, I need to talk to Kathy for a minute before we leave to go to the hospital."

"All right, honey. I'll be waitin' in the car, but hurry up, the midwife says you're bleedin' pretty good, and I wanta get you fixed up."

"Me, too, daddy. I'll be there in just a minute."

Turning to Kathy, who was still holding the baby, Sophie spoke softly. The midwife had gone home.

"Kathy, I need for you to do somethin' for me. You know I ain't gonna keep this baby, don't you?"

"I kinda thought so, Sophie, 'cause you didn't seem to be doin' any plannin' on it. No baby clothes or anything like that. What are you gonna do with it?"

"I'm bleedin,' and they're probably gonna want to keep me at the hospital for awhile. Daddy will stay with me. Just as soon as we drive off, I want you to call this number," Sophie said, handing Kathy a slip of paper. "Tell the man or woman who answers the phone that Tish—that's a secret name—said the time was right. They'll understand. They'll probably get here about an hour after you call them. Don't say nothin' else to them. They probably won't say nothin' to you when they're here. Just give them the baby. It's the last time any of us will ever see it.

"They're married, and he can't have any kids for some reason. They asked me could they have the baby. I met the woman at the county health department when I was goin' there 'cause I was pregnant. We waited in the waiting room a long time together one day. She was there to get a blood test 'cause they were gettin' married. They're fixin' to move somewheres a long way away from here. . . ."

"But," Kathy interrupted, "are you sure you want to do this. . . ?"

"Listen, Kathy, there ain't no other way. Now don't argue with me. Just do it. If you love me, just do it. I'd do it for you."

"Okay, Sophie. I love you. I'll do it."

"Good, I gotta go. I'm feelin' real weak. If you don't say anything to me about it when I get back, I'll know they got the baby okay. And I ain't never gonna want to talk about it after that. Okay?"

"Okay. Bye."

"Bye. And thank you. I love you."

"I love you, too."

Maurice was waiting on Sophie in the car. Walking was difficult, made even more so by the wash cloths the midwife had placed between Sophie's legs. Mud spun off Maurice's tires as his pickup truck cleared the front yard. Kathy dialed the operator and gave her the number on the slip of paper. The baby was sleeping soundly.

"Hello," the man said.

"Ah, this is. . . . Ah, Tish said to come get the. . . . Ah, she said the time was right. Tonight."

"Oh, wow. Great. Fantastic. We'll be there in less than an hour. Goodbye."

"Goodbye."

Frank Dailey was excited.

"Hello, this is Boudreaux Fontenot. Tell me what for."

"Evenin,' Boudreaux. This is Frank. I got news. I just got the call. I'll be where we planned to meet by dawn. You got the money?"

"Yeah, I do. I see you there." Then Boudreaux whispered, "Tailese gonna be so surprised and so happy, what chu mean! Tomorrow gonna be my lucky day."

"See you soon, Boudreaux. Goodbye."

"Goodbye to you, Frank Dailey, mm mmmmh!"

It had worked out perfectly so far. The baby had been born on a Friday night, and Boudreaux didn't have to work the next day. He told Tailese he was going fishing with some of his buddies real early and for her to sleep late; after all, Saturday was her birthday. Boudreaux told her he hoped he might bring her something home from the fishing trip that she would like. Tailese only half heard him. Alphonse was asleep. She was watching "All In The Family" on the TV. They said the funniest things.

It was approaching ten p.m. when Frank Dailey and Rena Kirkpatrick pulled into Maurice Minden's front yard. They were happy to see no other vehicles there. There had been no way to tell from the telephone call who would be there. Frank had been hoping Sophie's father would be gone. He didn't think there would be, but he sure didn't want any trouble. Further, he would just as soon as few people as possible saw his face. Frank and Rena parked the car in the front yard. It was still raining softly and Frank was hoping the car wouldn't bog down in the soft ground.

Just as they started to knock on the front door, it swung open. Kathy had the baby in her arms. It was wrapped, otherwise naked, in a small blanket. Sophie had not bought or otherwise obtained any clothes for the baby. Rena held out her arms. Kathy handed her the baby. Frank looked around nervously. Just as they started off the porch with the baby, there came a loud clap of thunder. The baby jumped and cried out. Kathy cried and ran back into the house. Rena jumped. Frank opened the door for Rena to get in the car. Frank ran to the other side of the car, jumped behind the wheel, started the engine, and backed slowly out of the yard.

Rena suddenly realized that she had no milk for the baby. She also realized that she wouldn't know what to do with it if she had some milk. She found herself hoping they got this baby to the rendezvous point before something bad happened to it or before it decided to go to the bathroom on itself and—worse—on her. She hadn't even looked to see whether it was a girl or a boy. About a mile down the highway, Frank began to gloat.

"What does it feel like to be holdin' five-thousand dollars in your arms, woman?"

"Oh, Frankie, this is making me so nervous. Are you sure this is going to be okay?"

"Hell, yeah, baby. They didn't want it. Boudreaux does. Who'll ever know? Who'll ever care? Say, I can stop sayin' 'it' now. What is it, anyway?"

"Ooh, Frank, it's asleep. I'm scared I'll wake it up if I start movin' it around. Let's just get it to that man as quick as we can. But don't you dare get stopped by no cops."

For Rena, the five-hour drive seemed an eternity. For Frank, it was just dangerous enough to be exciting. During the drive, Frank talked wildly about what all they could do with this $3,000 and another $2,000 later. Rena held the baby and fretted. All she could think about was gettin' rid of it before it woke up and peed or worse.

An hour or so before daybreak, Frank and Rena pulled off the main highway onto an oilfield road near Brickfield, Texas. It hadn't rained this far south, so the dirt oilfield roads were passable. Nobody would see them. The wells on this property had long since been drilled, and they were just pumping by themselves. Frank pulled the car around to the back of the first pumping wellhead he came to and turned the engine off. Even with the pumping wells, it was very quiet. Rena didn't say a word. The baby was asleep. It had slept almost the whole way down. Frank got out of the car, sat down on a corner of the wellhead and smoked a cigarette.

His third cigarette was about half smoked when Frank saw headlights coming up the road. He didn't recognize the car. When the car got close enough to him, he saw that it was a 1958 Chevrolet. Boudreaux pulled up beside Frank's car and stopped. Frank opened the door on Rena's side of the car and took the baby from her. He handed it to Boudreaux as he got out of the car. Boudreaux looked admiringly at the fidgeting infant.

"My, oh my, would you look at this little miracle of the Lord. Is it a girl or a boy, Frank Dailey?"

"To tell you the truth, Boudreaux, we ain't looked to see. You got the money?"

"Yeah, man, I got it right there," Boudreaux said, pointing with his eyes to his hip pocket. Boudreaux couldn't believe they didn't know the baby's sex. He thought that was real strange, but he didn't say anything about it. He was just happy beyond belief that he had this little baby in his arms and that he was going to be able to make Tailese so happy.

"I never seen a little baby that was what somebody might call pretty, but I do believe this one come real close," Boudreaux said, unwrapping the blanket and visually inspecting the child. He counted her fingers and toes and turned her over several times. "Jus' look at those big black eyes. You brung me a good, healthy, white baby girl, Frank Dailey. I gonna take this baby and give you the money."

"Great," Frank said. "I knew you'd want it. Here, I'll hold her while you get the money," Frank said, taking the baby from Boudreaux. Boudreaux fished in his back pocket. He took out an envelope and counted thirty one-hundred-dollar bills to Rena, who had exited the car and was standing beside them.

"I only got four thousand for my car, and I had to give one thousand for this one," Boudreaux said, nodding to the '58 Chevy he had driven up in. "I don't know when I get chu the rest of the money, Frank Dailey, but I gonna pay you, mm mmmmh! Don't chu worry 'bout that. If Boudreaux Fontenot say he gonna pay you, then you gonna get paid."

Frank handed the baby back to Boudreaux.

"Do you think you could pay me a hundred a month out of your checks, Boudreaux? I really am gonna need the money as fast as I can get it."

"I know I can pay you 'bout fifty a month, and I try to pay you the whole hundred. You jus' give me somethin' with your address on it, and I'll send you a money order every month, mm mmmmh, 'til I get chu paid."

"Okay, Boudreaux," Frank said, handing him the address he'd already written down for this purpose. It was a post office box in Barksboro, the Edge County seat. "I'll expect as much as you can pay every month 'til you get it paid. And I ain't gonna charge you no interest, hear?"

"That's a good thing, Frank Dailey, cause I couldn't pay you no interest no way. I never would get chu paid that way," Boudreaux said as he laid the baby in the bassinet on the front seat of his car. He had brought Alphonse's bassinet with him, having retrieved it from Alphonse's bedroom closet just before leaving the house an hour before.

"I'll see you, Boudreaux, and I'll be expecting to hear from you every month."

"You will, Frank Dailey, don't chu worry 'bout that none," Boudreaux said as he prepared to drive away. He hadn't even spoken to the woman. Out of sight of Frank and Rena, Boudreaux again unwrapped the baby from its blanket, peered lovingly at the sleeping infant and said out loud, "Mm mmmmh! Tailese Fontenot gonna be the happiest person on this planet in 'bout thirty minutes from now. What chu mean!"

Boudreaux Fontenot was talking to himself. He was talking to the whole world. He was one happy man. Frank and that woman were funny people, Boudreaux thought, but they did what they said they would do. And he was grateful to them. She was a beautiful child. Those big, big black eyes. . . . Mm mmmh!

"Tailese Fontenot, where are you in this house?"

"I'm right here, Boudreaux, feedin' Alphonse his breakfus.' What chu doin' here? You almost scared me half to death. I thought chu was out fishin.'"

"Well, Tailese, I tol' you a little bit of a story 'bout where I was goin this mornin.'"

"What chu mean?"

"I didn't go fishin.'"

"Where you been, Boudreaux Fontenot?"

"I been out gettin' your birthday present."

"Boudreaux, you know we can't afford a birthday present for me. And besides that, there ain't nothin' in this world I want but what I can't have. . . . I'm sorry, Boudreaux, I didn't mean to say I wouldn't be happy 'bout what chu went and got me. What is it? I could jus' paddle you for goin' and spendin' money on me. What chu bring me?"

"You have to come out to the car to see. Bring Alphonse with you."

Tailese got Alphonse down from his high chair and followed Boudreaux out onto the front porch.

"Let me have Alphonse. You go open the front door on the passenger side and see what I got for you."

Tailese handed Alphonse to Boudreaux and walked over to the car. She opened the door and saw the bassinet.

"Why you got Alphonse's bassinet in the car?" Tailese asked as she picked it up.

The baby stirred, and Tailese dropped the bassinet back onto the car seat. Her knees got weak, and Boudreaux had to set Alphonse down on the porch and help Tailese, who was leaning against the car, to the porch where she sat down on the steps. Then he brought the bassinet to her. Tailese was returning to reality.

"This is what I brought chu for your birthday, Tailese. What chu think?"

"Boudreaux, where did ju get this baby? Why do you have it? What chu mean this is my birthday present? I think I'm gonna faint all over again."

"Tailese, I gonna tell you somethin' and then we ain't never gonna talk 'bout this subject no more for the rest of our lives. This little baby girl here belong to you and me. She was borned last night to some real pore folks I know a way out in the country a couple of counties over. I used to work wit' the ol' boy who is the daddy of this child. He hurt hisself on a rig one day a while back and he can't never work no more. He tried to get some money from the company, mm mmmmh, but they tol' him to jus' get his family to take care of him cause they didn't have to and they wasn't gonna.

"His wife was sure 'nuff 'bout six-months pregnant with this baby and there weren't no way they could take care of this child, too, what with him not bein' able to work no more and them havin' three other kids already. So I talk to him 'bout it and we decide that he give the baby to me jus' as soon as it got born. I sure 'nuff thought about talkin' to you 'bout it, but I knew you would want the baby, mm mmmmh, so I decided to surprise you, what chu mean, and I can sure see I did that. All you have to say is that chu want this child and it is yours. If you don't want it, I'll take it down to the police and tell them I found it on the side of the road. What chu say?"

"Boudreaux, this is the prettiest baby I ever did see. And look at the way it kickin.' It a real strong baby. It look happy, too. Boudreaux, I don't know whether it's right to keep this baby or not, but I want to keep this baby. This is the happiest day of my life besides when I marry you and when Alphonse come. You are the sweetest man ever there could be. What is this baby's name?"

"It was jus' borned last night, Tailese. It don't have a name. You can call this child whatever you want her name to be."

The day before, Tailese had dug up a ginger root to use in a meal she was making Boudreaux. Ginger was good, and it was strong. Tailese saw the part of the root she had not used that was still on the front porch.

"I think we call her Ginger, Boudreaux. She is such a strong little girl. How does that sound? Ginger Fontenot."

"That sound jus' great to me. Ginger it be. Ginger Fontenot. You gonna give her a middle name?"

"I think her middle name should be jus' a letter, Boudreaux. The letter 'R.'"

"What that be for?"

"It could mean more than one thing. It means 'root' for how strong she is. And it means 'right' for this bein' the right thing for her and us. And it means 'rejoice' for all the pleasure this little girl gonna bring us in our lifetimes. I'm so happy, Boudreaux, I jus' don't know what to do."

"I gonna take off from work early on Monday, Tailese, so we can go down to the courthouse and get this little baby named Ginger R. Fontenot a birth certificate."

Sophie Minden had been home for hours. She was in bed, but she couldn't sleep. Only the night before, she had given birth to a daughter in that very bed. She hadn't even looked at the child, and now she never would have that opportunity. Sophie had told the emergency room personnel at the hospital in Rhinehart that she had given birth that night with a midwife attending and that the baby was fine.

There was no particular alarm or need to inform any authorities, the E-R folks knew, because country people used midwives for birthing all the time. Maurice Minden had told the nurse and intern on duty that Sophie's sister was watching the child. That no father was mentioned was a bit worrisome because of concerns about incest, but the doctor and nurse were nearing the end of their second straight shift apiece and were real tired. Besides, getting involved might mean paperwork.

When Sophie got home, about midnight, all that passed between Sophie and Kathy was a knowing look. Maurice Minden never inquired.

Chapter 15

Thursday, August 10th, 2000. Just under three months until the November general election. To say things were about to heat up was the understatement of the season.

Shannon sat on the couch in utter disbelief. There was a scene of Winford Thomas announcing at a recent press conference that he was "Mr. Fidelity" edited to video of him standing in the window of what appeared to be an apartment building with what more than appeared to be a young woman—not his wife. Thomas was slipping her clothes off while staring out the window with a look on his face that said his hand definitely was in the cookie jar and he definitely was getting away with it. The "window" video was date-stamped "July 27, 2000," and time-stamped beginning at "9:18 p.m." Obviously, Shannon thought, Thomas had no idea he was being videotaped. At that point, the screen went blank, but the audio, the date-stamp, and the time-stamp continued. Thomas and the woman clearly sounded as though they were making love. God, how invasive, Shannon thought. At the height of pleasure, the woman was heard to say: "Winford,

Winford, go for it, go for it. . . ." The date-stamp and time-stamp then changed to "July 28, 2000," and "3:46 a.m." Shannon heard what sounded like a second lovemaking session.

And as though that were not enough, the final audio segment on the tape, again juxtaposed to a blank screen, made it sound as though Thomas was...dare she think it?...masturbating; at least, all the vocalizing he was doing was accompanied by total silence. This third segment was date-stamped "July 28, 2000." The time-stamping of the third audio segment was "8:07 a.m." to "8:13 a.m." It was by far the most privacy invading and embarrassing thing she had ever seen or heard.

And that, she knew, was what would make it unbelievably good television. Was Texas ready for this? She would be the talk of the state for the remainder of the political season and then some. The debates over whether and how much of the tape should have been used would rage from the street to classrooms to boardrooms to legislative cloakrooms—and for a long time to come.

Was this a set up? It must be, she thought; after all, it surely wasn't Winford Thomas who had dropped this little piece of journalism awardsville in her lap. But who was setting him up? Was it the Republicans? They were the most likely candidate. And who was the girl? Probably, Shannon thought, just some high-grade hooker.

This was even better than when televangelist Sammy Jenkins had been seen with a hooker at a hotel in Las Vegas a few years earlier. Thomas was seen with a hooker, all right, Shannon thought, but these eyes were the non-lying eyes of a video camera. And speaking of video, she thought, why, if it was a set up, did they shoot the footage on Super Hi 8, a consumer-grade video format? Why not a professional-grade format, such as BetaCam?

Then it struck her. Maybe they did shoot it with high-quality gear and tape; that way, they could deliver a high-quality copy of it to her on consumer-grade tape and she might think it was a home-video job of some sort, like some amateur just lucked into it or something. Fat chance of that, she thought. No, this was a set up, and she might never know who had done it, but one thing was for sure—if she had anything to do with it, this tape would be the lead segment of Triple T's next show. For one thing, how did she know whether her mysterious benefactor also had benefitted her competitors, say, at the big local stations in Dallas and Houston.

Okay, she thought, what was the downside to this? First, was it faked? It sure didn't look like a fake, she thought, but she supposed it could have been digitally created or stitched together what with current technology. Was the video faked? Was the audio faked? Under the circumstances, some authenticating would have to be done, she knew. If it was real, she didn't see how her company could lose a libel suit because proof of falsity would be an absolute requirement of anyone suing.

But what about privacy invasion? The best defense to that type of lawsuit, she knew, was that the situation had to be newsworthy. In her mind, at least, this tape was as newsworthy as could be; after all, this man was a Congressman running for re-election and for election to the U.S. Senate. She asked herself whether video and audio of President Billartern's belatedly-admitted tryst with Lydia Melanson would have been aired by every television station in America a million times had such tape existed? And wouldn't such a huge and ongoing journalistic use personify the idea of newsworthiness? Of course this tape was newsworthy. Absolutely.

No, she thought, there was no way Diversicom could lose a lawsuit. Then she thought about how she would tell the audience where she got the tape. Obviously, her benefactor had no interest in being identified as the source. It would be best to say, she thought, that her source wished to remain anonymous; that, after all, while slightly misleading, surely was the case.

As she walked over to the Super Hi 8 player to retrieve the "Winford Thomas" tape, which she now believed to be extremely valuable, she glanced at the unlabeled tape that she had placed in her recycle drawer. How it had wound up in her purse, she didn't know, but since she didn't recall having placed it there, she thought she should just pop it in the machine to see what it was. This was an extraordinary day, after all.

The first images she saw were hot-air balloons. Just as she was about to pop the tape out of the machine, the balloons turned to images of two people sitting at a table in what looked to be a dimly-lighted restaurant. One of them was Jack Duvalier, Winford Thomas' Washington-office chief of staff. This was way too much of a coincidence, Shannon knew. Wherever this tape came from, she was going to watch it. She walked back to the couch and sat down once more.

As the conversation between Jack Duvalier and some woman named "Ginger" unfolded, Shannon thought she must be losing her mind. "This just can't be," she said aloud. "Unless I completely have lost my mind, there was only one tape in the locker at the bus station. Besides, whoever gave me the 'Thomas' tape would not have given me this tape, which shows that it was Thomas' own employee who set this whole thing up." The tape was downright explosive, Shannon thought.

When "Ginger" and Duvalier had departed the table, Shannon stopped the tape. She had to think. Where did this tape come from? It, too, was Super Hi 8. Was that a coincidence? Who shot it? Why was it given to her? Who was Ginger? Obviously, Shannon then knew, Ginger was the woman in the window with Winford Thomas, but she was a New York model who wasn't doing very well—not a hooker. Anyway, there was plenty of information on the tape that would quickly lead her to the woman's full identity, Shannon thought. "Hell," she said aloud, "Taz might know her; they look about the same age and he went to TCU."

Taz, she thought, Taz. What did he have to do with this? Nothing. Something in Shannon's mind, though, kept somehow connecting Taz to these tapes. She needed to ask him about Ginger—maybe even show him the tapes. Damn, she thought, this was the problem with dating people in government and politics; she knew better, but Taz had been so great, so great. He worked for the Democrats. Thomas was a Democrat. But, Lord, so was Jack Duvalier. None of this made any sense, Shannon thought, except that it was clear Jack Duvalier had hired Ginger to help him derail Winford Thomas' political career. If the plan was to catch Thomas on tape as an infidel and then give the tape to the news media—to her—the plan had been successful so far.

But who had taped the restaurant conversation? And how had it ended up in her purse? she thought. Had someone planted it there? That was the only logical explanation. Where had she been that her purse had not been with her. She remembered having cleaned it out just two nights earlier. Since then, it had been with her all the time. . . .

"Taz Sterling."
   "Hi, there."

"Hey, is this who I think it is? This must be my lucky day. First, I wake up with an absolutely gorgeous woman in my bed who asks me who I am but isn't mad about being there, and then she calls me the same day. How lucky can I get?"

"The only thing that would make you luckier would be two of me."

"Damn, I don't know if I could handle three women at once. There is 'the other woman,' you know."

"Nope, there's no 'other woman'—just me. Want to know why I know that? Because if there was another woman, you would've been with her last night and not me. Second, if there *was* another woman, *was* is the operative term because just one of me is as good as it gets."

"Wow. I knew I liked you for some reason other than your radiant beauty and your magnetic body. You also have a brain and a sense of humor. Dynamite combination. Makes me want to ask how you've remained single all these years."

"Listen, before I deal with those last insults, what do you mean by 'magnetic' body?"

"Simply that it draws mine to yours and won't let go."

"Damn. Well, bud, that was so good that I'm not even going to call you on my singleness and my old age. Except that I might ask you the same questions."

"Okay, here are the answers. I never have found anyone who deserved me. And I *am* two years younger than you, you know."

"God, this isn't getting me anywhere. With that silver tongue, you ought to have my job."

"Okay, sounds interesting."

"Well, speaking of interesting, I need to run something by you. Were you planning on calling me, or was I just another one-night conquest on your surely long string of them?"

"May I be honest?"

"Oh, God, I guess."

"Yes, I was going to call, and there's no string of one-nighters. Notwithstanding last night, that's not my thing."

"There goes that silver tongue again. Just keep it up. Since you were going to grace me with a call today, I will assume it would have been to ask me to dinner tonight, right?"

"Ah, right."

"Okay, how about Chinese at my place?"

"You cooking?"

"Hell, no."

"What time?"

"When you get there; the earlier, the better. Sevenish."

"See you then."

Shannon's place put Taz's apartment to shame. He was from a wealthy family but refused to live other than on his own resources, which were fairly meager given his government salary. He had a family trust fund, but none of his friends knew it because he dipped into it only rarely. Shannon, on the other hand, was a highly successful television reporter, who made big money and lived well—in a condo she had bought the previous year. It was tastefully decorated by a professional; Shannon had no time and little interest in decorating, though she very much enjoyed the condo's appointments as orchestrated by the decorator.

"Earlier" turned out to be just before seven p.m. Taz brought wine but had no intention of getting drunk. This time, he wanted to remember everything. Taz had been expecting the kind of Chinese take-out that he had brought home many times—in the white paper containers with the thin metal handles. One or two containers of rice, several other containers holding sweet and sour shrimp and cashew chicken and beef with peppers, all loaded with MSG. It sure was good. He could eat it all, not feel like he'd eaten a thing an hour later, and wish the next morning he hadn't eaten any of it.

Taz didn't know where the food he was experiencing at Shannon's condo came from, but to call it Chinese take-out did it a grave disservice. After dinner, he asked.

"You liked it? Great. It isn't something I do except on special occasions—that make you feel good?—because it's kind of expensive. It came from 'Yo Wang's' in the Bristol Building. No MSG. Cooked to order. Delivered on covered platters, as you can see. So you liked it?"

"It was delicious. You're delicious."

"I'll bet you're delicious, too. Wait 'til you see what's for dessert."

With that, Shannon slipped out of her chair and walked behind Taz's chair. As she pulled it back, he started to get up, but she bade him sit back down. With the chair a bit away from the table, Shannon—who was wearing a tight but comfortably-fitting light pink sleaveless sweater showing a hint of tanned midriff, darker-pink dress jeans, and no shoes—gently pushed Taz's legs apart and knelt between them.

"What are you doi...?"

"Shhh. This is dessert. Let me know if you don't like it."

Shannon's bedroom was large. In addition to an ample bed and accessories, there was a living area complete with couch and a home entertainment unit. One of the tape players was a Super Hi 8.

Taz was perched in Shannon's bed listening to music. Part of him wanted to turn on SportsTime, but most of him didn't. Shannon, dressed now in the most tastefully-sexy bed clothes he had ever seen, was opening a drawer in the home entertainment unit. Much as he wanted to make love to her again that very moment, he didn't want her to think him a sex addict, so he suppressed the urge as best he could. SportsTime was out of the question.

"Hey, I just want you to know that the dinner was excellent, especially the dessert. The Chinese was the best I've ever eaten, but the dessert...well...unmatchable."

"Thanks, killer, but right now I have something I want to show you. I've debated long and hard about whether to show it to you, but I have decided to. Now don't be insulted by what I'm about to say, but you do remember our conversation about confidentiality, right?"

"Sure. I'm not offended. It would take quite a bit to offend me tonight."

"Good. I'll remember that. Okay, do we have confidentiality on what you're about to see?"

"Well, I hate agreeing before I've seen it, but I can't imagine what the problem could be, so, okay, I won't ever tell a soul anything about this."

"Okay, here goes. After I came home from your place and then went to work, I got a call from a disguised voice telling me where to pick up this tape," Shannon said, holding up the "Thomas" tape. "I brought it home to look at it because I didn't want anyone at the office to see it at the same time as me. When I saw it, it just blew my mind. I'll show it to you in a minute, but that's not the whole story.

"When I got the tape out of my purse, there were two tapes, but I had put only one tape in there. Both were Super Hi 8. One of them was the one I had picked up; I had no idea where the other one came from. It wasn't labeled, so I tossed it in this drawer right here where I put tapes that can be recorded over. Because of what was on the first tape, I decided I'd better watch the second one even though I didn't know where it came from. If what was on the first tape was astounding, which it was, then what was on the second tape totally blew me away."

"My God, Shannon, let me see them." Why was videotape suddenly playing such a large role in his life? Taz thought.

"Okay, here goes." Shannon started the tape at the point where Ginger and Thomas reached the open window.

While Taz had never seen Ginger's New York apartment, he had seen her naked back hundreds of times. When he saw Winford Thomas peering out the window, so much blood vacated his brain that he thought for a moment he would faint. His heart was in his throat. He was nauseous. He started to speak but could not. Shannon was completely taken aback at his reaction.

"Taz. . . ."

He waved her off. He had begun to sweat profusely. The screen went blank. Minutes later, he plainly heard Ginger chortling to Thomas to "go for it," a phrase she had uttered to him in the same circumstances too many times to remember, including recently.

Taz never heard Winford Thomas masturbating even though Shannon played the tape through to the end. His mind was in another place—far, far away. The facts were too unbelievable to consider. Not only had Ginger actually engaged in a conspiracy with Duvalier by screwing Winford Thomas more or less on camera, but Duvalier had slipped the tape to Shannon Gillette, who undoubtedly would show it to Texas and the world—and soon. From the tape, he thought, Ginger was not identifiable, but he was fairly certain her identity would become public. What a shame for the Fontenots, he thought. Then he wondered if Duvalier had tried to blackmail Thomas out of politics before slipping the tape to Shannon. If he had, Thomas must not have agreed to go meekly into the night. But, Lord, did Thomas not think Duvalier would release the tape? This was too confusing to even begin to comprehend, Taz thought.

His stream of consciousness thinking was interrupted by Shannon.

"Ah, Taz. What's the matter, guy? I didn't quite expect this reaction from you. You look like you've seen a ghost of some sort. Do you know Winford Thomas personally? Is that it?"

"We've never met." Taz was sitting on the side of the bed now, running his fingers through his hair as he had done when Heather had shown him her restaurant footage weeks earlier.

"What is it, then, Taz? You look really bummed out."

"Shannon.... I can't explain to you everything I know about this. I'm sorry. It's real personal. Are you going to broadcast what I've just seen?"

"Unless you can tell me why I shouldn't, and don't take me wrong here, but I don't think you can. I'm a journalist remember. I've got a duty to bring newsworthy stuff to the attention of the voting public. My God, don't you think the people of this state ought to see this videotape?"

"Well, Shannon, I'm not sure I can answer that question. I'm just too involved."

"How, Taz? Tell me, please."

Tears were trying to escape his eyes. Shannon retrieved a box of facial tissue and sat down beside him on the bed. She continued.

"Hey, listen, I didn't mean to upset you. I've only known you for two days now, but I already feel like we've got something strong going. I really like you, Taz, and I sure wouldn't do anything to hurt you if I could help it. Tell me, please; what is it?"

In the spaces of her speech, Taz had decided that he could tell Shannon about his relationship with Ginger, but that was all.

"Shannon, do you know who the girl is?"

"No, do you?"

"Yes. Her name is Ginger Fontenot. She was my girlfriend in college our junior and senior years. We more or less lived together. We were supposed to be married, but Ginger decided when we graduated that she would leave me behind for a modeling career in New York. I've never been there, but the apartment where that...'event' took place probably is her apartment. I loved Ginger with all my heart, and it has taken me four years to get over her. I just can't believe that she would screw Winford Thomas."

Knowing it was the truth but not wanting Shannon to know he knew it to be true, Taz told Shannon he was wondering whether the tape was some kind of campaign dirty trick to politically assassinate Winford Thomas.

"Well, that's exactly what it is, Taz. Listen, I'm real sorry about your old girlfriend being the one in the tape. I had no idea. I did wonder if you knew her, though, because of her having gone to TCU."

That statement hit Taz like a clap of thunder.

"How did you know that, Shannon? I thought you didn't know who she was."

"Ah, well, I didn't know who she was, but I did know her name was Ginger and that she had gone to TC.... Oh, my God, you were the boyfriend they were talking about."

If the first statement was thunder, the last was lightning.

"Boyfriend. Who was talking about a boyfriend?"

"God, I'm not sure I want to show you the second tape."

The second tape. Taz had forgotten all about the second tape. What was it she had said—she didn't know where she got it?

"What's on the second tape, Shannon? Where is it? I need to see what's on it. Now!"

"Okay, but calm down, please. It will show you that Jack Duvalier of Winford Thomas' own staff hired your old girlfriend to do...well...what she did."

Those words sent a chill through Taz that was supernatural. The room began to whirl. It couldn't be, he thought, just before fainting, his lifeless body falling to the floor.

"Taz, wake up, please. For God's sake, wake up." Shannon was holding the back of Taz's head with one hand and gently dobbing his face with a cold, damp washcloth. Shannon had taken his pulse, so she wasn't worried that he'd had a heart attack, but she couldn't imagine why Taz was this upset. At the moment, all she wanted was for him to wake up.

"Please wake up," she virtually shouted.

First one eye came open, then another.

"Shit," Taz said, rubbing his eyes. "Did I faint?"

"Yes, you scared me half to death. Did you hurt yourself?"

"No..., I'm fine."

Taz eased himself up and leaned against the bed. Shannon looked at him directly.

"Taz, what is it about this that has you this upset?"

Taz was groggy but not so groggy that he didn't know that anything he said to Shannon now might reveal more than he ever would want her to know.

"I...I was just so in love with her, I guess. And now she's mixed up in all this shit. If you run this tape and tell who she is, it will just kill her parents. I feel so sorry for them. They're really good people. Shannon, I need to watch the other tape now."

"Ah, Taz, I don't think so; at least not now. I'm afraid you'll faint again."

"No, I won't. I really need to see it."

"Well..., if you're sure, I'll put it on. But get back in bed; at least if you faint this time, you won't fall on the floor."

Taz didn't hear Shannon's attempt at levity. He was contemplating that his worst nightmare was about to assault his eyes and ears. As Shannon switched tapes, Taz was struck by another realization. If the tape was what Taz feared it was, Shannon must have picked it up off the coffee table in his apartment living room that very morning—and not realized it—when she spilled her purse. Taz braced for the worst. He had recovered enough of his faculties to know that it would be a very bad move to somehow acknowledge that he knew anything about this tape.

When Shannon's fifty-two inch TV screen exploded into a picture of hot-air balloons, Taz had an extremely strong urge to scream at Shannon to turn it off. He wasn't at all certain he could sit through it, but he knew he had to—lest Shannon perhaps think he had seen it before. He tried not to watch. When it was over, Taz put his head in his hands, then looked up at Shannon, who was eyeing him cautiously as she hit "stop" on the remote control.

"Are there any circumstances under which you wouldn't run that tape?" Taz was fighting another urge now; the urge to jump up, grab the tape, and run. Just run.

"Taz, I understand your former relationship to her, and I hate to say it, but it looks at least a little to me like you're still in love with her. I also can understand your not wanting to hurt her parents, but I don't see how I can not run this tape. I don't have a clue how it came into my possession, but it did, and I have a clear journalistic responsibility to run both of these tapes. I hope nobody figures out you were the college boyfriend, but they might. Look at me. ... Are you mad at me? Have I blown in five minutes what I've been thinking all day might be a real good thing?"

"Ah, Shannon, I understand everything you've said. I like you a lot, and I'm going to try not to let this come between us, but I think you should consider whether the journalistic value of these tapes is worth the damage they undoubtedly will cause to a whole bunch of totally innocent third parties."

"Okay, Taz, I'll think about it, but I think I know the outcome of that already. I've faced situations like this before, and journalism always wins out."

Maybe if she knew it was his little sister who shot the tape, she wouldn't use it, Taz thought, realizing almost simultaneously that journalism would "win out" over Heather, as well. But those thoughts led him to another thought. Twice in the last two days—twice—Shannon had made sure he understood the concept of confidentiality before she would confide something in him. Maybe, Taz thought, what he needed to do to protect Heather—and his father—the best he could would be to obtain a promise of confidentiality from Shannon in return for telling her who shot the tape. Besides, if he didn't, Shannon would try to figure out where the tape was shot and any such investigation might lead her to Heather. He could grab the tape from her, but she'd really investigate everything then, he knew.

"What if I were to tell you I know where you got the tape?"

"What? Do you really know?"

"What if I do?"

"What do you mean?"

"What I mean is that you have been on your high horse with me about my sense of confidentiality twice in the two days I've known you. Is turnabout fair play?"

"Well, I'm not sure your question is particularly fair, but if you're asking me whether I can keep a confidence, the answer is just as much 'yes' as your answer was 'yes.'"

"Good. Then do I have your absolute word that if I tell you where you got the tape and who shot it that you will never reveal that information to a soul under any circumstances unless I or the person who shot the tape tells you it's okay?"

"Yes, yes."

"Are you certain?"

"Yes, damnit, except that I'm not sure you can speak for whoever shot the tape, unless it was you."

"It was not me, but I definitely can speak for this person."

"God, Taz, let's stop all this. I won't ever divulge the source to anyone without your permission. You have my absolute word, okay?"

"Okay. ... I can't be one-hundred percent certain how you got the tape because I didn't see what happened, but when I was in the bathroom at my apartment this morning, I heard you carrying on in my living room about spilling your purse, right?"

"Yes, I spilled a bunch of stuff on your coffee table. I didn't know you heard me."

"Yeah, you were swearing a little bit."

"Ah, yeah, I guess I was, but where are you going with this?"

"Well, the tape you just showed me was on my coffee table."

"God, you're kidding. How come? Where did you get it? Who shot it? And why?"

"You know the picture on my wall you saw of my mom and dad and little sister? ... She shot it."

"Your mother shot this tape?"

"Nope. My little sister Heather shot it."

"Heather? How old did you say she is?"

"Twelve."

"God, Taz, you need to explain. I'm real confused."

As Taz recounted the events of July 3rd to Shannon, it all came into focus. Weirdest set of coincidences she had ever heard of, she thought.

When he was through explaining, including the part about his father, Taz asked Shannon to repeat her pledge.

"Okay, Taz, I will because I can see what's going on here. You're just trying to protect your family. If I had one, I'm sure I would, too. So let me say it again. No one ever will discover from me that Heather shot the tape or anything about the circumstances of its origin. Okay?"

At that moment, Taz was thinking more about what in the world he would say to Heather than he was listening to Shannon. He really liked Shannon, but it was clear that her value system was differently configured than his. The more he thought about all of it, the more he realized that he would need to stay as close to the situation as possible so that he could continue trying to prevent Heather and his parents from getting caught up in this unseemly mess.

"Am I spending the night?"

"I hope so."

"Do you have any dope; you know, like a number-four codeine tablet or something?"

"Yes, I'll get it for you."

"Thanks."

Normally, strong medicine knocked Taz for a loop, causing him to have a difficult time getting up the next day. That night, the codeine provided some comfort, but his sleep was light and fitful. Shannon was sleeping like a baby, he thought, as he came awake during the night more times than he could count. Sometimes he stared at her a bit before returning to sleep. Dessert was the furthest thing from his mind.

Friday, August 11th, 2000. After work, Taz called Heather.

"Heather, I've screwed up real bad, and I have a very sincere apology to make to you."

"Gosh. What, Taz?"

"Well, to start with, I've never said anything about it, but I was real embarrassed that you had to hear about my sex life with Ginger on the tape you shot, especially because I'm always preaching to you about the sex life I don't want you to have too young."

"Taz, do we have to talk about this?" Heather was uncomfortable again, like she was when The Gatehouse's waiters wanted to put the napkin in her lap.

"Well, yeah, we do because—are you ready?—not only is your restaurant tape going to be on TV, but the reason it's going to be on TV has to do with my stupid sex life again."

"What? What do you mean?"

"Well, have you ever seen Shannon Gillette on TV on a show called 'The Texas Truth?'"

"Yes, I don't watch it, but I've seen her—she's real pretty."

"I'm glad you think so because she...she's my girlfriend now."

"So, what are you telling me? You just changed your mind about the tape because you're dating her and just gave it to her—without talking to me about it?"

"No, no, Heather, I wouldn't do that. Just calm down and let me explain it to you. I was gonna bring your tape to you, right? Well, no one ever comes in my apartment, so I just left the tape on my coffee table. Then I met Shannon a couple of days ago, and...well...we were drinking and ended up at my apartment, and...well...the next morning she spilled her purse on the coffee table, and when she put the stuff back in it, she must've put your tape in there, too. I didn't know it at the time."

"So she's your girlfriend and you met her two days ago?"

"Well, I know what it sounds like, and I'm sorry we're having to discuss this, but I need to tell you the rest of it." Taz didn't much like being scolded by his little sister, but he deserved it, he thought.

"Okay, go ahead."

"Well, yesterday morning, somebody—no doubt Jack Duvalier—anonymously gave Shannon a tape of Ginger and Winford Thomas at Ginger's apartment in New York. In other words, Ginger went through with what she and Duvalier are discussing on your tape. When Shannon saw that she had two tapes, and she didn't know where she got the other one, she watched both of them. The second one was yours. She showed both of them to me last night, not knowing at the time that I knew anything about either one of them. When I saw that she had your tape, I literally fainted, and she had to revive me.

"She now knows where she got your tape and who shot it. I had to tell her, Heather, so that I could extract a promise from her that no one would ever know from her lips who shot the tape. She's no doubt going to use both of them on TV—soon. She's not a bad person, Heather, but she is a journalist, and they sort of play by their own set of rules. I've decided that I need to stay as close to what she's doing as I can so that I can try to do anything I need to to keep it from becoming publicly known that you or dad is involved somehow. I promise you that I'll do whatever I have to to keep you from being involved. Okay? ... Heather? ... Are you there?"

"...Yes, I'm here. I'm just thinking."

"What about?"

"What do you think? I trusted you with the tape and now you've lost it—and I'm gonna get killed."

"Heather, I *promise* I won't let you be involved. Look, I know you're mad at me, and you have every right to be, but, please, don't worry about being in trouble. You aren't in trouble now, so just try not to worry about this, okay?"

"Sure, that's easy for you to say."

"I know, Heather, but there's nothing else I can say. Listen, whenever Shannon's program is on TV, I'll let you know. I think it would be good if you could watch it with mom and dad so you can see what their reaction is. There'll be some advance publicity about it, so I'm sure dad will want to see it. I'll call you after it's over to see what their reaction was, okay?"

"Okay, big brother, but I sure hope you know what you're doing."

"Well, I'm not so sure sometimes, but I am sure that I haven't meant to do anything to harm anyone."

"I know that, Taz. I still love you."
"I love you, too, sweetie. We'll talk soon. Gotta go. Bye."
"Bye."

Chapter 16

Monday, August 14th, 2000.
"Congressman Thomas' office. How may I help you?"

"This is Shannon Gillette. I need to speak with Jack Duvalier, please."

"I'm sorry, but Mr. Duvalier is no longer with this office."

"What? When did this happen?"

"Ah, the only information I have is that Mr. Duvalier is no longer on the Congressman's staff. Could someone else help you?"

"Yes, I'd like to speak with Congressman Thomas."

"He's not here at the moment. Would you like to leave a message for him?"

"Yes, tell him Shannon Gillette called and that I think he might want to speak with me—and I mean today. My number is 512.555.5666."

"I'll see that he gets the message promptly."

"Hello."

"Shannon Gillette?"

"Yes."

"This is Winford Thomas."

"Congressman, thank you for returning my call. Let me give it to you straight. I want your reaction to the fact that I'm pulling together a program which will have a videotape segment more or less showing you making love to a woman named Ginger Fontenot and another videotape segment showing a conversation between Jack Duvalier and Ginger Fontenot setting up your rendezvous with her to sabotage your political career."

Thomas knew he had been set up by Duvalier and Ginger, but he had no idea there was videotape of their discussion of the conspiracy. He was taken aback.

"You have videotape of Jack Duvalier and Ginger Fontenot talking about conspiring to end my political career. Is that what you said?"

"Yes."

"Where did you get that?"

"Well, sir, from an anonymous source that I can tell you nothing further about—but it's real. What's your reaction to all this?"

"My reaction is that you're crazier than I ever imagined. I met Ginger Fontenot at a beauty pageant years ago, and I saw her at an embassy party in Washington, D.C., recently, but I certainly never have slept with her. And if you are going to say on television that I have, I will sue your company for all it's worth. Do I make myself clear?"

"Abundantly, sir, but we're not going to just say it—we're going to show it on videotape."

"Well, whatever you're going to show must have been fabricated. I think you must've been sucked into a political dirty trick that someone is playing on me—and you. So just do whatever you're going to do. We both know I can't stop you, but I will be suing you."

"Yes, sir, but what about Jack Duvalier?"

"What about him?"

"He no longer works for you—as of quite recently—and we have videotape of him and Ginger Fontenot setting you up. What do you know about all that?"

"Ms. Gillette, I'm not going to comment further. You're a big girl who's soon going to be in a lot of trouble. Good luck to you now. Goodbye."

"Hello, this is Jack Duvalier."

"Sorry to call you at home, Mr. Duvalier. This is Shannon Gillette."

"Shannon. . . . Damn, news travels fast. How did you find out so quickly?"

"If you mean that you aren't working for Congressman Thomas anymore, I just called there a few minutes ago, asked for you, and the receptionist told me you didn't work there anymore. That took me completely by surprise, but I think I know why you're no longer there."

"Oh?"

"Mr. Duvalier, Triple T is going to broadcast a program tomorrow night which will show two pieces of video that have come into my possession. The first tape will show you and Ginger Fontenot having a conversation in which the two of you are conspiring to sabotage Congressman Thomas' political campaigns. The second tape will show Congressman Thomas and Ms. Fontenot in a highly-compromising situation. . . ."

"You're kidding. Your first tape will show what?"

"As I said, it will show you and Ms. Fontenot having a conversation in which the two of you are conspiring to sabotage Congressman Thomas' political campaigns.

Duvalier was shocked—and didn't quite know whether to laugh or cry.

"Shannon, I don't quite know how to respond. You obviously think you know something—that you have some kind of big story. Where you got your information, I don't know. You say you have footage of me having a conversation with someone named Ginger Fontenot. I know no such person, so I find that very hard to believe."

Duvalier's head was swimming. Shannon thought it sounded like Duvalier was talking to himself. He rattled on.

"What are you talking about? Damn. This is just too much. Sometimes you reporters just crack me up."

Duvalier was collecting his thoughts the best he could and was trying diligently to analyze them while he talked. Was this a bad development or a good one? Did it matter? If Shannon had what she said she had, and she must, what the hell difference did it make? What had he said to Ginger that might be on that tape that might compromise GAYPAC? Nothing that he could remember. But how the hell could such a tape exist?

"Okay, Shannon, I'll answer you this way. I have no intention of answering any of your questions. Please feel free to run whatever videotape you have in your possession that you think would be of interest to your viewers. I no longer work for Winford Thomas. I belong to the private sector now, and I don't feel nearly the need to answer reporters' questions that I once felt. Thank you for calling, but please don't call back. Goodbye to you."

"Hello."

"Ginger Fontenot?"

"Yes."

"My name is Shannon Gillette. I'm a reporter with 'The Texas Truth.' Do you know of the program?"

"Yes. How can I help you?"

Shannon then told Ginger essentially what the program would contain.

Ginger professed to be flabbergasted. She wanted Shannon to think she was flabbergasted that Shannon would even *say* such things, but the truth was that she was flabbergasted that Shannon *knew* everything. Ginger had known it was a calculated risk to let Duvalier tape her with Winford Thomas, but she had not dreamed that her participation in the conspiracy against Thomas would become public knowledge by the direct involvement of a journalist. Ginger decided to take the offensive, not knowing what else to do. And what was this restaurant tape? she thought.

"I have absolutely no idea what you're talking about. If this is someone's idea of a joke, it's a poor one."

Ginger could hear herself talking, but she wasn't sure what she was saying. How could this reporter know all this? Ginger kept thinking.

"Ms. Fontenot, I'm not the one playing games here. The question is what is your reaction to our intention to broadcast the program I just described to you."

Ginger decided there could be cover in "going ballistic."

"What in the hell are you talking about? You must be crazy? You must really think you're something? A TV reporter. You're a big deal, all right. Lady, you're really nothing. When you're through destroying lives, I hope you're real happy with yourself. You're gonna ruin mine, and you're gonna ruin the lives of some real innocent people, too.

"You don't know anything about me. You don't know anything about my life. My reaction to your program is that you should burn in hell and that if you put any videotape of me on TV, I will sue you and the company you work for for every dime any of you have. Goodbye, you poor, pitiful, little twit."

Later that day. . . .

"Mr. Duvalier, I believe all the parties are on the line now. Ms. Salley?"

"Here."

"Ms. Jamanski?"

"Yes, I'm on the line."

"Mr. Jasmine?"

"Yes, I'm here."

"Go ahead, Mr. Duvalier, and thank you for using Global Telephone and Video."

"Listen," Jack said, "you are not going to believe what just happened to me."

As Duvalier related his conversation with Shannon to the GAYPAC hierarchy, there was disbelief all around. Duvalier explained that he had absolutely no idea how Shannon could have gotten videotape footage of his restaurant meeting with Ginger but that, indeed, she seemed to have it.

"Look, I've thought this through. We needn't be worried about anything except any damage that might be done to GAYPAC directly. If she has what she says she has, she'll run it one way or the other. We couldn't prevent it if we wanted to, and I'm not sure we do. I'm quite confident that Shannon knows nothing of my personal life or my association with GAYPAC. She has no idea who was behind the 'Ginger' tape. If she'd known something about GAYPAC, she'd have confronted me with it. She has no idea why I wanted Winford Thomas out of politics, and I doubt she'll try to find out. She'll just run the tape and see what happens.

"The one thing we have to worry about is that Thomas will tell her about us when she confronts him with all this like she did me this morning. Hell, she could be talking to him right now for all we know—or she could have talked to him before she talked to me. If she did, it's a certainty that Thomas didn't tell her about us because, if he had, she would have laid it on me for sure. What I think we should do is that I should drop out of sight. Is our place in St. Croix open right now? I'll just go down there 'til this blows over. What do all of you think?"

"Sandy here. I think this is a bit scary. Our cause would be set back a long way if anyone discovers we're using political blackmail to get Thomas out of politics, not to mention the possibility of criminal indictments. But I don't know how we could have avoided this. Go on down to St. Croix, Jack. You've done a good job. We'll let you know what's going on. Besides, if Gillette puts all this on TV, I'm sure you'll see it down there."

"This is Harriet, Jack. I think we ought to just sit back, relax, and let this television reporter do our dirty work for us. The only thing we have to fear is Winford Thomas, and there's not a damn thing we can do about that."

"Jack, Tony here. Didn't you tell me you had taken a liking to Michael Fletcher over at the White House? Why don't you let me see if I can't get his boss, Marsha Johnson, to give him some time off. She's a real good friend of mine, and I'm sure you and Michael would enjoy yourselves in the islands. We might even keep you there until after the November elections. Is that agreeable with everyone?"

That night. Eight p.m. Shannon and Harry Daniels were sitting in a semi-darkened post-production suite at Triple T's offices in Austin. Putting together a long videotape program could be a world of fun. Good television reporters truly were in their element when they were in this environment, especially if they had a great story to tell and great footage to work with. Shannon believed she had both. Long stories didn't necessarily mean high-quality journalism, and short stories didn't necessarily mean poor-quality journalism. Some great stories took a long time to tell and some didn't. This one was closer to not needing a long time to tell than vice versa. Sex was sex. Everbody understood that. Government scandals were complicated and many viewers just didn't care about the details. It was a good thing that the story was "simple" because Triple T was a thirty-minute show.

To tell this sensational story, Shannon had been given the entire program—the first time in its history that Brenda Jordan, Triple T's executive producer, had devoted the entire program to a single story. But this one had "awards" written all over it. With non-program time subtracted, Shannon had right at twenty-two minutes in which to tell millions of Texans about Jack Duvalier and Winford Thomas and Ginger Fontenot. Once Shannon and Harry had spent several hours making all the computer-assisted content alterations to the various bits of video and audio that would make up the program, they began the process of assembling the final product.

Shannon finished her script for the show by one a.m. and recorded her parts on camera in a studio. Everything was coming together nicely. Shannon began the program with herself on camera explaining that the "restaurant" tape the audience was about to watch had just shown up in her purse—and that she had good reason to believe that its author wished to remain anonymous. In any event, she said to the camera, "The Texas Truth" had been able to verify scientifically that the tape had not been digitally altered or created.

Concerning the tape of the "Winford Thomas Affair," as it was dubbed by Shannon, she told the audience that she had no idea who the source was, that directions to where she would find it had been provided to her by an electronically-affected voice on the telephone, and that she assumed this source, too, wished to remain anonymous.

"It will be obvious to you," Shannon told the camera, "that the two tapes must have come from different sources, neither knowing of the other."

She told her audience that the second tape, too, had been verified not to have been digitally altered or created. She explained that Triple T had engaged in some slight computer-assisted content manipulation of some of the images and sounds in the tape from the restaurant so that the audience could view and listen to the tape with greater visual and aural fidelity, explaining specifically what she and her colleagues—and the computer—had done to the tape.

Shannon then placed the tape into context by explaining the two election campaigns that Winford Thomas was engaged in. She told the audience they would be seeing two people on the tape, and she explained to the audience who the two people were.

Finally, she explained that the old boyfriend discussed by Ginger Fontenot and Jack Duvalier was Taz Sterling, a staff lawyer for the state legislature who she recently had been dating. She told the audience that this fact was a complete coincidence and had no significance whatever in relation to the story. She would be criticized by some in journalism, she told the audience, as having an unavoidable conflict of interest, but the story, she explained, was much more important than any personal criticism she might receive. She had been the recipient of these tapes, she said, and she considered it her duty to tell this story.

About three a.m., Shannon directed Harry to edit in the two tape segments. For broadcast purposes, Harry and Shannon had used a common special-effects device to effectively block out Ginger's hips just as the cover-up fell from her shoulders. After that portion of the program had been laid onto the master reel, Shannon told Harry to insert the next segment of Shannon on camera. In that segment, Shannon told the audience that Jack Duvalier, Ginger Fontenot, and Winford Thomas had been given the opportunity to respond but that Duvalier had declined comment on the specific questions put to him and that Ginger Fontenot and Winford Thomas had responded that the program was a complete lie and that legal action against Triple T should be expected.

Shannon could have been somewhat more forthcoming about her conversations with Duvalier, Ginger, and Thomas, but she wasn't because she knew she would be doing follow-up stories, and she didn't want to tip the competition to any more information than necessary. There was a saying in journalism that good reporters always knew more than they reported at any one time. Shannon was relying on that wisdom.

After a two-minute commercial break was inserted, the next program element edited in was a sequence of Thomas in his various Congressional roles, ending with his "I've never cheated, and I never will" statement at the June 17th press conference, which Triple T had licensed from an independent television archive.

Shannon then explained that Triple T had endeavored to discover whether the "Thomas" videotape had been used by Duvalier or others in an attempt to blackmail Thomas out of the race. If any such blackmail or blackmail attempt had taken place, Shannon said, Triple T had been as yet unable to discover it. Shannon indicated that Duvalier no longer worked for Congressman Thomas, having recently resigned. Shannon also reported that the Republican party, when queried, had strongly denied any involvement in any kind of videotaping or political blackmail or dirty tricks or anything of the sort, emphasizing to her that, after all, Jack Duvalier was a Democrat.

In the final segment of the program, the three tape sequences of the media conference, the restaurant, and the apartment rendezvous were made into a single, connected segment, and repeated. Shannon then reiterated that each of the principals had been given the opportunity to respond but that each had refused and that Fontenot and Thomas had denied the truthfulness of the tape they had been told would appear in the program. Fontenot and Thomas also said they would file suit against Triple T if any such videotape was broadcast, Shannon repeated.

Shannon thanked the audience and encouraged them to watch Triple T in the coming days and weeks for news of developments in the story. Harry then edited in the program's close and the credits. At just before daybreak, the program was intact at exactly twenty-eight minutes and twenty-five seconds in length.

After watching the complete playback, Harry asked Shannon to explain all the legal stuff to him. Was he going to get sued? Shannon explained to Harry that she assumed Fontenot and Thomas meant they would sue the station for libel, that is, for broadcasting a program concerning them that was false and that injured their reputations and that Triple T, at the time it aired the program, knew the program was false or didn't care whether the program was false or not.

No journalist or journalism organization wanted to be sued, Shannon told him, but truth was an absolute defense in a libel case, and Triple T absolutely was telling the truth. Shannon explained to Harry that even though the program was appearing on nearly two-dozen television stations in Texas, those stations would have no fear of losing any libel action brought against them in the situation because they had no advance warning whatever of the nature of Triple T's program. She told Harry not to worry about being sued personally because Diversicom would pay his legal expenses and indemnify him against any loss he might suffer.

Finally, Shannon told Harry that Triple T also would win any lawsuit based on privacy, explaining that "newsworthiness" would defeat such a claim and that it had become clear over the years that the courts viewed the private lives of public officials as newsworthy. This footage, Shannon said, was dramatically newsworthy. Harry was satisfied as to the libel and privacy part, but he had one last question—did she know the source of the "restaurant" tape?

To Harry's question, Shannon's one-word reply was: "Yes."

Tuesday morning, August 15th, 2000. Nine a.m. There were just a couple more things to do before the program was broadcast that night. Shannon had to show the program to Executive Producer Brenda Jordan. Brenda loved it. Because some of the subjects of the program had told Shannon they would sue Triple T if the program were aired, Shannon told Brenda she thought it was imperative that she and Brenda show the program to company CEO Dave Browning before Shannon went home to get some sleep. Brenda called Browning's office, but his secretary said he was meeting with the sales department about last-minute sales for Shannon's program that night and would be tied up for an hour or so. Brenda told Shannon to go on home and that she would call her by noon if Dave Browning had any objections to running the program as constituted.

Shannon left. When Brenda hadn't called by noon, Shannon assumed Brenda had shown the program to the boss, that he had raised no objections to it, and that Brenda was just letting Shannon sleep. Brenda, however, had not shown Browning the program, believing the program not to be libelous or privacy invading. If there was one thing she hated it was non-journalist bean counters, like Dave Browning, messing with the journalism. Besides, like Shannon, Brenda wanted to be associated with an award winner. Real bad. This was it. Compared to New York, Texas was a backwater state and Austin was a puddle. She was ready for the big-time.

At precisely eight p.m., the program aired. Taz watched it with Shannon at her condo. At just before eight-thirty p.m., Shannon's telephone rang. Her number was unlisted. She answered it in the kitchen.

"Hello."

"Shannon?"

"Yes?"

"This is Dave Browning."

"Oh, hi, Dave. Helluva program, huh?"

"It sure as hell is, Shannon. We're going to be sued into oblivion by everyone involved and God knows who else and you didn't even have the courtesy of telling me about all that before you aired the damn thing."

He was roaring. Shannon's fur flew.

"Wait a minute, Dave. Bullshit. Brenda showed it to you this morning, right?"

"Wrong."

When Heather had not called by nine p.m., Taz called her on her private line using his cell phone.

"Hello."

"Heather, why haven't you called me? I've been worried to death about you."

"I'm sorry, Taz. I'm okay."

"What happened when you watched the program? Did you watch it with mom and dad?"

"They didn't think it was funny that your name got mentioned, especially the way it did, but I guess dad got over it because he laughed and laughed at the part about Ginger and that Congressman. Mom told him she didn't think any of it was a bit funny; that it was awful that Ginger was involved in such a bad situation. She said she just couldn't understand any of it. She tried to make me leave the room when she saw what it was going to be about, but I told her I was almost a teenager and that I'd just go watch it in my room, so she told me I could stay."

"Did either of them say anything about recognizing the video? Do you think either one of them has any clue that you shot it?"

"I was watching them as much as I was watching the show, especially during the part where the tape from my camera was shown. They were just glued to the TV. I don't think they know anything. They definitely would have said something to me about it by now. I thought maybe mom might have been thinking something but didn't want to ask me about it in front of dad. I don't think she knows. I was just about to call you to tell you that."

"Okay, sweetie, that's great. I hope it stays that way."

"I was real excited to see the video from my camera on TV and to know that it's now gone all over the country on a satellite. I taped the whole show on a VCR in my room. I wanted to say something about it real bad. Dad laughed a lot, but he also said the whole show invaded the privacy of Ginger and those people. He asked mom whether she still wanted Ginger as a daughter-in-law. Mom frowned at him real hard."

"Yeah, I bet. Well, I've gotta go, but I want you to promise to call me if anything weird or suspicious happens, you hear?"

"Yes."

"Do you promise?"

"Yes."

"Okay, sweetie, I gotta go. I'll talk to you soon. Bye."

"Bye."

Taz started to call his mom to apologize but thought better of the idea.

Shannon's unlisted number was ringing off the hook. The television-journalism world was congratulating her. Kudos all around. The only damper on her otherwise good spirits was that Dave Browning had told her to be in his office at eight-thirty the next morning. Taz wasn't sure what to make of any of it. After watching accounts of the program on the ten p.m. newscasts, Shannon switched off her telephone and Taz buttoned up his cell phone for the night. They had eaten Chinese take-out, but they hadn't yet had dessert.

Chapter 17

Wednesday, August 16th, 2000. Winford Thomas was still in the Texas cabin. It had a television—poor reception, but good enough. His family, horrified, had fled to his wife's uncle's summer home on a quiet lake in Wisconsin, having been flown there from northern Virginia early Wednesday morning in a private plane by a sympathetic church friend. Winford, figuring that's where they would go, had talked to his two daughters, Tori and Tanya, briefly by telephone. His wife, Linda, would not speak to him. He told Tori and Tanya that he loved them and that he would make this up to them. He told them he needed them to keep on loving him. They told him they would. The media were trying hard to find his family, but none of them knew anything of the Wisconsin cabin. Winford Thomas was pleased that Jack Duvalier and Ginger Fontenot had been exposed as co-conspirators in the deal, but it provided him little real comfort as against the major problems he was facing.

On Thursday night, August 17th, Winford Thomas prevailed on an oil-baron friend to fly him in his private jet from Rhinehart to Washington, D.C., where he stole away by car to a motel room that had been rented for him by another friend. He'd had his office schedule a media conference in the House television studios for ten a.m. on Friday, August 18th. At the appointed time, Winford Thomas strode through a private side door into the television studio. He walked briskly and formally to the gaggle of microphones adorning the lectern.

"Thank you all for coming. I will read a brief statement, and I will not take questions at this time. I hope you will appreciate why I cannot answer questions today after you have heard my statement. The statement is this. Effective at this moment, for the sake of Democrats and right-thinking people all over the great State of Texas, I hereby resign as the Democratic nominee to the United States Senate from the State of Texas. Also effective at this moment, for the sake of the wonderful people in my Congressional district who have elected me to the United States House of Representatives ten times, I hereby resign as the Democratic nominee to the United States House of Representatives, Thirty-first District, State of Texas.

"The people of Texas deserve the best representation they can get in the Congress, and I have concluded that I could not win either election in November on the heels of the program aired two nights ago. I have every confidence that the Democrat party of Texas will appoint candidates to take my place in these two important races who will defeat the Republican nominees for these offices.

"I want to make it clear that I am not resigning from the House; that I fully intend to serve out my term, which will expire at the end of this year. Finally, I want to say to you that within the next few days my attorney will be filing a lawsuit against 'The Texas Truth,' its parent company, Diversicom Corporation, and the various individuals who were directly involved, primarily Shannon Gillette. The wire services will be notified by my office exactly when the suit is to be filed.

Copies of the pleadings will be distributed by my office to all requestors at that time. Thank you very much, and I'm sorry I can't take your questions. This is on the advice of counsel. Thank you."

The media, of course, never hear words like "I won't be able to take your questions." Or maybe it's that they just can't conceive that anyone would refuse to answer their questions. At any rate, Winford Thomas was peppered with questions from a wad of reporters all shouting at the same time as he quickly retreated behind a "Members Only" door. He couldn't have answered their questions had he wanted to because none of the questions were individually decipherable above the din. As soon as he was out of sight, controlled journalistic bedlam broke loose. Some reporters punched on cellular telephones. Some ran for conventional telephones. Some stood before cameras—shouting to the others to stop shouting. Some bolted for the exits. The story was heating up.

Ginger Fontenot had spent the previous several days with her best friend in Manhattan. The media was camped out at her apartment. She was able to retrieve her telephone and e-mail messages. Most of them were from the media, but she was able to stay in touch with the friends she cared about. She hadn't heard from Pretty As A Picture since the program aired. They didn't call her much, anyway, so it wasn't a great shock. Manhattan had been a real struggle. She had spoken with the Fontenots. They were devastated but said they would get through it. They implored her to return home to Texas, but Ginger knew she never could go home.

Winford Thomas filed suit on Monday, August 21st, slightly less than a week after the broadcast. Thomas' lawyer, Barry Michaels of Dallas, an old buddy from law school, sued "The Texas Truth," its corporate owner, Diversicom Corporation, and Shannon Gillette, Brenda Jordan, and Harry Daniels, individually, in state court in Travis County, Texas. Thomas' lawyer could have filed the suit in a number of venues, but Austin, the county seat of Travis County, was ideal because every single district judge in the county was a Democrat and because, as Triple T's home base, Austin could not be argued by the defendants as being inconvenient to them or that Thomas had engaged in "forum shopping" to enhance his chances of finding a sympathetic judge—which, ironically, is exactly what Thomas and his lawyer had done. The particular judge would be assigned at random, but at least the judge would be a Democrat, Thomas knew. Thomas' pleadings set forth causes of action sounding in libel and invasion of privacy.

Diversicom, which owned a number of radio stations in addition to syndicated television properties, such as "The Texas Truth," had a Washington, D.C., law firm on retainer to handle its affairs before the Federal Communications Commission, and it had "local counsel" in all its markets to handle its routine legal work, such as worker's compensation claims, but it had no media-tort counsel anywhere. What it did have, though, was an insurance policy that covered up to $15 million in such damages. Thomas' lawsuit was for that very amount in compensatory damages. He asked for an additional $35 million in punitive damages.

When Dave Browning, Triple T's CEO and Diversicom's local agent for service, was served with Thomas' suit on Wednesday, August 23rd, he immediately contacted the corporate office in Atlanta, which, in turn, contacted the company's insurance carrier, America All-Risks. The second thing he did was summon Shannon Gillette and Brenda Jordan.

He had been beside himself with anger when he watched the program on the air and heard about the lawsuit threats for the first time. The next morning, he had demanded to know why he hadn't been told of the threats before the program was aired. Brenda confessed she should have told him and that she had promised Shannon she would. Lying, she said she didn't have an answer to why she hadn't told him in advance of the broadcast about the lawsuit threats. Browning knew she'd had a reason, but he also knew that she wouldn't tell him. Fairly new to the job, Browning had not been involved, prior to this, in any media-tort lawsuits."

Shannon, feeling a little better at Brenda's admission that Shannon thought Browning had been consulted and informed by Brenda, had told Browning it was entirely common for targets of investigative journalism to make such threats to try to keep truthful and highly-newsworthy information off the air and that the company would win any lawsuit because the legal deck was so stacked in favor of journalism and against public persons. She repeated this assertion at the post-filing meeting.

At the earlier meeting, Browning had not responded to Shannon's idea of media law; this time, he shouted, telling her he would fire both of them on the spot but for one thing—their firing two days after a big lawsuit was filed could too easily be construed as an admission of liability, and it even could attract lawsuits from Ginger Fontenot and Jack Duvalier.

Browning then asked Shannon where she got her license to practice law and, even better, when she began representing Diversicom. Where did she get off, he wanted to know, deciding it would be okay to get the company sued because it would win. Further, he told her, there could be a million reasons the company didn't want to be sued at that time that she could know nothing about. He then threw both of them out of his office.

Later that day, America All-Risks told Browning that the Dallas firm of Gentry & Sterling had just begun handling all its work in Texas and that because of the amount of potential liability in the case, it had referred the case directly to Rance

Sterling, the firm's managing partner and chief insurance-defense litigator, who had not been bothered, Browning was told, by his own son's tangential involvement in the case.

That same day, Rance Sterling called Browning. In reality, Rance was bothered by his son's involvement in the situation, however tangential, but he nonetheless was thrilled to get the case. Albeit indirectly, here was his opportunity to help George Parsons that someday could land him on the federal bench, perhaps even on the U.S. Supreme Court. He didn't know a thing about media torts. He knew most torts upside down and backwards, but media torts—libel and privacy invasion—were as unusual a set of torts as existed. The tort of libel was many centuries old, with a very murky legal history in the United States; murky because harm to reputation was intangible and, as such, a lot different than physical harm to person or property, the most usual kind of tort injury, and because the U.S. Supreme Court had entangled the tort of libel with federal constitutional law in a landmark case in 1964 by mixing it with the First Amendment. Privacy law was a creature of the twentieth century, but no less confusing.

Rance Sterling told Browning how happy he was to be representing the program. In truth, though, "politics make strange bedfellows" was the saying that kept running through his mind as he thought about representing Shannon Gillette and "journalism." He remembered having thought that Shannon's program, while potentially extremely helpful to Parsons' candidacy, had been a grotesque invasion of privacy. Luckily, he hadn't made such a statement publicly, only at home and at the office. In his heart of hearts, he was more than a little jealous of Winford Thomas for having had the opportunity to make love to Ginger Fontenot. More than once he had lusted to "know" her when he would come home to find the bikini-clad Ginger playing volleyball in the pool with Taz and others. His current envy subsided, though, when he snapped back to the reality that Thomas' one indiscretion with Ginger likely had cost him his political career and his family.

Like most old-money families involved in politics, the Sterlings had had their skirmishes with journalists. Rance Sterling generally, if privately, detested reporters—believing most of them to be "sleazy" and guilty of being obsessed with the journalistic notion of comforting the afflicted and afflicting the comfortable. Because the Sterlings were "comfortable" offered no conceivable reason why they therefore should be "afflicted" somehow by the news media, Rance Sterling thought. Consequently, he believed deeply that the second-best way to avoid unwanted publicity was to stay as far away from journalists as possible. The first-best way, he believed—naively—was for the owners of the various Metroplex news media to be beholden to him in some way. Even if such local relationships once could have protected him, it was true no longer because the conglomerates that owned so much of the news media in the Metroplex in 2000 were large companies based elsewhere. In terms of media ownership, "local" was no more—a product, ironically for Rance Sterling, of Republican deregulation of the media industry beginning in the eighties.

To say the least, the Board of Directors of Diversicom was not happy to learn of Thomas' lawsuit. Every one of its members was livid. The lawsuit was under discussion at a special called meeting on Wednesday night, August 23rd, in Atlanta. Diversicom was in the middle of serious negotiations to sell "The Texas Truth" and its other syndicated television programs when the program was broadcast. Diversicom had decided it liked the television business and was selling its syndicated properties in order to trade up to ownership of an entire television station, KZYX in Phoenix, which was for sale for a price Diversicom could afford if it could sell Triple T and its other programs for what it considered fair market value. Negotiations for the sale of the properties had been proceeding smoothly with the Kennecut Corporation—another large company wanting in the cash-cow television business—until the "Thomas" program and its lawsuit aftermath, at which point negotiations broke off, to resume only if the lawsuit could be quickly settled or resolved. It was difficult to sell a syndicated television program when it had contingent liability of $50 million in a pending lawsuit unless Diversicom was willing to indemnify the purchaser, which it was not. Kennecut was not interested in the package of programs unless Triple T, the flagship, was included.

Diversicom had two problems. First, Kennecut was in the mood to buy. The parent company of KZYX, Merlin Industries, needed to sell the station to pursue immediate opportunities in the cable television business, and it wasn't about to wait around on Diversicom. Diversicom's board had the uneasy feeling that Kennecut might end up owning KZYX—a bit of a financial stretch but probably doable—while Diversicom was left still owning its syndicated programs and millions of dollars in potential liability from a program that, in the hindsight and bean-counter view of Diversicom's board, never should have been broadcast because of the stridency of the lawsuit threats and confusing origins of the "anonymous" videotapes.

Diversicom wanted back on track as quickly as possible and so dispatched its general counsel on the corporate jet to fly to Dallas on Thursday, August 24th, 2000, to discuss the situation with Rance Sterling. Sterling did not like Diversicom's meddling in the case, even after Warren Rampy explained the problem to him that afternoon. After all, Rance Sterling had his own agenda, and it was to look good in the eyes of George Parsons. Further, Sterling and America All-

Risks were in control of the suit whether Rampy and Diversicom liked it or not.

"I'm sure you can understand, Rance, why Diversicom is interested in getting this case settled as quickly as possible."

"Of course I understand, Warren. And I'm sure America All-Risks would be happy to just completely bow out of this case if Diversicom wants to relieve it of liability. We've got a winnable case here, you know, and America All-Risks isn't going to pay the plaintiff several million dollars just so that Diversicom can get itself out of a tight. Now, if Diversicom wants to indemnify America All-Risks and let me negotiate a quick settlement on that basis, I'm sure that can be accomplished."

"Yes, well, thank you, Rance. I'll need to communicate this conversation to my board of directors. Could we meet here in the morning at nine o'clock for me to let you know my board's decision and to go over any other matters that may have arisen by that time?"

"Sure, Warren, I'll see you then."

Arrogant ass, Rampy thought, as he left Rance Sterling's office. He had known that Rance would make such an argument, but he had been ordered by Diversicom to broach the subject. That Rance Sterling's client in the case was Diversicom, and not the insurance carrier, meant that Sterling's legal obligation was to act in the best interests of Diversicom. But there was a hole in the tort system that everyone understood and no one but the insurance companies really liked. No matter the niceties of the "law," the truth was that tort defendants, absent unusual circumstances, never were in control of the litigation because it wasn't the defendants' money at risk. The law dictated one course of conduct, law practice and economics another; a legal conundrum that no one had been able to resolve.

When Rampy reported back to Diversicom's CEO Thursday afternoon from his Dallas hotel room, there followed a discussion between the CEO and the board by e-mail concerning relieving America All-Risks, but, in the end, the board wasn't comfortable enough with the idea to pull the trigger because no one had that much faith in being able to settle the lawsuit quickly for a reasonable amount.

No telling whether Thomas would settle, and no telling what a jury might award him if the case went to trial. Juries didn't like politicians much, but they liked journalists even less. The case could be won on appeal, but that could take years. When Rampy reminded the board that a jury just south of the Metroplex had in 1991 awarded the second largest libel judgment in history—$58 million—to a politician against a Metroplex TV station, and that a Houston jury had in 1997 awarded more than $220 million to a Houston company in a newspaper libel case—the largest libel jury award ever—the decision was made. America All-Risks would not be let out and could continue to control the litigation. Too, Ginger Fontenot and Jack Duvalier might file suit, as well, Diversicom's board knew.

Warren Rampy was dispatched to Rance Sterling's office Friday morning to inform Sterling of the board's decision and to see if an alternative could be worked out. Diversicom wanted the lawsuit to be expedited. In a media-torts case, the plaintiff normally would be delighted for the case to be handled quickly. It was normal defense strategy to drag out such lawsuits in hopes of wearing down the plaintiff so that the case might go away or at least be settleable for less than equitable. When Rance Sterling was approached by Warren Rampy on the subject of expediting the lawsuit, his initial reaction was the same as it had been to Diversicom's request that the case be settled.

"Warren, you know the answer to that question without even asking it. America All-Risks would be happy to expedite this case if you want to pay the tab; otherwise, there's just no incentive—and considerable disincentive—for America All-Risks to do such a thing. For the insurance defense to seek to expedite the resolution of a case like this would raise a red flag to the plaintiff that the defense was in some kind of bind or bad bargaining position. But you know that."

Rampy threw down the gauntlet.

"Of course, I know all that, Rance, but let me state to you the incentive you seem to have overlooked. Diversicom pays more than $7 million a year in premiums to America All-Risks through its various divisions. If America All-Risks can't see its way clear to expedite the handling of this lawsuit, Diversicom will immediately end its relationship with America All-Risks and take its $7 million in annual premiums elsewhere."

"Well now, Warren, you're talking to the wrong man," Rance said with a disgust-tinged voice. "I'm just a lawyer hired by America All-Risks to handle a case. Your 'proposal' would be better directed at America All-Risks itself. I'm in no way authorized to make any such deal. You know very well that what you're proposing is totally outside the authority I have in this situation."

"You might not be authorized to make such a deal, Rance," Rampy said sarcastically, "but we both know you can deliver the message."

"I'll be in touch with you real soon, I'm sure, Warren," Rance said tersely. "Good day to you now, sir."

"Good day to you. I'll be in my hotel room until late this afternoon waiting on your call. Do call personally, please," Rampy said with continuing sarcasm.

Rampy left Rance Sterling's palatial office feeling good—real good. Corporate counsel generally were condescended to by lawyers of Rance Sterling's station, being thought of as inferior to the major law-firm barons and litigators. Making Rance Sterling be a messenger boy made Warren Rampy's day. He felt even better when Rance Sterling called him at his hotel about noon that day to say that America All-Risks had agreed that the case should be expedited. Rance Sterling made about $2 million a year; Warren Rampy, about $200,000. At that precise moment, Warren Rampy didn't care.

Rance felt doubly odd in calling Barry Michaels just after he spoke with Rampy to tell Michaels that Diversicom would be happy to begin settlement negotiations. He knew Michaels would be wary if he pushed him to settle, so he tried to be as subtle as possible.

Michaels was surprised, but he still took the bait—in a sense. He was representing Winford Thomas on a contingent-fee arrangement; he wouldn't be paid a nickel unless and *until* there was a settlement or a final judgment awarded through the court system. Michaels didn't exactly know why Sterling was being so overly cooperative, but, for the moment at least, he wasn't going to look any gift horses in the mouth. He called Rance Sterling back late that day to say that he couldn't really begin settlement negotiations until he had deposed Shannon Gillette, star witness. They agreed she would be deposed on Monday, August 28th, just two days away. Michaels was bewildered but couldn't imagine what he had to lose. He would be required to burn the midnight oil to be ready for this deposition, but so be it, he thought.

None of the parties involved so far knew it at the time, but on that very day, Friday, August 25th, Ginger Fontenot had filed suit in Austin against the same defendants through her attorney, Lyle Branson. Branson had called her the week before and left a message on her machine. Ginger knew he was the Lyle Branson of Branson Danielson & Corning in the Texas Metroplex, the Colleen Etherington Foundation's law firm. She didn't know what he wanted, but she knew she would need a lawyer to sue Diversicom, so she called him back. Maybe he could recommend one. During the conversation, Ginger asked him whether he might be able to recommend someone to her. Surprisingly to Ginger, Branson offered to represent her himself, saying he would be delighted to take the case on a contingent-fee basis, meaning she would owe him nothing unless he collected damages in her behalf.

Branson expressed outrage that Ginger was, in his words, being used as a pawn in a high-stakes game of politics. She was quite flattered—especially under these circumstances—that someone as prominent as Lyle Branson would think enough of her to offer, and she didn't know any lawyers real well other than Taz, so she told him she would be happy for him to represent her.

He told her his original reason for calling her was foundation business, something to do with the IRS. He had a form he needed her to sign about her scholarship money. Just routine. He'd send it in the mail, he said, along with a contingent-fee agreement for her to sign. Just send them back together, he told her.

Suddenly, Diversicom was facing potential liability of $100 million as opposed to $50 million. Not that such amounts ever would be paid, but stranger things had happened. The syndicated properties were on the sale block for $200 million, with "The Texas Truth" accounting for about $50 million of that. Anything could happen.

Rance Sterling never had handled such an odd case before. An insurance-defense lawyer expediting a case was virtually unheard of. The legal strategies that would need to be employed to expedite resolution were strange. For instance, it was clear that Barry Michaels, in deposing Shannon Gillette, would want to know the source of the "New York" tape and the "restaurant" tape. Normally, the defense would make all kinds of arguments about why it would be impossible to divulge that information. In this case, however, the strategy would be to release the information to Michaels during the deposition. The individual defendant, however—Shannon Gillette—

could know nothing of this strategy. She simply would conduct herself in the lawsuit as requested by the company because the company was indemnifying her against any loss she might suffer. Rance Sterling met in his office with her on Sunday afternoon, August 27th, the day before her deposition was to take place. She had flown up from Austin on Southwest Airlines, the cheapest, best, friendliest, and most efficient airline flying.

Taz had told Shannon to be "cautious" of his father.

"But he's your lawyer; he'll be on your side. I don't know why you are being deposed this quickly, but, basically, just take his advice."

"It's nice to meet you, Shannon. Taz speaks highly of you. His family, of course, is sorry he's involved in this situation, but life takes some strange twists and turns. Knowing Ginger as I did, I never would have dreamed that she would conduct herself in this way."

"Thank you, Mr. Sterling. . . ."

"Rance, please. . . ."

"Rance. . . . I think a lot of Taz, and I, too, am sorry that he got involved—even in this small way. As I'm sure you know, other reporters have wanted to interview him about Ginger, but he has declined."

"Yes, well, this family has little interest in going public about much of anything. ... I guess we should get down to business here—big day for you tomorrow."

"Yes, sir."

"Shannon, Ginger filed suit against the same defendants on this past Friday. We haven't been served yet, but her lawyer faxed us a copy of her suit. It's virtually the same as the Thomas suit. Her lawyer is Lyle Branson of Fort Worth, which is quite odd to me, but...well. . . . He'll be at the deposition tomorrow, too. By the way, have you ever been deposed?"

"Yes, sir, I have."

"Good. Just answer every question they ask you as truthfully as you can. We have nothing to hide here. There was nothing untruthful about the program, so just tell them whatever they want to know."

"Yes, sir. You mean except the identity of the source of the restaurant tape?"

"No, Shannon, I mean that, too. Barry Michaels and Lyle Branson certainly will want to know where that tape came from. As you know if you've read the pleadings, Michaels has alleged that Ginger and Jack Duvalier had no such meeting; that the tape was created from whole cloth, as were the tapes we say were produced in Manhattan. Branson has alleged essentially the same thing.

"Now, you say you don't know the source of the 'New York' tape, and that's fine. If you don't know, you don't know. But you say you do know the identity of the source of the restaurant tape. If your source is as credible as you indicated in the program, and if this source would explain the circumstances surrounding the production of the tape in the first place, then Michaels and Branson would have a helluva time proving falsity, an essential element of the tort of libel.

"Thomas is a public person and Ginger may be a public person for purposes of this lawsuit and the story itself clearly is a matter of public concern, meaning that in addition to proving that what you said about them was false, they also would be required to show that you said what you said intending to lie or at least not caring whether you were lying or not. The source of the original tape can dispel all that—blow them completely out of the water concerning most of their allegations of falsity. So, no, Shannon, I'm afraid that question is the one we want you to answer the most forthrightly of all."

"Mr. Sterling, I'm very sorry, but sometimes I think no one has been listening to me. I promised the source of that tape confidentiality, and I intend to keep my promise. I mean no disrespect to you, sir, or to Diversicom, but I'm not going to tell anybody anything about who shot the restaurant tape."

"I'm *real* sorry to hear that, Shannon. I had no idea this meant so much to you. And it makes me a little nervous about where that tape came from. These folks are trying to nail us to the wall for millions and millions of dollars here, Shannon. This isn't some lofty journalism-class discussion. You don't have anything to lose here financially, but America All-Risks and Diversicom could lose millions. Clearly, you have an obligation to reveal the identity of your source."

"On the contrary, Mr. Sterling, I have a clear obligation to my source not to reveal his or her identity. I understand the position the insurance company and Diversicom is in, but they need to understand the position I'm in. 'The Texas Truth' has no written policy on the subject of confidentiality and no one ever articulated a policy to me, either. In journalism, that means its up to the individual reporter. The company then is supposed to stand behind its journalism. That's how it works. Maybe Diversicom hasn't been in the news business long enough to understand how it all works, but I can't help that. I've got to stand up to what light I have. My bottom line is that I'm not going to reveal the identity of the source of the restaurant tape."

"Well, Shannon, I hate to tell you this, but since you and Diversicom are now at cross purposes, it would be a conflict of interest for me to continue representing Diversicom and you. In a situation like this where I have to make a choice about who to continue to represent, my first allegiance is to the corporation. Under these circumstances, you'll have to find yourself a lawyer to represent your particular interests—and you, of course, would be responsible for paying that person. I'm going to have to call Dave Browning right now and tell him about this. Diversicom might not even want to employ you after this. And there'll be no deposition tomorrow because you'll need some time to find yourself a lawyer. I'll call Michaels and Branson and explain to them that I no longer represent you and that they should be hearing from you or your lawyer soon. They may want to contact you directly."

Journalists, Rance Sterling thought, journalists. . . .

What little money Shannon had accumulated over the relatively few years she'd been working certainly wasn't enough to pay the kind of legal fees she was about to incur. Plus, the next morning Dave Browning called her into his office and fired her for refusing to cooperate with the company. Shannon was devastated. She couldn't believe this was happening to her. Not only had she lost her job—which just two weeks before had seemed like a dream—she also knew she would exhaust her savings fairly quickly just living. Paying expensive attorneys' fees was out of the question. She called Taz first thing.

"Taz, God, your father was right."

"You get fired?"

"Yes, what the hell am I going to do now?"

"Well, I've been thinking about that. I just can't let you be unrepresented or spend your savings being represented. There's way too much at stake—for Heather, my parents, you, others. . . . Besides, I screwed this up, and I'm no longer mad at you about it if I ever was. So, with your permission, I will be representing you now."

"Taz, that's so sweet, but even if I'd let you, how could you do that and still keep your job?"

"I couldn't, but don't worry about it. My grandparents on dad's side left me a trust fund. It's substantial. Its assets became available to me when I was twenty five. I used a little of it to pay off law-school loans, but there's a whole lot left. I can't think of a better way to spend part of this money than to represent you in this situation. Besides, I've had enough statute drafting; I'm ready to practice law. This ought to be a helluva case to cut my teeth on. And, don't worry, if I get to a place where I'm more than a little unsure of myself, I'll hire an experienced lawyer as a consultant."

"Taz, are you sure you want to do this? I won't be able to pay you, and I would feel like I should."

"Shannon, let's just get all this over with. I just want to be sure you would want me to represent you."

"Of course I do."

"Okay, enough said."

At the dinner table that night, Rance Sterling asked Taz what he was doing in town on a Monday. "Are you here on state business, son? I didn't know you traveled much in that position."

"Actually, no, dad, I'm not here on state business. I flew up here this afternoon to let you and mom and Heather know that I no longer work for the state."

Everyone at the table was startled.

"What?" Rance Sterling said. "What do you mean you no longer work for the state? This was a little sudden, wasn't it? Who are you working for? Do you have a job?

God forbid with some other law firm. Lord, I hope you haven't embarrassed us that way. I never thought about how some of our competitors would surely view it as a real coup to hire the son of Rance Sterling. What's going on, Taz?"

As Rance Sterling spoke the words, they had gotten faster and louder. His tone approached anger.

"Well, dad, I see you're jumping to conclusions, as usual. You'll be pleased to know that I've taken on a real important client. I've gone into private practice on my own—as a solo practitioner—and I'm only going to have one client, at least for the foreseeable future. And, yes, my departure from my job was quite sudden, but that will make more sense to you when you know who my client is. My boss at the legislature understood the suddenness of my departure. No one there is mad at me."

"Solo practice? One client? All this is a little bewildering, Taz. I knew you wanted to prove your independence to me, and I had come to understand that, but I always just assumed you would come to work for us when you were convinced that I believed you were your own man. Who is this client? If this client is so important, why don't you just come to the firm and bring this client along with you?"

"I can't."

"Why the hell not?"

"Because that would constitute a rather obvious conflict of interest."

"What the hell does that mean?"

"It means you represent a client which is at cross purposes with my client in current litigation."

"What? Who the hell is your client? Do you mean you're representing a plaintiff that has sued someone Gentry & Sterling represents?"

"No, that's not quite right. I wouldn't disappoint you by representing one of those nasty plaintiffs whose lawsuits against those angelic insurance companies you represent make you all that money. Actually, I represent a former client of yours—Shannon Gillette."

Heather dropped her fork in her plate, nearly breaking a several-hundred-dollar piece of china. Reauxanne felt nauseated. Rance was greatly irritated at himself for not having thought of that, and he was mad as hell at Taz for doing it.

"What the hell are you trying to prove, son? I was happy to be representing her, but she opted to get on the wrong side of the case. I admire her principles, but she doesn't have a legal leg to stand on, and you don't need to be injecting yourself into this dispute in opposition to me, your family, and the firm. Damn, son."

"Look, dad," Taz said, dropping *his* fork on the several-hundred-dollar piece of china, "I mean no harm or disrespect to you, to the family, or to your law firm. Frankly, I don't see how my representation of someone possibly could be disrespectful to anyone. If you'd paid a little more attention to me over the years, you'd have some idea. . . ." He stopped short.

Reauxanne was stunned but said nothing. She was the one who would try her best to smooth things over as soon as possible. She was the one, like so many southern women, who tried so hard to keep the family from tearing itself apart.

Heather was crying softly. Rance and Reauxanne thought they knew why. But they were only partially correct.

Rance Sterling was mad at Taz, but he was madder at himself for letting the situation get out of hand. If Taz did that well in open court against him, Rance thought with some pride, he might just have a chance.

Taz excused himself from the table. He hugged Heather and told her he was very sorry if he had upset her, that everything would be just fine. He kissed his mom on the cheek, told his dad he'd see him around the courthouse, and left.

Chapter 18

Winford Thomas needed all the money he could get. His wife would be suing him for divorce, and he was afraid she would be awarded the vast majority of their marital estate under the adulterous and highly-public circumstances of the situation. He would like nothing better than to take GAYPAC down with him, but he knew he couldn't expose GAYPAC's blackmail of him and prove falsity at the same time. GAYPAC's executive committee, knowing that, was thrilled when Thomas sued Diversicom.

Tuesday, August 22nd, 2000. Linda Thomas left a message on the answering machine at their northern Virginia home to let Winford know she was divorcing him.

"I was able to forgive you for not telling me about the child you fathered until after we'd had our first child. And I'd been able to abide the charade of a marriage we've had these last years for the sake of our children, but for you to be videotaped making love to someone young enough to be your daughter was just too much for me. My lawyer will let you know where we have gone when we leave my uncle's. Right now, the girls are still so embarrassed that we haven't quite decided what to do or where to go, but they'll have to start school somewhere real soon. I could never go home to Rhinehart now. You've ruined that for all of us."

Winford didn't try to call her back. He wanted to speak with his children, but he knew they didn't want to speak with him at the moment, and he believed the time would come when he could re-establish a relationship with them.

If he were to win the lawsuit, he needed to prove that the program involved substantial falsity. He had every reason to believe there was nothing false about it, but he might learn something through discovery that he could hang his hat on, and he was fortunate that Shannon Gillette was refusing to tell where she got the restaurant footage—fortunate because the court might rule that unless Shannon identified the source of the tape, the court would declare that, for legal purposes, the tape did not exist. Should the court do that, winning a significant damage award against Diversicom would be much easier. For this reason, the privacy claim was much weaker than the libel claim. He might not even pursue it. Concerning privacy, politicians had very little, he knew, and what little he had probably was lost by virtue of removing Ginger's clothes in front of an open window. He probably had a reasonable expectation of privacy in relation to the audiotaping of the lovemaking session, but he didn't think most juries would be very sympathetic toward him given the context of the situation. Libel, he concluded, was the better approach for him.

In a word, Texas District Judge Arnold Ravinson was crazy. He was clearly the least respected of all the district judges in Travis County, and Taz was displeased to say the least that Judge Ravinson would be presiding over the case. So far as Taz could determine, Judge Ravinson had never sent a reporter to jail on a contempt citation for refusing to divulge the identity of a confidential source—or for any other reason, for that matter—but he had sent many persons to jail on contempt citations of various sorts, including, over the years, a number of lawyers.

To make matters worse, it was clear that Judge Ravinson hated the media. He'd had so many skirmishes with reporters during his sixteen years on the bench that Taz had decided to ask him to recuse himself from the case on that basis. When Judge Ravinson saw the motion for disqualification Taz filed, word from the inner sanctum at the courthouse was that he had gone wild and his bailiff had had to calm him down. Needless to say, the judge had denied the motion—and in short order. While filing the motion had not spared Taz from possibly being found in contempt by Judge Ravinson, it had provided him with the legal basis for an appeal in the event he was sent to jail by Judge Ravinson or in the event Shannon was sent to jail by the judge for refusing to disclose the source of the restaurant tape, as Taz expected would be the case.

Since Taz would not be able to use Judge Ravinson's extrajudicial tantrum against him in appealing any sentencing of Taz or Shannon to jail for contempt, he could only hope that the judges who sat on the court of appeals that would hear any appeal Taz might file would have heard about the tantrum through the grapevine, but he likely would never know. He had heard, though, that the latest stories about Judge Ravinson's courtroom behavior were always on the agenda whenever judges in Travis County got together privately.

The stories about him were legion. He loved to embarrass young lawyers, most of whom grew to dislike him intensely. As the young lawyers became older and more experienced in the courtroom, the judge stopped harassing them, but their dislike for him did not lessen much. A mistake of youth in his courtroom would subject the errant advocate to a loud harangue or lesson in the law—or both.

There was the time that a young fellow not too long out of law school was arguing to Judge Ravinson one day that the indictment against his client should be "squashed. . . ." That was as far as the poor fellow got. The proper term was "quashed," but it never would be known whether the young lawyer knew the proper term and suffered from a slip of the tongue or whether he would have had the rotund judge actually sit on the indictment until it hollered.

The truth never would be known because any mention of the incident to the now mid-career lawyer would bring a stare so icy as to surely be just short of a fistfight. For his part, the judge very likely would not remember the incident, so many there had been. In that example, the judge was said to have risen to his feet in judicial indignation and preached for no less than two excruciating minutes about the stupidity and grotesque ignorance of the young advocate. He even asked the young fellow who his civil procedure professor in law school had been so the judge could call the professor to let him know that one of his ex-students was making a fool out of himself and the professor in his courtroom.

As it happened, the lawyer's civil procedure professor from law school had become a member of the Supreme Court of Texas just before the courtroom incident. Hearing the new Supreme Court judge's name feebly spoken by the young lawyer in response to the judge's demand to know the professor's name, Judge Ravinson abruptly shifted gears and contented himself by preaching a lofty sermon on the subject of the low intellect of young lawyers generally, citing the trend of decline in the bar-exam "pass" rate.

Judge Ravinson's courtroom was fairly old and the space where he sat—between the bench and the wall behind it—

was not very large, especially given the fact that Judge Ravinson was...well...fat. Inexplicably, in the middle of a trial, the judge sometimes would turn his swivel chair around and face the wall—with his nose surely no more than six or eight inches from it. He sometimes would sit like that for extended periods, even sustaining and overruling objections from that point of view. Some courtroom observers thought he slept part of the time he was turned around, but he seemed to be awake whenever there was an objection; of course, the objecting lawyer objected rather loudly, so no one knew for sure just what the judge was doing or thinking when he was turned around like that.

Sometimes, he would spin his chair around suddenly and abruptly order the lawyers to approach the bench. Then, out of the hearing of all but the lawyers, including out of the hearing of the court reporter, the judge would, in hushed but excited tones, tell a dirty joke. The lawyers tried not to listen, but they were in a real quandary. If they didn't laugh at all, they might make the judge mad, even prejudiced against their side of the case. Folks around the courthouse said the judge could tell a whale of a nasty joke, so some lawyers also were afraid that if they actually listened to the joke, they would be hard-pressed to suppress laughter. Female lawyers were especially disgusted by this practice, but apparently not enough to complain about it officially.

Experienced counsel about to try a case against each other in Judge Ravinson's court usually discussed before the trial began what they would do in the event the judge wanted to tell them a dirty story in the middle of the trial. The usual consensus was that they would try to appear to be listening, laugh politely when the judge roared, and try very hard to return to the trial as quickly as possible. When this didn't work, it usually was because an unsuspecting lawyer, most likely from out of town, fell prey to the judge's crude behavior. It was said that a lawyer from Houston once laughed so hard at one of the judge's filthier jokes that the judge admonished him about inappropriate behavior in his courtroom.

It was in this kind of judicial environment, then, that Shannon refused to testify as to the identity of the source of the tape at her deposition on Thursday, August 31st, and was summoned before Judge Ravinson to show cause why she should not be held in contempt of court for refusing to be deposed on the subject.

"What's the problem here, Mr. Michaels. I'm a busy man."

"Your honor, my client, Winford Thomas, who is one of two plaintiffs in this consolidated matter...."

"Yes, Mr. Michaels. The whole world knows who your client is, and they know a whole lot more about him than they ought to. Sordid mess. Plenty of shamefulness on both sides."

"Ah...your honor...my client is seeking to depose Ms. Gillette here, but she...Mr. Sterling's client...this television reporter...insists on not answering certain questions lawfully posed to her."

"Yes, Mr. Michaels, I know who she is, too. These two do kind-of belong together. What questions won't she answer?"

"Questions, your honor, concerning the identity of the source of the tape broadcast by her in which a conversation was alleged to have taken place between a Mr. Jack Duvalier and Ginger Fontenot, who is the other plaintiff in this case, separately represented, your honor, by Mr. Lyle Branson here," Michaels said, gesturing at Branson.

"It is our contention, your honor, that the tape never existed, that there is, consequently, no source of the tape, that Ms. Gillette used special-effects equipment to create the tape from whole cloth for reasons of her own. Ms. Gillette insists that she did not create the tape from whole cloth, but she steadfastly refuses to deliver to us the original tape for our inspection or to tell us anything about where it came from except that she had and continues to have complete faith in the integrity of the tape and the source of the tape. That's fine, your honor, but we'd like to make an independent judgment on those accounts, and it's a bit difficult for us to do so without being able to see the original tape, if any, or question the source of the tape, if any."

"What would you have me do, Mr. Michaels? You know I can't subject Ms. Gillette to the *rack* to make her divulge the information. Unfortunately, the *rack* has fallen into disuse in modern society. Pity. It would do my heart good to see a few journalists subjected to it as payment in-kind for their perversions. But, alas, I cannot do that. Do you have any other suggestions?"

"Well, ah, yes, your honor, the plaintiffs respectfully request that you either hold Ms. Gillette in direct contempt of court for refusing to answer the questions and produce the tape and confine her to the county jail until she is ready to answer the questions and produce the tape, or that you issue a ruling stating that for purposes of the lawsuit against Ms. Gillette and her former employer, Diversicom Corporation, an irrebuttable presumption exists that the tape in question never existed."

"Yes, I see.... Do you understand what all this is about, Ms. Gillette?"

"Yes, sir, she does, your honor. I. . . ."

"Did anybody ask you to speak, Mr. Sterling? You're just exactly like your daddy over there was the first time he came in here," the judge said, alternately eyeing Rance Sterling and Taz Sterling. "Brash. Arrogant. I believe I was about to have a conversation with Ms. Gillette here. Do you have some kind of objection to that?"

"No, your honor."

"I didn't think so. Now, Ms. Gillette, please answer the question."

Even though Rance Sterling was in some serious respects on a different side of the case than his son, he nonetheless was incensed at Taz's rude treatment at the hands of Arnold Ravinson. Somebody ought to put the old son-of-a-bitch out of his misery, Rance Sterling thought.

"Yes, sir, I understand everything that has been said," Shannon replied.

"Do you fully understand what may happen to you if you refuse to testify?"

"Yes, sir, I believe I do. They are asking you to either send me to jail for contempt of court or issue a ruling that the tape never existed; in legal effect, that I made it up."

"That's correct, Ms. Gillette. Very good. You said that better than some of these lawyers would have. So, for the record, let me order you directly in open court to divulge the identity of the source of that tape and the circumstances surrounding your acquisition of it and its present location."

"I'm sorry, your honor, I mean no disrespect to your court or to the legal process, but I made a promise of confidentiality and I'm going to keep it, even if it means that I'll have to go to jail."

"Ever been in jail, Ms. Gillette?"

"No, sir."

"Well, there's a first time for everything, I guess. Mr. Michaels, I'm not going to issue any orders about any irrebuttable presumptions. I would if the only defendant were Ms. Gillette here, but the deep-pocket defendant, the television corporation, wants to do what's right but can't because its former employee, this reporter, has decided on her own that the law of civil procedure and the law of evidence ought to apply to everyone but her. To issue the order you seek would do harm to the television-corporation defendant, and I don't want to do that when it's trying to do what's right. And that doesn't leave me with but one alternative. Ms. Gillette, I hereby find you in civil contempt of this court, and I hereby sentence you to indeterminate confinement in the Travis County jail. I suppose your lawyer has explained what is meant by 'indeterminate confinement?'"

"Yes, sir, he has."

"Well, I'll tell you again just in case he hasn't been to court very many times, which it doesn't appear he has. It means that I could keep you there for a long time—until the trial of this matter is over, or until I decide you aren't going to testify no matter what and let you out in that the ends of justice would not be served by keeping you locked up any longer, or until some appellate court decides I don't know what I'm doing and lets you out.

"Don't expect me to be letting you out any time soon, young lady. And don't expect any preferential treatment at the county jail. You're in violation of the law, just like everybody else serving a sentence down there, and I won't view you any differently just because your violation of the law is contempt of court as opposed to stealing a car or something. At least those folks understand the difference in right and wrong."

"Yes, sir, your honor, I understand. I'd like to state that I'm not asking for any preferential treatment."

"Your honor...."

"What is it, Mr. Sterling?... I guess, for the record, I should say Mr., let's see, what's your first name...?"

"Taz, sir."

"Yes. I guess I should say Mr. 'Taz' Sterling. Anyway, what is it?"

"Your honor, I respectfully request that you stay the execution of Ms. Gillette's confinement until I can file a motion for a formal hearing on this matter."

"Fine, fine, Mr. Taz Sterling. I expected that. You just made the motion, and I just granted it. Your brief is due two days from now. The other side's brief will be due twenty-four hours after that. I'm hereby setting the hearing for Tuesday,

September 5th, at ten a.m. You all don't think it will take longer than two hours, do you? I've got a lunch date with my chiropractor that day. All of you already should be prepared. You all knew full well this was coming. I will rule from the bench after reading your briefs and hearing your arguments. Pending the outcome of that hearing, Ms. Gillette shall remain free on her own recognizance. Do you understand, Ms. Gillette, that if you fail to show up in court on the hearing date next week that I'll have you arrested?"

"Yes, sir, your honor. I understand. I'll certainly be here."

"Court is adjourned."

Tuesday, September 5th, 2000. Ten a.m. Judge Ravinson's court. The briefs were in. Judge Ravinson, of course, hadn't read them. Why should he, he always thought, the lawyers were going to argue it all in open court, anyway.

Taz Sterling's first argument in behalf of confidentiality was that for the court to require—on pain of jailing his client indeterminately—that she identify the source of the tape would be an unwarranted intrusion into the newsgathering process in derogation of the First Amendment. If reporters had to divulge the identities of their confidential sources of information, Taz argued, their ability to gather news would be significantly impaired, especially given the fact that so much reporting—certainly to include reporting about government and politics—came from confidential sources. If the process of news*gathering* were seriously harmed, Taz said, there would be less *dissemination* of news and what dissemination of news there was would involve less significant information. The First Amendment, he argued, was designed to protect reporters from just such intrusions by the government.

Barry Michaels and Lyle Branson countered in a jointly prepared brief that the U.S. Supreme Court had had the opportunity to make just such a broad ruling on several occasions and had declined to do so. Michaels and Branson argued that while courts were reluctant to intrude into the newsgathering process, they did so when not to would, for example, make a mockery of the need for evidence in litigation. Judge Ravinson agreed with them, ruling that news*gathering* as a First Amendment right was secondary to actual expression and that the First Amendment offered Shannon Gillette no protection from having to reveal the source of the tape, especially in the context of the matter at hand because of the importance of the evidence being withheld.

Taz then turned to the idea of common-law privilege. Journalists long had argued, only infrequently successfully, that there should be a "reporter-source" privilege against being forced by a court to divulge information given the reporter by the source just as there was such a privilege in the "clergy-penitent," "attorney-client," and "doctor-patient" relationships. In those situations, which journalists argued were analogous, the privilege rested with the penitent, the client, and the patient, meaning that *any* information given the member of the clergy, the attorney, or the doctor, respectively, could not be divulged without the express permission of the penitent, the client, or the patient, respectively. Taz argued to the court that such a privilege should attach to Shannon's confidential relationship with her source and that it should override the discovery process because of the importance of journalism to society.

Michaels and Branson countered that courts had found a number of problems with this theory, not the least of which was that while members of the clergy, attorneys, and doctors were considered "professionals," journalists were not; that, in fact, journalists could not be professionals in the legal sense because professionals such as attorneys and doctors had to be licensed by the government in order to practice their profession. Obviously, they argued, the government could not require journalists to have any kind of license to "practice" journalism since to do so would be as direct a violation of the First Amendment as was imaginable.

Further, they contended, society did not have nearly as great a need to protect reporter-source relationships as it had in protecting the other relationships discussed. As a result, most courts did not—and no court should—recognize a "reporter-source" privilege, they argued. The court agreed.

Taz's next to last argument—a fairly new one—resulted from a U.S. Supreme Court decision in 1991 which rocked journalism a bit, at least for a time. In that case, a PR advisor to a high-level party nominee in a midwestern state told two newspaper reporters, on agreement of confidentiality and just days before the general election was to be held, about a years-old minor criminal conviction on the record of the other party's nominee. The reporters then independently corroborated the information from public sources. When they showed the finished story to their editor, he wanted to know who the original source of their information was. They explained to the editor that they couldn't tell him because to do so would violate their pledge of confidentiality to their source.

The editor responded that they either would tell him the identity of their source or the story wouldn't run. Reluctantly, the reporters revealed the name and identity of the source to the editor. When the editor learned that the information had come from a PR person working for the opposing party—and at the eleventh hour, at that—he ordered the pledge of confidentiality broken and the source's identity included in the report. Over the strenuous objections of the reporters who had granted the pledge of anonymity, the story identified the source of the information—in the first paragraph. The PR person was fired not long after the publication of the story.

He sued the reporters, the editor, and the newspaper on the theory that he and the journalists had entered into a contract, albeit unwritten, and that the journalists, in divulging his identity, had breached the contract. At their simplest level, contracts have three elements—an offer, an acceptance, and some form of valuable consideration flowing from each side to the other side. Usually, there also is the need that the agreement be in writing. The plaintiff argued that he offered information to the reporters, that the reporters accepted the information, and that consideration flowed both ways—the information from the source to the reporters and the promise of confidentiality from the reporters to the source. The fact that there was not a *written* contract should not matter, the plaintiff argued, because of a legal theory known as *promissory estoppel*, which enforces an oral promise made where not to do so would work a fundamental unfairness on the party which had relied to its detriment on the promise.

On appeal to the U.S. Supreme Court, the defendants' attorneys argued that the situation presented a "damned if you do, damned if you don't" proposition for journalists, but the Court disagreed, ruling in favor of the plaintiff on the *promissory estoppel* issue.

Taz argued to the court that to force Shannon to release the identity of her source to the plaintiff could cause her to breach the contract she had with her source, even were the contract of the unwritten variety, which it was.

Michaels and Branson countered that even were Taz correct in his belief that Shannon's source had an enforceable agreement with Shannon, that fact should not deter the court from ordering Shannon to give up the identity of her source. To do otherwise, Michaels and Branson said, would mean that all any litigant need do to avoid divulging certain types of information in the discovery process would be to contract with a relevant third party not to reveal the nature of the information. This, they argued, would not serve the administration of justice and, in fact, would be a considerable impediment to dispute resolution. Judge Ravinson agreed. He knew he might well be wrong, but he was looking forward to sending Shannon Gillette to jail. An appellate court always could reverse him, Judge Ravinson knew, but for now, he was in control.

Taz's last argument to the court was that given the number of skirmishes the judge had had with reporters over the years, it was fair to conclude that the judge was generally biased against journalists, no matter the issue, and that, as a consequence, Judge Ravinson should not be hearing the case and that he most certainly should not be hearing this particular issue. Just as Barry Michaels rose to begin his refutation of Taz's argument on this point, Judge Ravinson rose from the bench and extended his hand, signaling Michaels not to speak.

Everyone froze, expecting one of the judge's patented tirades. Instead, the judge simply glared at Taz.

"Mr. Taz Sterling, I admire your guts. There aren't many lawyers who would stand here and say to me what you just did. Of course, you're wrong as hell in what you said, and I won't further dignify your argument with a response other than to say that if you think you're going to keep Ms. Gillette out of jail on that basis, you've got another think coming."

In its way, it was perhaps the most polite thing anyone could remember the judge saying from the bench in a similar situation. At any rate, all of Taz's arguments had failed to pass muster with the judge. The only remaining question was when Shannon would be going to jail.

Normally in such a situation, the court would impose a civil fine against the journalism entity and send the reporter to jail—media entities can't be jailed and reporters usually have little money with which to pay fines. But in the normal situation the journalism entity would have backed the reporter in not divulging the identity of the source. In this case, however, Diversicom had fired Shannon when she refused to reveal the source, so the court had no interest in levying fines against the journalism entity. Shannon Gillette would bear the burden alone. She would be going to the Travis County jail.

Even though she quite obviously was not a "normal" criminal, Shannon refused to allow Taz to ask the court for any special dispensation such as segregation from the general-inmate population.

Taz asked Judge Ravinson for a stay of execution of sentence pending Taz's appeal of the matter. Judge Ravinson had but two words to say on the subject.

"Motion denied."

He ordered Shannon to begin serving her sentence on Monday, September 11th. During the ensuing days, Taz asked the court of appeals sitting in Austin to expedite an appeal of the matter, but it refused. Taz also asked the court of appeals to stay the execution of Shannon's sentence pending appeal, but the court denied that motion, as well. Shannon would go to jail on Monday.

Chapter 19

Rena Kirkpatrick had lived a worthless life. She hadn't stayed in Demonbreun long after she and Frank Dailey sold the baby to Boudreaux.

Flush with cash, Frank had been drinking for weeks. One night, he came home to their house trailer so late and so drunk that a verbal fight escalated into a beating. Frank had taken to carrying a gun because he also was carrying a good amount of cash. During the fight, Rena wrestled the gun away from Frank and shot him. She then called an ambulance and the police. Frank died en route to the hospital. Demonbreun authorities arrested Rena, investigated the situation, and presented the case to a grand jury.

Rena testified to the grand jury that she had shot Frank in self defense and that he had beaten her on previous occasions. She said she was scared for her life every time he got drunk, which had become almost a daily event. The grand jury did not indict her.

Trailer trash, one grand juror said. Deserved what he got, said another. She's no "continuing threat to society," laughed another, "even if she 'offs' some other deserving piece of dirt."

When the property Frank had on his person at the time of his death was returned to Rena, his widow, included was a post-office-box key. Boudreaux Fontenot was a man of his word. Rena didn't know if Boudreaux knew Frank was dead. She figured he must not know, though, because he continued to send the money orders to the Barksboro post-office box. They were always made out to Frank Dailey. Each time she picked them up, Rena cashed them with the same teller at the same bank in Barksboro. She had shown the teller their marriage license and Frank's death certificate; that had seemed to satisfy the teller.

It wasn't always even $50, but Boudreaux sent a money order to Frank Dailey's post office box for at least $25 every single month until Ginger was paid for in full. It had taken him about four years. The main reason it had taken so long was that there was no way Boudreaux would want Tailese to find out that he had bought Ginger and was paying for her in installments.

Rena's life had become a downhill spiral. More or less, she had come to view herself as a worthless, baby-sellin' murderess with no future. She was clinically depressed over having killed Frank, the love of her life. Of the $3,000 Boudreaux initially had given them, $1,000 had gone to a down payment on the trailer, and Frank had drunk up most of the rest.

Rena couldn't keep a job because she had taken to drinking too much. Within a few months, the house trailer was repossessed, and she was on the street. She began drifting back and forth between Texas' major cities, including Austin. In a bar one night in Austin that same year, she went on a rampage, ending up in the county jail for public drunkenness, resisting arrest, and assaulting a police officer.

It was the first of many times Rena would find herself in jail over the next couple of decades. She wasn't bad, she just wasn't any good. She had never killed anybody other than Frank, but she had come close. Once, she had spent nearly two years in the "big house" over in Huntsville for attempted murder. It was a premeditated barroom brawl. Rena had cut the bitch pretty good with a knife, but she lived. To Rena, it was simple. The woman shouldn't have been messing with Rena's man, long since forgotten.

Every few months, when she'd had all the minimum-wage working she could stand for awhile, she'd light out for Frank's post-office box in Barksboro in whatever old junker car she was driving at the time; sometimes she'd come in and out of town on a bus. Just like clockwork, she'd find some postal-patron circulars and several money orders from Boudreaux. They always added to a hundred dollars, sometimes two hundred. It was always enough to stay drunk on and holed up in a cheap motel for a few weeks or so.

Rena was real good about keeping the rent paid on Frank's post-office box. Once, she had tried to pay it for two years instead of one, but the postal clerk told her she could pay for it only one year at a time. Postal clerks knew a lot of weird stuff happened through the mails, and the clerks in the relatively small town of Barksboro knew whatever Rena Kirkpatrick received every month in Frank Dailey's post-office box from somebody named Boudreaux Fontenot but with no return address probably was the result of some kind of no good.

Boudreaux did a funny thing when he sent Frank the money orders. He sent the money order *and* the receipt for the money order to Frank. Rena never knew why, but she really didn't care. The answer probably was that Boudreaux was taking no chances on Tailese seeing any evidence of what Boudreaux was doing. Boudreaux also never put a return address on the envelopes he sent. Until they became accustomed to seeing it, the postal clerks in Barksboro wondered why Boudreaux would bother to put his name on the envelope. Without a return address, his name would do him no good if the post-office box address on the envelope became obscured.

Rena did a funny thing, too. She kept all of Boudreaux's receipts.

There were a few pieces of paper in her life that Rena valued, such as her birth certificate and some high-school pictures. Since Rena was more or less a drifter most of the time, she kept a safe-deposit box at the bank in Barksboro. It was only $12 a year, and, for the first few years she had it, she paid the rent on it with one of Boudreaux's money orders, the same way she paid rent on the post-office box. There was plenty of room in the box for her birth certificate, her high-school pictures, and Boudreaux's receipts.

There were several other pieces of paper in the box—one was a picture of Frank and her. Whenever she would collect Boudreaux's money orders from the post office, she would go cash them and then put the receipts in her safe-deposit box. It gave her a reason to be able to look at the picture, and her two boxes were the only things in her life that were consistent. It wasn't much, but everybody needed to cling to something. After Boudreaux had paid off his debt to Frank, Rena kept the two boxes. They were her connections to reality. She would check them occasionally and pay the rent on them when due, usually when on her way to or from Edge County once or twice a year to see her old mama for a few days.

Rena had been in the county jails in Dallas and Houston almost too many times to remember how many it was. There was a time when they were okay, but they were getting too big and rowdy. She liked things a little quieter when she got convicted of some misdemeanor. For the last few years, she had been hanging around Travis County quite a bit. When she wasn't working, she was shoplifting or panhandling. She had worked as a prostitute some, but not in many years. Nobody wanted her in that way anymore, she knew.

The Travis County jail was not that bad; in fact, Rena kind of liked it. She was no longer the least bit violent. Age and tired bones had taken care of that. Had she any work skills, she might have quit petty crime altogether, but she had no skills, a horrible history, and she could stand minimum-wage jobs for only so long at a time.

She'd been in the Travis County jail four or five times in the last several years for a few months each time. She really could rest in there. She didn't have to pay rent. She got three meals a day. The TV worked. And it was an opportunity to dry out from any alcoholic binge she might have been on. Rena knew the difference in a felony and a misdemeanor. She knew the Texas Criminal Code pretty well, better than most habitual criminals and better than most lawyers who didn't practice criminal law. She was very careful not to commit a felony. One time in the big house at Huntsville had been enough. She never wanted to be raped by any prison guards again. Bad stuff went on in big county jails, too, but Rena pretty much knew how to avoid it by this time in her career.

Rena knew all the lawyers in the Travis County Public Defender's office by their first names. It was like old-home week when one of them would come to see her after she'd been arrested. But it usually was a short visit. Rena had no taste for trials whatsoever. Plea bargaining, she thought, was wonderful. Shoplifting was Rena's favorite crime, and she was good at it in two quite different ways. If she got away with it, she was able to enjoy the fruits of the theft. If she got caught, she knew she would be able to plea bargain her way into a few months in the county jail. She loved the system. Most of the time, she got away with her petty thievery, but July 4th, 2000, was one of those times she hadn't. She had been stopped by a security guard after walking out of a grocery store without paying for a carton of cigarettes. She offered no resistance. She never did.

The plea-bargained sentence was four months in the county jail. For about two months, Rena had been laying around in her cell and spending part of the day in the "rec" room watching TV or playing cards or reading. The inmates loved stuff on TV that exposed the miseries of other people. They particularly loved "investigative journalism" when it brought down the "big boys" a notch or two. Sex scandals were their favorite fare.

Rena had been among a number of jail dwellers watching Triple T the night Shannon's program was broadcast. There was a lot of hooting and hollering and carrying on about the show. Rena thought it was great that that sleazy politician from her growin' up neck of the woods had been caught with his pants down. She could understand why. The girl, this Ginger, was really a looker. Rena hadn't paid any attention to her last name until she saw it superimposed on the screen. But what really got her attention was when a local reporter the next day said this Ginger Fontenot had grown up in the little southeast Texas town of LeMieux.

Son-of-a-bitch, Rena thought. Could it be? How many years ago had it been? How many girls were there from LeMieux named Fontenot? Christ-o-mighty, she thought, if it were true, how could she use her knowledge of Ginger's birth and "adoption" to her advantage? First, she had to make sure it was her. But how could she do that? Rena had learned to be patient. Being in jail so much had taught her that. And she also knew better than to say anything to anybody about her suspicions. Besides, she needed time to think. A cell in the county jail was just where she needed to be.

The answer to Rena's question about whether Ginger was *the* girl was answered the next night when Boudreaux was interviewed on TV. There he was talking about how his only little girl could not possibly have said and done any such things no matter what they showed on the TV. Sweet Jesus, it's true, Rena thought. Twenty-four hours of thinking and seeing Boudreaux on TV was all Rena had needed. On the night of August 16th, Rena told the night jailer she needed to speak with Ted Jackson, one of the lawyers in the public defender's office.

When Ted got to the county jail the next day to meet with his several new clients, who had just been arrested for trying to cash several-thousand dollars worth of stolen lottery tickets, the day jailer told him Rena Kirkpatrick wanted to see him. Ted liked Rena. She was real easy to represent.

"Bring her in," Ted told the jailer.

"She's waitin' right outside," the jailer said, opening the door and calling Rena's name.

"Hey, Rena," Ted said, as Rena came into the room.

"Hey, Ted. How've you been?"

"Well, to tell you the truth, I've been better. Too many criminals. Not enough love. Know what I mean?"

"Yeah, this damn place is just full of 'em. I wish you'd talk to the management about that."

They both laughed.

"What can I do for you, Rena? You aren't wantin' out, are you? You've got another several months to go as I recollect."

"Yeah, that's right. Naw, I ain't wantin' out. I just need to ask your advice about another matter that might still be a crime that involves a friend of mine."

"A friend of yours? Right. Okay. Sure. Go ahead. What do you need to know?"

"Well, I'm certain that sellin' babies is a felony, but my friend don't know if it's a federal offense or whether it offends the peace and dignity of the good State of Texas or just what. And he particularly wants to know what the statute of limitations is on that particular crime. You wouldn't happen to know anything about the crime of sellin' babies, would you, Ted?"

"Damn, Rena, I hope we are talkin' about a friend of yours and not you, even though I somehow kinda doubt that. To start with, sellin' babies is obviously a serious felony that'll get most anybody convicted of it some time in the big house, especially if they have any kind of felony record. It's a state crime as opposed to a federal crime unless the baby was kidnapped in addition to being sold. The kidnapping would be a federal crime. That could get a person life. I'll have to get back with you on the length of the statute of limitations on the crime of sellin' babies. But I can tell you this. The longest statute of limitations for any crime in Texas is seven years unless the crime is murder. And, as I'm sure you know, there is no statute of limitations on that crime."

"So if the baby-sellin' took place twenty-some years ago and it didn't involve no kidnappin' or what, then the statute of limitations would have run out a long time ago?"

"Right."

"And the fellow that had done the baby-sellin' could walk down Main Street and say he done it and the cops couldn't do nothin' to him?"

"Right. Of course, Rena, you know as well as I do that if the cops can't get you for what they know you've done, they can always get you for somethin' else."

"Yeah, sure, but I...my friend ain't worried about that."

"Rena, this is big-time stuff. I think you ought to be real careful here."

"I appreciate that, counselor. I'll see to it that my friend seeks your advice before he does anything drastic. By the way, can you have private-payin' clients?"

"Yes, I can, as long as its civil work, not criminal work. My contract with the county allows that. Why?"

"Well, I just wanted to know, that's why. How much do you charge? Naw, wrong question. Would you help a client negotiate the sale of somethin'—I don't mean no babies, now—to somebody for a part of what the person got for sellin' it?"

"Well, I might, Rena. I'd have to know a lot more. When you want to tell me what the hell all this is about, you know how to reach me."

"Right. It'll probably take my friend a little while to figure out what to do, but I'll definitely get back to you. And oh, yeah, I would appreciate it if you could get back to me on what the statute of limitations is."

"I'll look it up this afternoon, Rena, and let you know when I'm back out here tomorrow."

Chapter 20

Monday, September 11th, 2000. The county jail in Travis County, Texas, while fairly new, was nonetheless a foreboding structure, especially for people like Shannon, who never thought they'd be seeing it from the inside out—and for an indeterminate length. As Taz and Shannon pulled into the parking lot of the county jail, they were taken aback by the number of reporters there to cover her going to jail. Shannon, who was beginning to learn firsthand what it was like to be on the other side of the microphone, so to speak, was amazed that her incarceration would attract this much media attention. She had become the news *maker*, not the news breaker.

There, perched on the front steps of the county jail was a bevy of reporters, including a dozen or so television reporters complete with camera crews. One station even had a live truck there. She wondered who the hell all those television cameras belonged to. As they got closer she saw who they were. Besides the stations in Austin and the four news networks, the other cameras belonged to the national tabloid shows, like "Inside Out." She hadn't anticipated those people having an interest in her going to jail, but given their brand of journalism, there was absolutely no telling what "angle" each one of them was pursuing.

As Shannon started to grouse about the media being there, Taz reminded her of several considerations. First, she needed all the publicity she could get because public pressure might cause her to be released from jail sooner than she otherwise might. Second, Taz told her that the local reporters surely were going to be supportive of her since most or all of them would be going to jail just like her if they had developed the same story. And third, Taz reminded her that it would be good experience for her to see how people felt when they were the subject of some kind of intense media scrutiny. All true, she thought, but not very comforting at the moment. As Taz pulled into a parking space and stopped the car, they were surrounded. The tabloid reporters already had begun to shout questions at her through the rolled-up windows.

"This is going to be a nightmare," Shannon said, "but I know how to get the situation at least somewhat under control."

"How's that?" Taz asked.

"Well, you'll have to get out of the car and leave me in here for the time being. I don't have to be in the jail building for another hour or so. Tell them that I will hold a media conference on the steps of the jail and try my best to answer all their questions if they'll calm down and go set up their gear at the bottom of the steps. Tell them if they won't do that, then we're gonna drive away and call the jail on your cellular telephone and ask the jailer to open the double doors in the back of the jail so I can be let off in there. Reporters aren't allowed in there. The jailer will have to let you do it because they allow prisoners to be brought in that way all the time."

"*Notorious* prisoners, you mean. You now notorious?" Taz asked, laughing.

Shannon shot him a deep frown but said nothing.

"You know," Taz said, "I once heard about a guy who was laughing real loud in the drunk tank one morning as he was sobering up and nursing his hangover. When he was asked why he was laughing, he said his situation was so tragic that it somehow seemed funny to him—you know, like the thespian masks that indicate how closely linked comedy and tragedy are. So before you jump me for laughing, I think that's the way I feel now."

"Yes, well, just please get out of the car and tell the beasts what I said before they start tearing your car up. This is tragic, all right, but I see very little humor in it. I don't think I'm going to do this 'time' very well."

Taz stepped from the car, shouting as he went, and repeating himself.

"Media conference. Bottom of the steps. Five minutes from now. Otherwise, no sound bites. Thank you."

The throng headed for the steps of the jail. Shannon thought to herself that more newsmakers should realize that the media was fairly controllable in situations like this if the newsmakers just knew what to do. Once all the gear was set up, which took just a few minutes, Taz pulled as close to the front steps as he could get and stopped. As Taz and Shannon got out of the car, Taz started to walk to the side, out of the way of the cameras, but Shannon would have none of that.

"No way, buddy. You, too," Shannon loudly whispered, enjoining him to stand by her side. "I might need to ask you whether to answer a question, and besides, they might want to ask you some questions directly. You need to get some experience at this, anyway, if you're going to be a big-time trial lawyer," Shannon said, forcing a smile.

"Right," Taz said, reluctantly complying.

No matter how much they tried not to be, they were nervous; they just hoped it didn't show. The media conference went normally given the various types of reporters there. The print reporters did what they usually did—standing around taking notes based on the exchanges between the broadcast reporters and the subjects of the media conference. The television reporters could be divided into three types—the local ones, who were very supportive of Shannon in the questions they asked her; the network reporters, who couldn't quite seem to decide why they were there or whose side they should be on—journalism at the television networks not being what it once was—and the tabloid television reporters, who obviously could not have cared less about Shannon or her plight, concerned instead with what they might get her or Taz to say that was somehow sleazy.

Triple T was not represented. Shannon would love to have heard the conversation between Brenda Jordan and Dave Browning, she thought, concerning whether Brenda would cover this event. Shannon knew that Brenda, left to her own devices, would cover Shannon's going to jail, but given the "no more coverage" edict from Dave Browning on the one hand and Brenda's nature on the other, there must have been at least some kind of discussion on the subject. Shannon had always wondered what went on in those conversations between the executive producer and management whenever the executive producer was summoned to the third floor. Shannon remembered watching Brenda get on the elevator to go up to the third floor on those occasions, and she remembered wondering about the nature of the journalistic sacrifices Brenda probably had to make when she was up there.

Now she thought she knew. For all her bluster about damning the corporate torpedoes and full journalistic speed ahead and all that stuff, Brenda's journalistic will had not been strong enough to allow her to defy orders not to continue covering this big story—or to quit in protest of such an order. Come to think of it, Shannon thought, while Brenda and the entire newsroom had professed shock to Shannon when Browning fired her for refusing to name the source of the tape, none of them had quit in protest or even offered her much real comfort. Shannon was brought back to reality by another question.

"How long do you think they'll keep you, Shannon?" asked Domingo Ramirez, a reporter for one of the Austin local stations.

"I wish I knew, Domingo. All I can tell you is that all of this mostly seems to be up to two people—the judge and me. If I were to name the source of the tape, I could be out of here today. But I'm not going to. So the answer to your question will have to come from Judge Ravinson. My lawyer tells me the judge could keep me in here until any trial in this case is over, at which time my testimony would be moot, or he could let me out sooner if he decides that even if he kept me here forever, I wouldn't name the source of the tape. And he would be right about that. I will stay forever before I name the source of the tape."

At that point, a tabloid TV reporter jumped in.

"Hey, isn't that a bit dramatically noble? Are you trying to set yourself up as some kind of journalistic martyr or what?"

"Even though your question is quite impertinent, sir, I will answer it. I don't mean to be dramatic or noble or a martyr or anything of the sort. The simple truth is that I had to make a choice in this situation—between hurting others or taking the heat myself. While the effect of my choice may be difficult for me, making the choice I made was not difficult at all."

"Sterling, you're her lawyer. Couldn't you keep her out of jail?" shouted another of the tabloid TV reporters.

"No, sir, I could not. I made all the arguments to Judge Ravinson I could make and then I explained Ms. Gillette's quite-limited options to her once the judge had ruled against her—and the whole of journalism, I might add. Ms. Gillette chose the option of silence, and I fully support her in her choice. Besides, the judge's finding of contempt is on appeal, and I have every belief that the court of appeals will release Ms. Gillette from jail. We're trying to be heard in the court of appeals as soon as possible."

"Do you know who the source of the tape is?" asked a reporter from an all-news radio station.

"I'm sorry, but that information is protected by the attorney-client relationship."

"Where is the original restaurant tape? Do you have it, Shannon?" another local TV reporter shouted.

"Let's just say I know where it is, and I couldn't imagine it being in a safer place."

"Now, thank you all for your questions," Taz said, stepping in front of Shannon, "but it's time for Ms. Gillette to report inside the jail. We wouldn't want her to be late. Thank you."

Taz and Shannon turned and walked up the stairs and through the front door of the county jail. Several of the television reporters had a second camera positioned at the top of the steps so the pair could be videotaped from the front as they entered the building. Taz could see and feel the prying eyes of the television cameras recording their every movement. There was something privacy-invading about it, even when the person being videotaped knew it was happening, Taz thought.

Shannon's thoughts at that point were a long way from journalism. She was about to face the scariest time of her life.

Sheriff Hank Gunther had a decision to make. He had received a call from Judge Ravinson telling him not to give Shannon Gillette any preferential treatment whatsoever. Gunther didn't like reporters much himself, but he resented the hell out of crazy Judge Ravinson telling him what to do in his jail. He, after all, not Judge Ravinson, had been elected by the people of Travis County to be the sheriff. Besides, Gunther didn't really want anything bad to happen to Gillette because she would be a high-profile inmate, and the sheriff didn't need any negative publicity; he was, after all, up for re-election. It hadn't turned out to be much of a race so far, but the sheriff knew anything could happen in politics.

With all this in mind, Hank Gunther was trying to figure out what to do when he saw Rena Kirkpatrick, trusty, walk past his open office door. Rena Kirkpatrick, the sheriff thought. Perfect.

"Say, Taylor," Sheriff Gunther hollered to an assistant, "does Rena Kirkpatrick have a cellmate at the moment?"

"Naw, sheriff, she don't," came the reply. "Rena snores so loud that nobody wants to bunk with her. She's real comfortable in here, you know."

"Right. Good. Well, I think Rena just got a new cellmate. Isn't that reporter, Shannon Gillette, due in here this morning?"

"She's being processed now, sheriff. Come in just a little while ago."

"Okay, Taylor. Do me a favor, will you? Go tell whoever's makin' the cell assignments today that I want Shannon Gillette to be Rena Kirkpatrick's cellmate. And go get Rena Kirkpatrick and bring her to my office. I want to talk to her."

"Rena, how's it goin' with you? We treatin' you all right?"

"Sheriff, you know I always get treated just great in here."

"Good, Rena, 'cause I've got a favor to ask you."

"You want a favor from me, sheriff? I don't know what I can do for you, but except for being a stoolie, I'd be happy to do anything for you I can."

"Naw, Rena, I don't want you to be no stoolie. We got plenty of scumbuckets down there volunteerin' for that assignment all the time. I just need you to take on a new cellmate today. I need you to sort of take her under your wing and teach her about how things work in a big county jail like this. It would be a big favor to me."

"Well, sure, sheriff, no problem. But who is she, anyway? Ain't she never been in jail before?"

"Rena, were you watchin' TV when that reporter named Shannon Gillette did a story about that Congressman from over in east Texas...ah...screwin' that New York model?"

Rena almost peed at the mention of the program and Shannon Gillette.

"Ah..., yeah, sheriff, I saw it, but what in the world does that have to do with me?"

"Nothin,' Rena, nothin.' It's just that that reporter, Shannon Gillette, has got herself sent to jail by Judge Ravinson for refusin' to tell the judge where some of her videotape come from. See, there's a lawsuit about it, and Gillette won't tell anybody anything—says she promised her informants that she wouldn't ever tell who they were. Now, see, Gillette is bein' processed in right now. I don't have no idea how long she'll be with us 'cause the judge sent her here to stay until she agrees to answer the questions they're puttin' to her. Now, Rena, I'm up for re-election right now, and the last thing I need is for somethin' bad to happen to this reporter while she's our guest. Know what I mean?"

Rena was relieved and fascinated at the same time. She had thought for a moment that the sheriff somehow knew what she had been talking with Ted Jackson about and had figured it all out, but the whole thing was just a coincidence. Like he said, the sheriff just needed a favor. Rena was only too happy to oblige.

"Oh, I see, sheriff. You don't want none of the bad girls down there doin' any numbers on Gillette, and you want me to keep her clear."

"Exactly, Rena, exactly."

"Well, sheriff, I got no problem with that at all. Just bring her to me. I'll tell her everything she needs to know about particular folks down there, and I'll explain to her how doin' time works. Don't worry, I'll take care of her."

"I knew I could count on you, Rena. And I'll make it up to you. If you help me get through having her in here, then whenever you need something really special the next time, you just let me know and we'll see what we can do."

Processing in hadn't been so bad, Shannon thought, but the walk down that damp, dark flight of stairs to the cell block had conjured thoughts of unspeakable horror.

"Gillette, meet your cellmate. Her name is Rena Kirkpatrick. Rena's a regular customer. The sheriff had you two put together special. Rena's gonna tell you how to stay out of harm's way while you're here. Get the picture?"

"I sure do," Shannon replied to the jailer. "Please convey my thanks to the sheriff."

"Ah, okay," the jailer said.

The big metal door slid shut and locked. And there she was. In jail. Orange jumpsuit and all. Shannon Gillette. Never in her wildest dreams did she think such a thing would ever happen to her.

"I don't guess we need no more of an introduction than the one we just got," Rena said. "You got told my name, and I already know who you are. We probably ought to get down to the deal here. We'll have to go eat lunch in a little while, and there's a bunch of stuff you need to know before that happens. The first thing to remember is never to let 'em see you sweat. Just like that TV commercial used to say. If they think you're scared, they'll be all over you."

Oh, Lord, Shannon thought, it must be true. That's exactly what Taz had told her no more than an hour ago.

"Thanks very much, Rena. I'm sure I'm going to need all the help I can get. And since I know you've already seen it in my face, I'll go ahead and admit to you that I'm scared to death."

"Don't worry too much, honey. Just listen real close to what I'm gonna tell you and stick real close to me. I'm pretty much respected in here 'cause I've been in here and other jails so many times. These girls know I ain't no stoolie, and they also know I can get a message to the sheriff and make it hard on them if they was to mess with me. Besides, as far as havin' to perform sexual favors, I'm an old lady to them now—not very attractive, know what I mean? So, with me, it's live and let live. I don't help 'em none, and I don't hurt 'em none. Dependin' on how long you're in here, I can probably save your bacon. I don't have but a couple of months to go this time, so I hope you can get out of here before then or learn how to get along without me."

"I hope so, too, Rena. I hope so, too."

Shannon listened intently as Rena explained the culture in a big county jail. And she listened even harder as Rena described to her which inmates in particular to watch out for. For Shannon, lunch was a nightmare. She stuck with Rena, but she didn't want to seem too close to her. There were lots of catcalls about the "TV pretty girl" and such, all of which scared Shannon a lot.

The movies and television-entertainment programs rarely actually reflect real life, Shannon thought, but the way life "inside" had been portrayed in the movies seemed right on target with what Rena was telling her and what she was observing. Most of the inmates were from a different world, Shannon thought, and they had a whole different value system. To them, Shannon was someone to be victimized, if possible. And there was only so much Rena, the sheriff, and the jailers could do to help her, she thought, especially given Judge Ravinson's "no preferential treatment" edict.

In the final analysis, she was on her own, and she knew it. She was more scared than she ever had been in her young life. During lunch, Rena had moved off to talk with a few of the other inmates. Shannon figured she was telling them to lay off, but Shannon reasoned that such a message could be a two-edged sword. Some of them might heed the subtle warning, but others might take it as a dare. Shannon thought she could handle any amount of verbal abuse; it was physical abuse that had her petrified.

When they got back to the cell after eating lunch, Rena told Shannon that everything had gone okay; that Shannon hadn't seemed real scared.

"I may not have *seemed* scared, Rena, but the truth is I was scared to death. Who were you talking to in there?"

"I was talking to the committee. Sylvia Alvarez. They call her the water king. She pretty much controls what goes on around here with the Mexicans. Leticia Smith. They call her the night rider. She's head of the blacks. And Mandy Carleton. They just call her Mandy. She tries to keep all the white girls in line. There's more whites in here than the other two. There ain't that many Mexicans in here, but they're definitely the meanest."

"God. Why do they call Alvarez the water king?"

"Well, they call her that because she likes to take her liberties with the weaker inmates in the shower room. She's real good at it."

"God, Rena, I was afraid that was what you were going to say. And why do they call Smith the night rider?"

"Same reason, basically."

"God. How much of that goes on?"

"Not a lot. The jailers will stop it if they know about it, but they don't always know about it."

"Why not? How could they keep from knowing? Doesn't the victim scream?"

"Mostly not. The bad girls know the 'victim,' as you put it, will start screaming, so they just tell her if she screams they'll kill her. Usually they don't scream much."

"Damn, Rena, this is a county jail; this isn't a prison. I didn't know stuff like that really went on in a county jail."

"Well, this is a big county jail for one thing. Lots of people in here are doin' a year or so, and they can get real horny, know what I mean? And, besides, there's lots of girls in here who are waitin' to be tried for murder and such, and then there's girls in here who've already been convicted and can't be sent to the state prison system 'cause there's no room for 'em there. There's lots of crime, you know?"

"So most of the sex stuff takes place in the community showers, is that right?"

"Yeah, well, that that don't happen in the cells after lights out, if you know what I mean? But for the other...stuff... the shower's the best place for it. The jailers aren't in there with us, you know. When a thing starts happenin' in there, most everyone leaves but the bad girls."

"Well, I don't know how long I'm going to be in here, but I think the thing for me to do is to just not take any showers."

"Yeah, that's what lots of rookies say, honey, but that won't work. See, the first time you don't take a shower when you're supposed to, they'll know you're scared, and they'll really be after you then. Besides, they're all wantin' to see your naked body. Plus the fact that the guards will make you take a shower once you start to stinkin' 'cause other people—not me 'cause I'd understand—would start complainin' about you smellin.' And it don't take long to start smellin' around here. Naw, girl, you'll have to go to the showers. I told the committee to have their girls leave you alone 'cause the sheriff said he's gonna make it real hard on anybody who fucks with you."

"What'd they say?"

"They said they'd try but that they didn't like the sheriff tellin' them what to do and they didn't like pretty girls like you bein' protected. But they said they thought they could control most everybody. See, they know they've got it pretty good in here, and they don't want the sheriff comin' down on 'em hard. So I think you're okay."

"What did they mean *'most'* everybody?"

"Well, there are some free-lancers in here. People who don't believe in following anybody's lead. Now they're subject to gettin' the shit kicked out of 'em by the committee if they mess with you, but that wouldn't stop you from havin' the problem in the first place."

"Can you tell me who the free-lancers are so I can try my best to stay out of their way?"

"Well, there's one in particular I've been thinkin' some about. Her name is Cleota Simpson. The reason I think you might have a problem with her is because she don't make it no secret at all that she hates reporters real bad."

"Oh, shit. Why does she hate reporters so bad?"

"Well, I don't know exactly. She just says that if it wasn't for reporters stickin' their fuckin' noses in other people's business, she wouldn't be in jail. Brings it up all the time when the TV news is on. Stays pissed off about it."

"Great. That's all I need. Point her out to me tonight, will you?"

"Sure, honey. I'm gonna do everything I can to help you."

"I wish I could do something to help you in return, Rena."

Before thinking, **Rena** blurted what she was thinking.

"Well, you just might be able to."

"How, Rena?"

"Well, I tell ya. I ain't no good at negotiatin' or anything like that. You're gonna get a call while you're in here from a friend of mine. If you can work things out with him, then we can talk. I think you'll be real interested. But for now, that's all I can say."

"Oh,...great. Well, I'll be happy to talk with him. You never know what's gonna happen, do you?"

Lord, Shannon thought, this woman is being so nice to me, but she probably wants some money for some wild story that doesn't amount to anything. Shannon knew, however, that she'd definitely play along, at least for awhile, with anyone who was trying to help her like Rena was.

For almost a week, things went okay. Shannon's first trip to the showers had been traumatic, but beyond the constant stares and the comments about her "tits" and "ass" and "muff," no one had approached her, including Cleota Simpson. She did notice, though, that Simpson had been watching her—in the showers, in the mess hall, in the rec room—everywhere. It made Shannon real nervous, but she didn't know what to do about it.

Rena had calmed down about the whole idea of Shannon being in jail. Shannon, Rena knew, was being treated with kid gloves by the other inmates. Apparently, the committee had gotten the word around to leave Shannon alone. Sheriff Gunther ran a real good jail, comparatively speaking. It was, within some loose rules, live and let live. But the sheriff could be provoked, and when somebody did finally make him mad, the offending inmate usually fell down and hurt herself pretty good and then ended up spending a good while in an isolation cell. When the sheriff was really interested in something, like he was in Shannon, he usually got his way—no questions asked.

No reporter or newsgathering organization could *control* a story; every reporter knew that. They knew it because every reporter who ever came across a great story wanted to be able to control it. But the fact was that just as soon as the reporter told the story the first time, it was fair game for everyone else.

And stories like the "Winford Thomas Affair" quickly took on a life of their own. It had all the markings of a story the tabloids—newspapers and TV shows—would just love to follow-up on. There was conspiracy, sex, politics, clandestine videotaping, covert operations, a reporter in jail, and Lord knows what else. The program that Triple T had broadcast might be just the first rabbit trail. A good tabloid TV reporter—and in 2000 they were plentiful—would love going down them. Some stories had been done since Shannon's original program, but none of them had added any significant new information.

The truth be known, the continuing nature of the story was the second-biggest reason Shannon wanted out of jail as quickly as possible. This story had wings, and she wanted to be on them. With her knowledge and involvement in the story, surely someone would want to hire her to follow up before there were no more rabbit trails to go down.

As the nineties had approached the mid-decade mark, conventional television news found itself in competition with a brand of journalism not previously in existence. With the emergence of "tabloid TV," as it had come to be called, things really got squirrelly. "Tabloid TV" was entertainment programming that looked like news shows. Its success caused the real news shows to look increasingly like entertainment shows. The "tabloid TV" shows, which were being produced mostly by people with entertainment—not journalism—backgrounds, resorted to the use of a device called the "re-enactment," where archival news footage was combined with acting to re-create a news event. "Reality" entertainment programs of all kinds were growing ever more popular, and in the midst of all this, some people in television news were still trying to be serious. Network anchorpersons had been heard to say to their audiences: "This is actual news footage you are watching...."

The media seemed to be converging on one another. The media conglomerates were growing—mass communication was coming to be owned by fewer and fewer companies. The media conglomerates were diversifying—becoming involved in the ownership of all the various types of media. And the media types themselves were converging—news was becoming entertainment and vice versa.

"Inside Out" was the latest—and most outrageous—entry into the nationally-syndicated "tabloid-TV" field. "Inside Out" was no stranger to lawsuits. Its latest legal skirmish involved one of its correspondents sneaking onto the private property of a prominent Los Angeles obsetrician to videotape the doctor's young child—a brain-injury victim at birth. The story was that the child's medical condition was the result of its own father having committed malpractice when he delivered the child. Rarely, the TV report had said, do obstetricians deliver their own children, but this doctor was too arrogant to allow anyone else to do it, leaving him as the sole culprit when "something went terribly wrong."

"Inside Out" knew the doctor probably would sue for invasion of privacy and libel—and win a jury verdict. But there was no way he would win enough to make the story a losing proposition for the company. First, the program had hyped the story and had a huge audience when the story aired. Premium advertising rates had been charged the companies advertising on that particular program. Second, the producers of the program knew that many of the viewers watching the program for the first time would become avid fans, translating into significantly increased revenue. Third, any lawsuit the doctor would file would just "fan the flames"—giving the program an excuse for running the footage of the child again and again and causing the program to have even more viewers. And last, should the doctor be awarded a mega-buck judgment against the company by some sympathetic jury and trial judge, an appellate court likely would reverse it—or at least reduce it significantly—in the name of the First Amendment and free expression. So no matter what it did, "Inside Out" just couldn't lose. It fed on that power.

Saturday afternoon, September 16th. Rena and Shannon were in the rec room watching college football on TV. Rena had told Shannon that the worst time to be in the showers was on Saturday nights, and Shannon was having a hard time getting that notion off her mind. Rena had told her there was just something about Saturday nights that made the inmates meaner than usual.

"Rena, I've been thinking about what you said about bein' in the showers on Saturday night, and I've got an idea. Why don't you and me go on and get our showers now?"

"Aw, come on, girl, can't you see ain't nothin' gonna happen to you in here. The word's out to leave you alone. Ain't nobody gonna want to screw with the sheriff that way. You're as safe as if you was in your mama's arms."

"Well, that's real nice to hear, Rena, but my mother's not with us anymore and, anyway, I'm not too sure that's not a bit of an overstatement."

"Look, girl, you want to take a shower now instead of tonight? I understand. But you don't need me to nursemaid you down there. Ain't nobody gonna bother you."

Shannon sat back in her chair. She needed to think. This was the first time Rena had not been totally helpful to her. Rena, she was afraid, had been lulled into a false sense of security by the fact that Shannon had been there almost a week and nothing bad had happened. Still, Rena was right that the word had seemed to go out to leave Shannon alone. What to do, what to do? Shannon thought. Finally, Shannon decided that to take a shower on Saturday afternoon with virtually no one there, but without Rena with her, would be better than to wait 'til night-time to do it with Rena there. If somebody in the showers that night really wanted to mess with her, Shannon concluded, there might not be much Rena could do to stop her.

Shannon looked around the rec room for Cleota Simpson. She was sitting by herself, flipping through a magazine and looking out the window. She didn't seem to be paying any attention to Shannon. But Shannon wasn't taking any chances she didn't have to.

"Look, Rena, I'll make you a deal," Shannon said as Rena stared intently at the tube. "What kind of deal? I'm trying to watch the football game."

"I just need you to do me one favor, Rena."

"What?"

"Just watch Cleota Simpson while I go take a shower. If she gets up to leave, come warn me so I can get the hell out of there. Can you do that for me, Rena?"

"Sure, honey, I can do that. Where is she?"

"She's over by the window flippin' through a magazine. See?"

"Yeah, I see her. Don't worry, I won't let her come get you."

"Well, please don't. I don't think the sheriff would be too happy about it, and I know I wouldn't. Don't lose sight of her, hear?"

"Yeah, I hear you, honey. Don't worry about it."

As Shannon left the rec room for the showers, she glanced in the direction of Cleota Simpson. She was staring out the window and seemed a million miles away in thought. Shannon just hoped she would stay that way for a few minutes more. Shannon had learned to shower quickly—real quickly—including washing her long hair. She never knew she could shower that quickly and feel at least mostly clean.

There were only three people in the shower room when Shannon walked in. Shannon didn't know any of them, but she didn't feel threatened by them. They looked at her when she came into the shower, then quickly looked away. Shannon figured that meant they had gotten the message to leave her alone. She had no more than turned the shower on and gotten wet when all three of them suddenly darted from the room. One of them still had soap all over her. Shannon knew why when she looked around. Her heart sank. A naked Cleota Simpson had just entered the shower room.

Looking around and seeing no one else there but Shannon, Simpson spoke.

"How many people have gone to jail because you're a nosey motherfucker, bitch?"

Shannon was petrified. Here she was with Cleota Simpson—alone. Rena had failed her. She didn't want to fight Cleota Simpson, but she wasn't going to be assaulted if she could help it. She was hoping that Cleota just wanted to fight. Shannon might lose a fight with her, but at least she wouldn't have been sexually assaulted; she could think of little worse.

"Look, Cleota, I've got nothing against you, and, to my knowledge, no one has ever gone to jail because of a story I've done. I wasn't a crime reporter, Cleota. I just did stories on things like government and politics," Shannon said as she shut the water off and moved slowly toward the shower-room exit.

Simpson moved a few feet and blocked her path.

"You don't think I'm gonna buy that line of shit, do ya, you lowlife whore? You may not have sent anybody to jail yourself, but you work with people who have, and you're a reporter, too, so you're just as bad as they are. I wouldn't be here myself if some motherfuckin' reporter hadn't done a story on drug dealin' that led directly to me. Just who do you assholes think you are, anyway?"

So far, Simpson was just talking. She had blocked Shannon's exit, but she hadn't moved any closer to her when Shannon stopped moving toward the exit. Shannon hoped she could talk Simpson out of whatever she was intending to do, but it was looking doubtful. She had blamed journalism for the predicament she was in, and Shannon was the first piece of journalism she might be able to get her hands on.

"Hey, Cleota, I can understand why you're upset at the reporter who did that story, but, like I said, I don't do stories like that. Like, I'm on your side. I'm on the side of the folks out there who're just tryin' to survive. The stories I did were about the fat cats in government and politics stealin' from people like you and me. You got me wrong. I'm not your enemy."

It was all bullshit, and Shannon knew it, but she was hoping Simpson would buy it.

She didn't.

"That's the biggest load of crap I've heard in awhile. You're nothing but a chicken-shit liar, bitch. Here you are insultin' my intelligence and thinkin' I'm gonna buy your line of crap. What you are is scared to death of me, and I'm gonna have myself a little piece of you that you won't soon forget."

Shannon braced. Simpson lunged at her. Shannon dodged, but Simpson caught Shannon's left arm with her left hand, and they tumbled to the wet and slick shower-room floor. For a minute or so, it was a good fight. Shannon was no fighter, but she was so scared that she was holding her own out of fear, operating on pure adrenalin. Simpson had gone completely wild. Simpson got Shannon in a wrestling hold. Simpson's front was to Shannon's back, and Simpson had Shannon's arms immobilized by interlocking them with her own. Simpson told Shannon that Shannon had fucked her and that she was gonna fuck her back. Maybe even do some permanent damage. Somehow, Shannon managed to break free of the hold just as Simpson attempted to tear her head off. Adrenalin only worked for so long, though, and Shannon was tiring. Simpson was a lot thicker than Shannon and much stronger.

Fatigued almost to the breaking point, Shannon got caught in another of Simpson's wrestling holds. They fell to the floor. Just as Shannon saw Simpson's clenched fist pull back to deliver a blow that Shannon thought surely would drive her head through the tile floor, all hell broke loose in the shower room. Shannon, bleeding from the nose, had turned her head away from the impending blow, and so, at first, she didn't see who had come into the room, but someone had just knocked Simpson off of her. As she turned and looked up, she saw Rena. In the corner of the shower room, Sylvia Alvarez, Leticia Smith, and Mandy Carleton were beating the hell out of Cleota Simpson. Simpson was having a hard time begging for mercy because Alvarez had one arm under her chin and the other arm on top of her head, squeezing her mouth shut. Simpson's tongue was caught between her own teeth, and she was bleeding profusely. It was ugly.

Rena helped Shannon up, and they headed for the shower-room exit. Shannon, stunned, was nonetheless amazed to find two jailers standing there taking in what was happening to Simpson.

"You dumb bitch. We told you not to fuck with her, but you didn't listen. So maybe you'll listen next time," Smith screamed.

Just as quickly as it started, it stopped. Simpson was sitting on the floor whimpering, bleeding. The jailers were smiling and glancing back over their shoulders every few seconds. Shannon was too close to shock at the time to realize exactly what she was witnessing. After collecting Shannon's jail uniform and more or less covering her with it, Rena helped her to their cell. The jailer who let them in just shook her head. People like Shannon Gillette ought not to get themselves put in jail, the jailer thought.

Chapter 21

Sunday, September 17th, 2000.

"Gillette, phone call for you," the jailer said as she opened Shannon's cell door.

Rena thought she knew who the caller was. Barely able to walk from the soreness of the previous day's events, Shannon followed the jailer down the hall to a small room where an old, black telephone lay on a nondescript table with the receiver off the hook.

"Hello," Shannon said, hoping it was Taz.

"Shannon Gillette?"

"Yes, who's this?"

"My name is Ted Jackson. I'm a lawyer in Austin. I have a client who has some information you would be interested in in relation to the story about Winford Thomas and Ginger Fontenot."

"Mr. Jackson, I'm in jail, as you obviously know. I've been fired. Why would I need such information?"

"I'll make this short and sweet, Ms. Gillette. Armed with the information my client possesses, we think you would do whatever it took to get out of jail. And we both know that there are a bunch of TV journalism outlets that would hire you in a minute and who understand, as your former employer seems not to, the value of storytelling."

"Okay. Let's say I'm interested. What does your client have?" Amazing, Shannon thought—in jail, half beaten up, and the journalistic juices were still flowing like hell.

"My client has direct evidence that Ginger Fontenot is not the biological child of her parents; that they bought her when she was an infant. Do you want this story?"

"If it's true, you know I do."

"It's true."

"How would I know that?"

"If I can prove to you that it's true, if I could provide direct evidence of it to you, what would it be worth to the tabloid TV show I suspect you'll call today."

"I don't know. Maybe five thousand."

"Right. I think you're missing a zero. I called you first, Shannon, because you are this story. But, damn, you're in jail. This is a big story. Wendy Bathurst is only a phone call away."

No way she was gonna let him give it to *her*, Shannon thought.

"So, you're asking fifty thousand?"

"Not a dime less."

"What would that buy anyone I might be working for?"

"It would buy you an exclusive interview with a person who was directly involved, and it would buy you direct documentary evidence of what that person would tell you."

"Is that all?"

"What else do you want? Pictures?"

"That would be nice."

"You'll have to create those in your computer. We don't have any."

"When do I get to meet with your client and see your evidence?"

"When we get paid."

"I'm sorry, but that's not how it works. No one would pay you that way."

"Well, there's no way you know who my client is or see any evidence until I have two things. One, the fifty thousand in an escrow account and, two, an escrow agreement signed by the president of the company that says the fifty thousand is ours when we give you the evidence and an exclusive interview to back it up."

"Pick your escrow agent and write your agreement. And hurry up. If what you say is true, other people know it, too. I'll do my best to get hired. I have some good ideas on the subject, but I don't know who's going to hire me if I'm still in jail. Call me tomorrow."

Monday morning, September 18th, 2000.

"Inside Out. May I help you?"

"George Cogbill, please. Shannon Gillette calling."

The receptionist at "Inside Out" knew who Shannon Gillette was. Everyone in tabloid TV, even in New York, knew who Shannon Gillette was. In the tabloid world and in the mainstream journalism world—what difference there was between the two anymore—Shannon was a hero for having gone to jail rather than divulge the identity of her source.

"I'll put you through."

"George Cogbill."

"Mr. Cogbill, this is Shannon Gillette calling from Texas."

"Shannon! Are you still in jail?"

"Yes, sir, I am, but I hope not to be here too much longer. My lawyer is working real hard on getting me out."

"Well, what can I do for you, other than thank you for sticking to your principles?"

"Thanks, but there's plenty else you can do for me—and for 'Inside Out.' What would you say if I could prove that

Ginger Fontenot was sold the day after she was born to the cajuns who raised her by a couple who was given the baby to raise by the mother of the child who couldn't raise it because she was poor and the child was illegitimate?"

"Whoa, whoa. Let me get this straight. You're sayin' that Ginger Fontenot is not the child of those cajuns, that she was sold to them by a couple who had been given the baby by the baby's mother, and that the baby's mother had given the baby to them to raise, but that instead of raisin' it they went out and sold it the next day?"

"That's what I'm sayin.'"

"I think I see where we're goin' here. You don't have a job, this information needs to be paid for, and you need a place to be employed so you can air the story, right?"

"Well, I was told very little got past you."

"Yeah, well, can you keep this source exclusive?"

"I think so."

"How much we talkin' about here and what do we get?"

"We get an interview from one of the people who did the sellin,' and we get documentary evidence of the sale—for fifty thousand. I've been contacted by the person's lawyer."

"Damn, Shannon, that would be a bargain if all they're tellin' you is true. But how do we know it is?"

"Well, if you'll put the money in escrow, they'll show us the proof and tell us who we get to interview."

"Did they know you were unemployed?"

"Sure. They just figured I'd get employed. They didn't care who with; anyone who would pay them, I suppose."

"When do you hear from them again?"

"Today."

"Tell them you have a job—you and I can talk about the particulars later—and to send the escrow agreement for our lawyers to go over. Does this sound legit to you, Shannon?"

"Yes, it smells right. For one thing, I don't know why I hadn't noticed how different Ginger is to those cajuns—just in appearance alone."

"Okay, Shannon, let's stay in close touch on this. Can you get to a phone fairly easily?"

"That doesn't seem to be a problem for me."

"Okay, and thanks for thinking of me. I think we're going to get along real well."

Ted Jackson's contract was simple, to the point, straightforward. When he got it back from the lawyers working for "Inside Out," he hardly recognized it. His had been five pages long. Theirs was eighteen. It was called "existence justification." He hated it. By mid-week, when the final document had been approved by both sides, he had twenty hours in a five-hour project. "Inside Out" needed a copy of that book on how to control legal fees, Ted thought.

As an inexperienced appellate lawyer, Taz didn't know whether it would be appropriate to argue to the court of appeals that Shannon should be released from jail as the victim of a jailhouse assault and, if so, how to go about doing it, but he knew he had to try, and he knew he didn't have time to find the procedure in a legal database. In law school at the University of Houston, he had taken appellate advocacy from Boris Raymond, a purported national expert on the subject. Taz had earned but a "B-" in his course and probably hadn't been one of his favorite students; worse, Professor Raymond might not even remember him—but Taz knew he had to pull out all the stops and fast.

The professor had been somewhat indignant on the telephone, Taz thought, but, then, most law professors didn't earn nearly what successful practicing attorneys earned, so they had to get their kicks some other way, and indignation about a practitioner needing help was one of those ways. At any rate, Professor Raymond told Taz to secure affidavits from as many witnesses to the events as possible, including his client, and petition the court of appeals to expedite the appeal of the contempt citation on that basis. Assuming the court of appeals allowed the expedited appeal, Professor Raymond said, the assault itself should be used as an additional argument that the petitioner should be released from jail because the government had an obligation to protect those in its custody from being assaulted by others in its custody; in other words, Shannon might deserve to be in jail, but she had not given up her right not to be assaulted.

Sheriff Gunther had been none too pleased when he learned of the assault. He was mad as hell at Rena Kirkpatrick for not keeping up with Shannon, but he was burning with anger at Cleota Simpson. The "punishment" she had received at the hands of Sylvia Alvarez, Leticia Smith, and Mandy Carleton was not enough. Soon, when things returned to normal, Simpson would fall down and hurt herself and have a long stay in isolation to get over it. Simpson was a convicted minor drug dealer awaiting transfer to the state prison system to serve a ten-year sentence, but the prisons were full and the sheriff knew she'd be in the county jail for quite awhile. All of this was a violation of her civil rights, but. . . .

And as though the sheriff were not mad enough at the incident itself, the next thing he knew, Taz Sterling was on the telephone requesting permission to take affidavits from all the witnesses to the incident. When the sheriff asked Taz why he wanted them and why so fast, Taz explained. His reason, Gunther thought, was two-sided. On one side, the jail would look bad letting something like this happen—and in an election year. On the other side, though, if Taz Sterling could get Gillette's case into court sooner—and win—Gillette would be released from jail and no longer a problem. The sheriff knew he couldn't protect Gillette indefinitely. In hopes of getting the problem solved with more than two months left to go in a less-than-exciting election campaign, Hank Gunther decided to take the lumps from the media and his opponent that would come his way when the affidavits became news stories.

On Friday, September 22nd, Taz filed four affidavits with the Third Court of Appeals in Austin. Two from jailers, one from Rena Kirkpatrick, and one from Shannon Gillette. The affidavits, in support of and along with Taz's petition again requesting an expedited appeal, were filed just after the clerk's office opened at eight a.m. The clerk called Taz just before noon to indicate that the court had granted his petition, that briefs were due by Monday afternoon with oral argument scheduled for ten a.m., Tuesday morning, September 26th. All the attorneys of record had been notified of the hearing, she said.

In his brief, Taz made essentially the same arguments for Shannon's release that he had made in Judge Ravinson's court for not jailing her in the first place, with the addition of an argument concerning the Travis County jail apparently not being able to prevent her victimization. Barry Michaels and Lyle Branson made essentially the same arguments they had made in their brief to Judge Ravinson on the same issues. They countered Taz's argument about the Travis County jail by citing cases indicating that while Gillette might have a cause of action against the county for not providing her adequate security, such a cause of action had nothing to do with the confidentiality issue.

At oral argument, the three-judge appeals panel seemed more interested in the attorneys' views on the "damned if you do, damned if you don't" case decided by the U.S. Supreme Court than in any of the other issues, including the jail-security issue. Taz even allowed himself a little excitement at the comment of one of the judges, Denise Johns, who said she didn't care much for a legal system in which there was no way to act appropriately no matter what you did.

As an analogy, Judge Johns cited the libel protection Congress had given radio and television stations when they were forced by law to run commercials for candidates for Congress notwithstanding that the commercials might be libelous.

"Congress," the judge said, "recognized the principal unfairness that would be visited where one law said the station had to run the commercial regardless of what it contained and where a tort said the station could be sued for any libelous matter any commercial might include. So to avoid the 'damned if you do, damned if you don't' problem, Congress simply made it impossible for anyone to successfully sue a station for libel under such circumstances. Problem solved."

Taz was chagrined that he had not made this argument himself.

At the conclusion of oral argument, Judge Henry Foreman, the designated chief judge on the panel, indicated that the panel would try to reach its decision by the end of the day. Judge Foreman told Taz to prepare a jail-release order for the court to execute in the event the court's decision went Taz's way, but the judge warned Taz not to interpret being asked to prepare the order as being presumptive of anything.

Taz told the judge he understood, but he nonetheless took it as a good sign. He started to tell Shannon about it when he spoke with her on the telephone at the jail a few minutes later, but he decided not to because he knew how bad Shannon wanted out of jail, and he didn't want to build up her hopes just to have them dashed. He did tell Shannon, though, that the judges seemed very interested in the "damned if you do, damned if you don't" issue. Taz was hopeful. Very hopeful. Shannon was hopeful. Very hopeful.

The session before the court had begun about ten-fifteen a.m. and had lasted an hour. After Taz called Shannon at the jail, he drove to his apartment to draft the jail-release order as instructed by the court. Orders like that were short and sweet and didn't take long to draft. But the drafter had to know exactly what to say. Taz never had written such an order before, but he'd had the presence of mind to stop by the clerk's office and make a photocopy of a similar one from another case. Taz had no idea in which of the thousands of cases in the clerk's office he might find such an order, but he had learned that if he simply treated the deputy clerks as normal human beings—some lawyers just didn't seem to be able to—they would bend over backward to help.

He'd had to make some alterations to the order he copied in the clerk's office to make it fit Shannon's particular situation, but it had not been a big problem, and by two p.m., Taz was waiting on the telephone to ring. It rang at three. It was Judge Foreman's law clerk, Lucy Bramble. She told him the appeals panel had voted unanimously to overturn Judge Ravinson's contempt citation and that if Taz could get over to the court building to get Judge Foreman's signature on the release order before the judge left for the day at about four-thirty, Shannon Gillette would not have to spend another night in jail.

Taz was ecstatic, breathlessly telling her that he had drafted the order and would be in the judge's office within the half hour. She told him she would give him a copy of the court's short opinion in the matter when he got there. Taz was interested, of course, in the court's reasoning, but at the moment he was more interested in calling Shannon with the good news and then getting her the hell out of that God-forsaken jail before the sun went down.

Shannon was thrilled with the news. She just couldn't believe it. She was having to pinch herself to make sure she wasn't dreaming. She wanted to scream, but she didn't want the other inmates to start screaming. Screaming in jail—she had observed—sometimes had a snowball effect with virtually everyone getting into the act.

Just as Shannon hung up the telephone from speaking with Taz, a jailer told Shannon to gather whatever belongings she had in her cell and to come with her to the sheriff's office. She figured Sheriff Gunther must have been faxed the order by the court, was happy at the news, and wanted to personally bid her adieu.

When Shannon and the jailer got to her cell, Rena was snoring. Shannon had to wake her up to tell her the good news. Rena was happy about it, too. She had grown tired of being responsible for Shannon—it was too much like work. Rena would be out soon, and she needed Shannon to be out, as well. So far, so good, Rena thought.

Shannon gathered her few cell-dwelling possessions—inmates traveled light—thanked Rena for helping her, said goodbye, and followed the jailer to Hank Gunther's office. The sheriff was waiting for her.

"I want you to know something, Ms. Gillette. I try real hard to run a clean jail here, but sometimes, in spite of my best intentions, things happen that. . . ."

"Pardon me for interrupting, sheriff, but let me put your mind at rest. First, I know you tried every way you knew how to protect me, and I appreciate it very much. Cleota Simpson is just crazy, that's all. It worked out okay. Nothin' happened. I'm still intact. I'm gettin' outta here. I learned a lot, and one thing I learned is that you do run a good jail. The vast majority of the inmates down there respect you tremendously. Second, I'm still a reporter, I guess, but I have no interest in publicly saying anything negative about my experiences in here. If I get asked by some member of the media, and I surely will, I'll just refer them to my lawyer, and he'll just refuse comment.

"You probably already know that the news media don't do a very good job of covering the appellate courts; I mean, for instance, the affidavits my lawyer took about what happened to me were filed with the court last week, but there hasn't been anything on TV or in the papers about it because so many reporters just kind of wait around to be told by some PR person or public information officer what's going on. It's easy for things to fall through the cracks because nobody notifies them about filings; they have to call or go there, and sometimes they're too busy or, for whatever reason, they just don't check it out. The only ones who routinely check filings in the appellate courts are the newspaper reporters, and they don't do it all the time, so that narrows it down a lot. Since none of them showed up at the hearing this morning, I don't think they knew about it.

"But when they see—probably not until tomorrow—the decision by the court releasing me from jail, they'll be all over the place; they'll be trying to find me—they won't—they'll be lined up outside here wantin' to talk to you about me gettin' assaulted in here. I mean, sheriff, it could even generate coverage by the TV tabloids. I'm real sorry about all this. Lord knows, I didn't want any of this to happen, and I'm the last person who wants it publicly known, but I had to use what happened in here to help me get out. I'm sure you can understand that."

"Sure. I'd've done the same thing. And I sure do appreciate your sayin' that you ain't gonna go makin' some big deal outta this with the media. I mean, I know it was a big deal to you when it happened, but it ain't the normal thing in here, and the media will probably try to make it seem like it is. I'd like to be re-elected, you know?"

"I understand, sheriff. You have my silence and my vote. Maybe it'll go away soon. I hope so. For us both."

An hour or so later, Shannon Gillette was a free person. To her delight, there were no reporters waiting when she and Taz walked out the same door of the Travis County jail they had walked in two weeks before. As they got in Taz's car, Shannon told Taz she was a little surprised there were no reporters there, that she thought somebody at the court building might call somebody in the media once they heard about the court's ruling.

"I hear you," Taz said, "but let me tell you why it didn't happen that way. When I got to Judge Foreman's office, his law clerk, Lucy Bramble, met me at the door and took the order in for the judge to sign. I waited on her in her office. When she got back, she gave me all the copies of the order and then she gave me a copy of the court's opinion in the case. You can read it later. Let me just tell you what it says. It's real short. It just says that the court feels there is a conflict between the law of evidence and civil procedure, on the one hand, and the law of contract and *promissory estoppel*, on the other hand, that needs resolution—and that you shouldn't have to sit in jail while the conflict gets resolved. Shannon, you can read that a hundred different ways.

"They could've been slapping Judge Ravinson in the face 'cause they don't like him; they could've been reacting to your problems at the jail but without saying so—they do that sort of thing a lot; they could've been telling all the trial judges not to sentence any more reporters for contempt of this kind until the conflict gets resolved; they could've been signaling the state legislature that it should resolve the problem at least as far as Texas is concerned—any of those things. Probably some others. Anyway, Lucy Bramble told me Judge Foreman personally had asked the clerk of the court not to put a copy of this opinion in the box that reporters check in the clerk's office until just before quittin' time. The right people seem to be on your side right now. They think you've suffered enough, I guess, and besides, most of them despise Judge Ravinson."

"Well, that's great. It's good to know I have some friends somewhere and that there's some sense of justice in the world. The media will be all over the story tomorrow, though. That gives me just enough time to go into hiding."

They laughed, but Shannon wasn't kidding.

Shannon stood under the shower in her condo until the hot water turned cold. Hank Gunther ran a pretty clean jail all right, but Shannon still felt dirty. Partly, it was physical; mostly, it was mental. No telephone calls. No one knew she was out. Shannon had purposely disconnected the answering machine attached to the telephone in her condo before she had "gone away." Taz had been collecting her mail and bringing it to her at the jail every couple of days.

"You do understand, don't you Shannon, that Michaels and Branson may very well ask the entire six-member court of appeals, sitting *en banc*, to re-hear the decision of the three-judge panel?"

"Well, I knew you were going to tell me some kind of nightmarish story about what my future might hold, but I was hoping it could wait a decade or two."

"Hey, we don't need to talk about this right now. There'll be plenty of time for me to explain it to you."

"No, I want to know. Go ahead."

"Well, I have no idea whether there'll be an appeal of this decision or not. They have thirty days to file a notice of appeal or a petition for re-hearing. It's possible that, eventually, the case could wind up being finally decided by the

Supreme Court of Texas. And at any one of the steps along the way, you could be sent back to jail."

"Damn, Taz, you could have talked all night and not said that."

"Well, you said you wanted to know."

"Do you think they will appeal?"

"I really don't know, Shannon. This case has been too crazy to be the least predictable, and, besides, I don't have enough experience to make any decent predictions."

As the night wore on, Shannon grew more and more amazed that no reporters had banged on Taz's apartment door. His apartment might not have been the best place to hide, but they were hoping it would do. Finally, she mentioned her wonderment to Taz.

"I've been thinking about something, Taz, and I want to run it by you."

"Shoot."

"I just re-read the court's opinion in letting me out."

"And?"

"And there's no mention in it whatsoever of the affidavits. It just says the court let me out because of the conflict thing."

"So?"

"So here's what I'm thinking. Let's add to what I just said the basic proposition that most of the media—except the tabloids—get lazier and lazier as PR people and government public information officers provide them with more and more of what they turn into news."

"Okay."

"Combine that with the fact that no stories came out when you filed the affidavits in the first place and that no one covered the hearing this morning."

"Okay, keep going."

"Even if there are stories on the TV stations tonight and in the papers in the morning about my release today, the basic information contained in those stories will have come from the opinion itself, which, as I said, doesn't mention the affidavits. In other words, unless some reporter actually goes into the clerk's office and asks to see the file on your appeal of the contempt citation, there's a chance that what happened at the jail never will become public knowledge."

For getting her out of jail, Shannon said, Taz deserved dessert. It was reciprocal. The whole night was delicious.

Neither the ten p.m. newscasts nor the morning papers contained any stories about Shannon's release.

About nine o'clock the next morning, Wednesday, September 27th, Taz's telephone rang. It was Domingo Ramirez, a local television reporter.

"Mr. Sterling, I've just received information that Shannon Gillette is out of jail. Can you confirm that for me?"

"I sure can. The Court of Appeals ordered her release yesterday, and I went and picked her up late yesterday afternoon."

"Where is she now?"

"That, I'm sorry, I can't tell you. I'm sure you can understand that. For now, she plans no public statements. Maybe in a week or two."

"What're the chances she'll have to go back to jail? Any?"

"Sure, there's a chance of it. Mostly, it depends on whether the other side appeals."

"Well, thank you, Mr. Sterling. I'd like your permission to call you back if I need something else for this story."

"Sure, Domingo. Call me any time."

No sooner had Taz hung up the telephone than it rang again. The next hour was filled with conversations between

Taz and various local reporters. Triple T did not call. The networks and the tabloids were off the story; nothing juicy going on. At "Inside Out," George Cogbill hadn't told his newsroom anything yet. All the conversations were basically the same. Not a single reporter said a single word to Taz about any affidavits or any trouble at the jail. Shannon was delighted.

She watched the noon TV newscasts with great attention. All of them, as with the morning papers, had stories about the court's opinion and her release, but none of them contained a word about any affidavits. Shannon could stand it no longer. She placed a call to Sheriff Hank Gunther.

"Ms. Gillette. What the hell is going on? I thought the media would be all over me like ugly on an ape by now. I didn't get a single call from a reporter yesterday, then nothing on the news last night, then nothing in the papers this morning. Did you do something or what?"

"I didn't do a thing, sheriff. I've been amazed, too, but I think I've figured it out."

After Shannon explained, the sheriff was incredulous.

"Well, I'll be damned. Wouldn't have thought anybody could miss this story after I read those affidavits and knew they were going to be a part of the public record. Let's keep our fingers crossed that this little oversight keeps on a-goin.'"

"Amen, sheriff, amen. Mine are crossed. See you."

About four-thirty, Taz called Heather.

"Hello."

"Hi, Heather. It's Taz."

"Taz," Heather exclaimed. "I'm so glad you got Shannon out of jail."

"Thanks, sweetie. How do you feel? Is everything okay with you?"

"Well, I have to tell you something."

"Okay."

"I've been pretty upset over all this, and I guess some of my teachers must have noticed it because they told mom and she made me go see Father McKenzie. Mom told my teachers and Father McKenzie that she had been noticing that I was acting funny, too—sort of like I was depressed."

"Well, Father McKenzie's a great guy. I've always liked being around him at the church. Did you confide in him, Heather?"

"I didn't want to, but I needed to talk to somebody. I was so worried about dad finding out I shot the tape and about that reporter being in jail because of me."

"Oh, Heather, I'm so sorry. I didn't know you were feeling that bad. Why didn't you tell me this before?"

"I just didn't want to make all this any worse by bothering you with how I felt."

"But, Heather, you promised you would tell me what was happening with you."

"I know, Taz, but there wasn't any way you could help me feel better, so I just kept it to myself."

"What did Father McKenzie say? Was he helpful to you?"

"He was real nice. It helped a lot just getting to tell somebody about how I felt and what was happening. He felt real bad about it, too, and told mom that he thought I needed to see a doctor to help me get through my problem."

"Was mom in the room when you were telling Father McKenzie the story?"

"No."

"So she still doesn't know why you were feeling bad?"

"No."

"Heather, you'll never know how sorry I am about how much trouble this has caused you. If I had it to do over, I would have destroyed the tape the first time you showed it to me. But that's hindsight. All that matters now is that you don't suffer anymore. So did mom take you to a doctor?"

"Yes."

"What kind? A psychiatrist?"

"Yes."

"How many times have you seen him?"

"Her."

"I'm sorry, her."

"Twice."

"Have you told her everything?"

"Yes."

"Has it helped you?"

"Yes, a lot."

"Good. Are you going to keep going to her?"

"She told mom that my problem could be solved and that it would be solved in time and that I should keep coming to see her once a week until then."

"What did mom say?"

"She asked me what I thought about it, and I told her that I liked Dr. Gray and that she was helping me."

"You haven't mentioned dad. What has he had to say about all this?"

"I think they talk about it, but he hasn't said anything to me. But he never talks to me very much."

"Yes, well, Heather, we're going to get this lawsuit over with just as soon as possible and then we can try to get back to living a normal life. It'll all die down and go away. It's just going to take a little time. I'm real sorry all this happened. I would never in a million years do anything to hurt you or dad. I'll make this up to you somehow, I promise."

"I know you'd never hurt me. I'm gonna be okay, Taz. I get to feelin' real bad about all this sometimes, but Father McKenzie and Dr. Gray have helped a lot. I'll be okay. I just hope nothing else bad happens."

"I do, too, sweetie. Listen, I'll call you every day or two, and you call me whenever you want to. Okay?"

"Okay."

"All right. Hang in there, and I'll talk to you real soon. Bye."

"Bye."

Chapter 22

Thursday, September 28th, 2000. Shannon had given George Cogbill at "Inside Out" Taz's telephone number. When he called late that afternoon to say the escrow arrangements had been made, he also told her that just as soon as Ted Jackson told her who the witness was, he would send a cameraperson to Texas.

Much as she didn't want to, Shannon knew she had to tell Taz about her new job and her new story; when he returned from the grocery store, she broke the news. Taz, still holding a bag of groceries, dropped it on the floor. Eggs ran. He was screaming.

"Damn it, Shannon, are you crazy? This is just shit, just shit! Fuck, just fan the flames some more. Stir the shitpot. Get Heather so fucked-up in the head she'll have to see her shrink forever."

"I knew you'd be mad, Taz. . . . What shrink?"

"The shrink she's been seein' since you've been in jail, damnit. All this has worried her so much that mom took her to a shrink."

"God, Taz, I'm sorry."

"Yeah, but it's the same old story, right? You're just not quite sorry enough to leave well enough alone? Right?"

"Taz, I don't know what to say. I'm a reporter. You know that. The bad comes with the good. I guess I'd better go home now."

"Maybe you should."

Taz walked away, slipping on the broken eggs and almost falling. "Shit."

His anger at Shannon's new "story" and new employment had been so intense that he almost forgot what she said the story was about. Boudreaux bought Ginger when she was a baby. God, how sad, he thought. And it's all going to be on TV. This will just kill Boudreaux and Tailese, he thought.

Shannon cried all the way home. She was conflicted. But she knew one thing—if Ted Jackson didn't sell the story to her, he'd sell it to someone. It was just journalism.

First thing the next morning, Friday, Shannon called Ted Jackson. When he told her that the baby seller was one Rena Kirkpatrick, Shannon was flabbergasted. Then, upon brief reflection, she told him that she remembered Rena mentioning something to her once about somebody getting in touch with her to negotiate something Rena wanted to sell concerning a story.

"Damn, I guess I'm dumber than a stump. I just never put that together when you called me."

"Well, it's her all right. She spent a couple of weeks convincing me to represent her in this situation and then I had to check out all kinds of ethics stuff and that took me awhile. But we were trying to figure out what to do even before you became her cellmate. That was an incredible coincidence."

"No kidding. ... So Rena Kirkpatrick sold a baby—Ginger—to the Fontenots when Ginger was an infant. Unbelievable. . . . And speaking of believable, how am I gonna know all this is true?"

"You just hang on tight. I'll have some great evidence for you real soon. Like tomorrow maybe."

Early that afternoon, Ted had Rena grant him power of attorney and give him the key to her safe-deposit box. Ted took a half-day of vacation and drove to Barksboro. The bank, as Ted had anticipated, wanted to verify with Rena that it was okay with her for Ted to get into her box at the bank. Ted explained to the vice president of the bank that Rena was in jail and that he was her lawyer, showing him the power of attorney, but the banker wanted more, so Ted had the banker call information for the telephone number of the Travis County jail. When the banker called the jail, Ted told him to ask for the jailer's office. Rena was waiting for the call. The banker thought it all most unusual, and it upset his stomach, but he couldn't think of a good way to be any more obstructionist, so he let Ted in the box.

Rena had not lied to Ted. The receipts were exactly as Rena had said they would be—scattered among her birth certificate, her high-school pictures, the picture of Frank and Rena, their marriage license, his death certificate, and some other papers Rena inexplicably was clinging to. Rena hadn't volunteered to Ted anything about the man in the picture, and Ted hadn't asked. It was obvious to Ted that Rena and the man were young and in love when the picture was made. Ted wondered if he could be the guy Rena shot and killed all those years ago. Her husband. And she kept their marriage license and his death certificate. Weird, Ted thought. Rena had asked Ted to bring her the picture. Ted put it in his briefcase along with the receipts and everything else. Weird, weird, weird, he thought.

That Rena was still in jail could have been a bit of a problem. The escrow contract allowed representatives of "Inside Out" to be able to interview Rena wherever in Travis

County they wanted to, including at a television studio. Anticipating the potential problem, Ted had made his unusual request to Judge Ravinson earlier in the week.

The judge had known Ted—and Rena—for a long time. He liked Ted, a straight shooter, and he didn't particularly dislike Rena. She was no account, but she never had given him any trouble, and she understood when she had broken the law. He'd take her over most criminals, the judge thought. So Judge Ravinson granted Ted's request. He would furlough Rena Saturday morning for the weekend in Ted Jackson's care and custody, and it would be Ted's butt if Rena wasn't back in jail by ten p.m. Sunday. Judge Ravinson hadn't even asked Ted what it was all about; he didn't want to know. Ted had volunteered nothing.

On Saturday, September 30th, Rena told her story on camera to Shannon Gillette. Ted had brought Rena to Shannon's condo. Rena probably never had been in a place like that, Ted thought, except perhaps as a burglar. Then Ted remembered Rena's aversion to felonies and dismissed that idea. When they had arrived, Shannon and Rena hugged like they were long-lost relatives or something. Funny, Ted thought. They must have bonded in jail.

Concerning Rena's information, though, Shannon was somewhat disappointed. The money-order receipts were nice, but they could've been for any debt Boudreaux might have owed the Frank Dailey to whom they were made out. The interview was great, but it seriously needed corroboration. Rena told Shannon every detail of the transaction on camera, including that the man in the picture's name was Frank Dailey, that it had been Frank and herself who sold the baby to Boudreaux, that she had killed Frank in self defense a short while later, and that she had cashed the money orders as they had come in from Boudreaux over the years. She told Shannon that she couldn't remember the real mother's name but that it sounded kind of like the name of a famous movie actress from back then.

Shannon had Whitney Johnstone, her cameraperson from New York, shoot some videotape of all the papers and the picture. All this information was wonderful, especially the murder part, but Shannon knew George Cogbill would want some corroboration. Not for legal reasons; it was just that the story would play better if, for example, Ginger's biological mother could be found. The escrow agreement spoke to this problem. At her option, Shannon had thirty days to corroborate. If she was unable to corroborate Rena's story and consequently did not want to release the money, Rena then would be free to sell her story to anyone else who would buy it and Shannon would be prohibited from using any part of it.

Rena thought all this was way too complicated, but Ted had assured her there was no other way "Inside Out" would buy her story. Rena stayed in a motel on Saturday night. Ted had spotted her a hundred. The beer tasted real good. By noon on Sunday, Rena was ready to go back to jail. She didn't have much of the hundred left, and she didn't have a car, and watching professional football games on TV in the motel room wasn't any different from watching them in the jail. Ted picked her up late that afternoon in time to get her back to the jail for dinner. Rena went back to jail without incident—except that she was fairly drunk when she got there. But she could hide that condition real well.

Chapter 23

Shannon needed a corroborating witness. She might confront the Fontenots at the right time, but not yet. It would be real nice if she could find Ginger's biological mother. Rena had remembered basically where she and Frank picked up the baby. As best she could, she drew Shannon a map. Armed with no more information than that, Shannon went to work. The place to start was Mason County, Texas, specifically near the Locust Grove community south of Rhinehart.

Monday, October 2nd, 2000. George Cogbill, excited, had provided Shannon with a producer. Shannon, her new producer, Tamara Jenkins, and her cameraperson, Whitney Johnstone, drove their rented van to Rhinehart where they got a couple of rooms at the Green Tree Inn. The search effort would be conducted from Shannon's room because she would have to stay inside most of the time. Her presence being known in Rhinehart might attract other journalists. Shannon believed she had an exclusive so far, and she certainly wanted to keep it that way.

The old Minden homeplace was in ruins. Clearly, no one had lived there for many years. Maurice Minden had been dead for fifteen years. Shannon found it by persistence. The map Rena had drawn her from memory was in error by the passage of twenty-six years, but Shannon and her crew just kept driving down country roads in the south part of the county until they spotted a place that just might be it. Shannon was disappointed that no one was there, but she had Whitney take some digital still pictures. On Tuesday morning, Shannon had Tamara hire a local title lawyer to trace the ownership of the property.

    The title lawyer, Tom Kirk, was a big success. By the next day, he had been able to tell Tamara that a man named Maurice Minden had owned the property at the time in question. In his latter years, Maurice Minden had sold the property to a corporation in return for monthly payments and the right to live on the property until his death. The corporation still owned the property, apparently holding it as an investment, Kirk said. On the brighter side, Kirk told Tamara there were a number of long-since-retired farmers and ranchers at a particular old-folks home in Rhinehart who might remember Maurice Minden if he had farmed or ranched the land. That turned out to be a good tip.

Thursday, October 5th.

    "Excuse me, gentlemen. Could I have a moment of your time?"

    "I don't know, missy," one of them said. "We're kind of busy."

    There was considerable laughter. The four nursing-home residents were sitting on the front porch. They didn't appear to be occupied by anything much other than maybe watching the grass grow. Tamara smiled.

    "I have a picture here I'd like to show you and a name I'd like to ask you about. Do any of you recognize this place. And have any of you ever heard the name Maurice Minden?"

"Old Maurice," one of them said. "I haven't thought about him in a helluva long time. Been dead a long time now. Died of loneliness, I expect."

"Was this where he lived?" Tamara said, showing the picture to the man who remembered Maurice Minden.

"Yep, that's where he lived. Used to ranch all that land around there, but after he went bust he was only able to keep that old house and a couple of acres. Worked at the old Barnes saw mill after that. Had two families, you know. Had one wife and a couple of boys, as I remember. The wife died, and the boys grew up and went away. I didn't know them much. Then Maurice married another woman. I believe her name was Nahlia Fern. She died birthin' the second of their two girls, I seem to recall. I sure do recall them two girls. Lookers, both of 'em. Don't know what happened to 'em, though. Been gone from around here a real long time."

"You wouldn't remember either one of them's name, would you?"

"Naw, I don't think so. Let's see. They were both lookers, I remember that. Let's see. One of 'em had real black hair and blue eyes. Almost eerie lookin.' Let's see...."

"Would her name have been anything like the name of any famous movie star from back then?"

"Let's see. Wait a minute. Yeah. She even looked like her, too. What was her name? Italian. Let's see. The girl's name was...Sophie. That was it. Sophie."

"Do you remember her sister's name?"

"Naw. Sophie was the older girl. Left sudden like and never came back. I remember old Maurice grievin' about it. I think he and the younger girl may have gone to see her a time or two wherever she went, but she didn't come around here again. Then the other girl went away and old Maurice just seemed to kinda wither away. Kinda like us old farts are doin' here."

There was laughter. Somebody told the speaker to speak for himself. More laughter.

"Do any of the rest of you remember anything about any of this?"

None responded. She thanked them all, especially the one who had provided all the information. Before she left, Tamara asked the talker his name. He said it was James H. Dooley. None of the porch sitters asked who she was, and she didn't tell them. Mr. Dooley hadn't even asked why she wanted to know his name. She was a bit puzzled that no one had asked her why she was asking all the questions.

When she was gone, one of the men in the group asked Dooley how he remembered all that stuff about Maurice Minden, allowing as how he barely remembered the man's name even after being refreshed by all that information.

"Lookers," Dooley replied. "They was lookers."

So far, this had been easy, Shannon thought, but the going probably was about to get tough. Ginger Fontenot's biological mother's name likely was Sophie Minden, but where was she? And who was the father? Maybe some of the middle-aged locals out in the county would remember her, Shannon thought. Much as she would have liked to go herself, Shannon sent Tamara to do the investigating.

Shannon was right—the going was getting tougher. Tamara had been stopping in general stores and grocery stores and at junk dealers for two days. On Saturday afternoon, it dawned on Shannon that they might not have been looking exactly in the right place and they may have been inquiring at the wrong time of day. The people most likely to know about Sophie back then just might be found in the honky tonks that dotted the county roads. Since they didn't get to going good until at least early evening, maybe Tamara should just rest up 'til about then, Shannon decided.

Saturday night, October 7th, 2000. Just a bit after dark. It didn't take long for Tamara to hit paydirt. Tamara was a slightly younger version of Shannon—less experienced but just as fearless. She didn't really think any of the rednecks she encountered in the clubs would give her any grief, but she was ready for them if they did. She was from New York City, after all. Some of them stared at her pretty hard, but she had expected that. The second joint she hit was called the Piney Paradise Country Club. The bartender appeared to be in his mid-to-late forties. Tamara ordered a bottle of beer and then asked him if he'd been around there long.

"You mean around this club or around here?"

Before Tamara had the chance to clarify her question, the bartender spoke again.

"Hell, I don't know why I asked you that. The answer to either question would be the same. I've been around here all my life. Two years out for the Army and 'Nam; otherwise, I've been right here. Just can't seem to get away. You sure ain't from around here. Where're you from?"

"New York, actually."

"Sounds right. Why do you want to know how long I've been here, anyway?"

"Well," Tamara said, "'cause I'm tryin' to find a girl that lived around here about twenty-five years ago—name of Sophie Minden."

"Sophie Minden," the bartender repeated. "I ain't thought of her in a helluva long time. What in the world do you want with her?"

"Well, I'm an investigator, and I really can't tell you that, but I sure would like to know everything you can remember about her."

"In the movies, the investigator always offers some money about this time. Ain't you gonna do that?"

"Sure," Tamara said, reaching in the pocket of her jeans. "How about twenty?"

"How about fifty?"

"How about sixty," Tamara said, handing the bartender three bills.

"Wonderful. What do you want to know? I ain't seen her in forever."

"Well, I'm told she left here in a hurry about twenty-five years ago. Would you know anything about that?"

"Not much more than a vague recollection. See, the boys around here had kind of a—what do you call it?—kind of a love-hate thing for her."

"What does that mean?"

"Well, see, she was damned gorgeous, and every old boy in four or five counties—includin' me—wanted to date her, but she wasn't havin' none of it. Kinda put us down. The worst of it was that summer she used to show up at the tonks all the time with that son-of-a-bitch that calls hisself our Congressman."

"Excuse me, who exactly do you mean? What exactly are you talking about?"

"Just what I said. That asshole Winford Thomas. His old man used to own a big chain of furniture stores around here. Yeah, Winford Thomas was a rich college boy from Rhinehart who liked to fool around with the country girls. I guess the city girls wouldn't put out for him like he wanted. So he'd date the country girls who didn't have nothin' and were all impressed by who he was and his money and stuff. I don't remember him gettin' in no fights over it but that was probably only because his daddy was such a powerful man that all the boys were a little afraid to rough up his son any. He sure needed it, though. Seems like he still does. That sure was some funny shit about him on TV a while back. I laughed my ass off.

"I do remember there was that one summer that him and Sophie saw a lot of each other. I think it wasn't too long after that that she took off. I don't recall ever seein' her again. I think she went to Dallas. Good lookin' as she was she probably married some rich bastard over there and lived happily ever after. That's the way it goes, ain't it?"

"Ah, yeah, I guess so. Say, thanks a lot for your help. You work here all the time?"

"Yeah. Why?"

"Ah, well, I might want to come back and drink another beer with you some time."

"Any time. Thanks for the tip."

"Yeah, you're welcome. Say, what's your name?"

"Sarge Sanford."

"Okay, Sarge. Thanks. See you."

When the state trooper finally got her pulled over, Tamara had to talk him out of giving her a ticket for failure to heed the instructions of a law-enforcement officer, but she had no problem accepting the speeding ticket. He had her on radar doing eighty-five miles per hour in a fifty-five miles-per-hour zone. The trooper, of course, had wanted to know what her hurry was. Tamara told him she was in the area visiting relatives, that she was staying at the Green Tree Inn, and that...well...she was hurrying back to the motel because...well...because her stomach was cramping really badly. He sent her on her way. The truth was that Tamara's mind was so far away that she hadn't heard his siren until he was directly beside her. She figured this little piece of information was worth a raise.

Shannon could not believe her ears. This was an awards-level story for sure now. Oedipus Rex come to Texas. This could turn out to be the story of the decade. God, if it was just true. She was having to pinch herself to make sure she wasn't dreaming or hallucinating. She had Tamara and Whitney listen to her thoughts to see if they could punch any obvious holes in what she was thinking. If all of it was true, Winford Thomas and Sophie Minden were the biological parents of Ginger Fontenot. Winford was the city rich kid with the political ambition who couldn't afford to let anyone know he'd knocked up a country girl. Sophie Minden was the pretty but ignorant country girl who got sucked in by the city rich kid.

Winford wouldn't marry her, and she was too damn poor to keep the kid, so she gave it to Frank and Rena Dailey to raise as theirs, but they sold it to Boudreaux Fontenot, whose wife could bear no more children. And Tailese Fontenot probably never knew the truth of where the baby came from; just graciously accepted it and thanked the Lord for providing it. And Ginger. If she knew she wasn't the biological child of the Fontenots, she obviously didn't know she was the biological child of Winford Thomas unless she was into incest. No chance of that, Shannon thought.

What was far more likely was that Ginger had no idea who her biological parents were. And maybe only a suspicion that she wasn't conceived by the people who raised her, Shannon thought. It just couldn't be. Stories like this could exist only in the imagination of a Hollywood script writer. And Rena Kirkpatrick. She had no idea that Winford Thomas was Ginger's biological father. Had she known, the price of her information would not have been a mere fifty-thousand dollars. This, Shannon concluded, could turn out to be the steal of the new century in tabloid journalism. Neither Tamara nor Whitney punched any holes.

Beyond any doubt, Shannon knew she had to find Sophie Minden. She was the key to everything. And Dallas was the place to start. Time was a wastin.' She told Tamara and Whitney to pack. She didn't care if it *was* after dark. They were driving to Dallas right then. If Sophie Minden was in Dallas, Shannon would find her.

It was one a.m., Sunday, October 8th, when Shannon, Tamara, and Whitney pulled into the parking lot of the Metroplex Manor in Arlington, between Dallas and Fort Worth. Tamara registered. Rooms for Tamara and Whitney. And a suite for Shannon. As the bell captain opened the door to Shannon's suite, Shannon thought to herself that she could own a hotel like this if she could just find Sophie Minden. They would do some preliminary work and thinking on Sunday, rest a bit, and be ready to hit the ground running on Monday.

Sunday afternoon. Ted Jackson was thrilled at the news from Shannon that she had corroborated Rena Kirkpatrick's story. There was no need to tell him anything more than that she was releasing the funds from the escrow agent and that she, as per their agreement, would like Rena to be available through the time the story aired on "Inside Out." Rena was beyond excited to hear the news from Ted. They had worked out their split at eighty/twenty. Ted had a lousy job and didn't make much money. With $10,000, he could pay off all his credit cards and take his wife on a trip to Maui. Hell of a deal. He wasn't even going to ask Rena for the hundred back.

Rena was only forty eight, but she was getting old before her time. All that drinkin' did that to a body. With this money, she was gonna buy a little house before she lost the money to booze or gambling or whatever. That way, at least she'd have a place to stay that nobody could take away from her. She was thinking about getting a job at a convenience store/gas station. She could make enough money to eat and keep the lights turned on, she thought, and she probably could steal a few beers from the store. Rena was excited about her new prospects. She, of course, hadn't considered that she would owe income tax on the money. Income tax was something she hadn't thought about in a long time. The IRS probably thought she was dead, she once had thought. "Inside Out" would send a 1099 for $50,000. They would send it to Ted Jackson's office. Ted would mail it to Rena's post-office box in Barksboro. Maybe Rena would put it in her safe-deposit box.

Chapter 24

Ginger Fontenot had been a happy child, but something wasn't quite right. She had no idea why, but she knew she just wasn't like her brother Alphonse and her parents. She spoke the cajun dialect of English that her family spoke, but it was never comfortable to her. She spoke the fractured French they spoke, too, but it wasn't comfortable to her, either. Many of the other kids she played with as a pre-schooler spoke cajun, but many of them didn't, and she somehow felt drawn to the kids who spoke "normal" English. Once in school, Ginger had leapt at the chance to learn mainstream English. By the time she was in the fourth grade, she had shed most of the cajun dialect in favor of regular English.

LeMieux was a small town, and everyone knew each other. Her teachers thought it quite odd that someone coming from a sure 'nough cajun home, where a heavy cajun dialect was spoken, would be so different from the rest of her family. Alphonse's cajun was exactly like Boudreaux's, the only contrast being that Alphonse's personality was a bit sullen, where Boudreaux was the opposite. There were other differences between Ginger and her family, as well. Alphonse was not dumb by any means, but his interests were one-hundred percent applied. He just wanted to know what was true and what wasn't; the abstract he could do without. He had a considerable mechanical aptitude and no creative flair whatever. Ginger, on the other hand, was quite the abstract thinker and highly creative. Abstractions just seemed to make more sense to her.

LeMieux had a decent public-school system. One of its better features was the introduction of all grammar-school children to foreign languages, even if just Spanish and French. Ginger loved it. She took to foreign languages like a duck to water. Her teachers were amazed at how quickly and how much she learned. It wasn't long until the grammar-school foreign-language lessons practically could have been taught by her. There was one real curiosity, however. While she excelled in Spanish, she had little interest in French. Coming from a cajun family, her disdain for learning French was at least an anomaly, but since she was so good at Spanish, and since she expressed such a serious interest in other foreign languages, her teachers didn't press her on the subject of learning French.

Ginger hadn't been in school long when the Fontenots noticed she wasn't talking much like them anymore. They would have believed it was just from interacting with all the non-cajun kids at school except that Alphonse went to the same school and he spoke cajun every bit as much as his parents did. Ginger's preference for regular English was okay with them, but it concerned them, too, because they knew she wasn't a cajun by birth and might end up having a hard time growing up in a cajun culture. Mostly, though, they didn't worry about such things. They just lived day to day, and as long as there was no major eruption, there was no problem. Clashing cultures and the long term simply were not concepts the Fontenots thought much about—or could do much about.

By the time Ginger became a teenager, she had become so annoyed with the "backwoods" way her family spoke that she had made snide remarks about it on occasion. Alphonse, just starting high school, loved his little sister, but he thought she was weird as hell. He was quite proud of his heritage, and for the life of him he couldn't understand why Ginger wasn't equally proud of hers. He just figured she'd spent too much time around too many non-cajuns, which is exactly what he told her whenever she said anything to him about his speech.

Boudreaux and Tailese were wounded whenever Ginger said anything to them about their speech. They loved her so much. She was so beautiful and so wonderful and so smart. They knew she wasn't "like" them, and they knew why, but the subject was absolutely taboo; they didn't even discuss it between themselves in the privacy of their own bedroom. Their response to her infrequent barbs about their speech was always that they hadn't had the opportunity to have the kind of education she was getting and that they were just too old and too far down the road to change the way they had been their entire lives. Inside, like Alphonse, they were extremely proud of their heritage and couldn't understand why, since they'd had Ginger from birth, she wasn't more like them. But they contented themselves with the idea that Ginger was just special and that everything would turn out fine in the end.

Ginger was as appalled at the bad grammar spoken by her family as she was at the cajun dialect. It was their whole culture. She just didn't seem to belong. It was like she was from outer space. Her parents had done everything in the world to make her the most loved child imaginable, but she'd still had a queasy, indescribable feeling for a long time. One day in ninth-grade literature class, as the beginning to a section on Greek tragedies, the teacher exhibited a film of the Greek play "Oedipus Rex," written by Sophocles in the fifth century b.c.

The play hosted one of the more tragic tales in Greek literature. In the story, which took place in the city-state of Thebes, Queen Jocasta had become pregnant by King Laius, her husband. Upon the birth of the child, an oracle came to Laius and told him what the future held for the child. When the oracle told him the child would grow up to kill his father, marry his mother, and father children by her, Laius and Jocasta decided that the child must be put to death to prevent such a tragedy. Laius bound the child's feet with rope and had a trusted shepherd take the child onto Mount Katyrun at the far reaches of the realm where the child would be left to die.

But the shepherd who took the child to this obscure location didn't have the heart to leave the child to die and instead gave the infant boy to a shepherd friend from the neighboring city-state of Corinth to raise as his own. The Corinth shepherd, knowing of the misery of his own king and queen over wanting a child but not having been blessed, decided to offer the child to them. The king and queen of Corinth, Polybus and Merope, took the child as their own.

Polybus and Merope called the child Oedipus, meaning swollen feet. One night at his parents' table, as Oedipus was reaching early manhood, a guest had a bit too much to drink and privately made the statement to Oedipus that he was not the blood child of Polybus and Merope. Later, Oedipus queried Polybus and Merope on the subject, but they were indignant at the mention of such a thing.

Not getting a satisfactory answer from his parents, Oedipus decided he would seek the truth from an oracle at Delphi, as the oracles possessed the wisdom of Apollo, the God of light. The oracle did not answer his question about his birth, instead telling him he soon would kill his father, marry his mother, and father children by her. Fearing such a tragedy, Oedipus determined that he would leave Corinth, never to return, as he loved Polybus and Merope deeply and wished them no harm, certainly not the tragedy predicted by the oracle.

On the narrow road to Thebes, Oedipus met several men accompanying the carriage of a nobleman. When the carriage would not allow Oedipus room to pass, Oedipus struck one of the men. As the carriage passed Oedipus, its occupant struck him. Oedipus, having no idea the occupant of the carriage was Laius, the King of Thebes—his father—struck back with his stick, killing Laius, who had been on his way to Corinth to seek the help of Polybus and Merope with a Sphinx that was wreaking havoc in Thebes. Oedipus, by that time enraged, then killed the other men present, save one, who fled in terror, returning to Thebes only after the passage of considerable time. Oedipus continued on his journey to Thebes, having no idea he had killed his father and having no knowledge of the Sphinx.

Arriving on the outskirts of the city, Oedipus was confronted by the Sphinx, a half-bear, half-woman who was ravaging the city and devouring its children. The Sphinx challenged Oedipus, as it did all comers, to answer a riddle. Should Oedipus accept the challenge and solve the riddle, the Sphinx promised to leave and never return, but should Oedipus be unable to solve the riddle, he would die. Oedipus accepted the challenge, whereupon the Sphinx asked Oedipus the riddle.

"What has four legs in the morning, two in the afternoon, and three at night?"

Oedipus thought but for a moment.

"Why, man, of course. A baby must crawl on its all-fours until it can walk. And a man walks erect during his adulthood until he reaches old age when he then must be assisted by a cane."

The Sphinx roared with anger but, true to its word, withdrew from the city it had left in near ruin. That it was the stranger Oedipus who had solved the riddle of the Sphinx soon became known to all in Thebes, and Oedipus became a hero.

About that same time, Jocasta received word that Laius had been killed. Soon after, she asked Oedipus to become her husband and assume the throne, which he did, becoming Oedipus Rex. When the survivor of Laius' slaying finally returned to Thebes and found to his shock and amazement that Oedipus was the new king, he revealed himself only to Jocasta. Lying, and in fear, he told Jocasta that Laius and the others had been killed by a band of robbers. He then asked to be sent to the fields where he might live out his days as a shepherd. Later, Jocasta bore Oedipus two daughters, Antigone and Agamemnon, thereby completely fulfilling the prophecy of both oracles. Many years later, when, through other circumstances, the truth was revealed to all, including Jocasta and Oedipus, Jocasta took her own life by hanging herself and Oedipus blinded himself by his own hand so that he might never again see the misery his life had wrought.

Adoption was not a subject that had occupied Ginger Fontenot's fourteen-year-old mind for more than a fleeting few moments from time to time. She knew, of course, that adoptions took place, but she didn't know anyone who had been adopted so there was nothing that caused her to relate to the subject. But there was something about the story "Oedipus Rex" that fascinated her. She didn't know what exactly, but she had been mesmerized while watching the film. She thought of little else the rest of the school day. In the solitude of her bedroom that night, she read the story of "Oedipus Rex" in her literature book. She read it twice. There was something she should learn from it—something in particular, but she didn't know what.

Finally, in reading it yet again, she came to the drunk man at Laius' table who had told Oedipus he was not the blood child of Polybus and Merope. Thinking about the differences in herself and her family, Ginger determined that she might be adopted, too. She decided to try to discover whether she had been adopted, and, in fantasizing about it, she determined that she would not make the same mistakes Oedipus had made if it turned out she had been adopted. She would do whatever it took to learn who her real parents were; she would never subject herself or her real parents to the tragedy that had befallen Oedipus.

But how would she discover whether she had been adopted? There was no way she could come right out and ask the Fontenots. If she hadn't been adopted, they would be incredibly hurt that she was having such thoughts, and if she had been adopted, they would be hurt that she suspicioned it. Further, there was no way they would tell her she had been adopted. She decided not to ask, but that didn't keep her from wondering, and it didn't keep her from paying even more attention to the contrasts as opposed to the comparisons.

Ginger loved the Fontenots, but, during her high school years, she began to grow more and more distant from them. She grew more distant from Alphonse, as well, but he never knew it, being far too interested in beer, motorcycles, guns, and girls—in that order—to notice. He just thought she was weird, smart, and not much like him, but it didn't bother him much because it didn't get in his way. Boudreaux and Tailese knew Ginger was not real close to them, but they had no idea what to do about it. It wasn't that Ginger was hostile toward anyone; she just didn't participate much in the good times of family goings-on. She mostly stayed in her room, studying, listening to the radio, thinking about boys—and thinking about knowing who she was and being far, far away from LeMieux.

Ginger always had thought it odd that her birthday was the same as her mother's. Such coincidences happened, of course, but it nonetheless struck Ginger as odd. She had no evidence that her birth certificate was anything other than accurate, so she never openly questioned it. She had evidence of other differences, however. Besides the obvious difference in speech patterns and mannerisms, there were considerable physical differences. Boudreaux was 5' 9," Tailese was 5' 2," and Alphonse was 5' 8"—all three were fairly short. Ginger—at 5' 8"—was tall and statuesque. Boudreaux's, Tailese's, and Alphonse's hair colors were all some shade of brown, while Ginger's hair was coal black. Ginger had bright blue eyes; Boudreaux's and Alphonse's were light brown and Tailese's were light green.

But perhaps the biggest difference was facial. Boudreaux, Tailese, and Alphonse were plain and ordinary looking; not bad looking, just ordinary looking. Ginger was strikingly beautiful. Once, after reading a book about thoroughbred race horses, Ginger thought that Boudreaux and Tailese being her biological parents made about as much sense as a Kentucky Derby winner having been born to a couple of ordinary work horses. Just as soon as she'd had the thought, however, she scolded herself hard and was instantly quite remorseful for putting the Fontenots down like that—and for making herself out to be something she probably was not. She loved them dearly and would do absolutely anything for them, but she couldn't escape the feeling that she wasn't their child. For the time being, she contented herself with the idea that the Fontenots had rescued her from death, as in Oedipus Rex, and that they loved her dearly. Of the latter, she was certain.

Ginger's interest in foreign languages continued throughout high school. She was an excellent student, at the very top of her class at the beginning of her last semester. With a 3.95 grade-point average out of a possible 4.0 and with an SAT score in the ninety-seventh percentile, she could be admitted to most any school, certainly in Texas. She was eligible for many scholarships, but none of them paid everything. One day while sitting in the waiting room of her high-school counselor's office, she read a brochure about a company that matched individuals with a national computer database of scholarship opportunities. The cost was just $20, no problem since Ginger had been earning money working part time at a local dress shop. She had saved almost a thousand dollars.

The Fontenots wanted her to go to college, of course, but they didn't understand why she didn't want to go to Trimeaux University in Demonbreun. It was a big, four-year university. All the smartest kids from southeast Texas went there, they told her, and she even could live at home and commute.

Ginger spent her own $20 on the computer scholarship match. The company sent Ginger a list of scholarships it had generated on the basis of comparing the data sheet Ginger had sent in with the criteria of the various scholarships in the database. Several of the better paying ones were attractive to her except that they would require her to attend particular universities, all of which were just a little *too* far from home—except one. She just kept reading the criteria for that scholarship over and over. It just seemed too good to be true.

Ginger wanted to get away from home, but not that far away. Trimeaux University at Demonbreun was a good school and all—most of her friends were going to go there—but Ginger had other plans. She wanted away from what she thought of as southeast Texas; she wanted to experience life in a faster lane. The scholarship she kept reading over and over and over said very plainly that every four years—the next year being the fall of 1992—the Colleen Etherington Foundation awarded a $100,000 scholarship to a female to attend Texas Christian University and major in foreign languages. The recipient had to meet all the normal criteria like financial need and exceptionally high grade-point average and SAT score, but the applicant had to be one other thing, as well—tall. The minimum height was 5' 8." Ginger couldn't imagine what height had to do with scholarship, but she was real happy that it seemed to matter to the Colleen Etherington Foundation, whoever Colleen Etherington was.

She knew she was 5' 8," but, just to be sure, she got in the old car she had bought herself and drove down to the dress shop where she worked part time during the school year and full time summers. There, she knew, was a very accurate measuring stick attached to a wall near the dressing rooms. It was mostly for mothers trying to figure out how many dress sizes too large to buy for their fast-growing little girls, but the measuring stick went all the way to six-feet even. When Ginger came rushing in, one of the full-time sales ladies at the store was happy to measure her, but she couldn't understand what the big fuss was all about. Sure enough, Ginger measured 5' 8 1/4."

Ginger thanked her and ran out the door praying out loud not to shrink before she could get her height certified by her family doctor and sent in to the Colleen Etherington Foundation. She had the need, the grades, the SAT score, and the minimum height requirement. She believed her high-school counselor and foreign-language teachers would write her good recommendation letters, as required. If she could just get by the two other hurdles—becoming a finalist and then interviewing well.

After Ginger sent in the completed application, which included several requested photographs of her, she began asking Tailese the very next day when she got home from her part-time job at the dress shop about what had come for her in the mail. When a package finally arrived from the Colleen Etherington Foundation about ten days later, Ginger was thrilled—but afraid at the same time. Tailese was excited for her. Boudreaux was still at work. Alphonse had moved away from home just after graduating from high school, having gone to work in the oilfields. He recently had been married. The first piece of paper Ginger pulled from the manila envelope was a letter addressed to her. She read it to Tailese.

"Dear Ms. Fontenot: We are gratified to inform you that you have been selected as a finalist for the 1992 Colleen

Etherington Foundation TCU Foreign Languages Scholarship. As you know, this scholarship is given only once every four years and is one of the richest such awards in the country. To have been selected as a finalist in this scholarship competition is an honor in itself.

"Your interview with the Colleen Etherington Foundation Board of Directors has been set for ten a.m., Saturday, April 15th, 1992, in the offices of Branson Danielson & Corning, the law firm in Fort Worth which handles the foundation's business and legal affairs. Please call Teresa Lake at (817) 555-5297 to make arrangements for transportation, meals, and lodging for yourself and your parents, should they be accompanying you.

"I wish I could tell you what to expect from the interview other than that it will last something on the order of two hours; alas, however, I am not permitted. Just be yourself and the competition will result as it should. If you have any questions, please let me know. Sincerely, Olive Martin, Executive Director."

Such a letter never had been received at the Fontenot household before. One-hundred thousand dollars was more money than Boudreaux knew how to contemplate. He was so thrilled he hardly knew what to do. At least he could take the family out to eat. Whether his Ginger actually got the scholarship or not, this was the best thing that had ever happened to them. And they would even go to that Mexican restaurant in Demonbreun that Ginger said she liked instead of the seafood place over by the Louisiana border that Boudreaux was partial to.

On Friday night, April 14th, 1992, Boudreaux, Tailese, and Ginger left for the Metroplex in the car Boudreaux had picked up at the rental office in Demonbreun. The foundation had rented them a Lincoln TownCar for the trip. Boudreaux had not driven such a fine automobile before, but he loved cars and felt like a million dollars driving it back to LeMieux to retrieve Tailese and Ginger. They had offered to go with him to Demonbreun to get the car since Demonbreun was more or less on the way to the Metroplex from LeMieux, but Boudreaux made up some excuse about needing to return to LeMieux to pick them up. Of course, the truth was that Boudreaux wanted a little time to familiarize himself with the car and its controls so he wouldn't embarrass himself in front of his family, and if any of his friends saw him driving through the streets of LeMieux in a Lincoln TownCar, well, that would be fine, too. The leather seats felt great, and it smelled so...new.

The Fontenots were staying in the Metroplex Manor in Arlington, one of the finer hotels in the Metroplex and surely the finest building Boudreaux, Tailese, and Ginger ever had been in. They arrived about midnight, Boudreaux very closely following the detailed Metroplex route map the foundation had sent him. The foundation had thought of everything. Olive Martin had sent Boudreaux $100 in cash for tips and such, and she had subtly suggested the amounts he might consider giving or leaving in various situations. Boudreaux had told Tailese and Ginger he understood all that when the letter had arrived, but, privately, he was quite happy about the money *and* the advice.

The valet parking service attendant got $5 and the bellman got $10. They were welcome to eat in any of the dining rooms at the Manor and charge the meal and a twenty-percent gratuity to the room. He could just tell the waiter to add the twenty percent. Ginger would be eating lunch with the foundation's board, after which time she would be free to be with her parents. The hotel reservation was for two nights and the car wasn't due back until Monday, so Ginger and her parents could see some of the sights in the Metroplex before they left for home if they wished, according to Olive Martin's letter.

They got up real early on Saturday morning. Everyone was excited. Ginger was in love. The car, the hotel, her room.

What more in life could there be? She wanted this scholarship real bad. But she was as anxious as she was in love. Boudreaux wore his only suit to breakfast. Tailese wore a dress that Ginger had bought her for the occasion at the dress shop where she worked. Ginger wore a dress, though not to breakfast, that cost her $150—and that included the discount the dress shop gave her. Everyone who knew about the scholarship situation was excited for Ginger.

Branson Danielson & Corning was in downtown Fort Worth, about a thirty-minute drive from the hotel, but Boudreaux was taking no chances. He was remembering everything. They left the hotel at eight-thirty a.m. No tip to the doorman unless he fetched a cab. The valet parking-service attendant got $5 every time he parked or retrieved the car. Ginger to be picked up at one-thirty p.m.

Ginger was nervous. No one was in the reception area of the law firm at nine-thirty a.m. when she arrived. As it was, she and the Fontenots had been parked outside on the street for thirty minutes. One of the giant double doors announcing the law firm had pulled open easily, but Ginger, anxious, was certain she had arrived at the wrong place. She went back out into the hall and looked around, but there were no other doors leading from the hall except doors leading to two restrooms. She knew she had the right floor—twentieth—she had memorized it over and over. So she went back inside and sat down, hoping they would take pity on her if she had gone to the wrong place. She strained and strained, but she could hear nothing. It was as though she was the only person in the entire building besides the security guard on the first floor, who had her name on a list. Whenever she got *real* nervous, which was every few minutes, she comforted herself with the idea that her name had been on that list.

At a few minutes before ten a.m., a woman walked from a hallway into the reception area. Middle-aged and stately, she extended her hand.

"Hello, Ginger, I'm Olive Martin. Welcome. How was your trip to the Metroplex?"

"It was terrific, thank you. The hotel is unreal. You've been quite generous to my family." Ginger was extremely relieved.

"Well, and we're delighted to be. Ginger, the people in the room you're about to enter are all on the board of the foundation. They'll introduce themselves to you and tell you a little bit about who they are. They're real important people, but don't let that make you any more nervous than I'm sure you already are. They just want to know about you. Who you are. What you think. Don't hold back. Just answer freely. And don't try to anticipate the kinds of answers they're looking for. Honesty in answering is very important, and they're pretty good at figuring out whether you really believe what you're saying. Are you ready?"

"Yes, ma'am, I'm ready."

The room had what seemed a twenty-foot ceiling. It also seemed dimly-lighted. It was completely paneled in some dark wood. There was a conference table in the room which seemed to Ginger forty feet long. Around it sat about a dozen middle-aged to older people, the nearest Ginger could tell from a glance. Olive Martin ushered her to the closest individual. All of them were standing. She shook hands with each one of them as they introduced themselves. She heard virtually nothing any of them said. After the introductions, Olive told her to sit at the head of the table. The leather chair felt great, Ginger thought.

The two hours seemed an eternity at first, but as time went by, she relaxed and realized that what Olive Martin had told her was true—they just wanted to know about her, what she thought about things and so forth. The only thing she thought funny about the whole two hours was that no one asked her about her interest in foreign languages, though they did ask about her interest in travel and athletics. And they seemed quite interested in her views concerning the clashing of cultures. Her answer in general had been that no culture had the right to impose itself on any other culture.

At a few minutes before noon, one of them thanked Ginger for coming, and Olive Martin, who had not been in the room at all during the two-hour interview, came into the room and ushered Ginger down an inside hallway and into a corner room with a view of the Fort Worth skyline. Except on TV, Ginger never had seen anything like it. When Ginger's awe had subsided a bit, she noticed there was a table for four in the middle of the room set up like the tables in the hotel's restaurant except that it was dressed for only three persons. She had assumed she would be having lunch with the entire board, as the letter had indicated. Olive Martin saw her looking oddly at the table.

"Relax, Ginger, your interview with the board is over. You're having lunch with Colleen Etherington and me."

Ginger had worried during the interview that Colleen Etherington herself was one of the people around the big conference table—there were six women—but she hadn't been able to remember the names well enough. A few seconds later her question was answered when a woman, probably sixty-five years old, elegantly appointed, walked into the room and introduced herself as Colleen Etherington.

"Sit down, please, won't you, dear, and I'll tell you all about this frightening business of talking to all those board members."

Ginger sat down. She instantly liked this woman. She was elegant, tall—probably 5' 10"—and very pleasant.

"It may not seem like it to you at this moment, dear," Mrs. Etherington said, pouring Ginger and Olive a glass of iced tea, "but we're a lot alike. I came from a very small Texas town. A Frenchman passing through my little town when I was a little girl left behind some illustrated French magazines by mistake, and I came into possession of them. I was fascinated by the language and the pictures of Paris and determined right then and there that I was going to learn foreign languages and travel the world. And I did. But it was a real struggle to go to college in those days with no money.

"I came to Fort Worth from my little town when I was graduated from high school. I got a job working as a maid in a sorority house at TCU. After I had worked there a year, I was allowed to go to school almost tuition-free, but I could take no more than a few courses at a time. It took me eight years, altogether, to receive my degree in modern languages. I had worked as a maid on campus the entire time.

"Slowly but surely, I embarked on an international career and was quite successful over time. But I never forgot those wasted years. These are some of the best years of a woman's life. So when I retired some years ago, having been financially successful, I decided to create this foundation and, among other things, give a scholarship in my name in foreign languages to TCU. But then I got to thinking about whether the school would follow my wishes to a 'T' and decided to award the scholarship personally. As you know, I award the scholarship only once each four years. TCU is quite expensive, but I want my girls to have to pay for very little themselves.

"I was quite excited when I received your application. Oh, yes, I hope you don't think it too terrible of me to subject you to the questioning of my board of directors, but I've found I like all the applicants so well that I really need the help of others to make an objective assessment of the applicants. And I hope you don't think it boorish of me that I was watching your interview with the board on a television screen in an adjoining room.

"You may be wondering about the minimum height requirement. As you can see, I'm quite tall. So I'm biased toward tall girls. There really isn't any other reason for it. It's just a matter of indulging the eccentricities of an old woman who wants to leave the world a little better off than she found it.

"Oh, one more thing before we eat, dear. You were the last of the applicants interviewed. You are the winner. The scholarship is yours. And I'm just delighted to have found the perfect person. Congratulations."

Ginger was dumbstruck. The speech had been fascinating, but she had not expected to find out on the day of the interview what the decision of the board—or Mrs. Etherington—would be. And to have been chosen. . . . To be $100,000-rich at this very moment was almost too much to comprehend. She wanted to scream, but she stifled it.

"Oh, Mrs. Etherington," Ginger said, almost too loudly. "I don't know what to say. This is more than any person ever could hope for, ever imagine. How can I thank you enough? I'm sure you have no idea what this means to me. . . ."

"Ginger," Olive said, smiling, "calm down. Mrs. Etherington very much understands what this means to you. We know you're the most appreciative person in the world at this moment, so you needn't feel obligated to express your appreciation now any more than you just have. There'll be plenty of time as the years go by for you to express your appreciation to the board and to Mrs. Etherington. Let's have lunch now, shall we?"

Olive pressed a small button on the table and lunch was served. The conversation during lunch was in and concerned foreign languages and cultures, especially Russian. Colleen Etherington told Ginger she had been curious as to why Ginger, with her background, had not been interested in French, but she never asked Ginger to explain, and Ginger didn't. While it wasn't a requirement of the scholarship, Mrs. Etherington said, she would appreciate it if Ginger would give some consideration to making the study of the Russian language and the Russian culture one of her principal undertakings in college. Ginger assured her that she would.

At the end of the luncheon, Colleen Etherington got up, shook Ginger's hand and told Ginger she didn't live in the Metroplex and that Ginger might not see her very often. She told her that Olive Martin, through the law firm, would handle all the details of the scholarship and any problems that might arise.

"Just sign the papers each year when we send them to you, dear, and the money is yours. Goodbye. And good luck."

With that, she walked from the room and disappeared.

Through four years of college and four years in New York, Ginger Fontenot had neither seen nor heard from Colleen Etherington again.

The money part was incredible. Including tuition, books, and living expenses, it cost right at $25,000 per year to attend TCU. Ginger needed a new—at least newer—car desperately because the one she'd been able to buy was old and shot, and she didn't trust driving it around the Metroplex. The money was unrestricted—the $25,000 was to go into her bank account each August 15th for four years—but if she bought a car with any of it, she knew she'd have to get a part-time job to make up the difference. The only reason she didn't want to work was so that she could excel academically. That was the least she could do for the foundation and Mrs. Etherington.

Some time during the summer of 1992 as she was discussing her plans with Olive Martin, the subject of her car problem came up. A week later, to Ginger's complete surprise and delight, Tailese called her at the dress shop to say two men had just delivered a car to her. Ginger rushed home. There in the driveway was a brand-new Ford Escort, blue.

There was a note in the glove compartment from Olive Martin.

"Just a little something extra for you. Do right by us. Olive."

Chapter 25

Monday, October 9th, 2000. The Metroplex Manor. Shannon had risen with the roosters. The executive producer of "Inside Out," George Cogbill, was salivating in his telephone discussions with Shannon about the situation. No expense would be spared, he told Shannon. Find that woman. He would send her two associate producers. Just find that woman. Shannon accepted the offer of the two associate producers. Several hours later, she dispatched Tamara and Whitney to the airport to pick them up. Jacque Panteen and Kirsten Powell knew what they were doing. This was a helluva crew. Together, they would find Sophie Minden in Dallas if she were there. They headquartered in Shannon's suite.

There were no Sophie Mindens in any of the telephone books. No way it would be that easy. But the telephone books offered possibilities, so Shannon assigned Jacque the task of making a list of every person in the telephone book with the first name of Sophie.

But what would the rest of them do? It was like hunting for a needle in a haystack. There were the standard sorts of techniques. They would go back twenty-six years and start from there and come forward. Much of public information was computerized by 2000, but only a small portion of public records had been computerized going back twenty-six years. Still, there was no better way. That afternoon, they would start at the Dallas County Courthouse using databases that went back that far. Marriage-license information could be the key to finding someone like Sophie Minden, but it had not been retro-computerized. Looking through the hard copies would take days. Kirsten got that job.

Had Sophie Minden ever been the subject of a news story? Newspaper morgues also were computerized, but neither the *Fort Worth Evening News* nor the *Dallas Examiner-Advertiser* had computerized their morgues very many years back. No matter, they still had to be gone through. Whitney got that job, starting Monday afternoon at the *Examiner-Advertiser*. Her task would be to check the clip file of every person whose first name was Sophie. That meant looking at the heading on every file. As a cameraperson, she didn't much like assignments like this, but this was the easiest of the assignments Shannon had given out.

Shannon's best researcher was Tamara. She got the public library. In journalism school, one of the courses she had taken was called "Information Gathering," in which she had learned how to traverse the modern databased library. If the name Sophie Minden was in the Dallas Public Library, Tamara would find it. By Monday afternoon, Tamara was scouring the library.

Earlier the same day, about mid-morning, Taz's phone had rung. It was Rance Sterling.

"Congratulations, son, I think you did a masterful job in getting Shannon Gillette out of jail. I'm quite proud of you, and I feel real bad about what happened to her while she was there."

Rance Sterling had seen the affadavits because Taz had mailed them to all other counsel of record, as he was compelled by law to do.

"Thanks, dad. I appreciate that a lot."

"Taz, I actually called for two reasons. First, I wanted to congratulate you. I've done that. Second, I wanted to ask you what you—and your client—would think about asking the court to appoint a mediator and let us try to settle this case that way. What would you think about that, son?"

"I think that's great, dad. I'm a big fan of mediation as an alternative means of dispute resolution, but I'm real surprised you or America All-Risks would be interested in mediation. We both know that when mediation sessions are successful, it's because there's been some kind of compromise reached. Dad, I have tremendous faith in Shannon's case. It's a winner. Your case is a winner. Ginger and Winford Thomas have sued us for a lot of money. What gives?"

Taz could have said much more but didn't. He had made his point.

"Nothing gives, Taz. We just believe we can talk sense to Ginger and Thomas if we have them across the table from us. Let's put it this way. You know you can get up and walk out on the mediation process any time you want to. You know the mediator is just a disinterested third-party facilitator. What do you have to lose? And one nice thing you have to gain is that you get to hear the plaintiffs' side of the case, more or less, and you get to talk directly to the litigants on the other sides. Get some idea of what they're thinking and feeling. Let them know what you're thinking and feeling. How 'bout it?"

"I'll talk to Shannon and get back with you by tomorrow. That okay?"

"Fine, son."

"And, dad, say hello to mom and Heather for me, will you?"

"I sure will, Taz. I'll tell them we spoke. They're real proud of you, too. Especially Heather. She just keeps talking about how happy she is that you got Shannon out of jail. I even think she's less depressed than she has been lately. I'll be waiting on your call. Goodbye, son."

"Bye, dad."

Taz called Shannon at the Metroplex Manor. She had left her number on his answering machine early that morning, and she had sent him an e-mail. In the e-mail, she had wanted to know if Taz still represented her. She told him she would understand if he did not care to continue as her lawyer. Taz wondered why she was at the Metroplex Manor, but quickly decided her personal life no longer was any concern of his.

Taz had considered the idea of seeking the court's approval to withdraw from the case but decided that Heather's interests were far more important than any personal considerations of his and that the best way he could protect Heather would be to continue as Shannon's lawyer. Their personal relationship was in the crapper, Taz knew, and he preferred to keep it that way. Shannon was pretty, had a great personality, and was great in bed, but her value system and his were just too far apart. Their attorney-client relationship was cordial.

"Shannon, dad has suggested mediation. I don't mind doing it, but I know my dad, and he has something up his sleeve."

"Well, even so, if it will help get this case over with, I don't much care what your father's motives are. Let's do it. What do mediators actually do, anyway?"

"Mediators have no authority to make the parties agree to anything. They're just there to hear all the sides talk and to facilitate a resolution of the problem, if possible. The mediator can't bind anybody to anything because the mediator is acting as a disinterested third party. The idea is that if you can get people together and get them talking, many times they'll find enough common ground to resolve the litigation short of going to trial *and* be able to have a relationship in the future instead of becoming bitter enemies. It's a real good system. You sure you want to do this?"

"Yes."

"Okay, I'll let dad know it's okay with us."

At the Metroplex Manor, a week had passed. It was Monday, October 16th, and Shannon Gillette and crew had nothing. Shannon was becoming antsy. Lord only knew who else was onto this story, Shannon thought. She was putting immense pressure on her crew.

Jacque had come up with one-hundred twelve persons with the first name of Sophie in the various Metroplex telephone books. She and Shannon had called them every one. To no avail. They knew from experience that the best approach was to ask directly, pleasantly, and confidently to speak to, for example, Sophie Andrews. Assuming they got Sophie Andrews on the telephone, they would then directly, pleasantly, and confidently ask: "Your maiden name was Sophie Minden, right?"

If the immediate response was something like: "I'm sorry, no, it wasn't" or "Ah, I'm not married" then that name went on the "highly unlikely" side of the ledger. If the response was: "Who wants to know?" or "Well, ah, I don't, ah..." then there would be follow-up questions. And even if the person then denied ever having heard of Sophie Minden, their name nonetheless would go on the "possible" side of the ledger. Such names would be investigated further as there was time.

Shannon and crew believed they would find her, and they were plotting their strategy to move in for the tabloidistic kill. But Shannon and Jacque had not gotten any "yes" replies, and they had listed but a few names under the "possible" category. Shannon decided to have Jacque search the telephone books once more and also write down everyone whose first name was Sophia. Jacque had asked Shannon about that in the first place, and Shannon had told her not to mess with them—to just list the "Sophies." Shannon was backtracking, Jacque knew, but she would have done the same thing.

The marriage-license search had turned up nothing. Shannon sent Kirsten to the Tarrant County Courthouse in Fort Worth to search those records. The Metroplex was a big place. For a courthouse search to be done properly, at least four county courthouses would have to be gone through. There were no Sophie Mindens to be found through the public library or through the newspaper morgues. Time was slipping away. Shannon was beginning to feel the heat from George Cogbill. She was growing desperate. What else could she do? Her crew was getting anxious.

There had been three-hundred eighty-nine "Sophias" in the telephone books. They had called them all, but they weren't excited about any of the responses. Shannon sent Jacque back through the telephone books one more time. Maybe she had missed a "Sophie" the first time through. It wasn't very likely, Shannon had said with an anxiety-tinged voice, that anybody who grew up "Sophie" would change her name to "Sophia" as an adult. Shannon had no idea whether that was true, Jacque thought, figuring she was just grabbing at straws. At any rate, back through the telephone books Jacque went. She would be real careful this time. She knew they were running out of time. Shannon had conducted a thorough cyberspace search, but it, too, had been to no avail.

Meanwhile, there was a development at the morgue of the *Dallas Examiner-Advertiser.* Shannon had ordered Whitney back to the morgues on Wednesday, October 18th, to expand the parameters of her search. Whitney had searched the news-clip files to no avail, but clips from the society section were maintained independently and had not been gone through. The routine stories from the paper's society pages, like weddings and wedding announcements, weren't clipped and filed, but anything that might have some historical or archival value was saved, like stories about the good works and deeds of volunteers in the community, people like Reauxanne Sterling.

In going over these clips, Whitney came across several stories about a Sophie Willingham who over the years had conducted numerous fundraisers to benefit a home for unmarried pregnant teenagers in the Metroplex. Whitney knew the Sophie they were looking for had herself been an unmarried pregnant teenager. This wasn't conclusive, but it was their best lead so far and certainly worth investigating. Excited, she made several photocopies and rushed back to Shannon's suite at the Metroplex Manor.

When she got there, Shannon and Jacque were calling the last few names on Jacque's latest list of "Sophies" from the telephone books. She had missed a few. They had started with the eleven she had missed in the Dallas white pages. Shannon was dialing the tenth name on the list when Whitney walked in. Whitney started to speak, but Shannon shushed her because the number she had just dialed was ringing.

"Hello."

"Yes, hello. Could I please speak with Sophie Willingham?"

Whitney's heart raced. She wanted to be the one to have found "their" Sophie. Was this the right one? Shannon needed the information she had brought back from the morgue.

"Shannon. . . ."

Shannon shot Whitney a serious frown and motioned hard for her to keep quiet.

"I'm sorry, she isn't in. Could I help you?"

"When do you expect her?"

"Not until later this afternoon. May I ask who's calling?"

"I'll just call back. Thank you very much."

"Damn it, Whitney," Shannon shouted as she put down the receiver. "You know better than to interrupt me in a situation like that. What if I'd had the lady on the phone? You might have blown it."

Nerves were fraying.

"I'm *sorry*, Shannon, but when I heard you ask for Sophie *Willingham*, I wanted you to see these before you talked to her. I'm glad she was gone. She may be our lady."

Shannon and Jacque read the clips carefully. Sweet Minerva, this could be it, Shannon thought. There were pictures of Sophie Willingham, several in color. She was about the right age. She had black hair. She was very attractive; gorgeous, no doubt, in her younger days. Could she be Ginger's mother? They certainly strongly resembled one another. . . .

"Damn, Whitney, you may have hit the jackpot. I take back whatever I just said to you. Damn, I'm glad Sophie Willingham wasn't home. I'm calling everybody in. We're about to find out about this little lady."

By mid-afternoon the next day, they had put together a respectable dossier on Sophie Willingham. She was forty five and divorced from Walter Willingham, a prominent surgeon. They had been married about twenty years ago. The marriage had lasted about fifteen years. They had two children, Barbara, eighteen, and Kristy, sixteen. Barbara had just started to SMU, and Kristy had just begun her junior year at Highland Park High School.

Apparently, Walter's and Sophie's marriage had been one of those doctor-marries-nurse kinds of things. The best

Shannon's crew could determine in such a short period was that Sophie had moved to Dallas from somewhere in rural Texas and had worked her way through school to become a nurse. She had gone to work in a major Dallas hospital as an operating-room nurse. There she met Walter Willingham. He had been married while in medical school, but he was divorced and had no children. No one Shannon or her crew had talked to could remember Sophie's maiden name. The only family anyone could remember her having was a sister who lived in the Washington, D.C. area.

Shannon was quite excited about what they had, but it still wasn't conclusive. She would go with it if she had to, but she really wanted to be able to match Sophie Willingham with Sophie Minden. The marriage license was the way, but there was no such marriage license in the Dallas County Courthouse or in the Tarrant County Courthouse.

Tamara was on the phone, talking with the public relations director at the home for unmarried pregnant teenagers that Sophie Willingham was associated with. Tamara told her that she was with a new cable television program called "High Society Works" and that she was gathering preliminary information concerning a story they might want to do on the significant homes for unmarried pregnant teenagers around the country that were supported by ladies of means. She asked the PR woman, Mindy Peel, about this Sophie Willingham who was such a big fundraiser for the home. Mindy gladly and willingly told Tamara everything she knew, including the fact that she and Dr. Willingham had been married at his ranchhouse in Denton County just north of the Metroplex.

Bingo. If Sophie Willingham and Sophie Minden were one and the same person, and Shannon was betting they were, this bombshell of a story would be ready for airing in a few days. Tamara was dispatched to the Denton County Courthouse. Denton was a confusing mixture of an old Texas town, the twenty-five-thousand-student University of North Texas, the ten-thousand-student Texas Woman's University, and the commercial growth up Interstate 35 from Dallas and Fort Worth and adjoining communities.

Tamara took the first Denton exit off the Interstate. When she stopped at the first red light, she rolled down her window and asked the kid in the car next to her, who looked to be a college student, where the county courthouse was. He told her he would show her, to just follow him. Southerners, she thought. Nothing like this would ever happen where she was from. When they got to the courthouse and pulled into the parking lot, she rolled down her window again and asked him his name. Mike Gamble, he told her. She asked him how to spell his last name. He told her. She thanked him for helping her and drove into a parking space.

Mike Gamble sat there for a few seconds. Finally, he shook his head and drove off. Why had she wanted to know his name? Who was she, anyway? Oh, well. . . .

Tamara was wondering whether Mike Gamble ever watched "Inside Out" on TV. If he did, she thought, he would know why she asked him how to spell his name when he saw it listed under the "And a special thanks to" credits at the end of the program. Bet that would freak him out, she thought. Sarge Sanford, too. And James H. Dooley at the nursing home, for that matter.

Tamara stepped quickly into the courthouse. The county clerk's office was right there on the first floor. All the ladies behind the counter looked like they had been working there a long time and long since had gotten past the problem new deputy clerks had of wondering why some stranger would walk in and want to see a twenty-year-old marriage license and marriage certificate. The lady that waited on Tamara was about sixty years old and had a name tag pinned on her blouse. "Stella Burns, Deputy Clerk," it read. She told Tamara that a marriage license that old would be in the back but that if it was supposed to be there it would be.

The files were old and dusty, but they were all in the right place and contained what they should, Stella Burns explained. It hadn't taken but five minutes for Tamara to strike gold. She had it. Sophie Minden and Walter Willingham had applied for a marriage license on April 1st, 1980, and had been married on April 6th, 1980, in Denton County. The application listed Sophie Minden's place of birth as Mason County, Texas. There was no way there could be two of them. Shannon had her story. In anticipation of receiving such good news, Shannon had dispatched Kirsten to the Dallas County Courthouse to search for the Willingham's divorce papers, which very likely were there. They probably wouldn't indicate Sophie's maiden name, but they might give up some interesting information.

There was more than one way to go about outing Sophie Willingham, maiden name Sophie Minden. Shannon could "ambush" interview her, but that type of interview was most properly used when the subject of the interview was not going to give the reporter any good information under any circumstances and when the person was a hothead who very likely would start screaming obscenities at the reporter on camera. It was great television, Shannon knew, but it probably wasn't the best way to get at this particular subject.

No, the best way to out Sophie Willingham would be to get her on a "bait and switch." It was easy for someone like Shannon Gillette. She had done it several times. It would be easy in this case because Tamara already had greased the skids with the PR lady at the unmarried pregnant teenagers' home. Shannon would just have Tamara call Mindy Peel and set up to do a story there. Tamara would say she was the reporter, and Shannon would slip in at the last minute to conduct the interview. Hopefully, Sophie Willingham never watched "The Texas Truth." Chances were pretty good that she didn't, but even if she recognized Shannon and got upset, bait and switch would become ambush. Shannon couldn't lose. It was a great business.

These PR people were pushovers anymore, Shannon's crew knew. Once upon a time, it was difficult to get hired on as a PR person without having spent at least several years as a regular reporter somewhere. It was an indispensable benefit because only by having been a reporter could a person know how journalists operated. Reporters-turned-PR practitioners had two distinct advantages—they knew how to use the news media, and they knew how to keep from being used by the news media. The Cecelia Rostroome Home's PR director, Mindy Peel, had a journalism degree, but she had taken mostly PR courses and never had worked a day for the news media, not even for the student newspaper while in college.

When Tamara called to tell her she wanted to do a story on the home, Mindy gave her access to everything but the girls themselves—she at least had some notion of privacy interests—including setting up on-camera interviews with officials and supporters of the home. Sophie Willingham was scheduled to be interviewed first. It had just worked out that way, Tamara told Shannon and the others. They all laughed.

Friday, October 20th, 2000. Mid-afternoon. The interview was to be done on the spacious and elegant rear patio of the mansion the girls lived in while waiting to have their babies. It was a beautiful day. Everything was set up and ready to go. Tamara was there early to put Mindy Peel at ease. When Sophie Willingham arrived, Mindy proudly introduced her to Tamara, who led her over to the spot on the patio where the interview was to take place. Tamara told Mrs. Willingham that the cameraperson, Whitney Johnstone, needed to have her sit for a few minutes in the chair she would be occupying during the interview itself so that the set-up would be just perfect. Sophie Willingham was happy to oblige. She had done TV interviews before.

At that point, Tamara told Mindy she really needed to get straight with her on the schedule for the rest of the interviews. Mindy, pleased, ushered Tamara into her office to work out the rest of those arrangements.

Shannon was in their rented van parked in the front drive of the home. On a cue from Jacque, she slipped out of the van and walked around the side of the mansion to the rear patio. Whitney's camera and recorder were fired up and running. Sophie Willingham was sitting placidly, chatting amiably with Whitney and Kirsten. When Shannon arrived, Kirsten became suddenly serious.

"Mrs. Willingham, this is Shannon Gillette, our boss. She'll be doing the interview."

Shannon was well-known by even casual watchers of Triple T. Mrs. Willingham either would know her or she would not. It appeared that she did not.

"Oh, I thought Tamara was going to do it?"

"I'm sorry, no, I am," Shannon said. "Hello, Mrs. Willingham," she said, extending her hand.

"Hello," Sophie Willingham said, shaking Shannon's hand somewhat uncomfortably.

They sat down. Shannon wasted no time.

"Mrs. Willingham. We're not doing a story about the home here. We're doing a story about you."

"What?" Sophie Willingham said. "I don't understand." She had done TV interviews before, but not like this. She was on camera. She was a dignified woman. She felt trapped. She didn't know exactly what to do. But she was strong, and her basic instinct not to be intimidated took over. She stood her ground. The scene was tense. Shannon was elated that she hadn't bolted; some people did.

"First, let's get one thing out of the way," Shannon said quickly. "Is your maiden name Minden, and did you grow up just south of Rhinehart on a small ranch?"

"Yes, I did, but. . . ."

"When you were about twenty years old"—Shannon was on a roll now—"did you have a child out of wedlock?"

"What is this all about? I'm not going to answer these questions. Who are you...?"

"And wasn't the father of that child Congressman Winford Thomas, like you, about twenty years old at the time?"

"Turn your camera off, please. If you don't, I will get up and walk away. What will you have then?"

Shannon appreciated her moxie. She was visibly shaken, but she had held her ground and had made an intelligent move. Luck, maybe, but effective nonetheless. Shannon looked at Whitney and motioned for her to kill the recorder. Whitney turned it off. Sophie was burning hot, but she was trying to be cool.

"Ms. Gillette—was that your name?—I don't know who you are or what you think you're doing, but you and I need to have a talk. No cameras. No one else. Just you and me. Right now."

She stood up, jerking off the lavaliere microphone that Whitney had showed her how to attach to her blouse so that the cord wouldn't show. As she jerked, a button midway up on her blouse ripped loose and fell to the ground. Sophie didn't notice.

Shannon stood up. There was no microphone appended to her. Her audio was being picked up by a boom microphone held by Kirsten. Running the lavaliere through Sophie's blouse had been tactical; with a microphone cord on the inside of one's blouse, it was difficult to bolt. That was part of the nature of the bait and switch.

"How about us just taking a walk down to that sitting area down there," Shannon said, nodding at an area about a hundred and fifty feet away on the grounds of the mansion.

"Fine. Let's go. And tell them to keep the cameras turned off."

"No taping," Shannon said to Whitney. That was code for no recording. "Do it" was code for Whitney surreptitiously using the telephoto lens and onboard unidirectional microphone to get anything she could. Shannon didn't want to make Sophie Willingham any madder than she already was by getting caught violating her word. Shannon and Sophie walked in complete silence to the sitting area at the far end of the mansion's grounds. When they got there, Sophie kept walking, ending up behind a small stand of spruce trees. It was quite secluded.

"Now. Just who the hell are you lady, and what do you want?"

Shannon explained who she was, who she worked for, and that she was doing a story on Sophie's illegitimate child with Winford Thomas. That was true, wasn't it? Shannon asked her.

"I get it now. Your program is one of those sleazy tabloid TV things. Filthy business. This is about Congressman Thomas getting caught cheating on his wife and lying to the public, isn't it? I'm beginning to understand now. You've been digging into his background since what was on television about a month ago to see how much dirt you could find, and you came up with me."

"Close enough," Shannon said.

"Well, your story stops here. I won't answer another of your questions. I'll have you thrown off this property, and I and the home will sue you and everyone concerned for this grotesque invasion of our privacy. This conversation is over."

"Ah, I don't think so," Shannon said, catching Sophie's arm as she started to walk away.

"Let go of me this instant."

"Okay, Mrs. Willingham," Shannon said, drawing her hand back, "but aren't you even the least bit curious to know what we've learned about your daughter. That's what it was, wasn't it, a daughter?"

Sophie Willingham, unable to keep a stiff upper lip any longer, burst into tears. Her mind took her far away. Oh, how she had later regretted letting her precious baby go. After she had been married to Walter Willingham for several years and had become pregnant with Barbara, she hadn't been able to get her first child off her mind. She had tried to find Rena and Frank Dailey, but the people she talked to in Edge County said Frank was dead and that they had not heard from Rena in years. Sophie had confessed it all to Walter one election night, just after Winford Thomas had been re-elected to Congress for the fourth or fifth time. Walter was aghast.

"Good God," he had said to her, "if anybody in Dallas finds this out, I'll be the laughingstock of the entire medical community."

Dr. Walter Willingham had forbade his wife to talk about it further, and he made her swear she would do nothing to find this low-class bastard child and embarrass him before his peers. For the third time in her life, a man had rejected this child. Sophie was bitter as could be, but she had tried to put her firstborn out of her mind. It had been easier after Barbara was born and easier still after the birth of Kristy. But it lingered. It was bitterness. It was hurt. It was not knowing. It was guilt. It was a lot of things Winford Thomas, Maurice Minden, and Walter Willingham couldn't or wouldn't understand. She hated Winford Thomas. Her daddy was dead and she just couldn't hate him. Walter Willingham she was growing to dislike intensely.

When Barbara was thirteen and Kristy eleven, Sophie could take no more of Walter's "God syndrome." Worse yet, he had been cheating on her for some years and she didn't care. They were well-to-do from his medical practice and from various investments. Sophie had had all she could take. She wanted out, and she wanted her share. She also wanted to make something of her life. She had no interest in going back into nursing, but she did have a sincere interest. She wanted to do something for teenaged girls who got pregnant and had no place to go. She wanted to comfort them. She wanted to make sure they understood their options. She believed as much in the sanctity of life as she had when she had refused to let Winford Thomas procure an abortion for her twenty-six years earlier.

Walter was ready for the divorce, and it hadn't taken long or been particularly acrimonious. The lawyers had wanted to prolong it, but Walter understood that little game. He hated lawyers. He was a surgeon. Surgery didn't always go exactly as planned. He was an excellent surgeon, but he just couldn't guarantee that every one of the hundreds of surgical procedures he performed each year would turn out perfectly. When one didn't, no matter the high degree of skill he had used, some ambulance-chasin' lawyer would sue him. How the hell did they get their medical malpractice clients? he had sometimes wondered. Did these blood-sucking lawyers stand outside the operating rooms and ask the departing O-R nurses how it went?

Sophie just wanted enough to be comfortable for the rest of her life. She didn't want to have to work for a living because she wanted to help unmarried pregnant teenagers and because she had grown accustomed to the good life. She wasn't worried about being able to support her two daughters. Whatever else Walter was, he did love his children. Sophie knew he would provide for them in fine style. They, of course, wanted to live with their mother. That was okay with Walter because he wanted to be middle-age crazy, anyway.

One day when Walter's divorce lawyer was explaining to him on the telephone about the extensive discovery in which it would be necessary to engage in order to get Sophie in a sufficiently negative negotiating position, Walter told him to just shut the hell up and to prepare a settlement document that would grant to Sophie whatever she wanted out of their personal and ranch homes, $2 million in cash, no alimony, and joint custody of their children with Walter being completely financially responsible for the children, including $5,000 per month in child support per child payable to Sophie.

When the lawyer objected to the generosity of the proposed settlement, Walter fired him on the spot. Then he called a medical-doctor friend and asked him didn't his son just graduate from law school and pass the bar exam. Walter then called Sophie and told her what he had done. She fired her lawyer. Several days later, Sophie accepted Walter's nice young lawyer's settlement agreement and the certified check for $2 million. The judge had no objection to the terms of the settlement because he never read it. If it was okay with the lawyers and the litigants, it was okay with him. Judges were that way.

After the divorce, Sophie settled into a quiet routine. She bought the smallest house for sale in the exclusive Highland Park area of Dallas, near SMU. It was just three bedrooms, but there were only three of them, she reasoned. The girls were very involved with school and friends. They didn't seem to have missed a click over the divorce. Both had new cars and cellular telephones, and they got to go to daddy's house in the Turtle Creek section of Dallas anytime they wanted. Besides, they had few friends whose parents weren't divorced. Being rich made not noticing considerably easier.

With no job to worry about and happy children with their own cars and cares, Sophie was able to turn her attention to the Cecelia Rostroome Home. She started to look for her own firstborn again, but decided after only superficial checking that she—and some pregnant teenagers—would be a lot better off if she would concentrate on the home's clients.

Given the prevalence and lawfulness of abortion clinics, unmarried pregnant teenagers wishing to place the child for adoption weren't so many as they were before, but there were enough of them that Sophie felt the call. She said nothing to them about abortion unless they asked. If they did, she described it as a lawful option but one that should be carefully considered. When one of the home's girls ultimately opted for abortion, Sophie helped make the arrangements. She didn't hate the pro-choice folks, but she did believe it was a child—not a choice. She was sorry the pro-choice folks hated her so.

She saw her sister, Kathy, occasionally. Kathy lived near Washington, D.C., where she practiced law. Her husband, Gary Poole, whom she had met in undergraduate school at the University of Texas at Rhinehart, was a senior Congressional staffer, having worked his way up to the top staff position on the House Appropriations Committee.

In effect, his boss was the second-ranking Democrat on the committee, Winford Thomas of Texas, who had gotten him a job on Capitol Hill a year after he graduated from the University of Texas at Austin with a Master of Public Administration degree. Kathy had received a law degree from the University of Texas at Austin, tops in her class. She was general counsel at the Novatech Corporation in Baltimore, which did DNA and human genome research. For her company, Kathy recently had acquired a patent on a device and process that made paternity identification foolproof.

Kathy, the mother of two boys, had no idea that Winford Thomas was the father of Sophie's first child. Her husband didn't know there had been a first child. Kathy and Sophie talked on the telephone with each other quite a bit and were close—though long distance—friends. Kathy didn't exactly know why, but Sophie wouldn't visit her in Washington, D.C. The reason, Sophie knew, was that Sophie didn't want to have to hear about Winford Thomas, but Sophie couldn't tell Kathy that, so she just said she didn't like to fly that much. Kathy didn't mind flying at all and so came to Dallas occasionally to visit Sophie and her kids. Neither Sophie nor Kathy knew of the whereabouts of their two half-brothers. Neither cared to know.

Finally, Sophie was jolted back to reality by Shannon. "Hey, Mrs. Willingham, we need to talk, right?"

Sophie composed herself. As she wiped away her tears, she looked directly into Shannon's eyes.

"Do you know the identity and whereabouts of my first child? Tell me straight."

"Yes, I do."

Tears streamed down Sophie's face.

"Are you going to tell me?"

"Not unless you cooperate. Of course, you might find it out on TV some night, but then again you might not. This way, I'll get what I want from you, and you'll hear from me, today, everything I know about your daughter. And I know pretty much everything."

"How will I know you're telling me the truth?"

"Let's start out with the names Frank and Rena Dailey. Ring a bell?"

A chill shot through Sophie. It permeated every fiber of her body. She began to cry again.

"Ms. Gillette, let's return to the mansion," Sophie said, composing herself as best she could. "I need to tell Mindy Peel there'll be no story done here today. To make sure you didn't photograph any of the residents, we, as you probably know, sent them on an excursion, so, hopefully, they won't know about any of this until your story is broadcast. That will give me some time to prepare them. I need to instruct Mindy to notify the employees here that there will be no interviews of them. As soon as possible, you and I need to talk. And if you want it to be on camera, fine. We'll do it at my home, and in a civilized way, if that's possible for you. I will tell you everything, but I will tell you nothing before you tell me what you know of my daughter."

"Tell you what, Mrs. Willingham, we'll meet you at your house in an hour. We'll turn the camera on. You answer a direct question of mine and then I'll answer a direct question of yours. Deal?"

"Deal," Sophie said, thinking that was the most reasonable thing she had heard come out of this woman's mouth yet.

"Come in. How many of your associates must you bring with you?"

"Just a few. Listen, I've been thinking about our deal, and I'm not sure it's gonna work."

Damn this woman, Sophie thought. She hadn't even come through the front door yet and she was already reneging on the agreement.

"Why not?"

Sophie was trying diligently to be dignified. She had recovered somewhat from the blow she had received at the mansion. She had called and called her children on their cellular telephones and at every place she thought they might be, but she could not find them. She was hoping they wouldn't walk in on this interview, but if they did, it couldn't be helped. She had no idea what their reaction would be to having a half-sister.

"Because I just need you to basically verify what I already know. When I tell you what I know about your daughter, it's going to shake you up pretty good, so I need to get my part of the deal over with first. You have no reason to trust me, I know, but I promise you that I will tell you everything I know just as soon as I'm through asking you questions."

"On one condition."

"What's that?"

"I get the feeling you will want to videotape my reaction to learning about my daughter. I'll trade you answering your questions first for your removing your cameras from my home before you tell me what I want to know."

Shannon hadn't thought of that. This was an intelligent cookie here.

"Yes, well, okay. I've got a story to do here, and your reaction to who your daughter is would be great TV, but I can live without it. Deal."

The cameras and recorders were fired up, and Sophie Willingham explained on camera to what would be an audience of millions how she had given birth to an illegitimate child as a nineteen-year-old in rural Texas and that the child's father was Winford Thomas, a twenty-year-old college junior at the time. Sophie explained why she felt she couldn't keep the child, and the anguish she had felt at giving it away. She had looked for her daughter in later years, she told Shannon, but to no avail. She always had hoped, she said, that Frank and Rena Dailey, the young married couple to whom she had given the baby to raise, had done a good job of raising her little girl. They moved away, she said, and she'd never seen them again. Sophie did not mention that she had heard that Frank was dead.

Sophie said she'd had no contact whatsoever with Winford Thomas since just after the child was born when she told him she had given the child away. He hadn't even asked the baby's gender, she said. She also explained that she had been working with the Cecelia Rostroome Home for the past decade because she had so desperately needed help when she had been an unmarried pregnant teenager but had not known where to turn.

Shannon basically just let her talk. This was absolutely great. She was pouring her heart out to Shannon's audience, but she had no idea yet who her daughter was. Shannon began to worry that this woman might have heart failure when she learned the truth. Since the cameras were going to be outside, she sure hoped Sophie didn't die on her when she found out her daughter had made love to her biological father. That would be the TV event of the decade for sure.

The interview was over. Shannon got everything she needed and more. This was the personification of corroboration. Rena Kirkpatrick had told the absolute truth. George Cogbill would crap his pants when he heard what she had. She would be the talk of the tabloids for months. Years. She would want to interview Winford Thomas, of course. And how would she break this to Ginger Fontenot? Would she do it on camera or beforehand? Probably on camera. Better television. And what about Ginger's parents, the Fontenots? Would they go on camera to talk about this? Probably not. It would be great television, though. She might ambush them. On second thought, she might not confront any of these people, including Winford Thomas, before breaking the story. That way, she could use their reactions to the revelations on subsequent programs. Tabloid TV was wonderful.

Sophie's crew loaded the camera gear into the van and loitered outside, waiting on Shannon to drop the news to Sophie babe that her first-born child had done a little incest on her way up the ladder of life.

Inside, Shannon was about to reveal to Sophie who her daughter was. For the first time in her professional career, she was nervous.

"I don't quite know how to say this to you."

"I'm ready, Ms. Gillette. Is she alive?"

"Oh, yes."

"Is she okay? Where is she?"

"Mrs. Willingham, did you happen to see my program on 'The Texas Truth' recently in which Congressman Thomas was more or less shown making love to a model named Ginger Fontenot?"

"I didn't watch the actual program itself, but I saw a shortened version of it on the news. You couldn't miss it. It was on every newscast for days. Why?"

"Because, Mrs. Willingham, Ginger Fontenot is your daughter."

Sophie Willingham thought she had prepared herself for the worst. She had not. She was paralyzed. She could not speak. She wanted to scream, but nothing was working. She was growing lightheaded, her body becoming numb. She felt faint and nauseous.

"Oh shit, she's doing it," Shannon screamed. She jumped up and ran to the front door. "Jesus, call 9-1-1, one of you guys. She's takin' out on us."

Tamara Jenkins punched 9-1-1 on her cellular telephone and told the dispatcher a possible heart attack was taking place, shouting out the Highland Park address she was reading from the curb in front of Sophie's home.

Her daughters were by her side. She was in intensive care at Highland Park Hospital. It had at first appeared a heart attack to the doctors, but it wasn't. Shock was a more accurate description. She would be fine. She was sedated.

Barbara Willingham had driven up just as the ambulance was loading her mother for transport to the emergency room. She had no idea who the people were with the television cameras, but there was no time to ask. At the hospital, after the doctors said it wasn't a heart attack and that she would recover, Shannon took Barbara aside and explained in full. There was complete disbelief. Shannon took her to the van and showed her a part of the interview with her mother. Barbara was bewildered. She had been as yet unable to find her little sister, but she had found her father. When Barbara explained to her father what Shannon had explained to her, he had just cursed—a lot. Barbara did not understand his reaction.

Shannon and the "Inside Out" crew could obtain no more interesting footage at the hospital, so they left. The videotape of Sophie Willingham being loaded into the ambulance and all the footage that came after that was just stupendous. It would make great, great television.

Chapter 26

Monday, October 23rd, 2000. Because Shannon and Taz were estranged—on a personal level—and because the Sophie Willingham story had yet to be broadcast by "Inside Out," Taz knew nothing of it, and Shannon wasn't telling.

The mediation had been scheduled. Taz wanted the case settled. He knew he could not control what Shannon might or might not do, and he simply wanted the entire affair to be over with for him, for Heather, for his parents, and for the Fontenots.

The mediator was Steve Boneri. The mediation was taking place at his offices in Austin. He had been conducting mediations full time for several years and had the process down to an art and a science. The art was the mediating itself. The science was the environment. Everything was designed to make the lawyers and the litigants just as comfortable as possible.

Boneri had the reputation for being able to facilitate the peaceful resolution of the thorniest of civil disputes, which is precisely why Rance Sterling recommended him to Judge Ravinson when the judge had inquired if anyone had a preference as to mediators. Rance Sterling, after all, had an incentive to get the case settled. America All-Risks hadn't been at all reticent to give him the authority, nay, the mandate, to get the case settled as quickly as possible after Diversicom's threat to change carriers. Boneri had been acceptable to Barry Michaels, Lyle Branson, and Taz Sterling. He was appointed by the judge, and the mediation was scheduled for Monday, October 23rd. It was quite odd that everyone necessary to be there would be available on such short notice, but once in a blue moon legal scheduling actually worked with some efficiency.

Mediating the consolidated cases of *Thomas v. Diversicom, et al.* and *Fontenot v. Diversicom, et al.* was complicated by the fact that there were four sides to the matter. Winford Thomas and Ginger Fontenot were both plaintiffs, but they had no interest whatever in interacting with each other. To Winford Thomas, Ginger was a prostitute who had engaged in political blackmail against him. To Ginger, Winford Thomas was a sleazy politician who deserved what he got.

Diversicom and Shannon Gillette were the remaining defendants, but Shannon had no interest in interacting with the company that fired her. Shannon had come to believe that her decision in not confiding in Brenda was an excellent one because, in hindsight, Shannon believed Brenda would have divulged to the company any information in her mental possession upon request by the company or its lawyers to do so.

Once the initial session was over and everyone was split up, Winford Thomas and Barry Michaels would stay in the conference room, Ginger Fontenot and Lyle Branson would take one of the two anterooms, Dave Browning, Rance Sterling, and Warren Rampy would take the other ante room, and Taz Sterling and Shannon Gillette would use Steve Boneri's private office.

It was nine a.m. Everyone was there. Steve Boneri sat at the head of the table. He began by explaining the mediation process.

"The first thing I'd like you all to know is that I am not a judge, and I am not an arbitrator. I have no legal authority whatsoever to bind you to any kind of agreement or to rule that any one side or whatever should win this case. I am what is called a disinterested third party. That doesn't mean," he said, smiling, "that I have no interest in this case at all. It just means that I have no personal stake in any particular way it might come out, that it would be all the same to me no matter what you folks decide as this process moves along. My only interest is that I want to help you come to a resolution of this case without it going to trial if that is possible."

As the attorney who brought the first suit, Barry Michaels began. Right out of the chute, he said one of the biggest problems he and Winford Thomas had was that a big part of Shannon's story was predicated on a videotape purportedly shot in a restaurant that might well have been concocted from whole cloth. If it did exist, he said, and if it did come from a person with the high degree of credibility Shannon Gillette said the person had, then it made no sense to him that Shannon wouldn't disclose the identity of the person and allow the tape to be examined. Who, he said, could have that much to lose by coming forward and disclosing their identity and the circumstances of the tape's production?

Michaels said the longer Shannon kept silent about the source of the tape, the more it was his position that no such tape existed, that her motivation in producing the entire program was to advance her career. Michaels said it was his belief that she used modern television technology to create whole portions of the program from scratch.

Michaels' theory was that the tape purportedly shot at the restaurant was a complete fabrication and that the footage from The Paul Senning Hotel was a complete fabrication, as well. These grotesque lies told about his client to what had become a national television audience had ruined his political career and his marriage and had damaged his reputation beyond imagination. Thomas would be willing to settle the case to get the entire affair behind him, Michaels said, but only for a very substantial amount. Irreversible damage had been done.

Lyle Branson spoke next. He said he agreed with Barry Michaels' assessment of the situation, but wanted to add his view of the case as it related specifically to his client. He went through Ginger's history, emphasizing that she never had demonstrated a particular interest in politics. Shannon's refusal to produce the original tape from the restaurant was proof positive, Branson said, that the program was fabricated.

Ginger Fontenot's modeling career had been seriously injured, if not completely ruined, by the adverse publicity, he said. They, too, would be willing to talk settlement to get all this behind them, but, like Barry Michaels, Branson said any discussion of amount would have to start high and stay there.

Rance Sterling cut to the chase. Given the highly unusual circumstances of the case, he said, his client, Diversicom, was willing to forego any discussion of affirmative or other defenses and begin settlement discussions immediately. While Diversicom had no interest in admitting liability in any way, it would seem, he said, that Shannon's continuing refusal to cooperate put the company in an awkward position. Under that circumstance, he said, he would not discuss the case itself at this mediation session, especially since neither Winford Thomas nor Ginger Fontenot had been deposed, but he would be prepared, after the initial statements had been made, to make a settlement offer.

It was Taz's turn. He was happy to be going last. He had, of course, anticipated the kinds of statements that Michaels and Branson would make, but the statement his father had just made about Diversicom being willing to settle the case without even so much as an argument about the truthfulness of the broadcast seemed quite odd to him. He, in any event, would speak to the merits of Shannon Gillette's case.

There was every reason, he told the group, that Shannon would not divulge the identity of the source of the tape or the circumstances of its production. The principal reason, he said, was that confidentiality in journalism was a time-honored concept to which Shannon had no intention of being disloyal. She had promised the source anonymity, and she intended to keep her word. Taz insisted that any theories about Shannon's motivation for doing the program were just that—theories—and that the reason the program had been produced was because it was true and because it was highly newsworthy.

Notwithstanding, Taz said, that the case was Shannon's to win on the merits, Shannon would be willing to settle the case if all the other parties would agree to three things: one, to stop asking Shannon to break her confidential relationship with her source; two, not to ask her to admit any liability; and three, that any financial settlement be between the plaintiffs and Diversicom.

Steve Boneri was delighted at these turns of events because everyone seemed willing to settle. Mediations which focused on arguing the merits of the case itself were less likely to be successful, at least in the early going, than cases in which the defendant was willing to discuss the idea that it owed the plaintiff something and in which the plaintiff was willing to discuss the idea that the amount was negotiable. This was where splitting everyone up came in handy. With all the parties in separate rooms, he could facilitate the negotiations.

In these situations, everyone wanted everyone else to be first to mention a figure. Defendants always had a fear of starting too high, and plaintiffs always had a fear of starting too low. Someone had to start. The easy thing to do was for the plaintiffs to start out asking for the figure they had asked for when they had filed the lawsuit, but when they did that they ran the risk of totally alienating the other side. Everyone knew all those zeroes behind some other numeral in lawsuit complaints mostly was just a figment of the plaintiff's lawyer's imagination. The defense always could start out offering a nominal sum, but that strategy could have the same backfiring effect. Someone had to start.

Rance Sterling broke the ice. He authorized Steve Boneri to offer Winford Thomas and Ginger Fontenot $250,000 apiece. When Boneri delivered the message to Michaels and Thomas, it was met with derision. That, of course, was to be expected, Steve Boneri knew. He paid no attention to it. At this stage of the game, he just wanted to know what the counterfigure would be so he could deliver it to the defendants after he had run the $250,000 figure by Branson and Ginger. The two plaintiffs, of course, were under no obligation to settle for the same amount. In fact, the negotiations would be separate in the sense that Ginger would not know what was being offered Thomas and vice versa.

Boneri took the initial offer to Branson and Ginger while Michaels and Thomas were deciding what their counter figure would be. But when he got there, he was met by a surprise. Ginger and Branson were having a rather considerable disagreement. Ginger was upset that Branson had indicated she would be willing to settle when they had never discussed the issue. Ginger had been under the impression that the case itself would be discussed at the mediation session.

In her heart of hearts, of course, she knew that everything Shannon had said about her in the program was true, but she nonetheless thought she might be able to cast some real doubt on the credibility of the program by playing her ace in the hole—Shannon's refusal to indicate where she got the tape. When she discovered that everyone at the mediation session, obviously including Lyle Branson, wanted to settle the case, she was mad as hell. She hadn't said anything in the open session, but she had jumped Branson just as soon as they had retired to the ante room they were using. Boneri interrupted Ginger's tirade.

Boneri apologized for the intrusion and asked whether he should come back. He had heard Ginger's loud and upset voice as he was about to knock on the door. Branson told him to come on in and report any communication from the other side. When Boneri then reported the $250,000 offer, Ginger spoke up before Branson had a chance to say anything.

"Just tell them that we aren't going to settle for that or any other amount. I thought we came here today to talk about this lawsuit, and I find out that everybody wants to wimp out and settle, but I have no intention whatsoever of doing that. I'll go to trial before I let it appear that this was all somehow just some kind of big misunderstanding and that we're gonna accept some money from them and just kiss and make up.

"Two hundred and fifty-thousand dollars is a lot of money to me, but money is not as important to me right now as it once was. You folks can sit around here playing paddy cakes with each other today if you want to, but I'm going back to New York. This was a completely wasted trip for me."

With that, Ginger got up and left. She called a cab from the reception area and waited on it outside. Within two hours, she had checked out of her hotel, taken another cab to the airport, changed her ticket, and was in the air and on her way back to New York.

Meanwhile, at Steve Boneri's office, the mediation session was over. Thomas and Michaels were incredulous that

Ginger would have walked out with the insurance carrier offering serious dollars to settle the lawsuit. They knew that an initial offer of $250,000 meant Diversicom would settle for an amount considerably higher than that, perhaps as much as $1,000,000 each. Thomas—and Michaels, for that matter—needed the money. Michaels had Boneri ask Rance Sterling to go ahead and negotiate a settlement with Thomas and worry about Ginger later, but Rance Sterling had no interest in doing that. Settling the lawsuit meant settling the lawsuit. It didn't mean settling the lawsuit against one of the plaintiffs; it meant both or neither. Diversicom's Warren Rampy was distressed at the news. Try to get her back to the table, he told Rance. Sure, Rance said, but how?

Taz and Shannon were disappointed, too. Shannon would have been happy for the whole mess to be over with so long as she didn't have to name the source of the tape or admit that she'd done anything wrong and so long as any settlement reached would not involve her owing either of the plaintiffs any money. Taz wanted the case to be over as protection and relief for Heather and his dad—and he would be pleased, as well, when his representation of Shannon Gillette was at an end.

Chapter 27

Thursday, October 26th, 2000. There was a knock on Ginger's door.

"Who's there?"

"Colleen Etherington."

"Mrs. Etherington!" Ginger exclaimed, throwing open the door to her apartment. "Come in. Come in. It's so good to see you. I haven't talked with you in all these years. When Lyle Branson from the law firm where your foundation is offered to represent me in the situation I'm sure you know all about, I asked him about you, but all he said was that you were fine and that he didn't see you much. I hope you got all my letters over the years. I graduated in modern languages with honors, you know, and I took every Russian course the university offered just like you asked me to that day I met you...."

"Ginger, please, dear, I know all that. May I please sit down? We have something to discuss."

"Of course.... I'm sorry.... Ah, please, sit down. May I get you a cup of coffee?"

"Yes, thank you. Black."

As Ginger returned from the kitchen with the coffee, she offered an apology.

"If it's about my conduct in this whole Winford Thomas business, I am very embarrassed and truly sorry. . . ."

"Ginger," Colleen Etherington said sharply, "I'm sorry that I don't have time for idle chitchat. I'm an old lady. I may not have much longer on this planet, so just listen to me. You're important. All my girls are important. I just want to explain something to you. When I told you there were no strings attached to the scholarship I gave you eight years ago, I lied. There are strings. But you must know by now that there are strings attached to most everything in life. You may not have realized it, but we've been keeping loose tabs on you. Unfortunately, we weren't keeping close enough tabs on you to keep you out of this mess you got yourself in, but that's neither here nor there.

"We want you to do something for us, Ginger. We can't tell you what it is right now exactly, but you'll be learning about it soon enough. What we don't need is for you to be entangled in a messy lawsuit that might last several years. We're very private people, Ginger. We play things real close to the vest. So here's what I want you to do. Call Lyle Branson and tell him that you want to settle your lawsuit against that television company just as quickly as possible. He'll understand. I would have contacted you sooner about this, but I have been out of the country. Do you understand what I want you to do?"

"I heard everything you said, Mrs. Etherington, but I have no idea what it meant. I want to explain to you that I have thought for a long time that I am adopted, and I've been trying to figure out how to find out about my birth without the Fontenots knowing anything about it. It would just break their hearts, and I have no desire to do that. I haven't made much money up here like I thought I would. Making big money fast was the only reason I came up here in the first place, so when I was offered the chance to make big money in this situation, I couldn't resist. The money Jack Duvalier paid me meant I would be able to pay off my debts, prop up my modeling career, help the Fontenots, *and* hire a private detective to investigate my origins.

"As for this lawsuit, I could have settled it recently for at least $250,000, but I didn't because I didn't want those people—any of them—to think I was going to be easy to get over on—ever again. I know I was taking a big risk of getting nothing from the suit by going to trial and losing, but it was a risk I was willing to take. Once I allowed myself into this very risky Winford Thomas situation in the first place, I found that I liked the risks involved. High risk, high reward.

"When I refused to settle this lawsuit and walked out of the mediation, it meant one of two things—either I would get little or nothing or I would get a lot more than they thought they could buy me for. I don't know what the deal is or why 'The Texas Truth' wants to settle this case so fast, but they must have some motive, and I was trying to take advantage of that."

"All of that is very understandable, Ginger. I wish you had confided in Olive Martin about your adoption thoughts years ago. We have lots of resources. We might have been able to help you. I do hope you learn the truth. And I'm not surprised at all by your sense of risk-taking. Our profile of you when you were a scholarship applicant suggested strongly to us that you would be an adventurous risk-taker as an adult. We've usually been right, and we were right on target with you. Your sense of justice comports with our thinking on you, as well. But for now, I don't believe I heard you say that you understood what I told you a moment ago about our calling on you to help us."

"I heard you, but I'm sure I don't understand."

"Well, you don't need to know everything right now. All that will come. You must settle the lawsuit. You set a low settlement figure in consultation with Lyle Branson, and I'll see to it that you're paid the difference in that and in what Mr. Branson thinks your part of the case actually was worth. Soon after you have been extricated from that situation, someone will be in touch with you to tell you what we need you to do for us. Believe me, you'll like the money and the adventure. Do I trust you'll call Mr. Branson the moment I leave here to indicate your willingness to settle for an amount that will be appealing to the television company?"

"How do I know...?"

"That we'll make up the difference? In any financial sense, have we let you down yet, Ginger?"

"No."

"Well, then?"

"I'll call Mr. Branson."

"Thank you very much, Ginger," Mrs. Etherington said, standing up. "You're a courageous, gorgeous, highly-educated young woman. The sky is the limit for you. Oh, if I could take your place," she said, shaking her head a bit as Ginger opened the door for her.

"Goodbye, Ginger."

"Goodbye, to you, Mrs. Etherington," Ginger said, closing the door.

For her seventies, Colleen Etherington was slim, attractive, sprightly, and elegantly appointed, Ginger thought. She hoped she would be doing as well at that age. Instinctively, Ginger moved to the window to watch Colleen Etherington leave the building. The back door to a black stretch limousine swung open. A nice-looking young man stepped out and ushered her in. The door closed behind them, and the driver pulled away. New York plates. The young man looked just like her stereotypical image of a member of the federal government's Executive Protective Service, which protected the president and others.

Ginger wondered if Colleen Etherington lived in New York. She wondered who she really was. For the first time, she wondered about the foundation itself. Had the whole thing been planned from the beginning? What had Mrs. Etherington meant by "all my girls" and all those other things she said about the foundation's profile of her and knowing she would become an "adventurous risk-taker"—is that what she called it?

All Ginger knew was that she didn't know anything. She felt a bit like a pawn on a big chess board. Everyone seemed to be having their way with her. She didn't like it, but she had learned from this experience how not to let it happen again, she thought. For now, she decided, she would just go along for the ride—with her eyes and ears open. The money was real good—$100,000 from Duvalier and a huge settlement from a lawsuit she probably would have lost in court, at least ultimately.

That afternoon, Ginger called Lyle Branson to indicate her newfound willingness to settle. He was out of town. Ginger left her name and number. When he called her back the next day, he was happy to learn, he said, that she had changed her mind.

Without benefit of further mediation, the case settled on Monday, October 30th. Diversicom paid $750,000 to Winford Thomas and $750,000 to Ginger Fontenot. Winford Thomas was obligated to pay one third, or $250,000, to Barry Michaels as per their agreement. Lyle Branson, however, waived his fee, leaving Ginger with the entire $750,000. He suggested to her that she not reveal that information to anyone. All of Shannon Gillette's conditions were met. The plaintiffs signed releases indicating they had no further dispute with Diversicom. Taz wrote Shannon Gillette a formal letter indicating that his representation of her was at an end. Heather was relieved.

Taz needed a vacation. At a Texas Drillers baseball game in late August he had met a breath of fresh air named Nicole White, the Drillers' media-relations director. Nothing high strung about her; real down to earth, Taz thought. He had called her after splitting with Shannon, and they had begun dating. When the lawsuit settlement was reached, Taz invited Nicole to go on vacation with him to Cabo San Lucas, Mexico. They had been there only a day when the call came.

Chapter 28

Wednesday, November 1st, 2000.
"Hello."
"Taz?"
"Mom, is that you?"
"Yes, it's me."
"Why are you calling me here, mom? Is there a problem?"
"I'm sorry, Taz, but there has been an accident, well. . . ."
"Give it to me straight, mom."
"Are you sitting down?"
"I am now."
"It's Ginger's parents, Mr. and Mrs. Fontenot. They're dead. They...they... committed suicide."

Taz slumped in his chair, dropping the telephone into his lap. He was nauseous. He was shaking. His body limp, numb. He felt as though he was about to faint. Nicole, startled, took the telephone from his lap and told Reauxanne that whatever she told Taz had caused him to become dazed but that he seemed to be recovering. Reauxanne thanked Nicole, said she understood, and that she would wait on the line for Taz to return.

When he could, he motioned for the telephone and slowly returned it to his ear.

"When?"

"Last night. Their son went to see about them and found them dead. From what I was told by the police in LeMieux, they locked themselves in an old car of theirs and ran a garden hose in through the window with the engine running. They died fairly quickly and painlessly, I was told. They were in each other's arms when they were found."

"My God, mom. I don't know if I can stand this. Did they leave a note or anything?"

Taz was wailing. Nicole sat close, wanting to help, not knowing what to do or what Reauxanne had said that was upsetting him so.

"Yes, Boudreaux wrote it, but it doesn't seem to make a lot of sense. It said something about the letter 'R' being about "ruin" and "revelation," something about the car they were found in not being so lucky after all, and something about the program Shannon broadcast last night being more than their hearts could stand."

"What program?"

"'Inside Out'—last night."

"What was the program about?" Taz thought he knew.

"I'm sorry to have to be the one to tell you this, Taz, but it appears that Ginger was adopted."

"I pretty much knew that, but why would that make the Fontenots want to commit suicide?"

"That's not all of it, Taz. The story on 'Inside Out' was labeled 'Oedipus Tex.' Ginger is the illegitimate daughter of Winford Thomas."

"Oh, my God, mom," Taz shrieked, now crying uncontrollably. "I just can't take anymore. How could that be?"

"Taz, I'm sure you feel absolutely horrible about all this. I didn't know them like you did, but I know they were fine people. I'm real sorry for everyone involved."

"My God, it's just too much...too much.... Why did a policeman from LeMieux call you to tell you about their deaths?"

"Because he was trying to find you."

"Why?"

"Alphonse."

"Oh, no. What has he done?"

"They said he and his wife were at the funeral home this afternoon making burial arrangements when all of a sudden he jumped straight up out of his chair, started screaming about killing you and Shannon Gillette and ran out. They haven't been able to find him. He's in his truck. His wife said it had a full gunrack. The LeMieux police have contacted the Metroplex and Austin police departments, who'll stop him if they see him, but you obviously needed to know. They're really afraid he'll kill you and Shannon if he can."

"Tell me about Shannon's program. I need to hear it from you."

Taz was calming slightly, but still crying. Nicole was silent, listening on an extension, as Taz had motioned her to do.

Taz was enraged when his mom told him that the woman who sold Ginger to Boudreaux was the same woman who had been Shannon's cellmate and the same woman who had sold her story about Ginger to "Inside Out."

Taz was looking for answers but could find none. He told his mom he didn't think Alphonse knew where he had grown up, but, just in case, he told her what he thought was the make, year, and color of Alphonse's pick-up truck, and he suggested she relay the situation and the information on Alphonse and his truck to the Highland Park police. She told him not to come anywhere near Austin or the Metroplex until Alphonse was located, but Taz assured her he would be all right. She would worry about him anyway, he knew.

Taz wanted to ask his mom about Heather's condition but thought better of the idea. He had to return home immediately, he knew.

Tuesday night, October 31st, 2000. Ginger had not seen "Inside Out" when it aired. Shannon had not sought to confront her with the "news," preferring to try to catch her reaction for her next program. Ginger was decorating her new apartment. The television was off. She never had been an avid TV watcher, and she had watched even less after Shannon's first program. Ginger's best friend in New York was Elizabeth Kamber, another model at Pretty As A Picture. Elizabeth saw the show.

"Hello."

"Ginger, my God."

"Elizabeth, what?"

"You didn't see it?"

"See what?"

"'Inside Out' on TV just now."

"No, why?"

"God, Ginger, I'm not sure I can tell you."

"Damn it, Elizabeth, tell me what? After what's been on TV about me, it would take a lot to shock me."

"Well, this is a lot. I think I should come over to tell you."

"Shit, this sounds really bad. Is it about me? Tell me now, damn it."

"You sure you want to hear it on the phone. I think I need to be there when I tell you."

"Yes, Elizabeth. Tell me now. I can't stand the suspense. You have me scared to death, so stop it and just tell me."

"Okay. . . . 'Inside Out' ran a program tonight that said. . . . Oh, God, I can't do it. . . . Shit, Ginger, it was about who your real parents are."

Ginger began to cry.

"God, Elizabeth, you must be kidding, but I know you're not. Oh, Jesus, who are they? How did they find them? Shit, tell me."

Ginger was crying hard now.

"Ginger, please sit down if you're not."

"I am." She was pacing the floor.

"Okay, your biological mother is a rich sort-of socialite in Dallas. She was a poor teenager who got pregnant with you and gave you up when you were born. The people she gave you to. . . . God, Ginger, I can't tell you the rest."

"Please, Elizabeth, please."

"Well, they...sold you to Boudreaux. Tailese didn't know he bought you. I can't tell you the money details—I just can't; you'll have to just watch the show or something."

"What's her name? Where was I born?"

"Her name is Sophie Willingham. Her maiden name was Minden. You were born near Rhinehart, Texas. You have two half-sisters in Dallas, and an aunt and uncle in Washington, D.C. They have two kids. Your aunt is your mother's sister. Oh, God, a whole bunch of stuff. Your mother is divorced from some medical doctor in Dallas."

Knees weakening, Ginger sat down.

"You haven't said anything about my biological father. Did the program say who he was?"

"Yes, but I just can't tell you that."

"Why not?"

"It's too horrible."

Ginger was crying hard again. Her stomach was in knots. She was convulsing, but, by God, she wanted to know who her father was. She was doubled over, one arm clutching her stomach, rocking back and forth rhythmically.

"How horrible could it be? ... Is he in prison or something?"

"No."

"Then what?"

"God, you're my best friend, Ginger. I just can't say this to you."

"Please, Elizabeth. If you are *my* best friend, you'll tell me. Don't make me find it out on the God-damned news."

"Look, Ginger, worse things have happened. You'll get over this, okay?"

"Please, please, just tell me."

Ginger was crying harder than ever. She was near collapse. Her head was reeling. She felt drunk, nauseated, on the verge of uncontrollable rage.

"Ginger, hang up the phone. I'll take a cab and be there in fifteen minutes. Talk to no one. Don't turn on the TV. Don't answer the phone. Okay?"

"Okay. Please hurry. I can't stand this."

Both arms now around her waist. Still rocking. Trying to hold in everything that wanted out.

When Elizabeth reached Ginger's apartment building, she was surprised that no media were there.

"Inside Out" had a crew at The Regency waiting to ambush Ginger when she left her apartment. Shannon Gillette didn't know that Ginger had moved, and the doorman at The Regency wasn't telling. What sleazebags, he thought. Ginger had always been good to him.

Inside Ginger's new apartment, Elizabeth was crying; Ginger was crying hard. They hugged, holding each other tight.

"Now tell me, please." Ginger's head was resting on Elizabeth's shoulder, Elizabeth's head on hers.

"Ginger, your biological father is Winford Thomas."

In the space of a nanosecond, Ginger was softly jettisoned from Elizabeth. There was no sound. She felt herself floating, as though moving slowly through the air, a bit above the floor. Her scream was primordial.

It would not be the last time in her life that Ginger Fontenot would issue a primordial scream.

Winford Thomas was in Hawaii. He had seen the show. Whatever else he was, incest had never crossed his mind. He threw up on the carpet of the condo. Head still swimming, he slowly turned off the television set, walked outside onto the lanai, and sat for hours, staring at the sea. The pain in his head was sharp. Finally, he walked down to the beach.

He hated himself. No one was to blame for any of this but him, he knew. He could face no one—not his wife, his children, his father, Sophie Willingham, Ginger. He contemplated swimming out to sea. He contemplated emasculating himself. At the least, he knew he could never go home. Never. He wasn't even sure where home was. He wasn't even sure he belonged on this earth. He was very alone; perhaps he always had been.

Nightfall, Thursday, November 2nd. Taz had returned to Austin.

"Hello."

"Mom."

"Taz, where are you?"

"I'm back in Austin."

"Well, you don't have to worry about Alphonse right now."

"What happened?"

"Well, apparently, when he took off after you and Shannon, he took a bunch of beer along with him. The police found him in his truck early this morning near Hempstead. They said he had failed to negotiate a shallow curve on U.S. 290, lost control, and ran off the road into a ditch. He must have hit his head on the steering wheel or something. Anyway, he was unconscious. He needed a few stitches. They're holding him in the Hempstead jail on a D.W.I. and for assaulting the officer who revived him, but they may not be able to keep him long. His wife has hired Miranda Buck from

Houston to defend him. Rance says that means he'll probably be out soon.

"The police at Hempstead notified the police at LeMieux that they had him, and the LeMieux police asked them to hold him as long as they could and to try to talk some sense into him. Supposedly, his wife will be in Hempstead with Miranda Buck in the morning. It's all a big mess. The LeMieux police told me Ginger was in LeMieux. The autopsies have been done, and the bodies have been released for burial, but Ginger won't make the final arrangements until Alphonse can be there. Alphonse apparently told the police in Hempstead that he wanted to kill Ginger about as bad as he wanted to kill you and Shannon. They may also charge him with terroristic threatening. It's just awful."

"Jesus, at least he's okay."

"I wasn't gonna tell you this, Taz, because you've got enough to be upset about, but I guess I should. Heather went into a serious state of depression yesterday and had to be hospitalized. We have no idea what caused it, and if Heather knows, she isn't telling anybody, except maybe her psychiatrist, who's been with her pretty much the whole time she's been in the hospital. The doctor said Heather could come home tomorrow, that she thought the problem would pass and that Heather would be okay."

The bottom line, Taz knew, was that something had to be done. Heather's suffering had to stop. Everyone's suffering had to stop. Now.

Chapter 29

Saturday, November 4th, 2000. Nine a.m. Heather was expected to be coming home some time after noon. Taz hoped he would be able to speak with her alone. He wanted to talk with her seriously about at least telling their parents that she was the source of the tape. At least that way, they would know what was going on and maybe Heather could stop feeling that the whole world was occupying her insides. If she agreed, Taz would unleash the secret to his parents. Something had to be done to help Heather before another single negative event occurred. He also had another plan. He would try it first. Taz was at the Sterling mansion. His parents were at the hospital with Heather.

Father McKenzie was opening his mail in the church office.

Dr. Noelle Gray was not on call. She was planning to be on the firing range by noon. She had a new forty-five caliber pistol she wanted to practice firing. Since the Texas legislature had passed a law permitting concealed weapons in cars, there had been so many second-degree murders that most everyone was buying a gun. It was sort of like the old west as erroneously portrayed in the movies. Life, more than a century later, was imitating art.

There had to be a common denominator, but what was it? he thought. Heather, of course, but that was what all this was about. Maybe that was it, though. The lure Taz needed was to concoct a story about Heather being in some sort of danger and needing their help. But what kind of danger? he thought. He would tell them that Heather had gotten out of bed just after her parents left her room after bringing her home from the hospital, that she had found a gun and was threatening to kill herself. Her parents were desperate.

Taz would tell Father McKenzie that Heather had asked for him, and Taz would tell Dr. Gray that Heather had asked for her. He would tell Father McKenzie and Dr. Gray that he was an employee at the Sterling mansion, calling at the request of the Sterling family.

The plan would work if everyone was near a telephone and would just run to their cars and drive immediately to the Sterling mansion. It also would require that his parents not come home with Heather for a while, but they had said they weren't bringing her home until early afternoon. It also would require Taz being able to hold the first to arrive until the second to arrive was there. It was a completely crazy plan, but Taz was going to do *something* this very morning. He would time the calls. Father McKenzie first. Taz knew he lived on the church grounds because he once had commented to Taz about his nice living quarters there. Dr. Gray next. She lived in Highland Park, just down the street from Sophie Willingham.

With no further thought, Taz executed the plan. Miraculously, he reached them both and they agreed to come instantly. Taz walked outside into the large semicircular driveway on Mockingbird Place and stepped into an archway at the side of the garage where he didn't think he would be seen. He waited. It seemed like forever. It was only a few minutes.

He heard squealing tires. Father McKenzie had arrived. Taz had hoped that would be the case because he thought Father McKenzie would be easier to handle than the doctor. As he stepped from his car, Taz reintroduced himself and explained that his call to him had been a hoax. Taz told him that he was needed in the house, nonetheless; to please go inside and wait in the study. Taz begged—and promised he would explain everything in a few minutes. Father McKenzie, a bit disgruntled and bewildered but charitable to a fault, went inside to wait.

Less than a minute later, Dr. Gray arrived. Rather than make any speeches to her outside, Taz simply received her and hurried her into his father's study. Once inside the room, Taz shut the door and stood against it. Dr. Gray was startled, but she let Taz speak.

"Before I begin, let me introduce everyone since none of us has met all the others. First, for your information, Dr. Gray, I'm Taz Sterling. This gentleman is Father McKenzie, Heather's priest. For your benefit, Father McKenzie, this is Dr. Noelle Gray, Heather's psychiatrist. I perpetrated this little hoax to get you both here—no questions asked. A very serious problem needs resolution, and we know what it is. Heather will be home from the hospital this afternoon, as scheduled. I was lying to you about her being home already."

Taz's eyes were blazing. Father McKenzie thought he understood what Taz was doing. Dr. Gray thought Taz was a bit maniacal, but in control of himself nonetheless.

"Everyone in this room knows a secret, but none of you know the whole story, which I'm about to tell you. I think you should sit down."

They complied.

"We all know Heather shot the restaurant tape. She didn't mean to. She didn't even know it until later. She gave the tape to me. Before I could destroy it, having decided it never should see the public light of day, Shannon Gillette mistakenly ended up with it. As we all know, things got out of hand from there. Nobody meant for all this to happen, least of all me. But it did. Shannon knew Heather shot the tape, but she couldn't tell anyone because she promised Heather confidentiality. That's a rule of journalism. Then Father McKenzie here got involved. I'm sure you helped Heather in the short term, father, but you couldn't tell anyone she was the source of the tape. That's a rule of religion.

"And finally, Dr. Gray here came to Heather's rescue. I'm sure you've been helping her in the short term, too, doctor, but you couldn't tell anyone Heather was the source of the tape, either. That's a rule of the healing arts. Until now, I've been unwilling to tell anybody Heather was the source of the tape. That's a rule of law. I may not know much, but at this point I do know one thing. My little sister has suffered enough. We simply cannot continue to let this totally innocent little girl suffer because of some well-meant but artificial rules.

"I know that the rule of confidentiality, in the case of each of our professions, was designed to protect people in Heather's position. And at first, it worked for Heather. But then Shannon went to jail. And then she was assaulted at the jail. And then the Fontenots committed suicide. And the rules failed Heather. We all thought we were being noble. We thought we were protecting Heather. And maybe we were, but not anymore. We need to make an exception to our rules, folks, and tell everyone what Heather's problem is. Or we need to advise Heather to allow us to announce that she was the source of the tape. Or we need to do something, anything but sit on our butts and philosophize about the sanctity of confidentiality, a concept I am totally sick of at the moment.

"There's a lot I could say about what has happened, but I won't, at least not now; instead, I'd like to say what I think should be done. I reached the conclusion last night that

Heather should let me tell the world what happened. I was going to tell her that this afternoon when she came home from the hospital. I don't know what kind of damage will be done to my dad's chances for a federal judgeship by letting people know Heather is the source of the tape. That's what Heather and I have been trying to protect all along; that and some other folks who no longer can be protected because they have killed themselves. Whatever happens, it can't be worse than what Heather is going through now.

"Obviously, Heather feels responsible for all this, and the Fontenots' suicides were just too much. For what it's worth, I started all this, and I take full responsibility for it. It snowballed, and I didn't know how to stop it. I had no idea that Shannon Gillette would do all the things she has done. I was totally shocked every time along the way that something bad happened. I always thought it would be the last bad thing that would happen and this would be over and no one would ever know that Heather was the source of the tape. I don't know what else bad can happen, but we need to stop the insanity here and now."

Taz moved away from the door and sat down. He closed his eyes and slowly rubbed both eyelids with his thumb and index finger. By his eyes, Father McKenzie deferred to Dr. Gray. She spoke.

"This is perhaps the most bizarre situation I've been involved in as a psychiatrist. Undoubtedly, it is testing the limits of the notion of confidentiality—in all of our professions, I suppose. As you both may know, I've been involved only for a short time. I fairly quickly concluded from talking with and examining Heather that her depression was episodic; in other words, that it was brought on by this particular situation and was not clinical or chemically-based or in any kind of state that would require long-term treatment.

"She was getting much better with therapy, but then there were these suicides and her depression deepened immensely. Again, it was episodic. I decided to keep her mildly sedated and to involve her in intensive therapy just as soon as she had recovered sufficiently from her deepest valley of guilt to meaningfully proceed. My plans were to check on her Monday and to begin therapy as early as then. I agree with Mr. Sterling about at least one thing. This last Shannon Gillette story was not foreseeable. The worst seemed over after she was released from jail. Heather's condition improved significantly and immediately on that occasion. I was joyous and felt the worst had passed.

"Heather is a strong little girl, but imagine believing, at age twelve, that you were directly responsible for all the grief these events have caused, the final straw being the two deaths. And, of course, should the public learn of all this, the senior Mr. Sterling's chances of becoming a federal judge might evaporate and that was on Heather's mind, too. She didn't want to harm her father, and she didn't want him mad at her, either.

"Where I disagree with Mr. Sterling here is with respect to whether Heather should totally come out of the closet now. Putting aside, for the moment, questions about our professional responsibilities, the question becomes what would be best for Heather at this point. And I'm not at all certain that letting it be known publicly that she is the mystery source would be helpful to her. I completely understand what you said about believing the worst was over each time one of the events occurred, Mr. Sterling. Perhaps the worst is over now."

Father McKenzie had listened intently to every word spoken.

"This is indeed bizarre," Father McKenzie said, finally speaking. "I perhaps hadn't realized just how much so until now. And Taz, while your methods are debatable, your purposes are not, and you are to be lauded for your intervention, in my view. But we can discuss that later. Right now, I agree, something must be done. I am willing to break my vow of confidentiality and tell the world what it wants to know. The rule of confidentiality is a necessary one. None of our professions could get along very well without it, but I fear it has failed us in this case."

"Well, then, this needs to wait until Monday. Heather should be up to it by then," Dr. Gray said. "May I suggest that we reconvene here early Monday morning. Later today, I'll tell Mr. and Mrs. Sterling that I'm going to stop by Monday morning to see Heather, and I'll suggest to Mr. Sterling that he be here. If she's up to it, we can talk to Heather about this and go from there."

Silence.

"Good," Father McKenzie said. "I suggest we leave Heather alone for the rest of the weekend. She'll probably be mostly sleeping, anyway. Is that right, doctor?"

"Yes. I think we should just let this lie until Monday morning. And Taz, I think your actions today were courageous, as well."

The visitors said goodbye and departed. Taz sat alone for a time.

Chapter 30

Sunday, November 5th, 2000. Two p.m. Reauxanne Sterling stood alone at the front edge of a small stage at The Redux, a hotel in downtown Dallas, just a couple of blocks from The Gatehouse.

"I'm Reauxanne Sterling. Thank you for coming. I have a statement I'd like to read to you."

Reporters from every news medium in the Metroplex had come to the media conference—only because of Reauxanne Sterling's prominence in the community and the mystery surrounding the refusal of her PR-firm representative to give any indication of the subject of the media conference. All Reauxanne had allowed her to say was that the media conference had nothing to do with any of the charities with which she was associated and that the news organizations might want to send their political reporters.

In that the general election was but two days away and the political reporters were out covering the last-ditch efforts of the various candidates to win election, most of the reporters there were not political types. All of them, though, knew of the Shannon Gillette stories.

Reauxanne read from a prepared statement.

"I have a twelve-year-old daughter. Her name is Heather Sterling. Inadvertently, Heather shot the tape of Ginger Fontenot and Jack Duvalier in The Gatehouse restaurant. Until this very moment, as far as I know, no one but my son, Taz Sterling, the psychiatrist Heather has been seeing because of all this, the priest at our family's church, and Shannon Gillette knew that Heather was the source of the tape. Her father and I learned all this only yesterday afternoon. The idea of confidentiality, it seems, prevented all these people, including her own brother, from telling Heather's parents what was going on.

"Boudreaux and Tailese Fontenot—two wonderful people—are dead, and my twelve-year-old little girl feels responsible. She can stand only so much. How this all started is quite strange, but must be told. Heather has a camcorder and loves to shoot videotape. She set the camera down on our table one day in July while we were having lunch at The Gatehouse. She must have inadvertently switched the camera into its recording operation. She shot the tape by mistake. When she saw later what she had done and what she had on tape, she gave the tape to Taz. Shannon Gillette—unwittingly and through no fault or intention of Taz's—ended up with the tape, and the rest is history. We must come together now to help Heather. Any other consideration, while perhaps itself important, is indeed minuscule in comparison with allowing Heather the opportunity to begin the healing process. We must help her suffer no more.

"One such consideration that must give way is this. As you may know, my husband once was nominated to a federal judgeship only to have the nomination withdrawn by a succeeding presidential administration. Should another Republican ever occupy the White House and were there a Republican senator from Texas, I'm certain my husband would look once more to be nominated. He has worked very hard his entire life to place himself in that position. He does so much want to serve his country in this way.

"Heather and I need you to understand that my husband had nothing to do with the videotaping of Ginger Fontenot and Jack Duvalier in the restaurant. Notwithstanding that fact, you in the media might reach a wrong conclusion before the situation could be thoroughly explained. Even should he have every opportunity to explain the inadvertence of Heather's camera's recording in the restaurant and that he had nothing to do with Shannon Gillette coming into possession of it, politics being what it is, any Republican occupant of the White House might shy away from nominating Rance just because he had been involved in this political controversy. The problem, of course, is that once you in the media associate someone with something, it doesn't matter how much disproving is done, the real truth never quite sticks.

"I am holding this media conference totally on my own. It was fairly easy to put all the pieces together once Heather took me into her confidence yesterday afternoon. She was mildly sedated from having been hospitalized in a state of depression. Her father and I were terribly concerned about her, but no one would tell us what her problem was. I, of course, now know that her latest and worst bout with depression was in reaction to the Fontenots committing suicide.

"Yesterday afternoon, as I was about to leave her bedroom after getting her settled in from the hospital, Heather rather groggily told me to look on her videotape shelf and bring her a tape labeled 'balloons.' I thought she was a bit delirious from the sedative she had been given, and so I basically just ignored her request. But she insisted. When I handed it to her, she pulled the tape from the box, looked at it for a moment, and then instructed me to watch it in a tape player in her room. When I did—and with some explanation from

Heather—everything suddenly began to make sense. There were Ginger Fontenot and Jack Duvalier having this conversation at what I then understood was The Gatehouse. I then called my son, Taz, and he explained everything to me. "I seem the only person involved in the whole situation who could or would act, and I have. I'm sure confidentiality is a necessary concept in journalism and law and religion and medicine, but it didn't work for Heather. I'm her mother. I brought her into this world, and I'm responsible for her. The only pause I had in deciding whether to call this media conference and make the announcement I made here today concerned my husband Rance's desire to be a federal judge. After careful thought, I decided that getting it all out in the open was the better choice for Heather if I could accomplish one thing. And that must come from you ladies and gentlemen in the media. Heather's health depends on your sense of fair play. You have your facts now. I have given them to you, but please, please, leave us alone. In the name of decency, please let my daughter overcome this and grow up to be a healthy adult. I trust you and your colleagues will observe this simple request. Thank you."

There were a million questions to be asked and every reporter there wanted to ask all of them at the same time. Any semblance of order was quickly lost. After all, this was a big story—and getting bigger.

Early Epilogue

After Reauxanne's disclosure, Heather became an instant and unwilling celebrity.

The news media worked themselves into a frenzy doing stories about the Sterlings, especially Rance. Had he put his daughter up to the original taping? Was he using Heather to cover his involvement in trying to sabotage the campaigns of Winford Thomas to ensure that George Parsons would be reelected to the Senate? The questions were endless.

Ginger requested, and received, an additional $250,000 from the Colleen Etherington Foundation in return for her willingness to settle the lawsuit.

Under the terms of the settlement agreement, "The Texas Truth" admitted no error in the broadcasting of the program. Diversicom promptly sold "The Texas Truth" and its other syndicated television programs to the Kennecut Corporation and bought KZYX from Merlin Industries. America All-Risks retained Diversicom as a client.

Alphonse buried the Fontenots. Ginger attended the funeral, but Alphonse would not speak to her. The Fontenots' simple will, written years earlier, named Ginger as executrix and split their assets equally between Ginger and Alphonse. Ginger settled the meager estate and placed the entirety of its proceeds—plus $500,000—in an account at the Bank of LeMieux in the names of Alphonse and his children.

Ginger had no interest in seeing her biological father ever again, nor did she wish to meet anyone in his family. But there was one person in his family who wanted very much to meet her—Winfred Thomas. Reluctantly, Ginger agreed to meet him, but made him come to New York. He apologized for his son and for his own part in Winford being what he was. Then he gave her $100,000 and told her he would understand if she never wanted to see him again. She thanked him for the money and didn't respond to what she might do in the future.

Ginger was interested, though, in meeting her biological mother. Sophie traveled to New York and brought Barbara and Kristy with her. Ginger and Sophie spent a lot of time together just crying. Barbara and Kristy mostly stayed away from their mother and half sister. Sophie begged Ginger to move to the Texas Metroplex but Ginger had other ideas. Sophie offered Ginger $1,000,000. Ginger accepted. Ginger had at that point amassed $2,200,000 (less the $500,000 she gave Alphonse)—tax-free because the compensatory proceeds of tort suits weren't taxed as income and because the rest of the money was received under the table or as unreported gifts. Ginger told Sophie she would visit her someday. Barbara and Kristy were happy Ginger was not coming to the Metroplex.

Sophie changed her last name to Minden and continued her work with the Cecelia Rostroome Home.

Ginger had her birth certificate changed to reflect her real birthdate—one day earlier. "Ginger R. Fontenot" remained her name.

George Parsons was re-elected to the U.S. Senate.

The Texas Democrat party replaced Winford Thomas on the Senate ballot with a doctrinaire liberal, Carl Hackman, who garnered only thirty percent of the vote against Parsons.

Moderate Republican Marlene Davidson, with fifty-two percent of the vote, won Winford Thomas' vacated east-Texas congressional seat against the Texas Democrat party's replacement for Thomas—Verne Atkins.

Rance Sterling still wanted to be a federal judge. He and Reauxanne separated briefly after her media conference, but they quickly reconciled and rallied around Heather. No one outside the family knew of the brief split.

Lyle Branson remained a partner at his Fort Worth law firm.

Hank Gunther was re-elected sheriff of Travis County.

The 2000 presidential election was the closest in modern history, nearly precipitating a constitutional crisis.

Winfred Thomas died peacefully in his sleep on Christmas Day, 2000. His wife had died some years earlier. Winford's sister remained a bank president's wife.

Kathy Poole joined her sister on the board of the Cecelia Rostroome Home.

Ed Land remained chief of the research and drafting arm of the Texas legislature.

Ted Jackson was back at work in the Travis County public defender's office after vacationing with his wife in Hawaii.

Reauxanne Sterling remained involved with various charities, now including the Cecelia Rostroome Home.

Alphonse remained in LeMieux with his wife and children. He continued to work in the oilfields.

Warren Rampy continued as Diversicom's general counsel.

Colleen Etherington continued living in Europe.

Later Epilogue

Heather recovered.

Winford Thomas moved to the island of Oahu and retired on the lawsuit-settlement proceeds and his Congressional retirement pay. He made a lump-sum settlement with his wife and children so they would not be bothered with him ever again. Shortly after arriving in Hawaii to stay, Winford formed a religious cult on a small piece of land on the northern end of Oahu which had been anonymously donated to him. He became the cult's leader, attracting a wide following among native Hawaiians interested in seceding from the United States.

Jack Duvalier got married to Michael Fletcher in Vermont. They moved to San Francisco where Jack was to head up GAYPAC's new and highly-secret political dirty-tricks division. Duvalier and Fletcher adopted a child.

Rena Kirkpatrick got her little house. She was right about the IRS. It didn't seem to know she existed. She went to work at the convenience store just down the street from her new home.

Shannon Gillette received various awards for investigative reporting. Triple T's new owners hired her back, giving her the moon and the stars to leave "Inside Out."

Judge Ravinson was elected to the Supreme Court of Texas and later was removed from office by judicial ethics authorities for the sexual harassment of female lawyers appearing before the high court.

Taz joined his father's law firm as its newest partner in the litigation section.

Bob H. Granger, Jr., was inaugurated as the 43rd President of the United States.

Quietly, Ginger moved to Paris and immersed herself in learning the French language and culture. Six months after moving to Paris, she disappeared. She finally understood what the Colleen Etherington Foundation was about. It was wonderful.

In Texas, all is well—and that's the truth.